SUPERNATURAL™
NIGHT TERROR

JOHN PASSARELLA

SUPERNATURAL created by Eric Kripke

TITAN BOOKS

Supernatural: Night Terror
Print edition ISBN: 9780857681010
E-book edition ISBN: 9780857685445

Published by
Titan Books
A division of
Titan Publishing Group Ltd
144 Southwark St
London
SE1 0UP

First edition September 2011
10 9 8 7 6 5 4 3 2 1

Visit our website: www.titanbooks.com

Did you enjoy this book? We love to hear from our readers. Please email
us at readerfeedback@titanemail.com or write to us at Reader Feedback
at the above address.

To receive advance information, news, competitions, and exclusive
offers online, please sign up for the Titan newsletter on our website:
www.titanbooks.com

A CIP catalogue record for this title is available from the British Library.

Printed and bound in the United States.

For Andrea, who kept our family on course while my writing routine drifted into the nightmare hours.

And in loving memory of my father, William Passarella whose absence/presence affects me every day.

HISTORIAN'S NOTE

This novel takes place during season six, between "Frontierland" and "Mommy Dearest."

PROLOGUE

Gavin "Shelly" Shelburn ambled along the tree-lined streets of downtown Clayton Falls, Colorado with enough conviction to avoid any charges of loitering. Occasionally, he sat on one of the secured wrought-iron benches to rest his perpetually sore feet, which had worn down the soles of his scuffed boots to the intimation of rice paper. Mostly, he spent the evening hours circling the restaurant district, eight square blocks encompassing the most popular sit-down restaurants, asking for handouts.

Whether people were about to sit down to a good meal, or returning to their cars after enjoying a fine repast, his strategy was to impart a touch of guilt on these more fortunate citizens. With a notoriously bad economy struggling to right itself, Shelburn remained on the bottom looking up. Not that it was much consolation to a man who had lost his wife to a lengthy illness, his job to subsequent neglect in unforgiving times, and his house to dispassionate bankers, but his current disenfranchised condition lacked the stigma of years past. With record unemployment and housing foreclosures "There but for the grace of God, go I" had become a familiar refrain.

The decline and fall of Gavin Shelburn had begun in advance of the so-called Great Recession, but he wasn't above accepting the sympathy of those still gainfully employed to keep his stomach, if not full, then at least occasionally mindful of its gastric function. To that end, he made his nightly rounds wearing a battered fedora—which he unfailingly tipped to the ladies and regularly flipped over to accommodate folded donations—along with a rumpled overcoat that also served as his blanket and fell to the top of his second-hand combat boots. His gaunt torso gained some bulk from the two button-down shirts he wore, one over the other, though he switched the layers each day in lieu of regular laundering. Combined, the two shirts had a complement of buttons sufficient for one. His threadbare jeans retained a hint of their original black color.

On most nights, the reliable combination of sympathy, guilt and polite panhandling kept Shelly's stomach fed and, yes, his spirits warm, while steering clear of Chief Quinn's holding cell. But the lingering effects of a poor economy led to slow evenings in the restaurant district, especially on weeknights. He'd reached the outskirts of his bread-and-butter zone, near the smaller pizza joints which offered slim pickings at the best of times, and was about to head back, when a middle-aged woman rushed out of Joe's Pizza Shack with a large pizza box and a two liter bottle of Coke.

"Good evening, Madam," he said, tipping his multi-purpose fedora.

"Oh," she said, startled, pausing in her dash to her car, a white Nissan idling at an unfed parking meter. "All right." She set the pizza box on the hood of the car, fished a crumpled dollar bill out of her purse and dropped it in his hat. "Here ya go."

"Thank you, Madam," he said, graciously accepting the dollar, which he stuffed into his left pocket since the right had a hole that had traveled the entire length of the seam.

With a careless wave she gathered up her pizza box, jumped in the car, and sped off.

A fine white mist roiled in her wake, seeming to seep in from the side streets and roll past him, lending an unearthly quality to the gritty areas that lay beyond the reach of the urban gentrification of the downtown district. More than isolated, he felt… abandoned, as if reality, along with the suburban woman, had decided to move on without him.

He stood for a moment, staring after her car, before pushing the fedora back down over his thinning, prematurely gray hair, and turned back the way he had come. Despite momentary delusions to the contrary, his reality had not changed. Though it had become routine, his life remained unpleasant, with no guarantees. *But these days*, he thought, *nobody has any guarantees*.

Over the course of the slow evening, he'd collected enough to pay for a few slices of pizza and a beverage to call his own, but it was too soon to reward himself with a meal or a drink—alcoholic or otherwise. Within the next hour, the last wave of sated diners would be heading home to park themselves in front of their high-definition plasma screens. Surely a few would spare a buck or two for a neighbor who had fallen on hard times?

Ignoring a protracted grumble of protest from his stomach, he continued his trek back toward the heart of the restaurant district. He hadn't gotten far, when he heard another sound behind him, a scrape like steel on concrete followed by a sudden, slurping hiss.

Startled, he whirled around. And staggered backward in disbelief.

"What the hell?" he whispered.

It wasn't possible.

His right hand patted the flask tucked into his overcoat pocket. Almost full. He hadn't touched the stuff. Was saving it for later, when he would hunker down for another fitful night's sleep. But even if he had drained every drop, it couldn't explain what he saw.

It was easily as long as two Nissans. A giant lizard, with a black pebbled face, its long powerful body and massive tail banded with bright orange. A name bubbled up from his subconscious, planted there in his grade school years and not quite forgotten.

Gila monster.

Its forked tongue, long as a pink yardstick, flickered out toward him, tasting the air. Then its jaws spread open, revealing a row of sharp teeth lining a mouth that could accommodate his head and entire torso in a single bite.

He remembered something else about Gila monsters.

They released venom in their saliva, a nasty neurotoxin that would paralyze their prey.

"Sweet Jesus…"

Unable to tear his gaze away from the monstrous lizard, Shelly stumbled back several paces. These creatures were supposed to be slow—but they were also supposed to be less than two feet long. This one was twenty times that size.

It took a step toward him, one set of sharp claws scraping the pavement beneath it. The tongue flicked out again. Then all four legs began to churn forward in an alternating stride that covered ground much too quickly for Shelly's liking.

Turning his back on the enormous creature, he ran almost doubled over, out of control. Behind him, the raking claws stuck the concrete in a frightening, metronomic rhythm that gained in volume as the distance between him and the creature withered away.

"Help! Somebody, help me!" he screamed breathlessly.

His voice seemed lost in the night, silenced by the blanket of mist and his total isolation. Never had he felt more alone on the streets of Clayton Falls than at that moment. Gasping in a breath to scream again, he felt the monster's long, forked tongue, sticky with what he imagined a lethal dose of venom, strafe his stubble-covered cheek.

He squealed in uncontrolled fright, his heart pounding so hard he thought it would burst in his chest like a blood-filled grenade. Claws slapped down on his right heel and the combat boot was wrenched off his foot, twisting his ankle painfully to the side. Staggering, he barely managed to maintain his balance, but knew his time had run out, so he veered left, into an alley behind a Chinese restaurant.

The hot breath of the giant Gila monster washed over the back of his neck.

Shelly heard a loud thump as the creature's enormous tail stuck a parking meter.

The alley ran all the way through to Bell Street, but he couldn't outrun the creature here, either. In seconds he would be devoured close to where he often scavenged for discarded food himself, right out of the—

He veered to the left, raised his left arm up to the edge of the shadowy bulk of the restaurant's Dumpster and heaved himself over the lip and down into the damp and malodorous refuse.

No sooner had he landed in the cushion of garbage than something, probably the Gila monster's head, stuck the side of the Dumpster and propelled it down the alley. Metal shrieked against the brick wall opposite the rear of the Chinese restaurant. The Dumpster trundled spastically as its undersized wheels squealed in protest.

Abruptly, the jittery motion stopped.

Shelly held his breath. All he heard was the thunderous beating of his overtaxed heart. As he pushed himself up to a sitting position, something powerful struck the side of the Dumpster, dimpling the steel right between his feet, and rocking the container back into the brick wall. Another protracted screech as the creature's claws raked the exterior.

Shelly remembered another unfortunate fact about Gila monsters.

They could climb.

And this one was large enough to raise itself over the edge of the Dumpster.

He was cornered.

Frantically, he swept his hands through the slimy and sticky refuse, searching for something sharp or hard, anything that could serve as a weapon. His search became more desperate when he saw the creature's claws wrap around the rim of the Dumpster like a matching set of butcher knives. The trash bin began to tilt forward as the creature's weight pressed down on it. Shelly heard an explosive pop as of one of the wheels sheared off the base. It was only a matter of seconds before the pebbled head, beady black eyes, and grotesquely long, forked tongue would rise over him and block out the sky.

Shelly's foraging hand slammed into a wooden slat. He blindly traced its dimensions because he refused to look away from the Dumpster's opening. *A produce crate!* he realized. Flimsy, but if he broke it apart he could use one of the slats as a makeshift dagger. Poke its eye out and maybe it would go elsewhere for its next meal.

Abruptly the Dumpster eased back and bumped into the brick wall.

Long seconds passed before Shelly realized the claws were gone. One moment they'd been pressed against the steel, the next they were absent. He waited a minute, motionless, listening intently for any sound. Gradually, he became aware of the ambient noise of the night. The rumble of passing trucks, the hiss of tires on asphalt, the toot of distant horns... his own ragged breathing.

He rolled onto his hands and knees and reached for the edge of the Dumpster, slowing pulling himself up out of the garbage, his head rising above the surface like a periscope in enemy waters. He peered along the length of the alley, left and right.

Nothing. As if the lizard had dropped off the face of the earth.

"I'll be damned."

"This town is so lame."

Eighteen-year-old Steven Bullinger drained his second can of beer, crumpled the empty aluminum can and tossed it into one of the decorative bushes that ringed the tarnished bronze statues of Charles Clayton and Jeremiah Falls at the center of Founders Park.

Tony Lacosta shook his head. "You say that every night."

"Yeah, Bullinger," Lucy Quinn said. "You need new material." She stood between them, facing the opposite direction, hands stuffed into the pockets of her hoodie, which was hot pink and densely patterned with tiny black skulls. She was the lookout.

The bronze nineteenth-century pioneers were depicted astride their horses, angled away from each other in a V-shape, illuminated by recessed floodlights. Clayton pointed into the distance, possibly indicating the site of the present municipal building, while Falls pulled up on his horse's reins. But the three teens did not choose their loitering spot out of any sense of civic pride. The benches directly behind the bronze horses were obstructed from view and cloaked in shadow at night, beyond the harsh glare of the monument's floodlights.

Steven grumbled, "Making sure you were paying attention."

"You could leave."

"Thinking about it," Steven said sullenly. "Weighing my options."

"Right," Tony said. "Toss me a beer before you drink them all."

Steven slipped his hand into the open backpack he'd set on the park bench next to him and tossed a can to Tony. He looked at Lucy. "You want one?"

She shook her head. "I'm good." Drinking was the furthest thing from her mind.

"You don't drink no more, is that it?"

"No," she said defensively. "It's not that."

"Worried your dad will catch you?" Steven persisted.

"No," she said, then sighed. "Maybe. He *is* the chief of police."

"And you have him wrapped around your finger."

She scoffed. "I wish."

"What's the real reason?" Tony asked, index finger poised over the tab, waiting to open the can.

"I don't know," she said and shrugged. "The timing."

"What? Not late enough for you?" Steven asked.

Tony heaved an exasperated sigh. "She's talking about Teddy, you dumbass."

"Yesterday was the one-year anniversary," Lucy said. "You guys don't think about the accident?"

"Sure I do," Steven said defensively. "Don't see me driving, do you?"

"Jackass!" Lucy said, kicking him in the shin.

"What the hell?" Steven seemed more upset about dropping his third can of beer than about the kick. He scooped it off the ground before much had spilled. A thin white mist had rolled across the park grounds, progressing in eddies and swirls. Steven only gave it a moment's notice. "I didn't mean anything by it!"

"So being a jerk comes naturally?"

"More like constant practice," Tony said, smirking.

"Shut up," Steven said to him. Then he turned to Lucy. "Look, a year ago that's all people talked about. Every time they saw me. Any of us walk into a room or if they passed us on the street. Can't say I miss that. Ever since the factory fire... All I'm saying is, I get to deal with it on my own terms now. Without people shoving it in my face all the time."

Lucy crossed her arms and glared at him. "Excuse me if I don't want to forget about Teddy."

"I don't—I didn't say—Tony, talk to her."

"None of us want to forget Teddy," Tony said. "He was your boyfriend, but we knew him since grade school. And we were all... stupid that night. But dwelling on it? I don't think that's.... What's wrong? Cops?"

Lucy was staring at the statues. Her eyes were wide, her green irises ringed with white. She pointed. "Three—three horses."

Tony followed her gaze. Steven twisted around on the bench, looking over his shoulder. Moving within the V created by the horses of Clayton and Falls was another horse, a black stallion. Its hooves clopped on the marble base of the life-sized monument and it snorted as its rider steered it away from the bronze tableau, between two benches and through a gap in the decorative bushes.

"It's coming for us," Lucy said.

"What?" Steven looked from her to Tony.

Tony dropped his beer can. "What the hell?"

The rider was clad in black, a riding cloak, shirt, trousers and boots. But the first thing Lucy noticed was his head. Rather, his lack of a head. The cloak was tied around the trunk of his neck, but the neck ended in a ragged, bloody stump. No head… and yet she had the feeling he could see everything. He seemed to be staring right at her through invisible eyes.

The rider held the horse's reins bunched in his left hand because his right hand held a gleaming sword.

"Run!" Tony yelled.

Lucy was paralyzed. In that moment, she was sure she would have stood still as the headless horseman shoved the sword straight through her heart. But Tony grabbed one of her suddenly clammy hands and tugged her sideways. She stumbled after him, looking back, unable to take her eyes off the nightmarish apparition that had materialized out of thin air.

Steven trailed behind them, mainly because he had paused to grab his beer-filled backpack.

The horse whinnied and reared up on its hind legs. The rider kicked spurs into the horse's flanks and it dropped down to all fours and galloped after them, its hooves pounding the earth with deadly determination. Lucy could feel the vibration in her shins and thought she would throw up any second. She realized she was sobbing.

Steven hadn't paused to zip up his backpack. Every few strides a beer can slipped free and tumbled to the ground, letting out a protesting hiss of pressurized foam. Finally, he cursed and tossed the backpack aside.

Lucy couldn't help glancing back every other step. She stumbled again and again, but Tony's momentum kept her upright. She saw the horseman bear down on Steven and swing his sword in a whistling arc, determined to reduce the young man to his own headless condition or perhaps remedy his cranial loss by random substitution. Lucy gave an involuntary shriek.

The gleaming blade missed Steven's neck by a whisker.

Steven must have felt its swift passage. He clapped a hand to the nape of his neck, as if checking for blood.

They were near the edge of the park, within sight of the municipal building, when Lucy was jerked to the side. She stumbled and fell against Tony for a moment before he led her to the right.

"What—?" she began.

"We need to split up," Tony said, his breathing ragged. "Can't chase all of us."

"But Steve…"

The vibration in her legs was gone. She glanced back but could no longer see the headless horseman. In his gray sweatshirt and faded jeans, Steven was a blur of motion running and stumbling toward Park Lane.

"C'mon," Tony said, pulling her attention back. "Think we lost him."

"What was that?"

"Sure as hell wasn't the neighborhood watch."

Steven had never run so fast in his life. At some point, between tossing aside the backpack he'd used to smuggle beer out of the house and feeling the horseman's sword whistle past his neck, he forgot about everything that had led up to the nightmarish chase. He stopped questioning the impossibility of a man without a head riding a horse that had appeared out of nowhere. Every iota of his concentration focused on racing from his imminent death, while suppressing the powerful urge to vomit up every last ounce of beer he had imbibed. A single hesitation, for whatever reason, would mean the difference between life and death. Even so, a man, even a sober man, couldn't outrun a horse for long. Steven veered close to tree trunks, favoring those with low hanging limbs. Unseat the horseman and the chase turned in his favor. But it seemed he couldn't shake the headless rider, only postpone the inevitable. The thunderous rumble of hooves was never more than one false step away.

Face contorted in a rictus of pain, he burst from the edge of the park, bounded across the wide sidewalk and sprinted onto Park Lane. Several steps into his panicked flight across the blacktop, he stumbled and almost fell to his knees. Doubled over, he cringed, waiting for the hard steel to bite into his flesh. Then it occurred to him that the thundering noise of hooves had stopped. He looked back and saw that the headless horseman had vanished. He had never followed Steven out of the park.

Steven straightened and peered behind him. Nothing moving between the trees. No horse. No headless rider. Looking left and right, he couldn't see Tony or Lucy. Vaguely he recalled them veering to the side, away from his mindless, straight-line flight. Sensible strategy, but he would have had their back.

Or would he?

Staring back at the park, he wondered if the horseman was confined within its boundaries. If his friends remained in the park now, were they in danger? Would the rider seek them out after his solo target had escaped? Steven could go back and warn them... but he had no idea where they had gone. Was the horseman even real? Could they have imagined the whole thing? When you really thought about it, it made no sense. How could it? Unless...something in the beer? Product tampering? LSD in the cans? No, because Lucy had seen it first and she hadn't had any beer. Then how—?

BEEP!

A battered Ford pickup truck swerved around him, the driver leaving behind a string of curses with the truck's pungent white exhaust.

Steven looked down at the painted line and realized that he'd pulled up in the middle of Park Lane. Fortunately for him, traffic was light in the evening. And the white exhaust was really spreading...

Not exhaust. The white, cottony mist he'd barely acknowledged in the park had spread out across the road, swirling around his ankles.

An accelerating motor—a deep-throated roar—drew his

attention up again but this vehicle didn't swerve.

He had a moment to register the color red, with a white stripe across the hood leading his eye to the driver, but—

Air exploded out of his lungs as his legs shattered and his body flipped through the air, bounding across the hood of the car, skipping past the windshield and tumbling up and away from the roof as if gravity had suddenly released any claim to his mass. But just as suddenly, it reclaimed him with punishing force, slamming him down onto the blacktop as if swatted from above by a giant hand. His head struck and his skull seemed to lose its rigidity, his vision splitting into two separate views a split second before one side went completely dark and the other began to fade.

Somewhere he heard a woman scream.

A man looked down at him, shock on his face.

"Oh, God," Steven heard him say.

Steven wanted to tell the man not to worry, but the words came out jumbled and seemed to originate far away. Didn't help that he was shivering as he spoke.

"I can't believe—that guy—he hit you on purpose!" the man declared.

Steven tried to shake his head. Big mistake. Pain knifed through him so fiercely he blacked out for a second. Maybe longer. When the man's pale face returned, this time with a cell phone pressed to his ear, Steven tried to explain what he saw before the moment of impact but only the last two words made it past his numb lips.

"…nobody driving."

"What—?"

A young woman stepped into Steven's diminishing field of vision. She grabbed the man's arm.

"I—I can't believe it!" she said. Her voice sounded distant and hollow.

"I called an ambulance," the man told her.

"—tried to get the license plate," she said, glancing briefly at Steven, long enough for him to see the horror and disbelief on her face before she looked away. "Blake, I—I couldn't."

"That's okay," he said. "It happened so fast."

"That's not what I mean," she said. Her words were out of sync with her lips, as if she were an actress in a poorly dubbed foreign film. Movement began to leave smears of color across Steven's vision. "I was looking right at the car and it… vanished."

"Vanished how?"

Like the headless horseman? Steven wondered.

"I don't know how," she said. "One second it was there. And the next it was gone."

Steven blinked, but when he opened his eyes there was only darkness. He thought they might still be talking above him but the only sound he heard was a soft, rhythmic thumping, fading and slowing and then nothing…

ONE

The beam of Dean Winchester's flashlight played over the pair of stained manacles dangling from an eyebolt mounted in the back of a stall in Cletus Gillmer's horse stable. He didn't need a forensic kit to guess the nature of the stains.

"Sick bastard kept the victims chained back here," he said.

Across the aisle, his brother Sam examined the tack room, dominated by a sturdy wooden work table with eyebolts screwed into the surface at each corner.

"And chopped them up over here," Sam responded.

"Not what old man Gillmer had in mind when he asked junior to take over the family farm."

They'd found Cletus Gillmer in the farmhouse, sprawled on an old recliner patched with duct tape, his eyes bulging and bloodshot, his tongue protruding and his throat savagely crushed. On the round table beside him, he'd left behind an old, loaded revolver and a curious, apparently interrupted, to-do list. After "siphon gasoline from generator," "bury body," and "burn stable," he'd written "burn" a second time before dropping the pen on the floor. Dean guessed that "burn farmhouse" would have been next, followed by "insert revolver in mouth" and "pull trigger." Apparently old man Gillmer had grown weary of chasing thrill-seeking teens off his property, but not before somebody else decided to punch his ticket.

A local newspaper's piece on the five-year anniversary of the machete killings and the sudden, mysterious disappearance of Cletus' murderous son, Clive Gillmer, had created an urban legend to test the mettle of a new crop of teenagers. From deranged serial killer to phantom bogeyman in five years. The old man tried to scare the kids away, garnering "crazy old coot" status, but some had gone missing nonetheless. Dean suspected the old man knew what the Winchesters did: bogeymen have teeth.

On their way out of the farmhouse, Sam spotted the pink sneaker in the high grass beside the front porch steps, bathed in moonlight. Their flashlights had revealed the young woman with a broken neck stuffed under the crawlspace. And so the to-do list had led them to the horse stable…

As Dean walked toward the second stall—duffel bag hanging from his left shoulder, shotgun loaded with rock salt cradled under his right arm—he heard Sam open and search one of the tack trunks under the table.

"Dean!" he called. "Found a machete."

"Keep looking," Dean said absently. "Junior's body's gotta be here."

He opened the next stall door with the tip of his shotgun.

The eyebolt in this one was angled down. Dean grabbed it, wiggled it back and forth, felt the wood planking give, bits of rotted wood falling away like damp mulch. His flashlight flickered—

A loud crash broke the eerie silence of the stable.

Dean whirled. "Sam!"

Looming over him was the six-foot-seven, three-hundred-pound vengeful spirit of Clive Gillmer, in mottled whiteface, wearing the traditional black-and-white striped shirt under blood-stained bib overalls. "The Machete Mime," as the press had dubbed him.

Dean swung the shotgun up, but the Mime clubbed his arm away and rammed him against the back wall with enough force to split the weakened boards. The shotgun fell from his numb fingers along with the flashlight.

"Sam! Little help!"

Before Sam regained his soul, Dean was never sure when his brother would have his back. But that was before. Now…

The Mime picked Dean up and slammed him against the wall to the right and then to the left. Both were in better shape than the rear wall, if the sharp pain in his ribs was any judge.

"Marcel Machete here has anger management issues!" Dean yelled.

He dodged a fist which punched a hole in the wall next to his head, but caught a knee in the gut and dropped to the ground, stunned.

The crash he'd heard earlier, after Sam discovered the machete...

"Sammy!"

Face it. Sam's out of commission.

Dean heard a clanking of chains, then felt cold steel encircle his neck, bite into his flesh and inexorably tighten.

He managed to slip his fingers under the chain and alleviate the pressure long enough to suck in some air and clear his vision. His other hand scrabbled across the matted straw of the dirt floor until his fingers closed around the barrel of his shotgun.

The Mime's booted foot kicked Dean's arm against the wall and once again the shotgun slipped from his grasp. Dean's vision began to dim again, fading to black at the edges, when he heard a shotgun blast from above.

In an instant, the pressure of the chains around his neck was gone and he was stumbling forward onto hands and knees, coughing and gasping for air.

Sam stood in the aisle, shotgun braced in his hands. His jacket was torn at the shoulder seam and a line of blood trickled from his scalp.

"He surprised me," he stated.

Dean nodded. "Makes two of us," he rasped.

Dean grabbed his own shotgun and Sam helped him to his feet. Brushing straw off his clothes, Dean scanned the ground for his flashlight and found it near the back wall of the stall.

"Let's find the body before Baby Huey comes back," he said, scooping it up.

"Don't think it's here," Sam said.

Dean didn't respond.

"Dean?" Sam said.

Dean stared through the gap in the broken back wall. He kicked a split plank out of the way.

"Behind the farmhouse," he said. "You see that?"

Sam looked past his shoulder. "Wooden shed."

"We assumed the old man planned to burn the farmhouse after the stable."

Sam nodded. "Clive knew his father's real target."

They slipped through the gap in the wall and raced along the corral fence, behind the farmhouse to the unprepossessing tool shed in back. Ten feet square, it was open in front, revealing three walls with hooks for various farm implements long ago removed. The floor was covered with mismatched scraps of outdoor carpeting littered with old leaves, yellowed sections of torn newsprint and snack food wrappers.

"Nothing," Dean said flatly. "More nothing."

Sam walked into the shed, probing the corners of the single room with his flashlight beam. Boards squeaked under his weight. He stopped, looked down, then back up at Dean.

"You thinking what I'm thinking?"

"Root cellar?"

Sam crouched, lifted a few uneven squares of carpet and tossed them aside, revealing twin wooden doors secured by an old padlock with an elongated shackle.

"Bolt cutters?"

"Try this," Dean said, passing him a crowbar from his duffel.

Slipping the straight end under one of the door handles,

Sam levered it up and out of the rotting wood until the screws popped out. He repeated the process on the other handle and wiggled the padlock free.

"Here goes."

He wedged the crowbar under the edge of the right-hand door and raised it enough to slip his fingers under it. He flung it open to the squeal of protesting hinges.

"Whoa!"

The stench assailed them like a physical presence.

Left hand pressed against his nose, Sam leaned over and flipped open the other door. Dean's flashlight beam speared the darkness at the bottom of the rickety staircase and revealed the hulking corpse in the remnants of a striped shirt and bib overalls, curled on its stomach, with a pitchfork buried in its back.

Deep enough to puncture lungs, Dean thought. *Or skewer his heart.*

"Old man put him down five years ago. Left him to rot," he said.

"Let everyone assume he'd run off," Sam said.

He reached down for his own duffel bag and so was caught by surprise.

Flickering into existence between them, the Mime's spirit charged—

"Sam!"

—and shoved Sam down the stairs.

Both root-cellar doors slammed shut.

Junior spun around and rushed Dean, his marred white face stretched wide in a hideous grin that revealed years of dental neglect.

"I've seen your act, Tiny," Dean said grimly, taking a step back to pump the shotgun's action and level the barrel at the killer Mime. "It blows."

He blasted a round of rock salt into the spirit's torso.

The Mime vanished, buying them some more time.

Dean slammed the action bar down and back to chamber another round.

Then, rushing into the shed, he flipped the doors open and aimed his flashlight into the darkness.

"Sam! Sammy!" he called.

"Here, Dean," came the reply. "I'm okay."

Dean negotiated the rickety stairs, sweeping the underground room with his flashlight to reveal sagging multi-tiered wooden shelves lining the walls, filled with an assortment of mason jars and plastic containers, rotting vegetables and rancid salted meats long since abandoned. On the floor, sitting beside the decaying corpse, Sam massaged his neck with one hand while shielding his eyes from the light with the other.

"Let's end this," Dean said, tossing his brother a canister of sea salt. He rifled through his bag for the container of lighter fluid.

Sam climbed to his feet, pressed a hand to his lower back and winced. But he shook off the residual aches and pains of having rolled down the stairs and spread salt liberally over Clive's remains.

"What is it with mimes anyway?" he wondered. "Clowns with a vow of silence?"

"This one forgot the rule about 'no props,'" Dean replied.

Dean squeezed the aluminum container and flicked the stream of lighter fluid back and forth over the corpse, head to toe.

"Machete Mime." Sam shook his head. "Light him up."

Something took shape in the darkness.

Their flashlights dimmed.

"Dude, we're not alone!"

Out of the shadows a beefy arm snaked around Sam's throat and pulled him back into the darkness. They crashed into the shelving in the back of the root cellar, busting shelves and sending jars shattering against each other on the floor.

Blocking out the frantic sounds of Sam's dire struggle, Dean fished his Zippo lighter out of his jacket pocket, flicked it to spark a flame, then tossed it on the Mime's remains. As the fire caught hold, Dean heard Sam gasp and stumble forward across the shattered glass. The wooden handle of the pitchfork protruding from the Mime's back caught fire and the racing flames quickly ignited the shelves to the right. In seconds, the fire swept along the back wall and then spread to the left. Dean realized that if it reached the stairs they'd find themselves trapped in their own private inferno.

"Sam!"

"Go!" Sam yelled, veering unsteadily around the burning corpse.

Dean caught Sam's upper arm long enough to steady him, then shoved him toward the wooden staircase. Sam took the stairs two at a time. One of the boards cracked under his weight but Sam was up and out. The heat had become unbearable. Dean shielded his face with his arm, holding his breath and squinting through the roiling black smoke as he followed his brother. Flames scorched his heels as the hungry fire roared up out of the ground. He rolled clear of the shed, which was engulfed moments later, and gulped down huge mouthfuls of fresh Nebraska air.

Dean left the Impala parked at the curb and walked into a local tavern. With his ribs aching and his mouth tasting of bitter smoke, he wanted nothing more than a cold one or three to apply the layer of numbness he needed to sleep through the night.

It was a few hours before closing time, but the barroom was deserted. Tables, booths and stools were empty, the lone pool table unemployed, and the jukebox silent. A flat-screen TV angled over the bar displayed a soccer match in some other part of the world, the volume turned down to white noise hum. Other than Dean, the middle-aged bartender was the only person in the place.

Tapping the eraser end of a pencil against his teeth, the bartender was hunched over a pile of papers on the countertop with the concentration of someone working on his taxes. As Dean neared the bar, he saw the object of the man's concentration was a horse racing form. The man looked up at his approach.

"Get you something?"

"Whatever you got on tap," Dean said, sitting on the nearest stool. He rested his forearms on the padded edge of the counter and sighed. "Maybe a few peanuts."

"Sure," the bartender said, taking down a glass. "Quiet night, huh?"

"Didn't start out that way."

"Problems?"

"Same old same old."

The bartender held the glass under the chrome faucet and pulled the brass lever. Amber liquid flowed into the glass, rising toward the brim. But at the halfway point, the beer level began to fall.

"That's odd," the bartender murmured.

"Hole in the glass?"

"No, no, the glass is fine." Nonetheless, the bartender released the lever, set the glass aside and began to fill a replacement. Same result. As fast as the beer flowed into the glass, it seemed to... evaporate. "This makes no sense. Let me try another one." He sidestepped to the next draft lever and repeated the process. Beer flowed into the glass and was as quickly gone. The bartender passed a hand over his close-cropped blond hair. "This has never happened before."

"First time for everything, pal."

"Maybe it's the CO2 tank. How about a bottle?"

Dean nodded. Tapped the countertop in front of him.

"Domestic? Import? Microbrew?"

"Let's start with domestic and go from there."

The bartender grabbed a long-necked brown bottle from under the counter, popped off the cap, releasing thin streams of vapor, and slid it across to Dean with the glass from the tap.

Dean decided to skip the middleman and raised the tip of

the cold bottle to his lips. He tilted the bottle back and...
nothing came out.

"What the hell?" he declared.

"What's wrong?"

"It's empty."

"That's impossible."

Dean upended the bottle over the glass. Not a drop fell
out.

"Let me try that," the bartender said, grabbing a fresh
bottle. He eased it back and forth and liquid sloshed within
the bottle. He then popped the cap and titled it over Dean's
glass. Wisps of vapor escaped the bottle and dissipated.
A few drops of liquid struck the bottom of the glass and
promptly evaporated. The bartender pushed the empty
bottle aside and tried a third, and a fourth, different labels,
all without success.

"Cans," Dean said. "What about cans?"

The bartender opened a door behind the counter into a
back room, and returned a moment later with a six-pack.

"These were delivered today," he stated.

He pulled the tab off the first can and they heard a faint
hiss as vapor spiraled out the opening. One can after another,
the glass remained empty.

Dean shook his head. "This is not happening."

"I'm sorry," the bartender said. "What can I do?"

"Try something else," Dean said. "Anything. Whiskey,
rum, vodka. Peach schnapps!"

Nothing worked. The bartender tried Irish whiskey,
Russian vodka, and Jamaican rum.

"I can't explain this," the bartender said, incredulous. "What does it mean?"

Dean noticed the audio hum emanating from the television set above the bar had changed. He glanced up and saw a news bulletin had replaced the soccer match. A telegenic news anchor in her late twenties spoke while a news crawl informed Dean one letter at a time that the world's supply of alcoholic beverages had become unstable.

"The volume," he said. "Turn it up!"

The bartender pointed a slim remote control at the set and raised the volume.

"...the scientific community remains baffled by the sudden and complete volatility of alcohol in any form."

Dean stared aghast. "You gotta be *kidding* me!"

"This bar's been in my family for sixty years," the bartender said morosely. "And it's all gone?"

The news anchor continued in an upbeat tone, "...face the new reality that we have become a nation, indeed an entire world, of teetotalers."

"She's smiling," Dean said, pointing accusingly. "Why is she smiling? She can't smile about this."

"Oh, well," the bartender said, now strangely at peace with the family-business-ending news. "How about something nonalcoholic?"

"No," Dean said, backing away abruptly and knocking over his stool.

"Pop? Or milk?"

"No!"

"Juice box? Bottled water?"

"No!"

"Got it," the bartender said, snapping his fingers. "A Shirley Temple. No alcohol in that!"

"Dude! Seriously?"

Dean backed up to the door, tugged on the handle but the door wouldn't open. In frustration, he pounded his fists on the wood panels.

"An egg cream?"

"Noooo!"

Dean sat upright, heart racing. A fleeting sense of displacement faded and he remembered where he was. The nondescript motel they'd checked into in Lincoln, Nebraska. He sat in the dark and fought the ridiculous urge to turn on CNN to confirm the safety of the world's alcoholic beverages.

Across the room, sprawled on his bed as if sleep had been an afterthought, Sam mumbled something about hunters.

Dean stacked pillows against his headboard and laid back gingerly, enduring sharp protests from his ribs with each awkward movement. Felt as if he'd been kicked repeatedly by a mule with a sour disposition. Bedside clock radio told him he'd been asleep less than an hour. He'd need at least a few more before they hit the road. Coffee would take care of the rest.

"But no more dreams."

TWO

Sam Winchester stood in the root cellar again.

The underground storage room was empty. No shelves or mason jars or plastic containers. Even the Machete Mime's corpse and the pitchfork that had killed him were gone. No evidence of the all-consuming fire.

He stood at the bottom of the wooden stairs, moonlight spilling across the floor on either side of him, but not reaching far enough to penetrate the darkness that shrouded the back of the room. And though the room seemed empty, Sam was not alone. A shape of equal height and mass stood within the shadows staring back at him.

"What do you want?" Sam asked.

"To replace you."

"Why?"

"Because I'm better at it than you are."

Sam wanted to step forward, to reach into the darkness, but he was paralyzed where he stood, as if balanced on a precipice. One false step and he could fall; maybe never stop falling. He was close to something dangerous here. Had to be careful. He'd lost his way before. How many times could he go astray before it became impossible to find his way back to... himself?

The *other* took a step forward, emerging from the shadows. Like looking in a mirror, Sam stared at another version of himself. Sam without a soul. And that Sam was smirking at him.

"Your soul is a burden. It makes you weak."

"You were out of control. You tried to kill Bobby to save yourself."

"Self-preservation is an admirable trait in a hunter." Soulless Sam walked around him in a loose circle while Sam struggled to move his legs. He was pinned to the spot.

"You were no different from the monsters you hunted."

"Keep telling yourself that, Sammy," he said. "We both know I was the more effective hunter."

"Doesn't matter," Sam said. "You're done."

"Am I?" Soulless Sam asked. "Or... could be that soul of yours is a poor fit these days. Damaged goods. Might not stick around for the long haul. One little *push*—" Soulless Sam poked him in the chest with a forefinger and Sam staggered back a step before regaining his balance—"and *poof*! I'm back in the driver's seat."

"No," Sam said. "That's not gonna happen."

"You'd be surprised," Soulless Sam said. "You're not free of me. Never will be. I'm still in there, itching to get out."

"No!"

Sam was frozen to the spot while Soulless Sam had complete freedom of movement. He walked behind Sam and paused at the staircase. Sam twisted his head around to keep Soulless Sam in view.

"Not as safe as you think you are."

Soulless Sam climbed the creaking stairs. Before he disappeared into the night, he turned back and shook his head.

"Better watch your step, Sammy."

With a sense of impending doom, Sam looked around the dark root cellar. Soulless Sam's parting words had been a warning, no mistaking that but what—

Through the soles of his feet, he felt vibrations, as if the ground was pulsing. And with that chthonic disturbance, he regained control of his feet. But the moment he shifted his position, the cellar floor began to sink from the center outward, the concrete crumbling to the consistency of gravel—or sand. Even the walls began to slide down, funneling into the widening hole. Sam leapt toward the wooden staircase, falling forward to grab the bottom step with his hands. The ground fell away so quickly it offered him no support. He pulled himself up the stairs far enough to get his knees, and then his feet under him. But without the floor to brace the staircase, it was unable to support his full weight. The tread beneath his feet cracked down the middle, separating from the riser. As he jumped up to the next step, he heard a sharp crack and saw the top tread separating from the front wall. Sam lunged toward the exit—

—and struck an invisible barrier.

He pressed his hand against what appeared to be a glass

barrier, several inches thick. After pounding his fists against the glass to no effect, he rammed his shoulder against it and almost fell off the teetering staircase. Catching his balance he pressed his back against the transparent barrier and tried to push it out of the way. His gaze dropped to the center of the root cellar where a whirlpool of sand sank into darkness.

Suddenly the staircase collapsed under him.

Falling, he flung out an arm and caught the shattered wooden framework, clinging to the wood as if it were a life preserver in the swirling ocean of sand. Soon he was caught in the current, cycling around and down, ever closer to the darkness that would consume him—

"Whoa!"

Sam sat up on the motel bed, heart racing as he tried to remember where he was. Middle of the night, but cold light cast from the motel parking lot sliced through a gap in the curtains and split the room in half. On the other side, he saw Dean propped up against his headboard. Too dark to tell if his brother was awake.

"Dean?"

"Yeah."

"Ribs?"

"Waiting for the aspirin to kick in."

"Right."

"Bad dream?"

"That obvious?"

"Case of the three a.m. shakes," Dean said. "Had a doozy

myself. Terrifying."

"Really?" Sam had the unsettling idea that Dean had witnessed Sam's dream. Or had the *same* dream. They'd seen stranger things. "What about?"

Sam listened with a growing incredulity.

"…and to top it off," Dean finished. "I was trapped there with that guy."

"*That* was your terrifying nightmare?" Sam scoffed.

"All the beer, Sam. In the world. *Gone!*"

"Wow."

"What? Tell me yours was worse?"

"No—I—no," Sam said. Actually, he was relieved that Dean didn't know what had plagued his subconscious. As it was, Dean thought his brother's psyche was too fragile. No need to add fuel to that fire. "It was—was fine."

Dean's demeanor changed. He climbed off the bed with a soft grunt of pain, and walked toward Sam, the slice of light momentarily painting a swath of illumination across his concerned expression.

"Sam, if this is something serious, maybe I oughta know about it."

"Look, Dean, I get it. You're worried about me. But this is… nothing. Really. Nothing at all. Okay, man?"

"Then tell me."

"It was the Mime, all right? I was back in Gillmer's root cellar." At least that part was true. "Too close to the clown thing."

"Stealth clowns," Dean said, nodding. "Right."

"You don't sound convinced."

"No. I'm convinced. But that don't mean we should forget you have a wall inside your head keeping a hell storm of memories bottled up."

"Dude, do you seriously think I'd forget about the wall in my mind?"

"No. You're right. Thing about a scab is, you pick at it."

"I'm not picking at anything," Sam said in exasperation. "I was sleeping. Dreaming. That's normal, right? Something I couldn't do when my soul was MIA." Sam took a deep breath. "It's not like I can control my dreams."

Dean thought about it for a moment and nodded. "But, you notice any cracks in the wall, you tell me. Right?"

"Sure, Dean."

In the dim lighting, Sam couldn't tell if his brother believed him.

A cell phone rang.

Dean grabbed his jacket, pulled out his mobile and glanced down at the display.

"Bobby," he told Sam and answered the call.

THREE

"You boys up for a drive to Colorado?" Bobby Singer asked in Dean's ear. Dean punched a button to put him on speaker.

"Machete Mime's in our rearview. What's in Colorado?" he asked.

"Clayton Falls," Bobby said. "Giant lizards. Headless horseman. Hit-and-run car with no driver. Definite weird-meter stuff."

Sam got up from his bed to position himself closer to the mic.

"Mass hallucinations?" he said.

"Wasn't no hallucination that run down a kid fresh outta high school," Bobby responded.

Sam frowned.

"We'll check it out, Bobby," Dean said, ending the call. He turned to Sam. "I'll get coffee. Wanna see what you can find online before we hit the road?"

Sam nodded. "Sure. Wi-Fi hotspot here's not half bad." As he opened the laptop and powered it up, he added wistfully, "Now that I can sleep again, I can't find the time."

Dean paused in the doorway on his way out.

"Sleep's overrated, right?"

Several hours later, the sun was up, the coffee was long gone, and Dean was behind the wheel of the Impala, riding I-80 West out of Nebraska. In the passenger seat, Sam had the laptop computer open to review the pages he'd downloaded for offline viewing before they'd left the motel.

Dean glanced over at him. "Anything?"

"Not much more than what Bobby gave us."

"So Spielberg wasn't in town filming giant lizards?"

"Homeless man complained to a beat cop that he was chased by a giant Gila monster."

Dean raised an eyebrow. "Homeless guy?"

"That's what it says. Gavin Shelburn."

"Anyone else see Godzilla?"

"No."

"Maybe chalk that one up to Gavin hitting the sauce a little hard."

"Maybe," Sam said noncommittally. "Steven Bullinger, eighteen, hit-and-run victim. Head trauma. Pronounced dead at the scene. Before he died, Bullinger told a witness the car had no driver."

"You did say 'head trauma?'"

"Yeah," Sam said, conceding the point. "But… another witness tried to grab the license plate number on the car."

"Okay, that one sounds clear-headed."

"She says the car disappeared. There one minute, gone the next."

Dean tapped the steering wheel. "Phantom car. Okay. What about the headless horseman?"

"Apparently he chased the daughter of the chief of police. Lucy Quinn."

"So we got something."

"Something," Sam agreed. "Dean, I've been reading through old articles. Lot of press about a garment factory explosion six months ago. Gas leak. Partial building collapse. Trapped a lot of people. Sprinklers malfunctioned. Those who weren't killed by the initial explosion and fire died from smoke inhalation."

"How many?"

"Thirty-two dead. All locals," Sam said. He clicked on another saved page. "Lots of editorials. Worst catastrophe in town history. Human interest stories about each of the victims and their families. Petitions for a memorial. Public debate about the location of the memorial. At the site of the explosion or opposite the town hall. Articles on the bidding and construction. Looks like the town hall location won."

"Public grieving," Dean said. "Think there's a connection?"

"It's something to consider."

The Winchesters reached Clayton Falls by early afternoon and, after a brief stop at the Liquor Barn, checked into the StarBrite Motel, their room an instant sixties flashback with framed flower-power prints on the walls, tie-dyed pillowcases, bedside lava lamps, peace sign drawer handles and mirror decals, and a colorful beaded curtain doorway for the closet.

Clutching a brown paper shopping bag in one arm, Dean took in the rainbow color scheme with a frown.

"Place looks like they provide LSD tabs instead of complimentary soap," he said.

"Might explain some of the weirdness in town," Sam replied with a shrug.

Reaching into his Liquor Barn bag, Dean removed three bottles of whiskey and two six-packs of beer, lining them up on the dresser beside the secured television.

"Planning a bender tonight?" Sam asked.

"No," Dean said, determined to avoid any further mention of his evaporating alcohol dream. "This is my… strategic reserve."

"Worried about a shortage?"

"Keeping my options close at hand. Timesaver. That's all."

"All right," Sam said, smiling as he nodded. But he let it go.

They changed into their FBI suits and drove to the municipal building to check in with the chief of police. Zeppelin's "Kashmir" was playing on the local classic rock station when Dean turned off the Impala's engine.

They climbed out of the car and crossed the parking lot. The sky was a crisp blue with a staggered line of cottony clouds. To the west, the Rocky Mountains loomed but their edges seemed muted, slightly out of focus.

"Look," Sam said and pointed to a curved brick wall, five-feet high, fifteen-feet wide, with flagpoles at each end, one flying the US flag, the other the state flag of Colorado. The concave front of the wall faced the brick municipal building, with a lofty white clock tower rising from the middle, on the other side of Main Street. "The curved wall's the memorial. I recognize it from the online photos."

They circled around to the front of the memorial. Mounted in the center of the wall was a bronze plaque which listed details about the explosion. On either side of the main plaque were smaller bronze plaques, side by side, with portraits of each of the victims, their names, ages, birth and death dates. The death dates were identical. At the base of the wall fresh bouquets of flowers, along with stuffed animals and framed portraits of the victims or their relatives, filled the open space and spilled out onto the sidewalk.

"This new every day?" Dean asked.

"Flowers are fresh."

A sign directed them to the police entrance in the back of the municipal building. A short corridor led to a small lobby adjacent to the dispatcher's elevated area behind bulletproof glass. A gray-haired woman sat on a chair wearing a lightweight headset while she knitted. Next to a microphone in front of her, a nameplate read "Millicent Perkins."

Dean tapped the glass to get her attention and flashed his counterfeit FBI credentials.

"Ms. Perkins," he said.

She leaned forward, switched on the microphone.

"Oh—oh, my! How can I help you?"

"FBI," Dean said. "Agents DeYoung and Shaw. We need to see Chief Quinn."

"Just a moment. I'll see if he's available."

She turned to the side, picked up a phone and spoke into it. With the microphone off, her voice was too muffled for him to distinguish individual words.

Dean looked around. The lobby held some framed newspaper articles highlighting the police department's activities in the community. A wall-mounted display rack held various informational pamphlets: how parents could recognize drug use in their children, how to form a neighborhood watch, emergency preparedness checklists, and gun safety tips.

The inner door, beside the dispatcher's booth buzzed, then opened to reveal a trim man with gray hair in a charcoal-gray police uniform.

"I'm Chief Quinn," he said. "You are?"

Dean flashed his ID again. "Agents DeYoung and Shaw."

"Didn't realize we had a Federal matter here in Clayton Falls."

Dean exchanged a glance with Sam, who cleared his throat and said, "Homeland Security. We believe—"

"That's quite enough." Chief Quinn held up his hand to interrupt. "Let's take this back to my office."

Quinn led them down a short hall, past a row of desks with computers, two of which were occupied with uniformed police officers, and stopped at a door with a gold nameplate: "Chief Michael C. Quinn." He ushered them into his spartan office: law books and police manuals on one bookcase, several framed photos of Quinn at community events or posing with local dignitaries, coat rack in the left rear corner, US flag on a stand in the right.

Quinn closed his office door and motioned them to the two padded chairs in front of his desk. He sat in the much more comfortable chair behind it.

The contents of his desk formed an organized triangle, a desk blotter holding a monthly calendar with a Cross pen in the center, a stack of file folders at the right corner, and a high school graduation photo of a young woman with red hair and green eyes to the left. *The chief's daughter, Lucy*, Dean surmised.

Chief Quinn leaned forward, forearms angled against the edge of his desk, hands loosely clasped.

"Apologize for cutting you off out there. Millie isn't the town gossip, but not for lack of trying. You were about to mention something related to Homeland Security."

"We need to question any witnesses to the unusual… events of last night," Dean said.

"And read any statements that were taken," Sam added.

"As far as I know the only *real* incident was a hit-and-run fatality," Quinn said. "Hardly a Homeland Security matter."

"We read reports of a giant Gila monster, and a head—" Sam began.

Quinn held up a hand. "Let me stop you right there, Agent Shaw. There is no giant Gila monster in Clayton Falls."

"Gavin Shelburn…" Sam stopped as the chief's hand came up again.

"Shelly isn't the town drunk but—"

"Not for lack of trying?" Dean finished.

"Exactly," Quinn said, not taking offense. "Nobody else saw such a thing. How far is it from pink elephants to giant lizards? One bottle or two?"

"Lucy Quinn, your own daughter, reported being chased by a headless horseman."

"My daughter…" Quinn sighed. Leaned back in his chair and stared off into space for a few moments before he spoke again. "Lucy is an only child. She came to my wife and me later in life. A surprise. Pleasant one, mind you, but we never thought…" He cleared his throat. "Lost my wife to breast cancer when Lucy was five. That was hard on Lucy, hard on both of us. Don't think you can come out of something like that unchanged." He picked up the Cross pen and tapped it against the paper of the calendar. "Then, last year, Lucy lost someone else close to her. What I'm trying to say is… I don't think Lucy would intentionally lie about this, but…"

"What? You think she imagined it?" Dean asked.

"I'm not so foolish to think that she might not experiment… that she might have been involved in something she'd rather not tell her old man about."

"Headless horseman's one hell of a cover story," Sam said.

"The boy who was killed by that driver ran out into the middle of the street and stopped there," Quinn said. "He'd been with Lucy and another boy in Founders Park. I know for a fact that drinking was involved. We certainly found enough beer cans out there. Possibly drugs."

"A witness said the car disappeared," Dean said.

"Witnesses are, as a rule, unreliable," Quinn said. "No surprise to a couple Feds, I'm sure. All of which brings me back to my first question. What's the connection to Homeland Security?"

"We don't want to alarm you or the citizens of Clayton Falls," Sam said. "We know this town has been through a lot."

"The factory fire," Quinn said, nodding. "Many residents lost someone, or know someone who did. Hell of a thing."

Sam cleared his throat, about to launch into their cover story. "We have information from credible sources indicating a terrorist cell might be testing a weaponized airborne hallucinogen here."

"Weaponized airborne hallucinogen? In Clayton Falls? Why?"

"Small population, out of the way location, easy to monitor results," Dean said with a shrug.

"Obviously, we don't think Clayton Falls is the ultimate target," Sam said. "Their ultimate objective would be a large metropolitan area."

"And how, may I ask, did you come by this information?" The chief looked startled, as though uncertain how to react to the information.

"Most of the details are highly classified, but…" Sam said and paused for a moment, as if debating how much to tell the local police chief. This was also part of the plan. "What I tell you must be handled with the utmost discretion."

Quinn leaned forward and nodded. "Of course."

"We're relying on some ECHELON chatter and reports from some deep-cover operatives."

The chief nodded and leaned back in his chair.

"I'm convinced you're convinced," he said and cleared his throat. "But I'm a skeptic at heart."

Sam reached into his suit pocket and produced a credible

facsimile of an FBI business card and pushed it across the desk.

"Our supervisor, Agent Tom Willis, working out of the St. Louis field office, can clear up any jurisdictional concerns," he said. "Possibly provide you with more detailed threat assessment information than we're authorized to reveal."

Quinn picked up the business card and examined it for a long moment with one eyebrow arched before sliding it into a shirt pocket.

"Thank you. I'll take that under advisement." He stood abruptly; Dean and Sam rose with him. "Regardless, I see no reason why you can't read the statements or interview witnesses."

Dean glanced meaningfully at the photo of Quinn's daughter. "Even…?"

"Legally, she's an adult," Quinn said. "Might do her good to learn the… consequences of this type of report."

He shook hands with both of them.

"I do have one reservation."

"Which is?"

"This is a quiet town," Quinn said. "I'd like to keep it that way. Wasn't always like this though. As I'm sure you're aware, Falls Federal Prison is just outside the town limits. Couple of years ago, they added a supermax wing. Worst of the worst locked up in there. Had folks in town jumpy as frogs on a hot skillet. Protests, picketing, demonstrations—and not always peaceful. Time passed. Falls remained secure. Life goes on. That's where we are now. Peaceful, quiet, and orderly. What concerns me is that talk of a terrorist attack here could cause a panic."

"Understood," Dean said.

"But if we're right, Chief Quinn," Sam added, his deep voice serious, "this could turn dangerous."

"Noted. Keep me informed."

"Of course."

Chief Quinn opened the door and looked out into the bullpen area. Only one uniformed cop remained along the row of desks: mid-twenties, buzz cut, earnest.

"Jeffries. Give these FBI agents—DeYoung and Shaw—copies of the witness statements from last night."

"Everything, Chief?"

"Warts and all."

"Yes, sir. Oh, and Lucy's…?"

"Everything, Jeffries."

FOUR

"Well, that's everything," Officer Richard Jeffries said, dumping the stack of folders on the edge of his desk. "Sorry it took so long. Copier jammed. Office assistant usually takes care of this stuff, but she only works mornings. Budget cutbacks, you know."

Dean picked up the pile of folders, itching to get out of the building.

Jeffries hooked his thumbs in his belt. "You're taking all of this seriously?"

"Very seriously," Sam said. "Why?"

"Even Shelly's giant lizard?"

"No stone unturned," Dean said.

"You hear stories about people dumping pet alligators down the sewer and they supposedly grow down there to full size. Live off rats. But that stuff's urban legend, right?"

"One of the great mysteries," Dean said.

"Think somebody dumped a Gila monster down the sewer?"

"You never know," Sam said. "Are you familiar with these reports?"

"Read them all. For entertainment value, sure beats traffic citations."

"Impressions?"

"Hard to take them seriously," Jeffries said and shrugged. "Well, except for the hit and run. Bullinger stood in the middle of the road. Driver of the car should have seen him, but… who knows? We're looking for a red car. Don't know make and model. Not even a partial on the plate. Not much to go on, really."

"What about Lucy Quinn's statement?" Dean asked.

Jeffries hesitated, glancing at the police chief's office, perhaps unwilling to speak negatively about his boss's daughter.

"Sticking with her story. Stubborn, like the chief. She was hanging out with Tony Lacosta, who backed up her story. Bullinger was with them earlier. Obviously we never got his statement. But, really, a headless horseman?" He shrugged again. "My first thought was—" he glanced toward the police chief's door again and lowered his voice—"controlled substances."

"Thanks for your help," Sam said. "Anything weird happens, keep us in the loop. We oughta get going."

"Sure. Right. Didn't mean to hold you up."

As they walked back toward the lobby, Jeffries called after them.

"You need anything, let me know."

"Will do," Dean said, waving an arm without looking back.

He exchanged a glance with Sam. "Won't be stumbling over any police follow-up."

"Not anytime soon."

Minutes after Dean drove from the municipal parking lot, Sam's phone rang.

"Bobby," Sam said and put the call on speaker.

"You jokers put Guinness on speed dial?" Bobby said. "In town less than an hour and already you got somebody checking up on you."

"Chief Quinn rang the bat phone?" Dean asked.

"Of course, ya idjit," Bobby snapped. "Who else would I be flapping about?"

"Just saying," Dean replied. "That man has a distrustful soul."

"And whatever you two were selling in there," Bobby continued, "he ain't exactly inclined to rush to the checkout lane."

"But…?" Sam said.

"What I gather, he's willing to play out enough rope for you two to hang yourselves."

"Well, that's encouraging."

"My advice," Bobby said, "don't go too far off the reservation on this one. Or expect a guided tour of county lockup."

"Right," Sam said. "Low profile."

"Bobby," Dean said. "Any luck with the phoenix ash situation?"

"Besides their place of honor on my mantel?" Bobby said.

"Fat lotta good they are when I can't find hide nor hair of Eve, Mother of All."

"Something will turn up," Sam said.

"Ain't you the Pollyanna," Bobby said and ended the call.

Sam looked a question at Dean.

"What? Keeps his mind off Rufus."

"Considering one of Eve's creatures was responsible for Rufus' death," Sam said, "not sure that will do the trick."

"It's Bobby. What's he gonna do? Look the other way?" Dean asked. "Besides, I'd prefer directed anger over grief any day."

He parked the Impala on Welker Street near the Mandarin Palace restaurant. He and Sam walked along the side of the restaurant and turned down the alley that ran behind a bunch of storefronts in the business district of Clayton Falls between Welker and Bell Street.

"Here?"

Sam nodded. "According to the report."

After looking for Gavin Shelburn to no avail at the local homeless shelter, food bank, and soup kitchen—housed in two adjoining buildings—they had decided to visit the site of the alleged giant Gila monster attack.

"Police never bothered to check the scene," Sam said. "Figured Shelburn had one too many."

"Let's say Shelburn wasn't hallucinating. What are we looking for exactly? People around here would notice a giant lizard."

"Yeah, but they might not notice this."

Sam crouched beside a battered Dumpster with a missing front wheel.

Dean stood over his shoulder. "Banged-up Dumpster?"

"Banged up and…" Sam traced his fingers along two sets of deep parallel grooves that scored the blue paint of the trash bin. "…scratched. Dean, Shelburn said he jumped into a Dumpster to escape."

Dean nodded, lifted the lid of the trash bin.

"Score marks on the edge," he pointed out.

"Busted that wheel off, too," a voice said from behind them.

They turned to face a grizzled man in a misshapen fedora, creased overcoat, threadbare jeans and battered combat boots standing at the entrance to the alley. He kept his distance from them, a wary look in his eyes, as if he would never again trust what he saw.

"Gavin Shelburn?" Sam asked.

"Shelly's fine," the man said, making no effort to approach them. "You with the government?"

"FBI," Dean said. "Okay if we ask you a few questions, Shelly?"

"I'm not crazy," he said.

"Good to know."

"It happened right here. Quinn's boys think I'm nuts. But I ain't nuts. Sure, I drink. Who doesn't? But I see what I see… at least I…" He stuffed his hands in his overcoat pockets. "It was a Gila monster attacked me. But big. Size of two cars back to back! I know that ain't right. But I can't explain it."

"Did you see where it came from?" Dean asked.

Shelburn shook his head. "I was walking back from Joe's Pizza Shack and I heard it. Heard something. Turned around and there it was. Chased me. I ducked in here and, well, jumped in there. Guess you could say Dumpster diving saved my life."

Sam pointed at the scratch marks. "Then it attacked the Dumpster?"

"Yep," Shelburn said, finally coming a few steps closer. He walked along the brick wall and showed them scrape marks at Dumpster height. "Pushed it, slammed into it, then tried to climb inside after me. That's when the wheel busted off, under its weight, I guess."

"But it gave up and left?" Sam asked.

"That's the weird thing. It never walked—crawled away. I would've heard that, with its claws scraping the ground and that tail thumping everything in sight. But nope. Nothing. One minute it was there, the next it was gone."

"Anything else you remember?"

"Seemed mighty hungry."

"Right," Sam said with a slight smile. "Thanks for your help."

"You know what caused it?"

"No," Dean said. "We're here to find out."

"Bet it was radiation," Shelburn said. "Or toxic chemicals. Illegal dumping. Or... some top-secret government experiment? Is that it?" He backed up a few steps. "That why they sent you FBI types to Clayton Falls? A cover-up? They send you to kill all the witnesses?"

"Whoa! Nothing like that," Dean said. *Batting a thousand*, he thought. *First witness already panicking*. "The 'I' is for investigation."

Shelburn nodded slowly, as if trying to convince himself, calm himself.

"Okay, all right. I'm not a conspiracy nut. Never was. But you see a giant Gila monster and you start to rethink everything, right? Down is up; up is down."

"You might want to steer clear of this alley," Sam suggested.

"You believe me?"

"Yes."

"Thank you," Shelburn said, suddenly smiling broadly. "I may be down on my luck, but I ain't crazy." He doffed his hat and extended it in his arm. "Wouldn't mind a donation…"

Sam smiled.

Dean reached into a pocket, peeled off a twenty and dropped it in the hat.

"Mighty generous of you," he said, tucking the bill into a pocket. "I'll take your advice as well and clear out."

"Wait a minute," Sam said. "You're out most nights?"

"About every night. Why?"

"Wait here," Sam said. He walked to the Impala and returned with a pair of two-way radios from the trunk, handing one to Shelly. "You know how to use these?" The man nodded. "Keep it on channel five. You spot anything weird, out of the usual, call me."

"You deputizing me?"

"Think of it as neighborhood watch activity."

They spent a moment checking the battery levels, sending and receiving messages. Shelly adjusted the volume on his unit and nodded, satisfied, and stuffed it in his pocket. "Anything weird or unusual. Got it."

"Don't put yourself at risk," Sam said. "Just call it in."

"No worries on that account."

As Shelly sauntered off, Dean shook his head at Sam.

"What?"

"Dude, you realize that radio's headed for the nearest pawn shop."

"Not like I gave him the pair."

Shelly paused at the entrance to the alley and looked back at them.

"Remembered one other thing," he called. "White mist, clinging to the ground. Noticed it right before the beast attacked."

FIVE

Blake Dobkins, marketing manager at an organic food company located in an industrial park at the south end of Clayton Falls, met Dean in the lobby and led him to a conference room where they could speak in private.

"Not much to tell, Agent DeYoung," Dobkins said. "My wife and I were out celebrating our fifth anniversary at this Italian place where we had our first date. Actually, we were leaving the restaurant to go home, when I saw the speeding car hit that young man in the middle of the street."

"Police report said the car was red. Any other details?" Dean asked.

"Not really a car enthusiast," Dobkins said apologetically. "It was an older car. Maybe one of those muscle cars from the sixties or seventies. Gone before I had a good look at it."

"Nothing unusual about it? Spoiler? Fancy hubcaps? Tinted glass? Anything?" Dean pressed.

Dobkins shook his head, almost a reflexive gesture. But

then he closed his eyes. Dean waited, resisting the urge to drum his fingers on the shiny surface of the conference room table. He could imagine Dobkins trying to visualize those brief seconds as the car sped up to Bullinger, struck him, and raced away from the scene.

"White," Dobkins said at last, opening his eyes and nodding. "A streak of white."

"But you said the car was red."

"Yes, it was," Dobkins said, "but it had a wide line—a racing stripe—on the hood. *That* was white. My eyes tracked the boy when the car struck him. Everything happened so fast, but yes, I remember a streak of white on the driver's side of the hood."

"Good," Dean said, trying to sound encouraging. "That could help us find the car." Assuming the car was real and had a human driver. "What happened after Bullinger was hit?"

"I ran into the street, to see if he was okay, but I… when I got up close… it looked bad. I called for an ambulance, but…"

"Before he died, Bullinger spoke to you?"

"He said nobody was driving. Didn't make sense, but considering his condition, I wasn't surprised."

"Were those his exact words?"

"He said, 'nobody driving.' That's all I heard."

Sam flashed his FBI credentials at the front door of the Clayton Falls Child Care Center and was buzzed in by a middle-aged woman with frizzy brown hair and a distracted demeanor. She introduced herself as Mary Horton, the manager. She wore a white smock with dozens of colorful giraffe silhouettes dotted across it. They stood in the middle of a spacious room with scattered activity centers for children, including a mini puppet show theater, art supplies and easels, a stocked bookcase, jigsaw puzzles, blocks and bins filled with toys and action figures. All the tables and chairs were scaled down for children, but the room was empty. Judging from the commotion Sam heard out back, they were all enjoying the playground equipment.

"Oh, no! This isn't about a kidnapping, is it?" Mary Horton said, eyebrows dancing with concern.

"No, Ms. Horton," Sam said. "I'm here to talk to Linda Dobkins."

"She's not in any sort of trouble, is she?"

"I have a few questions about an accident she witnessed."

"Oh, yes, she told me about that. Horrible. Who could do such a thing?"

"That's what we're trying to figure out."

"Wait here. I'll get her," she said. "One of us has to stay with the children at all times."

Sam followed her to the back door and waited there in the relative silence.

Mary talked to a younger woman with a blond ponytail wearing a white smock with monkey silhouettes over faded jeans and sneakers. Compared to the chaotic appearance of her boss, Linda Dobkins seemed almost serene in the middle of the childhood frenzy whirling around her, kids racing from sliding boards to swings to seesaws and back again. Linda nodded, brushed her hands on her jeans and came in through the back door.

She offered her hand. "Agent… Shaw, right?"

"Yes."

"Well, you know who I am, obviously," she said, flashing a smile. "Of course, I want to help, but I'm afraid I told the police everything I saw. Or, rather, didn't see."

"The disappearing car."

"Yes," she said. "Crazy as that sounds."

"Tell me everything you saw, from beginning to end."

"We—my husband and I—were leaving the restaurant. I heard the roar of the car's engine. I swear the car accelerated. Like the driver was *trying* to hit that boy. It was a split second, a flash of motion, then the impact. I was shocked, stunned, but Blake ran out there to help. No hesitation. I tried to get a look at the driver, but the car was already past me, so I tried to catch the license plate number. Even part of it. I've seen television shows where a few digits are enough to find a car."

"Did you see any digits?"

"No," she said and frowned. "I mean, it was a second or two at most. Before my eyes could focus on the license plate, the car vanished."

"You're sure about that?"

Sam noticed several of the children had become curious about his presence, pressing their faces against the glass door for a better look. One girl, about five years old, waved at him. A boy not much older stuck out his tongue. Mary Horton took notice, rushed up and shooed them away from the door.

"Yes, I'm sure," Linda said. "The car started to turn the corner. I was losing my angle on the license plate and then it was like it… winked out of existence. Blake thinks I must have looked away, distracted by the injured boy, but I never took my eyes off the car from the time I tried to catch the license number."

"Could another vehicle have passed between you and the car?"

"No," she said. "Traffic was light. No other cars or trucks passed by during the few seconds before, during, and after the accident."

"I see."

"You think I'm crazy, don't you?"

"For what it's worth," Sam said. "I don't."

Timing was everything. Dean managed to snag a corner booth in C.J.'s Diner before the sizable dinner crowd rolled in. Considering how popular the place was, he had high hopes for the quality of his ordered cheeseburger and fries. Sam arrived at the tail end of the rush, spotted Dean from across the crowded restaurant and joined him.

"Quiet little place?" he said.

"Until about ten minutes ago," Dean replied. "Who knew?"

Their energetic waitress—Betsy, according to her nametag—arrived with two identical plates, smiling broadly as she placed them down on the Formica table.

"Careful, boys," she said amiably. "Food's hot and so are the plates."

Dean nodded at the food.

"Kept it simple. Ordered two of everything."

"Which, if I don't eat, gives you two of everything?"

"C'mon," Dean said. "It's a burger. Won't kill you. Look, she put lettuce on it."

After a moment, Sam shrugged. "Fine. But next time, I order."

Betsy put her hands on her hips, her smile maintaining its high wattage, as if she were the chairperson of the Clayton Falls welcoming committee. She certainly looked official in her server uniform, white blouse and black slacks topped by a navy blue vest with four red buttons and "C.J.'s" embroidered in gold thread script opposite her nametag.

"You're them FBI agents. Am I right?"

"How did you know?" Sam asked.

"Bit overdressed for this place," she said. "Plus, word gets around."

In the next booth, an elderly man with a few days' growth of stubble laughed.

"Let them eat before their food gets cold, Betsy. And I'm still waiting on my onion rings."

"Oh, you'll get your onion rings, Phil Meyerson," she said. "But if you want them now, you'll eat them raw."

"What's taking so long?"

"Put the order in two minutes ago," she said. "You're retired, Phil. Relax."

"Not in my nature."

"Don't worry, dear," she said. "Any super viruses come along, we'll kill them in our deep fryer."

Dean and Sam exchanged a look.

"Super viruses?" Dean asked. He looked down at his

half-eaten cheeseburger and fries then back up at Betsy. "Anything I should know?"

"Oh, nothing," she said with a dismissive wave of her hand. "Phil worked at the C.D.C. in Atlanta. Don't think he brought anything contagious with him."

"Phil?" Sam said.

Dean could see the wheels turning.

"Microbiologist," Meyerson said. "Retired seven years ago. Only contagious thing I've had since then was a nasty head cold. Now, look at this. My coffee cup is empty."

"Relax, Phil," Betsy said. "I can take a hint."

Before she turned away, Dean said, "We were hoping to talk to Lucy Quinn. Said to meet her here."

"Oh, right! Girl said she had to hang around."

"Hang around?"

"Shift ended a few minutes ago," Betsy said. "She's in the break room. I'll send her out."

After Betsy left for a coffee pot, Meyerson slid out of his booth and headed toward the restroom. Dean took the opportunity to compare notes with Sam.

"Anything new from Linda?"

Sam finished a fry, and shook his head.

"Nothing that wasn't in the police report."

"What are we looking at here? After the possessed love doll thing in Jersey, I'm keeping the Impala far away from any vengeful spirits."

Through the front window, Dean saw an ambulance roll into the diner's lot and stop behind a row of cars without pulling into a parking slot.

"Linda said the car vanished. I believe her."

"Meaning?"

"Not a vengeful spirit."

"Poltergeist? Some kind of haunting?"

"I don't know, Dean," Sam said. "Headless horseman, giant lizard, phantom car. Not seeing a common thread. What about the husband?"

"Remembered the red car had a white stripe on the hood," Dean said. "Otherwise, no revelations."

A rail-thin EMT entered the diner and walked over to the counter under a "Pick Up" sign dangling from two chains made out of interlocked paper clips. He drummed his fingers impatiently on the countertop and looked around with quick darting motions.

Hummingbird metabolism, Dean thought. *Or an addiction to amphetamines*. A waitress in her fifties working behind the counter brought him a grease-stained bag and a large coffee.

As the EMT paid for his order, a young woman with red hair came through a gap in the counter and spoke to him briefly, patting his arm. She looked around the diner until she saw Dean and Sam and made a beeline for their booth. She wore a cropped denim jacket, a black T-shirt and jeans, with a lime-green canvas bag slung over one shoulder. Dean saw the edge of a blue C.J.'s vest poking out of the bag.

"Agent DeYoung?" she said, guessing right. She offered her hand. "Lucy Quinn."

Dean stood, shook her hand.

"This is my partner, Agent Shaw."

She turned to Sam, repeated the gesture.

"Scooch over," she said to Sam, who obliged. She sat next to him and snatched one of his fries. "Not really supposed to hang around after my shift, but I'm sure my boss will make an exception for the FBI."

On his way out to the double-parked ambulance, the wiry EMT called over to her, "Bye, Lucy."

"Later, Roman!" She waved at him.

"Friend of yours?" Dean asked.

"Neighbor," she said. "Roman Messerly. Babysat me years ago, when my dad took my mom to her chemo… Anyway, he's kind of like the older brother I never had. Worry about him. That job is all wrong for him. Way too stressful. Jeez, I'm rambling." She clasped her hands together and sat up straight, as if practicing good posture. "Sorry. Nerves."

"We have a few questions," Dean said. "About the horseman."

"My dad warned me," she said, then quickly added, "I mean, he told me you'd ask about what I saw. I asked Tony to meet us here—'cause he saw it too—but he's a no-show. Time challenged. So, questions?"

"You were in the park—" Sam said.

"Yep. Founders Park. By the monument. Just hanging out, minding our own business."

"And the headless horseman appeared out of nowhere?"

She nodded. "I was facing the statues. The town founders. They're both on horses. So, two horses. Next thing I know, I see three horses. But the third horse and rider are moving, and they come around the monument and start chasing us."

"And the rider had no head? You're sure."

"Definitely! He was dressed in black head to toe—well, neck to toe—but there was no head attached to the body."

"Maybe his face was hidden," Dean suggested. "A dark mask?"

"Nope. His neck was all ragged and... blood-crusted, like whoever lopped off his head took several whacks to finish the job."

"And he came after you?"

"All of us or... I don't know, maybe one of us was the target, but we ran away together and he charged us with a sword. Until..."

"What?" Sam asked.

"We split up," she said slowly. "Tony pulled me to one side. Steve kept running straight ahead. The horseman followed Steve, not us. We were so scared. We kept running through the park until we came out on the north side, and headed home. Later, we called Steve but got no answer on his cell. He never made it home. My dad called me after he found out about the hit and run, to make sure I was okay." She took a deep breath. "That... thing chased Steve into traffic. It's the reason he was killed."

"Did you notice anything unusual before the horseman appeared?"

"No. It appeared out of nowhere..." She paused. "Oh, wait. There was some kind of white ground mist. I noticed that first when Steve dropped his... What? Why are you guys staring at each other like that?"

"Second time somebody mentioned white mist before seeing something... weird," Sam said.

"So, that's significant, right?"

"Maybe," Sam said. "Have to ask. Any illegal substances involved while you were hanging out in the park?"

"Drugs? No!" she said defensively. "Steve swiped some beer from home, but I didn't have any. Wasn't in the mood. I was thinking about…" She shook her head, as if she was mentally shifting gears. "I was sober. Completely."

"Your father tell you the car that hit Steve vanished?" Dean asked.

"No," she said. "He said it was a hit and run. Steve was in the wrong place at the wrong time. Vanished how?"

"Into thin air," Sam said. "According to a witness."

"What's going on?" she asked. "Things appearing and disappearing." She leaned forward and whispered. "My father said you guys think a terrorist is testing a hallucinogen."

Dean tried to hide his surprise.

"He told you that?"

"Yep," she said, still hushed. "He's all about total communication with his daughter. Figures I'll reciprocate." She shrugged. "But he sounded skeptical."

"We got that," Sam said.

"Whatever it is, you think the car is connected to the headless horseman?"

"Possibly."

"But what do they have in common? Anything weird about the car?"

"Before he died, Steve said the car had no driver."

"Hadn't heard that either," Lucy said somberly. "Horseman without a head. Car without a driver."

"Otherwise, it seemed like a normal red car."

Dean added, "With a white stripe on the hood."

Lucy grabbed Dean's wrist, her green eyes widening. "What?"

"Red car with a white stripe," he repeated.

Her grip tightened.

"Oh, my God! What—what kind of car?"

"Is that important?"

"What *kind*?"

"Older model," Dean said. "Muscle car. Sixties or seventies. That's all we know."

"Could it have been—? No, that's not possible. It's crazy."

"What?"

"A '68 Dodge Charger?"

"Maybe," Dean said. "Why? Have you seen it?"

Lucy released Dean's wrist. She glanced down at the table, nibbled on the edge of her thumbnail. When she spoke again, her voice was so soft Dean had to strain to hear her words.

"That was Teddy's car."

Before Dean could ask about Teddy, she slipped out of the booth, rushed across the diner and out the door without looking back.

"What just happened?" Sam said.

Dean stood, removed thirty dollars from his wallet and slapped it on the table. He glanced wistfully at his half-eaten meal.

"Damn," he said, "That cheeseburger was good."

They found her in the parking lot, pacing behind a row of cars, still nibbling at the edge of her thumbnail. Dean had the impression she wanted to run away but was fighting the urge. He looked sideways at Sam, who shrugged.

"Lucy?" he called. "Everything okay?"

"Fine," she said, her voice pitched higher than usual. "I'm—it's fine. It's insane, right? Can't be Teddy's car."

"Teddy?" Dean said.

"Teodor Kucharski," she said. "He is—was my boyfriend."

"Let us talk to him."

"You can't," she said. "He's dead. He died a year ago."

"Sorry. I…"

"It's okay. I'm fine."

Cleary, she wasn't fine. Dean looked at Sam and whispered, "Vengeful spirit?"

Again Sam shrugged.

"The car," Dean said, taking a few steps closer to her. "Who has it now?"

"That's the thing," she said, finally making eye contact. Her eyes were red, her cheeks moist. She'd been quietly crying since she hurried out of the diner. "Teddy was driving his '68 Dodge Charger the night he died. The car was totaled. So, this… vanishing car couldn't be his. Could it?"

"Don't know," Dean said. "Maybe somebody fixed it."

She shook her head. "I was in that car when it crashed. We all were."

"We who?" Sam asked.

"Teddy, Steve, Tony, and me," she said. "I broke my arm against the dash. Tony broke both legs. Steve needed surgery on his hip. I managed to climb out the passenger window. They needed the Jaws of Life to get Tony and Steve out. But… Teddy… he got the worst of it. Steering column crushed his chest."

"That's horrible," Dean said.

"It was stupid," she said. "We were all stupid. Drinking. We let Teddy drive. He loved that car, inherited from his dad. Washed and waxed it every week. Kept it spotless. Nobody else could drive it. Ever. That night… well, it was the same as always, except we'd all been drinking. Goofing off. None of us should have gotten behind the wheel. But Teddy… It was always Teddy. I have nightmares about the accident. All the time. I wake up as if I'm about to go through the windshield. Sometimes I wake up screaming." She wrapped her arms tight around herself, shuddered and shook her head. "So believe me, that car was totaled."

"Listen," Sam said. "It's getting dark. Let us give you a ride home."

"Take me to Tony's house," she said, wiping away a fresh tear. "You should talk to him about the headless horseman. He can confirm what I saw."

She'd already put herself through an emotion wringer. Dean had no desire to make it worse. Not like they needed her to make introductions. "That's okay. Just give us his address."

"No," she said quickly. "It's fine. I want you guys to figure this out before I start thinking I really am nuts. Besides, Tony lives a couple blocks from me. I can walk home from his place."

"Sounds like a plan," Dean said.

A silver Lexus pulled into the diner's lot and parked in a spot close to where the trio was walking towards the Impala. Before they could walk around the car, a tall middle-aged man in a charcoal-gray pinstriped suit, with more salt than pepper in his hair, climbed out of the car and placed a hand protectively on Lucy's shoulder. Though he spoke to her, his suspicious gaze lingered on Dean and Sam.

"Lucy," he said. "Everything all right here?"

"Fine, Uncle Alden," she said, smiling at him. "These men are with the FBI."

"Agent DeYoung," Dean said, resisting the urge to pull out his fake ID.

"Agent Shaw," Sam said with a slight nod.

Uncle Alden raised an eyebrow. "FBI?"

Maybe that was an ID-flashing moment after all, Dean thought.

"It's cool, Uncle Alden," Lucy said. "They've already talked to Dad."

"I see," he said, nodding without surrendering his suspicions yet. He held her chin and tilted her face up. "You've been crying."

"I'm fine," she said. "Talking about Teddy. That's all." She cleared her throat. "Agents, this is Alden Webb. Friend of my father. He's the warden at Falls Federal Prison."

Webb offered his hand, shook each of theirs.

"Chief Quinn spoke of resentment in town about the prison," Sam offered.

"There was some… concern when we opened the supermax wing. But that's in the past," Webb said. "The town and the prison have reached… an accommodation. They know the prison is here to stay but the inmates—especially those in supermax—represent no threat to Clayton Falls. There's a peaceful coexistence."

"Anyway, Uncle Alden, the agents were about to drive me home," Lucy said. "So, enjoy your meal. And I'll see you later."

"Certainly," Webb said, nodding to them. He gave Lucy a quick hug and a peck on the cheek. "Take good care of this one, gentlemen."

"You bet," Sam said.

Dean nodded and, after Webb entered the diner, led the way to the Impala. As they climbed into the car, Dean asked Sam, "You get the feeling he'd like to toss us in a cell?"

"Don't take it personally," Lucy said, chuckling. "He's suspicious of everyone. Says it's part of his job description."

She directed them to Tony Lacosta's house, which was a little over a mile away from the diner.

"Right there," she said. "Yellow siding, white trim and posts."

"Got it," Dean said and pulled in at the curb. The house had a covered front porch with a white railing three steps up from the ground. Behind a few small shrubs, he spotted a latticed porch skirt. He flashed back on the image of the young woman's body they'd discovered under the Machete Mime's farmhouse.

"There he is." Lucy led the way up wooden steps to the porch.

Tony Lacosta sat on the first of two white Adirondack chairs, asleep with his crossed feet propped up on the porch railing. When Lucy unceremoniously knocked his feet down, he jolted awake and jumped out of the chair.

"What the hell!? Lucy?"

"Are you stoned?" she asked.

"No," he said quickly. "Yeah. Maybe. Had a few brews. Who's asking?" He glanced at Dean and Sam in their FBI suits and leaned closer to Lucy before whispering loud enough for all three of them to hear. "Jeez, Luce. Narcing on me with the FBI guys?"

Lucy punched his upper arm.

"I asked you to meet me at the diner!"

"Oh, right. Damn, I forgot."

"Forgot? I called less than an hour ago!" She shook her

head in disappointment. "You're such a jackass."

"Don't be a bitch," Tony said. "Besides, what's it matter? I saw the same thing you saw."

"That's the point!" Lucy said, exasperated. "Everyone thinks I'm crazy. I thought you had my back."

"I do," Tony said, chagrined. "I saved your ass in the park, didn't I?"

Lucy sighed, dropped down in his chair while he stood looking down at her.

"Yes. I was an idiot. That thing would have lopped off my head if you didn't drag me out of there. Sorry, Tone."

"Apology accepted," he slouched against the wooden post beside the stairs. "Sorry about not meeting you."

"Okay. So tell Agent DeYoung and Shaw what we saw."

"DeYoung and Shaw, huh? Like a Styx reunion." When he got no reaction to his quip from Lucy, he continued. "Fine," he said, focusing on Dean and Sam at last. "Lucy's right. This sounds crazy. But it happened…" He told them his version of the headless horseman story, which basically matched Lucy's with the significant exception that his back was turned when the horseman supposedly appeared out of nowhere. "When I turned around it was already there. Freaky as hell. Looked like it was out for blood, so we bolted." The rest of his account matched Lucy's and offered no additional information.

"Any idea why the horseman continued after your friend?" Sam asked. "Instead of you two?"

Tony shook his head. "Totally random. When I pulled Lucy with me, I guess I forced him—it—to make a decision. Maybe it knew it couldn't chase all of us if we split up." He shrugged. "Could have come after us. Steve kept running straight ahead. Thing didn't have a head. No eyes. Maybe it was easier to keep riding straight." He shook his head, ran his hand through his dark hair. "Hey, you guys want a beer or something?"

Dean thought a beer sounded like an excellent idea, but they had to keep up their cover. Especially since they would be hanging around Clayton Falls for the foreseeable future.

"I'll pretend I didn't hear that," he said. "But thanks for your help. Both of you."

"No problem."

"Thanks for the ride," Lucy said. "I'll hang here for a while."

"Cool," Tony said. He sidled past Lucy and plopped down in the matching chair.

As Dean walked back to the Impala with Sam, he glanced over at his brother and said, "Could go for a beer."

"Figured."

Ten-year-old Daniel Barnes lay in bed with the covers pulled up to his chest and asked his mother to check the closet.

She opened the folding doors wide, slid the clothes on plastic hangers to either side and declared the closet empty of bogeymen. "However, there is a lot of boy clutter on the floor."

"Mom!"

"Just saying, Danny. Wouldn't hurt you to clean up this mess every once in a while."

"I don't have anywhere to put my stuff."

"Because you have too much stuff."

"Check under the bed now," he instructed her.

This was his nightly ritual: cup of water, closet check, bed check, nightlight on, kiss goodnight. The repetition comforted him. He watched as his mother got down on her knees, lifted the edge of the covers and peered under the bed.

"Oh, no!" she said.

"What?"

"They're back," she said in mock terror. "Dust bunnies!"

"Is that all?" he asked, smiling.

"And some fallen action figures," she said, climbing to her feet to stand at attention. "Otherwise, all clear."

"Okay, then."

She leaned over and kissed his forehead.

"Time to go to sleep, young man."

"G'night, Mom."

"Goodnight, honey." She switched off the bedside lamp. The darkness triggered the sensor in his nightlight, which flickered on in response and spread a warm glow of illumination across the floor.

"Love you," she said as she leaned against the doorjamb.

"You, too," he said and succumbed to a yawn.

Quietly, she slipped out of his room and closed the door.

In a few minutes, Daniel slipped into a light sleep, unaware that a light wind had begun to gust—until the branches of the white oak tree outside his bedroom window began to tap repeatedly against the glass. He opened his eyes, completely awake now but unsure what had roused him. A moment later, he heard the *tap, tap, tap-tap* on his window. He sat up in bed and looked out into the night sky. In his mind, the tree branches transformed into monstrous arms swaying before him, the tips of the branches now hands reaching for him, blocked only by a thin layer of glass…

"Mom!" he cried out.

A few seconds passed.

Tap, tap-tap, TAP!

"Mom! Where are you?"

He heard a rush of footfalls from the hallway outside his room. His mother burst into the room, looked left and right for any potential threat before her gaze settled on him.

"Daniel? What's wrong?"

"The tree… it was moving…"

She approached the window and stood there for a few moments. Suddenly, the tip of a tree branch swayed far enough to scrape along the windowsill. To Daniel's ears it sounded like fingernails—or claws. He shuddered.

"It's nothing," she said in a soothing voice. "Getting breezy out there. The tree branch brushed your window, that's all."

"It scared me," Daniel said. "Looks creepy."

Hands on her hips, she stood over him and shook her head. "Daniel, you're perfectly safe here. You can't be afraid of every little shadow and bump. Okay?"

"Okay," he said glumly.

"Be a brave boy for me?"

Daniel nodded. "I'll try."

"That's what I like to hear," she said and kissed his forehead again. "I'll ask your father to trim that tree in the morning."

"Okay."

This time, on her way out, she left his door ajar, so she could hear him better if he called for her. Accepting the compromise, Daniel tried to sleep again. He rolled onto his side, back to the window so he wouldn't see the shadows, and drew his knees up close to his chest.

Wind and shadows, he told himself. *No reason to be scared…*

Another yawn, wider than before, and he was drifting off to sleep much sooner than he would have expected after his scare.

With his eyes closed and sleep tugging him down into unconsciousness, he failed to notice the nightlight flicker and wink off. Seconds later, he was oblivious as a splotch of darkness in an upper corner of his bedroom uncoiled and drifted toward him like tendrils of obsidian and impenetrable smoke. The darkness flowed across his bedcovers, passed over his face and gathered over his bed's headboard. Slowly, as the darkness condensed, a shape began to emerge, like a silhouette, but in three dimensions. First a head formed, dark and unknowable and, beneath it, a pitch-black arm extended from the center mass, the tip stretching to coalesce into a hand and shadowy fingers that splayed across the boy's forehead.

Outside Daniel's home, the wind picked up, gusting as with a coming storm and the white oak's branches stirred and swayed and became agitated, reaching for the house and the boy within…

Dean brought a cold six-pack of beer back to the motel room, stuffing a few bottles in the packed ice bucket to keep them chilled. Considering he had two other six-packs, he needed a much bigger bucket. Or an ice chest. The local supermarket would have a cooler. He sipped from a bottle as Sam perused old news stories on the laptop computer.

"Found it," he said eventually and spun the computer around for Dean's benefit.

"That accordion was a '68 Dodge Charger?" Dean asked.

"That's what it says."

Dean peered at the screen.

"Color matches. Cherry red, white racing stripe."

Sam turned the laptop around again, scrolled down through the story.

"Hit a retaining wall. Driver's side took the brunt of the impact."

"Even if it was possible to repair that damage," Dean said, "doesn't explain how the car can disappear. Could be a lookalike car but unless it belongs to a magician…"

"Maybe it's a vengeful car, not a vengeful spirit."

"All we need. Car with a grudge. Christine comes to Clayton Falls."

"Kid lived with his paternal grandmother," Sam said, relaying information as he skimmed through articles. "Mother died in childbirth. Father and son lived in New Jersey. Father died five years ago. Massive heart attack. Heavy smoker. Grandmother only surviving relative. Took the boy in."

"Lot of tragedy in that family."

"That dead teenager is the only connection we have to any of these sightings."

"If it's not a vengeful spirit," Dean said. "Maybe we need to concentrate on the living."

* * *

Daniel Barnes squirmed in his bed.

Lost deep in REM sleep, his eyes darted back and forth beneath his eyelids, tracking the stuff of nightmares. Removed from the waking world, he was unaware of the shadow-hand and fingers pressed to his forehead. He was equally oblivious to the creature of darkness taking form over his bed. The creature's head continued to solidify, with glowing red eyes pulsing in its sunken cheeks. Beneath a long, malformed nose, its mouth opened wide to reveal a row of black, fanglike teeth. As the young boy moaned in distress, the creature hissed in delight.

Outside the boy's bedroom window, a rush of wind pummeled the house. The white oak's branches heaved up, and dropped, twisted and shook, flailed in the night, striking the house's siding, scraping the windowsill and rapping against the windowpanes with a ragged drumbeat of persistence.

When a branch struck the window with enough force to crack it, the shadowy creature emitted a gurgling hiss of satisfaction and withdrew its hand from the boy's forehead.

Daniel's head whipped to the side and a startled cry escaped his lips. A moment later, he awoke and pushed himself up from the tangled bedcovers as if he were coming up for air. Staring across the dark room, without even the benefit of the nightlight's meager glow, he called for his mother again.

Behind him, the shadowy form lost its cohesion, thinning to irregular splotches of darkness that climbed up the wall and slid across the other shadows, once again invisible and unknowable.

"Mom!"

This time his father came down the hall and pushed the door open. Even in the best of times, Daniel's father had less patience for his nighttime fears than his mother. Daniel hung his head, ready to apologize despite the feeling of dread that kept his heart racing.

"Daniel, your mother asked me to come up here," his father said, standing at the foot of the bed, arms across his chest. "You need to stop this nonsense."

"I'm scared."

"It's just a storm. You don't—"

"The tree broke the window."

"What?"

"Look!"

But Daniel's father had already crossed to the window to assess the damage.

"You're right. It's cracked. Hard to see." Daniel's father walked over to the doorway and flicked on the light switch. Nothing happened. He tried again. "Try your lamp."

The wind gusted and rattled the house. Outside the damaged window, the tree branches danced in the wind.

Daniel leaned over and tried his bedside lamp to no effect.

"Broken," he said.

"No. Looks like we've lost power."

His father returned to the window, ran his hand along the crack.

"Okay," he said and turned back to face Daniel. "I'll put some tape on this. Tomorrow, I'll trim the branches so they don't—"

Suddenly the wind howled with renewed ferocity and a thick branch thrust forward, shattering the window with a loud crash. Daniel jumped out of bed with a cry of alarm. Then he noticed his father hunched over, making choking noises as he tried to say something.

"Gah—gah—guhgh!"

For a moment, Daniel's imagination tried to fill in the blanks. He thought his father had grown a third arm—that it had sprouted from the center of his chest and was dripping on the floor. But as he took a step toward his father in the dark room, the true nature of the shape became apparent. The branch had come through the window and speared his father, whose blood was now running down the length of the branch and dripping all over the floor.

"Dad…"

His father's head rolled to the side, almost resting on his shoulder. Blood leaked from his mouth, forming little bubbles that spread like foam across his chin.

"Dad!"

The house shook, vibrating beneath Daniel's feet.

Outside the window, the white oak seemed to heave against the house, all its branches surging upward. Daniel's father was lifted by the branch that had impaled him, up to his tiptoes, and held swaying there. His gleaming eyes seemed to stare at Daniel, even as his head flopped from side to side. Hands that had grasped the bloody tree branch now fell limp at his sides. The branch then pulled him to the right and back to the left, forcing his dragging legs to perform the plodding steps of a macabre dance.

Daniel backed away until his own numb legs bumped against his bed. Then he dropped to the floor and wrapped his arms around his knees, head turned to the side as he screamed over and over again.

"Mom!"

Before she returned and without his notice, the splotchy darkness slipped out of the bedroom window and into the night.

SEVEN

Another sleepless night was what the gray-haired woman had come to expect. She hardly ever slept well in her bed. Maybe an hour here, a half-hour there, tossing and turning. Aches and pains too numerous to categorize contributed to her long nights. But not all the aches were physical. Memories had a way of keeping her awake into the wee hours. Invariably, she would surrender the idea of sleeping in her bed and, instead, settle into her musty recliner and watch television. If she was lucky, she'd catch a few hours of sleep spread over the long night.

Lately, her level of exhaustion had become more pronounced. Throughout the day, she would bumble through her inconsequential routines and by evening, she had so little energy it was a wonder she didn't collapse simply from climbing the stairs or completing a minimal amount of housework. Nothing seemed to matter much to her anymore. She wondered how long she could go on simply marking time. Living had become a reflex, a habit. She found no joy in it, and hadn't for some time.

She reached for the remote control and her hand, with veins and liver spots more prominent than they'd been a week ago, trembled with the effort. Such a simple act was almost beyond her current level of physical stamina. Maybe it wasn't physical. Maybe it was a neurological issue. Health problems plagued the elderly, became the focus of their twilight years. Marking time in the interval between taking one pill and the next.

She turned the television on and leaned back in the recliner, her eyelids already heavy with a sleep deficit she could never pay. It would do her good to see the doctor. Another routine to pass the time. Of course, he didn't care if she got better. Wouldn't know her name if she bumped into him on the street. But he tried to shock her with predictions of death and disease. Inevitable, but he made it entertaining. A jolt to remind her she was alive and not yet worm food.

Yes, she'd pass some time with the doctor again because, oddly enough, he was a comfort to her. He was as familiar with death and violence and tragedy as she had become…

Images flickered on the television set and she was only half conscious of them. As she slipped in and out of her troubled sleep, she was unaware of another image, an expanse of darkness that slipped under her door like a trick of the light, then flowed up her wall, slid across her ceiling and descended to the back of her chair, dyeing the ivory antimacassar on her headrest deepest black. And there it began to swell into a roiling mass of darkness with a head and glowing red eyes rising from the center and arms growing from the sides. Spindly, crouched legs formed beneath the torso. These were new but improving, strengthening. As were its abilities.

The darkness became as comfortable as the old woman in her recliner. The house and the chair and the woman had already become familiar to the monster. It had mined a rich vein of darkness with this one. But soon their collaborations would come to an end. It sensed time was running out. Yet all was not lost. The town presented so many intriguing possibilities. And the night was young.

As twin red eyes burned in its obsidian head, it reached out with fingers of solidified darkness and draped them over her forehead. In moments, it began to feed.

In keeping with his nightly routine, after grading the eighth-grade science homework and preparing a lesson plan for the next school day, Harvey Dufford jogged along Welker Street, turned left on Main, past the municipal building and the factory fire memorial and then turned left again onto Bell Street.

He followed Bell past the commercial district and into the business district at the west end of Clayton Falls. Most of his jogging route kept him in view of the restaurants, nightclubs, and shops with evening hours. Though the crime rate in town was generally low, he thought it prudent to remain in high pedestrian traffic areas for his daily cardio workout. And so it was always with a little trepidation that he concluded his nighttime run by crossing through the cluster of professional buildings across from his townhome community. Most of these offices closed at five or six o'clock with the exception of the scattered general practitioner or dentist who offered evening hours once or twice a week.

Streetlights shone down on the modest parking lots, revealing an eerie absence of cars and people. Sometimes Dufford experienced an otherworldly vibe from the professional buildings, as if he had slipped out of the normal time stream and had lost contact with the rest of humanity.

On more than one occasion, he had considered planning a new route to avoid these "dead" spots, but ultimately he thought they provided motivation for him toward the end of his run. He was closing in on fifty-five years of age and his legs lacked the spring of youth, had for some time, and that leaden-leg feeling regularly overcame him toward the end of his route. Probably psychological, knowing he was almost finished making his body crave rest. So why not counter the physical exhaustion with a burst of adrenaline derived from his anxiety when jogging through this deserted section of town.

As he approached the cluster of professional buildings, the bright lights of open stores became scattered, the sounds of pedestrian activity became hushed, the rush of cars separated into the passage of individual vehicles separated by increasing intervals, as if the heartbeat of the town weakened and slowed, nearing a flatline. That was when Dufford picked up his pace, placing one foot in front of the other faster and faster with each long stride, forcing himself into a last sprint to feel his heart rate quicken. His mouth opened and he sucked down air in great gulps to satisfy his demanding lungs.

He leaned into a left turn and entered the parking lot of the first structure. To his right, the beige one- and two-story buildings presented dark lobbies behind Plexiglas doors with official office hours posted in the form of black stencils on the glass or on freestanding message boards. To his right, beyond the parking islands, grassy mounds rose to vinyl privacy fencing. For Dufford, taking the shortcut back to his townhome instilled the claustrophobic sensation of running through a long tunnel.

A two-lane entranceway adjoined the next block of offices without providing any street exit. At regular intervals, signs were posted discouraging through traffic. Pedestrians were limited to narrow grass-covered gaps between clusters of connected buildings. The layout discouraged street and foot traffic for anyone without official business or a medical appointment. In the evening, hourly patrol car sweeps deterred loitering teenagers and would-be vandals.

But a lot can happen in an hour.

So focused was he on maintaining his brisk pace that several moments passed before Dufford noticed the thin layer of mist that puffed and swirled around his running shoes. Because he turned his attention to the unusual phenomenon, he failed to hear the padding sound coming up swiftly behind him until it was almost too late. The hairs on the back of his neck stood on end and he had a premonition someone was about to jump him.

Being mugged while jogging was something he often worried about, especially since he carried no wallet while exercising, relying on the emergency contact bracelet he wore in case of an accident. A mugger faced with a penniless victim was likely to react with extreme prejudice. Another reason he avoided deserted sections of town. But he couldn't have been less prepared for his attacker, not in his wildest imaginings.

As he whirled around, raising a forearm for protection from a blow he was certain was imminent, he stared in horror at the monstrous shape bearing down on him. Its body was the size of a minivan, each of its eight red-banded legs as thick as a fire hose.

One part of his science-teacher brain identified the giant spider as a Mexican red-kneed tarantula while another part rationalized that it couldn't survive at that extreme size—it would be crushed under its own weight. But somehow it *did* exist and it was chasing him. The most primitive part of his brain triggered his flight response.

Unfortunately, he had effectively run himself to near exhaustion before the threat had materialized. His heart raced wildly, he had a stitch in his side, and his legs felt like blocks of wood fastened awkwardly to his hips. He'd never felt closer to sixty years of age before.

He spun on his heel and veered to the right, narrowly avoiding a swipe by one of the creature's hairy front legs. But one of the retractable claws at the tip of the leg tore through his soaked sweatshirt and caused him to stumble. Catching his balance on the round cement base of a parking lot lamppost, he placed the vertical obstacle between himself and the enormous spider—and immediately realized his mistake.

The tarantula wouldn't have to move. Its legs were long enough to reach around the pole.

* * *

Lucy Quinn sat on one of the matching pair of Adirondack chairs, with her feet up on the porch railing, mirroring the relaxed posture of Tony Lacosta. The weight of the long night kept prodding her to get up and walk home. Inertia kept her seated. Tony's parents had come home from work hours ago, whipping together a mix-and-match dinner of several nights' leftovers to which they had invited her. Afterward, they had retired to the family room to watch TV, while Tony and Lucy returned to their porch chairs, each with a can of Coke. From the look Tony gave her when he took them out of the fridge, she could tell he wished they were beers.

Lucy didn't think his parents minded her hanging out here with their son, even if they would never think of her as a good influence. But they probably figured he had fewer opportunities for trouble or mischief if he stayed close to home. And after what had happened to Steve, they were a bit traumatized by the occasional randomness of fatal accidents. Of course, Tony and Lucy, along with Steve, had been complicit in the accident that had cost Teddy his life. They had somebody to blame for that. And it made sense, when you factored in the carelessness of teenagers and driving under the influence. But Steve... run down by a stranger, out of the blue, like a bolt of lightning that could strike down anyone. How could a parent rationalize that? Or come to terms with it?

Lucy took a sip of her Coke. Shook the can. Not much left.

"So, have you talked to Steve's parents?" she asked.

"Earlier," Tony said. "They're messed up about it, naturally. Weird thing is, I felt like I should apologize."

She turned to look at him, his face almost amber in the wan streetlight, and he had a faraway look in his eyes.

"You feel guilty," she said. It wasn't a question.

"Yeah. Don't you?"

She nodded. "They call it survivor's guilt."

"It was him or us, right?"

"Right."

Tony tilted his Coke back, finished it off.

"Maybe we should have stayed together."

After a long moment, she said, "Maybe."

Reluctantly, she dropped her feet to the wooden porch floor and pushed herself out of the low chair.

"So... I should go."

"Want a lift?"

"That's okay," she said. "A walk will clear my head. You going in?"

"In a few minutes."

"See ya," she said, taking the three stairs slowly, as if she had been drinking alcohol instead of a soft drink for the last few hours.

Tony waved when she glanced back from the bottom of his driveway.

"Later, Luce!"

After a few blocks, the weight of sadness she carried whenever she was around Tony eased. It wasn't his fault. She'd felt the same sadness with Steve, though it hadn't seemed as bad when all three of them were together. Now

Steve's absence reminded her of Teddy's absence, not that she ever needed a reminder of that. Though they put her in a melancholy frame of mind, she craved those connections. They helped her keep Teddy in her thoughts.

A fine white mist drifted across the street, undulating across the asphalt, spreading across the sidewalk like a living veil.

She hugged herself against the chill night air, rubbing her arms to generate some warmth and missing Teddy's arm across her shoulders. It came as a surprise to her that she was trying to live in the past, trying to recapture those days of a year gone by, before the accident. And that past was forever lost to her. Her town, her neighbors, had that in common with her. They built a memorial to help them remember the past, but their past was fresher, only six months gone.

Every day, they placed flowers and stuffed animals at the memorial and lingered in their lost past as she lingered in hers. But few placed flowers at the site of the factory fire. The scorched brick of the crumbled building surrounded by the teetering wrought-iron fencing was too harsh a reminder of what had been lost and how horribly it had been wrenched from them. She would have to decide how long she'd cling to her memories of living while Teddy was still a part of her life. Would a day come when she looked forward to the future more than she longed for the past?

Ahead of her, a car engine raced with a throaty roar. A moment later, high beams flared, blinding her. She raised her forearm to shield her eyes. The car, a dark boxy shape cloaked behind its headlights, sat in the middle of the street, unmoving. She wondered how long the driver had been sitting there. Lucky somebody hadn't crashed into him already. The street wasn't busy but cars passed at regular intervals.

The engine raced again, and the car lurched forward.

"Jackass," she whispered.

As if the driver heard her disparaging remark, the car swerved across the street toward her, along the shoulder and—

—jumped the curb!

As the car barreled down the sidewalk toward her, she had a horrifying thought. *He's trying to run me down!*

EIGHT

If not for the parking lot lamppost between Harvey Dufford and the giant tarantula, the creature was close enough to pounce on him. Any move to the right or left and the spider would be on top of him in a heartbeat.

The tarantula brought its front pair of legs down on either side of him, boxing him in. For a moment he stared at the eye mound, the size of a cake box, with its two rows of four beady black eyes. The tarantula hunted by sensing vibration and sound rather than detecting movement with its relatively weak eyes, but they were alien and unnerving nonetheless. Dufford imagined they saw well enough to classify him as a meal.

Abruptly, the spider raised its two front pairs of legs high in the air, elevating its cephalothorax in a threat posture. Its pedipalps, bristling feelers that also served as food handlers, waved in front of his face like a pair of truncated legs, just out of reach. The spider's double-segmented chelicerae extended, twin fangs at the tips dropping down but too far away to inject him with venom.

The venom from a normal tarantula wasn't fatal to humans, but a tarantula of this extraordinary size would produce a proportionate amount of venom. Dufford figured he would fare no better than a field mouse. And if this monster managed to grab him, the chelicerae would coat him with corrosive digestive juices. The spider would wait for his flesh to liquefy, then suck it into its straw-shaped mouth.

Dufford barely had time to catch his breath before the tarantula dropped down onto all eight legs and scampered around the pole. Backing away, he put distance between himself and the giant spider before turning his back and running full speed. As he scanned ahead, looking for a weapon or a gap between blocks of buildings, he saw a rust-pocked blue Ford F-150 pickup truck parked in front of an orthodontist's office. A white rag tied to the door handle indicated the truck was disabled and awaiting a tow, or possibly that the driver planned to return with a container of gasoline or a replacement part.

Harvey tugged desperately at the passenger door handle. Unfortunately, it was locked.

He circled around the truck and tried the driver's side— also locked. Ducking behind the bed of the pickup, Dufford listened for the sound of the tarantula and marveled at how stealthy it was despite its enormous size. On hands and knees, he peered under the truck to track its movement. Thick bristling legs pranced around the other side of the Ford, but too few of them. Not nearly enough on the ground, with more rising out of view by the second.

The pickup creaked on its worn shock absorbers a moment before a broad shadow fell across Dufford's hiding place. Almost too late, he dropped to his back and looked up. Bristly pedipalps swept over his head, while the creature's fangs sliced the air, dripping venom as the tarantula strained to reach him from its perch in the truck bed.

As one leg, then another came down on the driver's side of the Ford, Dufford rolled underneath it. When the spider seemed committed to his side of the truck, Dufford rolled twice and emerged from the passenger side. He climbed to his feet and pumped his exhausted legs back the way he had come.

Behind him, the truck's suspension groaned under the weight of the monstrous spider. Dufford tried to put the sound out of his mind and focused on getting the hell away from the area. Nearly doubled over from exertion, his breathing became harsh in his ears, his stride erratic. But he was almost out in the open again.

Once he exited onto Bell Street, he could flag down a car or, even better, a police cruiser. He could find a store that hadn't closed yet, a nightclub or tavern, and take shelter there. The tarantula was too big to fit through a doorway but not big enough to burst through walls. At least he hoped that was true. If its strength was proportionate to its size…

He chanced a look back over his shoulder—

—and nearly screamed in terror.

The tarantula was close enough that he could make out the individual hairs on its waving pedipalps. The red-banded front legs were a blur of motion, their tips touching down several yards behind him. And the gap was closing.

Ahead, he saw Bell Street. A white panel truck zoomed by before he could even raise an arm to try to catch the driver's attention. But that flash of contact gave him hope that he could escape—

He stumbled, the sole of his right running shoe sticking in the asphalt as if he had stepped in deep mud. He pulled it free, but lost the shoe. Then his left foot became mired. Tugging against that resistance, he lost the other shoe—and promptly planted his right foot into more clinging softness. The ground gave way under him. Incredibly, he was sinking into the asphalt, knee deep, then mid-thigh, then up to his hips before it stopped.

The ground was solid again, and he was trapped.

Pounding the asphalt until his fists were bloody, he twisted around and moaned as he saw the tarantula looming over him, rearing up on its two back pairs of legs in its threat posture. It slowly lowered itself over him, the cephalothorax coming down like the lid of a coffin.

For a brief moment, he hoped—prayed—that it would lose interest in him, and move away. A moment of stillness in which Dufford heard another car breeze along Bell Street, then the ominous rustle of the descending pedipalps.

He took a deep breath and yelled, *"HELP!"*

A dark flash of the chelicerae preceded twin white blurs as the hollow fangs plunged into his back like a pair of butcher knives. White hot pain sliced through his body. He convulsed, whether from shock or pain or from the effects of the venom, he couldn't know. The pedipalps curled around him, the bristling hairs raking furrows in his skin as the appendages tried to pull him up against the grinding teeth under the chelicerae. But his body was trapped in the hardened asphalt and offered too much resistance.

Instead the tarantula pressed down against him, the chelicerae rubbing roughly against his skin, pushing him bodily left and right. Sticky fluid coated his bare neck and back, where it was exposed from the tears in his sweatshirt. It soaked into his wounds, into the fang punctures, and burned worse than alcohol. It felt as if gasoline had been poured into those cuts and ignited. His flesh bubbled and hissed, lighting his nerves on fire until unbearable white flared behind his eyelids blinding him with screaming pain.

Again the tarantula pressed down on him, but now it was feeding. His ears roared with the harsh sucking sound of his liquefied flesh being consumed, siphoned away through the spider's straw-shaped mouth. Again the chelicerae washed over him, this time pressing against his face and throat.

A more intense round of burning pain filled his shrinking universe. He tried to scream but his left cheek dissolved, leaving a hole that exposed all the teeth on that side of his head, so that only a panicked, gasping hiss emerged from his burning throat. In seconds his left eyelid was gone, and the exposed eyeball went dark a moment later, dribbling down what was left of his cheek.

When the chelicerae pressed down again, he raised his arms to hold them back. But his hands were bare and soon coated in the sticky digestive fluids. With his remaining eye, he watched as the flesh of his fingers and palms and forearms ran down his sleeves like hot candle wax. But not for long. The suctioning mouth was greedy and wanted more of him. When his arms were useless, the chelicerae pressed down, enveloping what was left of his face as the pedipalps gripped him in a single-minded embrace.

Briefly, he became aware of the bass rumbling of a truck engine and a flare of light washing over him, bathing the tarantula's bristling body and appendages in sharp contrast. But those sensory cues were overwhelmed and forgotten as the suffocating pressure of the spider's mass bore down on him.

Sight abandoned him, and then hearing, and finally his nerves, so long on fire, fell silent as his exposed brain was given the spider's special attention.

The tarantula savored every liquid morsel—until it abruptly vanished.

Lucy stared in horror as the car bore down on her. She briefly caught sight of the distinctive grill, with the chrome bumper below it, but had no time to process the memory. An image of Steve's face flashed in her mind and that, more than anything, spurred her to action. She dodged to the left and hurled herself over the waist-high picket fence fronting the nearest house.

The car swerved again, even further across the sidewalk, and the front bumper clipped every slat and post in the fence in quick succession with a rapid series of explosive cracks, like machine gun fire.

Lucy rolled across the grass and sprang to her feet.

The owner of the house, a woman in a bathrobe, poked her head out the front door.

"What the hell was that?" she demanded.

"Call the police!" Lucy yelled, her gaze tracking the receding taillights. "That car tried to run me down."

"Who? What kind of car?"

Lucy walked across the wooden debris out to the sidewalk, deep in thought as she stared back the way she had come. She turned back to the woman, her eyes wide in realization.

"A '68 Dodge Charger!"

"Wait! Where are you going?"

Lucy sprinted back toward Tony's house. The car had killed Steve and had nearly killed her. But this time it hadn't disappeared. She had a terrifying feeling that it hadn't completed its night's work.

She had Tony's house in sight. She saw the Charger's brake lights flare, the tires screaming against the asphalt as the car made an abrupt ninety-degree turn to face the front of the house.

"Tony!" she screamed.

As she ran, she shoved her hand into the pocket of her jeans, pulled out her cell and speed dialed her father. He answered on the second ring but static drowned out his voice.

"Dad! Come to Tony's house now! It's urgent!" she shouted, hoping he could hear her over the squawking interference, but a moment later the phone went silent. The light of the display and behind the buttons winked out, as if her battery had died in an instant.

Tony stood on the porch, leaning over the porch railing, confused as the Charger revved its engine.

"Hey!" he called, shielding his eyes from the bright headlights. "What the hell?"

"Tony, get inside!"

Instead of following her instructions, he looked over at her and shook his head.

"Lucy?"

The Charger lurched forward, engine roaring as it again jumped the curb, barreled across the front lawn, demolishing the small bushes Tony's mother had planted, and slammed into the porch skirt.

Wood creaked and the porch sagged in the middle.

Tony staggered, grabbing onto the twisted railing to catch his balance.

The Charger reversed, nearly to the curb, then rushed forward again, smashing into the white planking of the porch floor. The center collapsed, in a V, and Tony pitched forward onto the hood of the Charger.

Lucy screamed.

The Charger reversed again, tires spinning and digging up clods of dirt from the lawn as Tony fell from the hood and whacked his head against the shattered planking. Dazed, he climbed to his feet and staggered in one of the long ruts in the dirt.

Tony's father flung open the front door of the house, a baseball bat gripped in both hands. Behind him, Tony's mother appeared, looking past her husband's shoulder, her face stark white with fear. In the time it took Tony's father to take in the scene, the Charger had roared forward again. Tony was pinned in the lights, trapped between the ruin of the porch and the oncoming front bumper of the car.

Tony raised his arms—

The Charger rammed him back into the shattered porch, the grill and bumper of the car crushing him against unyielding wood.

Lucy looked away from the horrifying image of Tony's chest bursting open, broken ribs entangled with jagged shards of wood as his blood splashed everywhere. She dropped to her knees and sobbed.

Tony's father yelled, an unintelligible sound of rage and anguish, and swung the bat like an axe, cracking the windshield of the Charger and pounding the hood. The bat shattered but he continued to smash what was left of it against the Charger until his hands bled.

With a roar, the Charger reversed, spinning into a turn so that it faced Lucy. The engine raced and she realized she was next. She was too distraught to move. Nothing could stop this car. It would kill her just as it had killed Steve and now Tony. She wondered if she'd been living on borrowed time for the past year. Maybe they were all supposed to die in the crash that had killed Teddy. And this was just fate cashing in its unpaid bills.

Tony's mother ran down to her son's broken body, dropping down beside him in her bathrobe and cradling him in her arms. Sirens wailed in the distance.

Before the Charger moved toward Lucy, Tony's father jumped in front of it and pounded on the hood with his bare, bloody fists. Once, twice, a third time—

—and his fists came down on nothing but air.

The Charger had vanished.

NINE

"We've been driving around aimlessly for fifteen minutes," Sam said. "What exactly are we looking for, Dean?"

"It's like the definition of porn."

"What?"

"I'll know it when I see it."

"Don't you think Chief Quinn or Jeffries will call if anything weird happens?"

"Maybe," Dean said. "But by the time they get around to it, might be too late to do anything. Hey, nap if you want. I see a headless horseman, I'll be sure to wake you."

"Funny, Dean," Sam said. "But if we're gonna do this, I need coffee."

"Place up ahead," Dean said, nodding toward a white sign with red letters at the corner of a parking lot: "Mack's Qwik Mart." "Says it's open twenty-four seven."

Dean flicked on his turn signal as he neared the convenience store's parking lot.

Beside him, Sam sat up straight, leaned forward.

"Wait, what's happening?" he asked, peering ahead of him.

"Don't know."

A group of agitated people in the parking lot were yelling at each other, pointing at the ground, and backing away. A woman with facial piercings, wearing a distressed leather jacket and jeans, ran to the front of the store and pounded on the windows, screaming, "Get out!"

Walking on wobbly legs, an old man fell against the side of his Buick sedan, fumbled for his keys, then gave up and hustled out of the parking lot. A young woman with bleached blond hair dropped two plastic bags filled with soft drink bottles and unhealthy snacks and raced across the parking lot as if a Hellhound was on her heels. A few people dashed toward their cars, minivans, and SUVs, while others simply followed the blonde's lead.

"Dude," Dean said. "*This* is porn."

As the old-timer who'd lost his keys lumbered heedlessly out into the street, Dean stomped on the brake pedal to avoid hitting him. Under bushy gray brows, the man's eyes were wild.

"Get back!" he yelled. "Get back while you can!"

After that frantic warning, the old man continued his retreat.

Dean slowed to school zone speed and drove up to the parking lot. He was halfway up the entrance ramp when he hit the brake again—hard. Dean would risk his own life before he would imperil the chassis of the Impala. After all, the Impala couldn't defend itself.

"Sinkhole!" he said.

"You think?"

Sam was right: the word 'sinkhole' didn't begin to cover what was happening in the convenience store's parking lot. The ground was falling away at an alarming rate, from the center of the parking lot outward, the blacktop was crumbling like burnt toast.

Dean shifted the Impala hurriedly into reverse. The cars lined up behind the row of cement bollards protecting the Plexiglas front of Mack's Qwik Mart tilted backward as the back wheels lost their support. A metallic-blue Nissan Murano was the first to fall. It landed with a resounding crash, shattering the back and side windows. A silver Dodge Durango followed soon after, slamming into the Nissan with a concussive *whump* and a protesting screech of metal. The theft alarm whooped and wailed.

Dean twisted around to look through the rear window of the Impala. Seeing the road clear, he gunned the engine and the Impala lurched backward and accelerated away from the convenience store.

"Dean?"

"You'll get your coffee, Sam."

"That's not what I—"

"That sinkhole's eating cars," Dean said. "Keeping my baby clear of that."

Sam shook his head, rolling his eyes. "First things first, right?"

"Damn straight."

Dean spun the wheel and backed into a parking space

along the curb on the far side of the street, a couple of hundred feet from Mack's Qwik Mart. A few moments later, they were out of the car and sprinting back to the site of the chaos.

Some of the people who had fled the store or abandoned their cars in the unstable parking lot stood on the shoulder of the road, staring in disbelief at the ongoing devastation. The Winchesters shouldered past the line of gawkers, repeating "FBI" and "Move aside" until they reached the parking lot.

Sam turned to the people and held up his FBI laminate.

"I need everyone to back up to the far side of the street," he stated firmly. "For your own safety. Move!"

A few nodded, others grumbled, but they all backed up.

From the edge of the parking lot, Dean looked down into the sinkhole. *More like a friggin' abyss*, he thought. A few cars parked on either side of the lot were within a few brittle blacktop inches of falling into the hole, but what concerned him more were the two people standing at the entrance to the convenience store. An attractive blond woman no more than thirty, with a panic-stricken look on her face, straining to pull away from the wiry teenaged boy wearing a nametag and green polyester shirt that probably served as a store uniform. The teenager had a firm grip on her upper arm to keep her from running headlong into the pit.

Dean called across the chasm.

"Ma'am, you need to stay where you are."

"My son's asleep in the van!" she yelled back.

Glancing to the right, Dean saw a blue Chevy conversion van. Aside from the windshield, which faced away from him, all the windows were tinted. If the kid had any sense, he would have lit out soon as the first car crashed in the hole.

"How old?"

"Three!"

Damn, Dean thought. "Sam! We got a problem. Kid trapped in a van."

Dean pointed at the Mack's employee. "Young man, what's your name?"

"Anson."

"There a back exit out of the store?"

"Yes," Anson said. "But there's a wall behind the store."

"Can you get over it?"

"No. Wait, yes, we have a ladder for changing lights."

"Great," Dean said. "I want you to take this woman and go out the back."

"I'm not leaving my son!" the woman cried.

"I'll get your son," Dean responded.

"I'm not leaving until I know he's safe."

Dean sighed. He looked at the strip of sidewalk they stood on. At the moment, it seemed secure. The blacktop had crumbled away almost to the bollards. Maybe they provided some extra support.

"First sign that sidewalk's failing, you leave. Okay?"

After a moment, she nodded reluctantly.

Beside him, Sam said, "What do you have in mind?"

Dean noticed a four-foot high chain-link fence ran along both sides of the convenience store parking lot. Easy enough to climb over it to get to the van.

"You take the passenger side. I'll take driver's side."

"Figures."

Sam started to run along the outside of the fence. Dean was a step behind him when he noticed the conversion van shudder. The blacktop under the left rear tire was crumbling. He veered to the right, but stayed on the inside of the fence, running along a thin strip of sidewalk that abutted the chain-link fence. The ground shook beneath his feet. A quick glance at the van and he saw it drop a few inches and rock side to side.

The front bumper of a late seventies gold Pontiac Firebird was close enough to kiss the fence. Without a moment's hesitation, Dean jumped on the hood of the car and crossed over it.

Someone across the street yelled, "Hey!"

"You gotta be kidding me," Dean muttered. Joker's car was ten seconds from joining the vertical demolition derby and he was worried about a ding on the hood?

Dean bounded across the hoods of two more cars and landed beside the Chevy van as Sam was leaping sideways over the fence. The passenger side doors were locked. This close, he could hear a frightened child crying inside the van. Dean circled around to the driver's side, which was also locked.

"Here," the young mother called. "The keys!"

She tossed them underhand to Dean.

The van lurched as more ground gave way.

Dean staggered, but snatched the keys out of the air by the dyed-pink rabbit's foot keychain. He opened the driver's door and was about to hit the button to unlock all the doors when he was flung forward against the steering wheel.

The woman screamed. Dean felt the van sliding violently backward. Sam's startled face flashed by the passenger-side window and was gone a second later.

A moment or two of eerily quiet free fall and then a jarring impact.

First Dean was tossed up against the steering wheel, banging his already bruised ribs. Then he came down hard against the driver's seat. With one leg hanging outside the van, the door slammed painfully against his knee, but provided enough resistance to prevent him from hurtling through the interior of the van. He kicked the door with his other leg to free himself, and promptly sprawled across the front seats. Twisting around, he peered down.

Fortunately, the three-year-old boy was buckled into a child safety seat strapped to the passenger side captain's chair in the second row. Terrified, his cheeks streaked with tears, the boy stared at Dean as if he were an alien life form. The sudden drop and impact must have stunned the crying jag right out of him.

"It's okay, kid," Dean said trying to sound calm. "I'm gonna get you outta here."

"Where's Momma?"

"Your mom's fine. She's up—back in the store."

"I want Momma."

"I'm gonna take you to her. Okay?"

The boy nodded. "Want Momma."

"We've established that," Dean said. "But I need you to work with me. Okay?"

Another nod. This time the kid gave him an expectant look.

"What's your name, kid?"

"Hunter."

Dean smiled. "No kidding?"

The boy nodded solemnly. "Hunter Riley Fields."

Gravel and chunks of blacktop pelted the exterior of the van like hailstones with biblical aspirations. One particularly large chunk stuck and starred the windshield. A few more *plinked* and *plunked* against the hood. Dean tried not to think about what might happen if a big enough rock—or even another car—came through the windshield at that moment. Or what would happen if a fuel tank ruptured and something sparked. No, he wouldn't think about that at all.

"Okay, Hunter," Dean said with a serious nod of his own. "Let's do this."

He reached between the front seats and stretched his arm to the far seat in the second row, pushing the release button on the kid's safety seat. Accustomed to the seat routine, the boy pulled the V-straps up over his head without any prompting. Dean smiled reassuringly.

"Great job, Hunter. Now, let's get out of here."

The boy started to climb out of the seat.

"Whoa!" Dean said. "Careful, now. Give me your hand."

Dean stretched to meet the kid's small hand but adjusted his position to get a better grip on his arm.

"One, two... *three*!"

With one quick tug, Dean pulled the boy up to the front— top—row of seats.

Dean backed out of the door, propping it open with his back as he stood in the dirt and gravel slope of the sinkhole.

The van rested against the side of the hole at a sixty degree angle. With one arm wrapped around Hunter, he moved away from the van and let the door slam shut. The back end of the van rested against a beige Camry that was almost completely submerged. Even as Dean watched, the van's tires were sinking into the dirt and crumbled blacktop.

"Dean!" Sam called from above.

Dean spotted his brother braced against the chain-link fence in front of where the van had been parked, his forearms hooked over the fence so he could clutch it while leaning forward for a better view. Sam was almost twenty-five feet above.

"We're fine," Dean said.

"Hunter!"

"Momma!" Hunter said, waving at his mother who stood beside the store clerk. The bollard nearest the pair tilted at a forty-five degree angle. The sidewalk wouldn't last much longer. But they had a more immediate problem.

A banana-yellow Mini Cooper that had been parked one space closer to the store's entrance was inching backward and leaning at a precarious angle. Clumps of dirt and chunks of blacktop broke away from beneath its back tires. With a scrape of metal on asphalt, the Mini Cooper pitched backward, listing to the left as it hurtled toward Dean and the boy.

Dean whispered, "Oh, crap…"

TEN

Ehrich Vogel shuddered in his sleep, rolled to the left and a few moments later rolled to the right, becoming tangled in his sweat-soaked sheets. Mumbling softly, his words unintelligible, the tone of his voice escalated from concern to agitation to fright. His distress culminated with him shouting, "No! No! *NO!*"

With the last protest, his eyes opened wide and he swung his tangled legs over the edge of the bed, breathing harshly. Pressing his good hand to his chest, he felt his heart hammering beneath his ribs. He could imagine himself having a fatal heart attack at that moment. Widowed, retired, alone. Nobody would miss him for days. While he waited for his heart rate to return to normal, he leaned over the bed, forearms resting on his thighs, head hanging.

Because of his huddled posture, he neither saw nor sensed the mass of darkness dispersing above his bed, thinning itself into deep shadow and drifting along the walls and out through a narrow gap in the windowsill.

His thoughts turned inward, to the nightmare. The same one that had visited him on a regular basis for the past twenty years. Only worse. The explosion, the partial cave-in at Croyden Creek began the same, but this time more than his right arm had been crushed. He'd been standing in a new section, next to a support beam and the explosion blew it clear.

Coal dust and methane. Bad combination.

He shook his head.

One moment he'd been standing, the next he was buried under an avalanche of rock and dirt, his ribs crushed. In the nightmare, he couldn't escape, couldn't breathe. Felt his life slipping away down in the darkness.

Vogel stood on weak legs and walked to the bathroom, bending over to splash water on his face with his trembling left hand. The fingers of his right hand were mangled. He couldn't do much with the muscles of that arm and, as a result, it had atrophied. After the cold water cleared the fog of sleep, he stood up straight and took several deep breaths.

The real explosion and cave-in at Croyden Creek Mine had been bad, but the nightmare scenario had been far worse. Nevertheless, *bad* had been bad enough. After the accident, he never set foot in that mine or any other mine ever again. That didn't stop the nightmares from haunting him through the years.

Outside, the wind howled and his bedroom windows rattled in their frames. A flash of lighting lit the room in stark black and white. The rumble of thunder shook the eaves of his house.

This troubled night, with the cave-in images especially vivid in his head, he decided he'd had enough sleep. Staying awake, whether watching a movie or reading a book, was his only guarantee that another nightmare wouldn't finish the course of the first, and this time see him buried alive in a deep, dark pit.

If nothing else, his heart would thank him.

As the yellow blur of the Mini Cooper fell toward him, Dean clutched the three-year-old boy against his chest and flattened himself against the driver's door of the Chevy conversion van.

"Hold on!" he said into Hunter's ear.

The Mini Cooper slammed into the partially submerged Camry with a booming clash of metal, and a popping crunch of breaking safety glass. The yellow car's roof missed Dean and Hunter by less than a yard.

Hunter's mom screamed and the boy started to cry again.

"Everybody calm down!" Dean shouted. "I've got this." He took a deep breath. "Hunter, can you hang onto my neck?" The boy nodded. "Good."

Dean shifted Hunter to his back, with his small arms wrapped around Dean's neck. But he didn't trust the boy's ability to hang on as he climbed, so Dean kept his left hand clamped over both of the boys' fists. He scrambled up the steep slope high enough to climb onto the side of the Mini Cooper.

The small car's undercarriage had sunk into the side of the sinkhole facing the front of the store, so Dean jumped onto the slope, with an awkward three-point landing. His shoes immediately began to sink into the soft earth and his free hand couldn't find any reliable purchase.

He realized two things at that moment: No way was he climbing out of the sinkhole unassisted; and that strong odor assailing his nostrils was definitely gasoline. Somewhere in the mangled pileup of cars, a fuel line had been compromised or a gas tank ruptured.

He looked to where Sam was inching along the fence to track their movements.

"Sam!"

Their eyes met and Sam nodded grimly. He looked over to the store clerk.

"Anson! You sell rope in there?"

"What? Rope? No, we don't—wait. What about clothesline?"

"Clothesline is perfect."

"We have packages. Hundred feet."

"Good. Get one."

While Anson ran into the store, Sam made his careful way along the fence and then hurried along the sidewalk to join Hunter's mother. Anson came out and handed Sam the shrink-wrapped package of white clothesline, which Sam quickly ripped open to play out the coiled line.

"Hey!" Anson yelled. "Bad idea, man!"

Dean looked to the far side of the parking lot and saw one of the bystanders, a balding man in his forties, edging around the back of the gold Firebird.

"The hell's he doing?" Dean called.

"Sir!" Sam yelled. "Get back!"

The man tossed a dismissive wave in Sam's direction.

"I'm saving my car!"

Dean shook his head. "You believe that guy?"

"Dude, seriously?" Sam said.

"What?"

"You... and the Impala."

"Totally different."

"Right. Because you have all your hair," Sam said, then shouted at the man. "You can't move your car! It's trapped."

The back wheels of the Firebird were two feet from the edge of the expanding sinkhole. The front bumper was too close to the chain-link fence. No room to turn or maneuver. The car was as good as gone.

Ignoring Sam, the man started and gunned his engine. Then the Firebird edged forward, pressing into the metal fence. It seemed he intended to run over the fence and drive off the side of the lot. But the center of his front bumper pressed against one of the vertical support posts, which was anchored in cement and wouldn't budge. He floored the accelerator, which caused the back wheels to spin and squeal against the compromised blacktop. What he couldn't see was that the wheels were accelerating the erosion process. He threw it in reverse and backed up a bit, expecting to ram the fence. But the back wheels hit the lip of the sinkhole before he expected and they dropped over the edge with a loud squeal as the undercarriage slammed into the ground.

"Sam! The rope!" Dean shouted.

With the sound of screeching metal behind him, Dean reached up and caught the end of the clothesline. Sam was about to secure the other end to a bollard, but noticed the one leaning dangerously forward and backed up to loop the line through one of the store's door handles. Meanwhile, Dean had looped the other end around Hunter's body, snugging it up under his arms and making a few quick knots.

He checked it was secure, then called, "Ready!"

Sam stepped out to the edge of the sidewalk and pulled the line up end over end, lifting Hunter out of the pit. He caught the boy in his arms and the mother cried out in relief. Rather than fussing with the knots, Sam took a folding knife from his pocket and cut the rope behind the boy's back and handed him to his mother.

"Oh, thank God," she said, squeezing her son against her chest and kissing him repeatedly on his cheeks. "Thank you. Thank you, both!"

"Anson, take her and the boy out through the back," Sam instructed.

Dean looked over his shoulder, wincing at the protesting squeals of metal. The Firebird slipped inexorably backward, tilting up like a breaching whale captured in slow motion video. Sparks showered across the blacktop, reminding Dean of the gasoline leaking somewhere in the pit beneath him.

"Gonna get hot down here, Sam!"

The loose bollard broke free, arcing down toward Dean's head. He jumped to the side, sprawling in the dirt as the cement post crashed through the side window of the Mini Cooper. The small car and the Camry beneath it settled deeper into the pit.

The joker in the Firebird opened the door of the car and

jumped out. The door slammed shut, clipping him on the shoulder as he fell and sent him sprawling toward the back of the car. The treacherous ground gave way beneath him. He shouted in alarm as he toppled head first into the pit in what amounted to a half somersault. Landing with a thud on the passenger door of a half-submerged black minivan, he stared up into the night sky moaning.

Sam looked from the teetering Firebird to its owner twenty feet below.

"Oh, no."

"Hey, Ass-hat!" Dean shouted. "Move!"

The man rubbed the back of his head. Then it suddenly dawned on him.

"My car…"

The Firebird dropped straight down like a hammer on an anvil. And the owner had the misfortune of lying between the two.

The crunch of shattered bones was almost completely masked by the collision of steel driving into steel. Almost. Slick gobs of burst flesh and an arterial spray of blood splattered over the black minivan. The Firebird toppled over with another crash, revealing a red pulpy mess barely identifiable as human remains.

Grimacing, Dean looked away and not simply because the Firebird had taken its name all too literally. Active tongues of flame roamed along the undercarriage, hungrily seeking a more plentiful fuel source.

With renewed urgency, Dean wrapped the clothesline around his waist several times and tied it off. He climbed hand over hand, scrambling up the loose earth to keep from losing ground. Sam pulled on his end, taking some of Dean's weight away.

Red and blue lights flashed across the expanse of the sinkhole, accompanied by the brief *whoop-whoop* of a police siren. Dean recognized Chief Quinn's voice over the police cruiser's loudspeaker. "Everyone clear the area! Stand clear! Now!"

Dean spared a quick glance over his shoulder and saw the police chief exiting his cruiser and waving everyone back, across the street.

"Agents," he called. "Fire truck's on the way."

"Sinkhole's clear," Dean yelled. "Everyone's out."

"Good," Quinn said. "Now you'd better get the hell out of there."

"Working on it," Dean said.

He heard a woman call out to Quinn. "That man saved a little boy."

Dean was halfway out of the pit when he noticed the crumbling dirt was gradually revealing the underside of the sidewalk. Cracks formed in the cement and sections started to break away and slide past him on the steep slope. Utility pipes, possibly cable, water and gas lines, ran under the sidewalk. To his right, a second bollard pitched into the hole.

In the distance, Dean heard the wail of police sirens.

By the time he reached the edge of the sidewalk, Sam was standing with his back pressed against the glass storefront, hauling on the thin clothesline but monitoring the disintegrating walkway. Sam caught Dean's arm and pulled him up and out. At that moment, several sections of sidewalk tilted forward, pitching them toward the sinkhole.

The door securing the line had been pulled open by Dean's weight.

"Go!" Dean said. "I got the line."

Sam threw himself backward, through the open door and into the Qwik Mart. Dean's feet started to slip out from beneath him, but he continued to support his weight with the clothesline until Sam caught his arm and tugged him inside. A glance back showed black smoke curling up from the pit, but the flames were beneath his line of sight.

An explosion blasted up from the sinkhole, followed by another, and a third—a chain reaction of automobiles exploding. The noise was deafening and debris sprayed everywhere. Chief Quinn took cover behind his cruiser. Bystanders were shouting and screaming, racing to the far side of the highway. No doubt they'd witnessed the Firebird owner get himself killed. If nothing else, the man had helped by serving as a cautionary tale for others.

"That was close," Dean said.

"Too close."

Another explosion roared outside, this one rocking the convenience store. Overhead, the fluorescent lights flickered. Snack bags and aluminum cans crashed to the linoleum floor.

"Not good," Dean said.

The vibration was only the beginning. The store itself was shifting, creaking, groaning. Dean recalled the utility lines running under the sidewalk out front. Natural gas. Maybe a propane tank out back. *Crap.*

"We're not out of the woods yet, Sammy," he observed.

They sprinted to the back of the store, kicking the fallen shop goods out of the way, past metal racks of chips and bread and boxes of doughnuts and assorted candy, and ducked through a door marked "Employees Only" into a cluttered stock room, and out through the rear exit.

Another explosion sounded, seeming even closer and with a bigger wallop. The back wall of the store shook and the ground beneath their feet shuddered. They couldn't underestimate the instability caused by the sinkhole. For all Dean knew, the whole convenience store might drop onto the crushed cars at any moment.

"There," Sam said, pointing to an eight-foot ladder propped against the cinderblock wall behind the store.

A few moments later, they had climbed over the wall and dropped down to the grass on the other side. They were shielded from the blast zone, but how far the sinkhole would spread was an open question. Anson, the store clerk, stood there awkwardly with his hands stuffed in his pockets, but Hunter and his mom were nowhere to be seen.

"Kid and his mom?" Dean asked.

"Gone," Anson said, a clear tremor in his voice. "She wanted to hang around to thank you again, but after the first explosion…"

"Good parenting," Sam said. "No place for a kid."

"You okay?" Dean asked Anson.

"Yeah, fine," the clerk said, nodding a bit frantically. "Called my manager. Told him I'd wait for him. Don't think he believes me, how bad it is."

"Picture's worth a thousand words, right?" Dean said.

"If I were you, Anson, I'd wait a block or two away," Sam said.

Then his cell phone rang. He glanced at the display and showed it to Dean. It said: "Clayton Falls Police."

Sam answered and listened. He mouthed the name "Jeffries" to Dean.

"Yes. Yes, we did. Yes, I would classify that as weird. That too." He listened for a few moments. "I'll need addresses." After a few moments, he said, "We found something weird as well." Sam described the sinkhole, the subsequent explosions and one death. "Your chief's here. Got his hands full with crowd control." A short time later, he pulled the phone away from his ear.

"Well?" Dean asked.

"Walk with me," Sam said, with a discreet nod in Anson's direction.

They cut through someone's backyard and circled around to the street, heading towards the Impala.

"Short version?"

Dean nodded.

"Giant tarantula. Killer trees. And the phantom Charger returned. Killed Tony Lacosta. And other reports are coming in, attempted home invasions, masked gunmen."

"Busy night," Dean said grimly.

"I'll say. Police are spread thin," Sam said. "But some of these… apparitions disappear in front of the witnesses or are gone by the time patrols arrive at the scene."

"Fits the MO of whatever the hell this thing is."

Lightning flashed across the sky, followed by a prolonged rumble of thunder. A gust of wind whipped around them, shaking nearby treetops. Behind them, another explosion rocked the night.

"Sam," Dean said. "Don't think this night's done yet."

ELEVEN

"What's closest?" Dean asked as soon as they were back in the Impala.

"Stay on Bell Street," Sam said. "This takes us to the office buildings on the left, where the giant tarantula attacked."

Dean shook his head and had to smile.

"What?"

"Just the fact that you said what you just said. With a straight face."

Sam smiled. "Yeah. See what you mean."

"Next stop, eight-legged freak."

Ahead, a traffic light blinked to yellow, then red. Dean slowed, ready to run the light as soon as he checked the cross street. He craned his neck over the dashboard for a quick look and hit the brake hard.

A dark blue Honda Civic raced into the intersection going in excess of seventy miles per hour. The driver, apparently unaccustomed to high speeds on city streets, took the turn too wide, tires screeching in protest, and slammed broadside into a parked Dodge Ram pickup truck. The left side of the Civic rose off the ground, and would have rolled over a lower barrier.

"What the hell?" Dean said for what seemed like the tenth time that night.

The driver looked stunned, but uninjured. Fortunately, he was alone, because the passenger side had taken the brunt of the impact.

"Dean," Sam said, pointing down the length of the cross street. "Look!"

"Is that—? No, that's not what it is. Is it?"

"A pack of Velociraptors."

"Velociraptors? As in *Jurassic Park* Velociraptors?"

"Actually, they're from the Cretaceous per…" Sam cleared his throat. "Yes."

Four Velociraptors bounded along the street on powerful hind legs in apparent pursuit of the Civic. Their reptilian heads—predominantly jaws lined with sharp teeth—darted side to side as they neared their prey, eyes that reminded Dean of alligators scanning for other predators.

The white-faced driver stared through his side window, watching slack-jawed while the hunting pack sprinted across the intersection and surrounded his wrecked car. Not that he had many options. Safest place at the moment was inside the car. But the Civic's engine was still running, if roughly, so the driver floored the accelerator. The car tried to move, but the wreckage of the passenger side appeared to be entangled with the Dodge Ram. He shifted into reverse and the vehicle shuddered, immobile.

Ignoring his failed attempts to flee, the first Raptor scrambled onto the roof of the small car, the large sickle-shaped claw on each rear foot tapping the metal, perhaps probing for weakness. Another Raptor shoved its head at the side window, fracturing the glass. One more strike and it would break through, giving its fearsome jaws access to the interior of the car.

Dean swung the Impala onto the shoulder of Bell Street. He jumped out with Sam right behind him. In their FBI guises, they both carried handguns, but Dean thought they might need something more powerful from the arsenal they stored in the trunk.

"Time travel, Sam?" Dean said incredulously. "These things come through a friggin' wormhole? Even Cass is gonna have trouble sending them back to the... Crustacean period."

Sam shrugged. "So we put them down."

Dean nodded emphatically. "Simple. I like it."

He unlocked the trunk and raised the lid, peering inside.

"Dude—" Sam said.

Dean glanced to the left, assessing. "Where's the fourth Raptor?"

"Vanished. It just... *winked* out."

One of the remaining three Velociraptors jumped on the hood of the Civic, leaned toward the windshield—and vanished.

Two remained. The one prowling on the roof, and the other attempting to poke its head into the car.

With a screeching roar, the second Raptor struck at the

window, shattering the glass and darting his head inside with one quick motion. The driver huddled against the passenger door, as far from the driver's side as possible. With the passenger side pinned against the Dodge Ram, he was, for the moment, safe.

"Something's not right," Sam said thoughtfully.

Dean stared at his brother. "When has this *not* been wrong?"

They armed themselves swiftly.

The Raptor on the Civic's roof leapt down to the windshield and its weight crunched through the safety glass, detaching the whole window from the frame. Spinning around, the Raptor ducked forward, trying to shove its large snout into the interior of the car.

Sam was already walking across the street, his automatic raised in both hands as he drifted to the left for a better angle. He took two quick shots. Blood blossomed on the head of the Raptor crouched on the car's hood. As it toppled sideways, it disappeared. The last raptor swung its head around to track Sam with its alligator eyes.

Screeching, it bounded toward Sam, picking up speed at an alarming rate.

Sam took two more shots. The first missed. The second clipped the outside of its left foreleg. Neither slowed it down.

Dean had his own automatic out, but Sam blocked a clear shot.

"Sam! Down!"

Sam dropped, just as the Raptor leapt, covering the remaining distance between them. As Dean sighted along the barrel and applied pressure on the trigger, the creature was gone.

Sam climbed to his feet, brushed himself off and gave Dean a look.

Dean shrugged, holstered his gun. "I had the shot."

"Look on the bright side," Sam said. "You saved a bullet."

The Civic's driver tried his door, found it jammed, so proceeded to climb out through the windshield frame. Sam helped him down.

"You okay, man?"

"Yes, I'm fine. I mean, considering what the hell just happened," the driver said, his voice shaky. "You guys cops?

"FBI."

"My name is Paul Hanes. Swear I wasn't drinking," the man said. "Although I could use a drink right now. It's just—those things came after me and—what were they?"

"Velociraptors."

"Dinosaurs? But they're extinct…"

"Maybe," Dean said. "Starting to have my doubts."

"Any idea where they came from?" Sam asked.

"No. I mean, I had a fight with my girlfriend—Cathryn Rowsell at 142 Allen Drive if you need to verify this—and I noticed something coming out of the shadows when I unlocked the car door. I thought mugger, or carjacker, you know? Jumped in the car, locked the doors, and drove away fast as I could." He spoke rapidly, propelled by nervous energy he couldn't contain. "When I glanced in the rearview, I saw them—those four… lizards racing after me. I was so startled, I actually slowed down. One of them caught up to me and jumped on the trunk of the car. That was enough for me. I floored it and that one fell off. I didn't slow down until I, well, until I crashed into the pickup."

"Notice anything unusual before you got in your car?"

Hanes pursed his lips. "May have heard rustling in the bushes before I saw the shadows against the wall. But not on—fog. There was mist or fog along the grass and walkway on my way out. Didn't remember seeing it when I got to her place after work."

"Thanks," Sam said.

The wind gusted again. Lightning arced across the sky, like a pulsing vein in the darkness, followed by a rolling crash of thunder. For a moment the streetlights went dark as far as they could see. Then they flickered fitfully back on.

"Oh, man…" Hanes said, staring at his car and the Dodge pickup. "How do I explain this to my insurance company?"

"Worry about that tomorrow," Sam said. "Find shelter before they come back."

"Jeez!" said the guy. "You think?"

Dean steered the Impala into the professional building complex. Once he neared the entrance, he had only to follow the flashing red and blue lights. A patrol car, an ambulance, and a wrecker were parked in a rough half-circle around the crime scene—although an attack by a giant tarantula could hardly be called a crime. Make that an incident scene.

A pair of confused EMTs—a woman and a man— stood on either side of Officer Jeffries, as if awaiting instructions. Two men stood near the wrecker, their fidgety body language betraying impatience or discomfort with the situation. The taller of the two wore a baseball cap with an embroidered company logo over an apparently bald head; the other man had a shaggy mane of greasy hair.

"Trying to find a pattern here," Sam said pensively. He seemed preoccupied with the Velociraptors' attack rather than focusing on their present situation.

"Besides the white mist?" Dean asked. "And the nighttime? And giant lizards in general?"

"A tarantula isn't a lizard," Sam said, glancing up at Jeffries and the paramedics. "And the Velociraptors were big, but not gigantic."

"Count your blessings."

Dean swung around the emergency vehicles, and parked the Impala in the island of light under a lamppost. Finally, he saw what the paramedics and Jeffries had obstructed from view when he pulled into the lot.

"You see that?" he asked Sam.

"Human remains."

"It's… sticking out of the ground."

Jeffries walked toward the Impala as they climbed out.

"Hey, guys," he said. "Hope you got strong stomachs."

He waved them toward the victim.

"What have we got?" Sam asked Jeffries.

"Victim was an adult male," Jeffries said. He grabbed an evidence bag from the hood of his patrol car. "Harvey Dufford, according to the metal plate on what's left of this emergency alert wristband we found beside the body, which no longer has any wrists to speak of."

The upper torso—what remained of it, at least—looked as if it had been doused with highly corrosive acid. The head was little more than a crushed skull with a few strips of inflamed flesh around the neck. Most of the flesh on the arms and torso was gone, the internal organs missing or partially dissolved into a loose jellylike substance. With no ligaments to connect them, some of the bones had fallen in a loose circle around the torso. The man's body seemed to end at his waist, but closer inspection revealed flesh and organs embedded in the asphalt of the parking lot.

"Where's the giant tarantula?" Dean asked.

"Vanished."

"Was my first guess. And we know it was a giant tarantula because…?"

"Marcus Epps, owner of the wrecker over there, brought his brother-in-law, Otis, here to retrieve his pickup truck, which is a few lots down from here. Soon as they turned into this lot, they saw the giant spider hunched over the victim. I told them to stick around. Figured you'd want a word."

"Appreciate the cooperation, Jeffries… Hold on," Dean said. He stepped back, crouched down and ran his hand along the surrounding blacktop. He felt ripples in the surface leading away from the remnants of the corpse. Even further away he found misshapen lumps merged with the asphalt. After a few moments, he identified the objects. "Running shoes."

"You're right," Sam said. He walked from the embedded shoes toward the corpse. "From the ID and what's left of his clothes, looks like he was jogging. Sees the giant tarantula, starts to run away, but then… sinks into the ground."

"What? Giant tarantulas can melt asphalt?" Dean stared up at Sam. They knew weird, the brothers lived and breathed weird but this case was getting way beyond weird.

"Maybe Marcus and his brother-in-law know how this happened," Sam suggested.

They walked over to the wrecker and the two men waiting there. The bald man's cap advertised "Epps Service Center" in red script letters on a white field. That settled which one was Marcus.

Dean flashed his FBI laminate.

"Agent DeYoung. This is Agent Shaw. You saw a giant spider?"

Otis responded. "It was a red-kneed tarantula."

"That sounds specific," Sam said.

"Growing up, buddy of mine had one," Otis said. "Fed it live crickets from the pet store. Let me watch."

"And, as far as red-kneed tarantulas go, this one was big?"

"Hell, yeah!" Marcus said. "Thought it was a bear at first. Hunched over. My headlights swept over it, and I saw those red-striped legs."

"Damn near had a heart attack," Otis continued. "Doc keeps telling me my cholesterol is too high."

"What happened?" Sam asked. "Exactly."

"I could tell it was feeding," Otis said. "Saw enough crickets eaten by my buddy's tarantula. This thing had something wrapped up in its feelers while it went to work on it. Couldn't tell what it was at first. You know, spiders can't eat solid food. They digest it outside of their body then suck up the fluids."

"Helluva way to check out," Marcus said, shuddering.

"What happened next?" Dean asked.

"Not much," Marcus said. "Couple seconds after my headlights hit it, damn thing vanished. Poof! Like a magician's trick. Thought maybe I'd imagined the whole damn thing. But, obviously, Otis saw it too."

"After it disappeared," Otis said. "That's when I saw what it had been eating."

"Don't know what to make of it," Marcus said. "Thought it ate the lower half. Then saw the guy stuck in the ground, like he was… planted there."

Dean thanked them for their help, gave them his business card in case they remembered any other details. The men then piled into the wrecker and drove deeper into the series of linked parking lots to retrieve Otis's pickup.

The Winchesters joined Jeffries and the paramedics near the impacted body.

"Thanks," Dean said. "Got what we need."

"We want to talk to Lucy Quinn," Sam said. "Apparently she witnessed the Lacosta hit and run."

"Spoke to the chief. Said he was on his way there when he spotted you two at that sinkhole," Jeffries said. He removed his cap and ran a hand through his hair, staring down at Dufford's remains. "Nothing in the manuals or academy training about this sort of thing. We're waiting on the county medical examiner, but…"

"We can't move the body without construction equipment," the woman paramedic said. "Jackhammer minimum." She took a deep breath. "Christ!"

The other EMT scratched his jaw. "Maybe we should cover the body."

"Better not," Jeffries said. "Might contaminate evidence. Some of that flesh is liquid." He looked toward Dean and Sam. "A word?"

The three of them took a few paces away from the paramedics. Jeffries turned down the volume on the radio clipped to his belt, reducing the police chatter to white noise.

"Listen," Jeffries said and cleared his throat. "When I heard about Shelly's giant lizard before, well, I assumed he'd had a bit too much joy juice, you know?" He took a deep breath and sighed. When he spoke again, his voice was hushed. "Chief told us you Fibbies—sorry, Feds—think this might be terrorist-related. Some cell testing a kind of hallucinogen weapon, right?"

Sam glanced at Dean before he spoke. "We had some information along those lines."

"Right, so, a hallucinogen makes you see weird stuff. Giant lizard, headless horseman, okay, that fits."

"Giant tarantula," Dean said.

Jeffries snapped his fingers. "Exactly what I thought when this call came in! Another weird one. But—" he looked back at the mostly dissolved body embedded three feet deep in asphalt—"*that* is not you or me *seeing* something. That *is* something."

"And you want to know what that something is," Sam said.

"Exactly."

"We don't know yet," Dean said. More or less the truth.

"There's more here than we thought," Sam added.

"Goes double for me," Jeffries said as he turned to walk back toward the paramedics. "Hell, triple!"

The Winchesters headed back toward the Impala. Behind them, Dean heard Jeffries turn up the volume on his belt radio. A lot of squawking and excited chatter. With the sinkhole and subsequent explosions, the car crash and Velociraptor attack, the brewing lightning storm, and who knew what else, the police were on high alert and apparently unprepared for the chaos befalling their sleepy little town. But two words stood out in the stream of reports and assignments.

Dean stopped, turned toward Jeffries.

"She did not just say Nazi zombies?" he called.

Jeffries looked over at him. "So you heard it too?"

"On Main Street?"

Jeffries threw up his hands in surrender.

"Why the hell not?"

TWELVE

Ignoring posted speed limits, Dean raced the Impala east along Bell Street, reluctantly tapping the brake pedal as he rolled through each red traffic light. No guarantee the Velociraptors hadn't returned to hunt another car and driver. He shook his head in disbelief.

"This is what I meant," Sam said. "This is all wrong."

"You mean the Harvey Dufford smoothie back there? Or the *Dead Snow* sequel on Main Street?"

"Everything."

"I'm not arguing."

"Those Velociraptors don't match current fossil records," Sam said. "Real Velociraptors were smaller."

"So are tarantulas and Gila monsters."

"They had feathers."

"Tarantulas?"

"Velociraptors," Sam said. "More birdlike than reptilian."

Dean nodded. "So we rule out wormholes and time travel."

"Along with the return of the Third Reich."

"You got a theory?"

"These… manifestations are real," Sam said. "But inaccurate."

"I'm listening."

"They're more like perceptions," Sam continued. "Or misconceptions."

"Put it that way," Dean said. "Sounds like a tulpa."

"Dozens of tulpas?" Sam suggested and dismissed the idea with a shake of his head. "No, I don't see how—"

"FBI? You there?" said a familiar voice punctuated by an electronic squawk.

Sam pulled the two-way radio from his pocket. "Shelly?"

"Couple of cars drag-racing west on Welker," Shelly said. "Thought you should know. Least I think they're drag racing."

Sam frowned.

Dean shook his head. "Don't look at me. He's your deputy."

"Thanks, Shelly."

"Actually, they might be driving under the influence, weaving all over the road like that."

Sam leaned forward, intent now. "Where are you?"

"Near the restaurant district, of course!"

"Did I hear screaming in the background?" Dean asked. "Restaurants… He's a block or two from Main."

"Shelly, listen to me," Sam said urgently. "Get away from there."

"Whoa, lady," Shelly said as the sound of a screaming woman passed by his mic. "What the hell are they supposed…"

"Shelly, get out of there!"

"Some kind of invasion. Soldiers. Nazis? They ain't right." Shelly's breathing was ragged; they heard the rustling sounds of him running. "FBI, I'm sorry. I'm sorry! This ain't for me. I quit!"

Sam tried the transmit button several times, rewarded with only silence.

"Don't worry, man," Dean said. "He got away. Probably tossed your radio down a sewer—"

The Impala pulled to the side, buffeted by a savage gust of wind. Lightning flashed repeatedly, revealing a thick mass of thunderheads. Then a jagged lightning bolt struck a corner lot, hammering a cottonwood with an explosive crack. A large branch, split from the trunk, toppled sideways, crashing through the windows of a two-door garage.

A couple blocks farther east, a curtain of heavy rain slashed across the Impala's hood and pounded the windshield. Though Dean turned the wipers to their highest setting, he felt as if he were driving underwater. Smears of lights streaked across the safety glass and the world seemed to melt around them. Poor visibility forced him to decelerate to a crawl. For all he could tell, another sinkhole loomed a hundred feet ahead. Maybe a cliff. At this point, anything was possible.

Dean gripped the wheel and ploughed on.

Just when the downpour eased a little, another lightning bolt struck one block ahead of the Impala and skittered across all four lanes of Bell Street, finally blasting a freestanding mailbox. A shower of sparks erupted from the scorched box, which had been dislodged from its cement mooring. Flames flared through a twisted gap in the side of the box as letters and packages burned until doused by the unrelenting rain.

Dean loosened his white-knuckled hold on the steering wheel.

"That was close," he said. The close encounters seemed to be stacking up.

Ahead, on their right, a searing white flash preceded a fiery explosion.

"Transformer hit," Sam said.

Dean tried to blink away the afterimage of the lightning bolt from his retinas. The damaged wooden utility pole teetered toward the road. Engulfed in flame, the pole-mounted transformer at the top showered sparks like the world's largest welder's torch.

"Dean, it's coming down!"

Burning at the top, severed near the base, the utility pole swung down toward the street, trailing snapped live wires. Dean floored the accelerator and swung the Impala into the oncoming lanes, which were, fortunately, empty. Glancing in the rearview mirror, he saw the pole come to rest in the middle of the road, still burning and spitting sparks in every direction.

"That was closer," Sam said.

"This storm have a personal grudge?"

They passed a street sign for Arcadia Boulevard on the right, one block before Main Street. Dean looked ahead into the rainy night, made more difficult by a dead row of streetlights. Sam turned in his seat, looking back down Arcadia.

"Hold up," Sam said. "They've reached the row of restaurants back there."

"You saw them? Actual Nazi zombies?"

Sam nodded. "At least a half-dozen hungry zombies looking to dine on the diners."

The repeated booms and ongoing rumble of the thunderstorm woke Roman Messerly. He experienced a few moments of disorientation as he took in his surroundings. His head rested on the pillow, but his bedcovers were relatively undisturbed. And he still wore his EMT uniform. Last thing he remembered was going off duty, driving home. After that, his memory was a blur.

Pressing his forearm across his forehead, he closed his eyes.

Not quite a blur. He remembered exhaustion sweeping over him as he entered his townhome. He'd skipped preparing a small meal for himself, instead heading for the bedroom. For some reason, he thought he'd take a nap and then eat something... before going to sleep? Made no sense to him. Usually he had trouble sleeping, which he attributed to drinking coffee nonstop during his waking hours. Occupational hazard. His job entailed long periods of boredom punctuated by short periods of action, the aftermath of mayhem visited upon others. His actions could mean life or death for somebody, so he tried to remain alert at all times. Accidents were caused by carelessness, and he could not afford a moment of distraction.

Some nights he tossed and turned for hours—probably sweating out the last dregs of caffeine—before he fell asleep. And he was not a heavy sleeper. He kept his pager and cell phone close to the bed. Never knew when they might need him. Sometimes he dreamed the pager was buzzing. He'd wake up and grab it only to find it quiet and still in his hands. Rare was the night he slept more than three hours in a row or five hours total.

Lethargic, he forced himself to climb out of bed and walk to the window. To the west, he saw the lights of downtown. And stretches of darkness marking a power outage. Flashes of lightning opened the black sky, revealing masses of angry clouds. As he stood there, he thought about how comfortable the bed had been. It pulled him like a gravity well. At that moment, he wanted nothing more than to sleep for ten hours straight. He had almost convinced himself to give in to the unnatural exhaustion when he saw the lightning strike and heard the boom. From experience, he thought a pole-mounted transformer had been hit. Above the trees, a flare of fire illuminated the night. Looked to him like Bell Street.

Hurrying to his bed, he reached for his pager and cell phone and experienced a moment of dizziness. Again the urge to climb into bed and sleep it off hit him. He teetered on the moment of indecision, weighing duty against personal weakness. Lightning flashes bathed his bedroom in stark, shifting shadows. For a moment, the shadows over his bed seemed to slide and race across the wall, as if with a mind of their own. Then the room plunged into darkness and he attributed the strange motion to tricks of the weird lighting.

His pager vibrated, shimmying across the tabletop.

When he checked the display, he saw he had five queued messages.

Strange that he hadn't heard it once.

The cell phone display lit up. A quick check revealed he had received several calls and a half-dozen text messages. As he walked out of his bedroom, he shook his head in disbelief. Nothing like this had ever happened to him before.

Must have slept like the dead to miss all those alerts, he thought.

Unfortunately, it hadn't helped. He was exhausted.

"Hold on."

Dean checked the oncoming lanes and his side view mirror before spinning the steering wheel hard left, while accelerating, making a sweeping three-sixty turn to loop back to Arcadia Boulevard and dart down the wide street until he had a visual on the World War II-era zombies. He parked in a loading zone in front of Mama Ferracci, an Italian restaurant.

While Dean parked illegally, Sam released the partially spent magazine from his automatic and replaced it with a full one.

The rain had eased to a light shower.

Arcadia Boulevard sought a measure of old-world appeal with a row of ornamental horse-head hitching posts that alternated with faux-gas street lamps along the length of the sidewalk. Each storefront and restaurant had a different colored vinyl awning, and some businesses announced daily specials or sales on chalkboard sidewalk signs. Unfortunately, the proliferation of LCD parking meters conspired to spoil the turn of the twentieth-century illusion. Then again, add a dozen shambling Nazi zombies to any setting and you have more than enough anachronistic confusion.

As they exited the Impala, Dean looked over the roof of the car at Sam.

"What do you think? Silver stake through the heart?"

"No," Sam said. "Perception is reality."

"Ah," Dean said. "Romero school. Headshots."

Dean took a quick count of the zombies. No less than nine soldiers in green helmets and uniforms with black jackboots. An SS officer stood out in the black uniform, peaked cap with the SS eagle and a red armband with the black-and-white swastika prominent. A graying field marshal also wore a peaked cap but with a full-length leather trench coat, while a younger officer wore a white summer tunic, stained with blood, due in large part to a gaping abdominal wound exposing a loop of intestines. All of them had blood caked around their mouths and on their hands. Impossible to know if they had appeared bloodied out of thin air, or if they had already begun snacking on the citizens of Clayton Falls.

Red and blue light pulsed from the light bars of two police cruisers parked at hurried angles farther down the street. Both cops—a burly man with dark hair and a pale face, and a trim blond woman in her mid-twenties—were slowly approaching the zombies with their guns drawn and braced with both hands, held down at a forty-five degree angle. Thankfully, the immediate area was clear of civilians. But Dean spotted frightened faces behind the glass doors and windows of several restaurants.

"Freeze!" the male cop yelled at the nearest undead soldier.

Ignoring his command, the soldier rammed his helmeted head into the glass door of a coffee shop decorated with a blue-and-white striped awning. The glass shattered and Dean heard startled screams coming from inside the building.

The cop fired a round into the back of the soldier, who immediately turned around and staggered toward him. One of the soldier's eyes looked as if it had been clawed from the socket. As he lumbered toward the cop, the other police officer fired, hitting the zombie in the side, to little effect.

"Headshots!" Dean yelled.

Both cops immediately swiveled, turning their raised guns toward the Winchester brothers.

THIRTEEN

"FBI!" Sam shouted, producing his laminate in one smooth motion while keeping his gun hand down at his side. "Agents Shaw and DeYoung."

"Right," the female officer said. She glanced at her fellow cop. "It's okay, Cerasi. Chief mentioned them."

"Affirmative," Cerasi said, taking two steps back from the advancing zombie soldier. "You two know about this?"

"Headshots," Dean said again. "Nothing else will stop them."

"You're serious?"

"And don't let them bite you," Sam warned.

Dean turned to him, eyebrow raised. "You think?"

Sam nodded. "Perception is reality."

During the back-and-forth conversation between the living, the young Nazi officer in the blood-stained white summer tunic with exposed intestines had worked his way behind the female cop. About two strides away from her, he stared hungrily at her exposed neck.

"Wild! Check your six!" Cerasi said.

Dean had closed the distance to the cops and had a bead on Summertime Nazi. He squeezed off a shot and watched as the zombie took the round through his right temple, his head whipping to the side. As he dropped to his knees and pitched forward, Officer Wild jumped back.

Beside Dean, Sam fired two rounds in quick succession. Two zombie soldiers teetered and fell—one with a neat hole in his forehead just above the bridge of his nose, the other losing rotted bits of brain matter after the back of his skull was blown away, along with the shattered remains of his helmet.

Cerasi sighted along his automatic and fired a shot at the first soldier, almost point blank. The zombie's nose seemed to vaporize and the back of his neck exploded. As the zombie swayed on unreliable legs, Cerasi raised his foot and kicked him in the abdomen, knocking him to the ground, his helmet rattling around on the ground behind him. The zombie's head twitched back and forth for a few seconds, until Cerasi stepped forward and put a bullet through his forehead.

The gray-haired Nazi field marshal in the full-length leather trench coat targeted Wild. With his mouth gaping and his chin resting on his chest, his red-rimmed eyes stayed as fixated on her as his outstretched arms and twitching fingers.

She took a step back, almost tripping over the dead zombie in the white tunic, then sidestepped and raised her firearm. "Stop!"

"Too damn civilized," Dean scoffed. He raised his automatic.

Wild let the zombie take one more step before she pulled the trigger. Twice. One shot burst through the field marshal's left eye, the other blew off his peaked cap and the top of his skull. His legs crumpled and he fell to the side.

The rest of the zombies shambled around the broken window of the coffee shop, trying to gain entrance. Somebody inside was shoving them back with a coat rack, but there were too many zombies to keep at bay. The soldier bearing the brunt of the coat hooks wrapped his arm around it and staggered sideways, dislodging the pole from the coffee shop patron's hands.

The cops and the Winchesters rushed forward. Coming from the side, Sam had the best angle. If the cops fired at the zombies and missed, their rounds could maim or kill somebody inside the coffee shop. Dean's line of sight was obstructed by Sam, so he stood ready, guarding Sam's back.

Gun down at his side, Dean waited as Sam methodically delivered headshots to the soldiers, above the nose if they faced him, at the base of the neck if their backs were turned, behind the eyes if they stood in profile. If they twitched at all after falling to the ground, Cerasi or Wild came forward to deliver a *coup de grâce*.

While Dean had Sam's back, he forgot nobody had his.

If not for a wet grunt too close to his ear, he might not have reacted in time.

He whirled around, leaning back to avoid a pale, bloody hand missing half its fingernails. The black-uniformed SS officer had emerged from behind one of the rain-streaked sidewalk signs. The zombie's mouth was stretched impossibly wide, strands of bloody flesh lodged between chipped teeth, as it leaned forward to take a chunk out of Dean's neck.

Before it winked out, the bedside lamp failed to dispel the coalescing oily shadows above Trevor Deetz's sleeping body. A humanoid shape resolved from the roiling darkness. First the head with glowing red eyes appeared, followed by a torso and arms before the emergence of spindly legs and nascent clawed feet, gripping the headboard.

Unaware of the intruder in his bedroom, Trevor mumbled in his sleep, his brow damp with perspiration while his clammy left hand rested on the graphic novel he'd been reading before slipping into unconsciousness.

The dark shape above the bed reached out a shadow arm and placed its unnaturally long fingers on Trevor's forehead. The face sculpted from the darkness sighed in pleasure as its fingers began to ease downward through the membrane of flesh and the armor of bone.

Trevor's mumbling became agitated, the volume of his voice increasing. Beneath his eyelids, his eyes twitched furiously in accelerated REM sleep, while the muscles in his arms and legs shuddered as if experiencing repeated electrical shocks.

The graphic novel slipped from beneath his hand, exposing a lurid cover. In the foreground, a fleeing woman screamed. Behind her, a zombie in a black Nazi SS uniform with a bloodstained face had torn out the throat of a man in a business suit. The title of the book was splashed across the cover in oozing red letters: *Hitler's Zombie Force.*

Trevor's left arm rose from the blankets in a quick backhand motion, catching the edge of the graphic novel, which fell to the hardwood floor with a thud. At the sudden impact, Trevor became still. His eyes fluttered open and he stared at the ceiling. Noticing a slice of unusual darkness in his field of vision, he reached up and rubbed his eyes, then wiped away the film of perspiration on his brow.

While he was distracted, the solid darkness expanded, becoming vaporous, and retracted to the wall above his bed. When Trevor next opened his eyes, everything had returned to normal. Taking a deep breath, he sat up, looked around his room and swept his hands across the blankets, searching.

His bedside light flickered on, momentarily blinding him. That's when he remembered. He'd been reading the graphic novel that included the first twelve issues of *Hitler's Zombie Force* when he fell asleep. Couldn't beat zombies for über gore factor. He thought it was awesome. Supposedly they were turning it into a movie, but his mom would never let him see it. She monitored his movie consumption like a hawk, but never looked twice at the stack of comics he brought home from Greg's Comic Vault each Wednesday.

Even though his comic books flew under her maternal radar, Trevor wasn't stupid enough to test her inattention. Anything with a gory cover he kept in his bedroom and read there. The best comics he read at night, right before going to sleep. Never when he should be studying, because she might choose the exact wrong time to check on him.

For a fleeting moment, he wondered if his mom had come into his room after he nodded off and confiscated the zombie book. That could explain the eerie sensation he'd had when he first woke up—the feeling that he wasn't alone. He glanced at the door to check that it remained closed.

Shaking off the sense of being watched, he leaned over the right side of the bed and checked the floor. Nothing. Then he scanned the left side and saw the graphic novel on the ground, exactly where he must have dropped it. Mystery solved. Scooping it up, he stared at the cover for a few moments, deciding if he wanted to continue reading.

A powerful yawn interrupted his internal debate, so he had his answer. Setting the book down on the bedside table, he reached up and switched off the lamp. But he could hardly wait for tomorrow. The story had been getting good. Really bloody.

Dean fired a wild shot into the zombie SS officer's chest in an attempt to gain some separation. If Sam was correct about perception being reality with these manifestations, Dean's odds of survival were nonexistent if he suffered so much as a single skin-breaking nibble from the undead Nazi storm trooper. Backing up, Dean found himself pushed up against the glass storefront.

The zombie leaned forward, its ashen face contorted in equal parts rage and hunger, arms outstretched, fingers twitching in anticipation. Pink drool slipped from the side of its mouth.

Dropping to his knees, Dean raised his automatic in both

hands and fired straight up along the line of the zombie's torso. The round caught it under the chin, piercing the soft palate and the roof of the mouth to burrow into its brain. The Nazi's head whipped backward, his black peaked cap sailing to the sidewalk. Dean fired a second round for good measure and turned his head aside as the Nazi's face erupted in a misty pink shower of gore.

How dumb am I? Dean wondered. Avoid the lethal bite by creating an infectious mist he couldn't help but inhale. *Genius.*

But his concern proved unwarranted. A moment after the second bullet struck home, the SS officer, along with all remnants of his presence, either solid or aerosolized, winked out of existence.

"They're gone," Officer Wild said, marveling. "How the hell do they just disappear?"

"Same way they appeared," Sam said.

"And how's that?" Cerasi asked.

"Hell if I know."

"But we're working on it," Dean added as he climbed to his feet, figuring it was his turn to trot out the company line.

For the first time, he noticed how all the stores and restaurants along the street displayed large black ribbons, wreaths with black bows, or photos of victims of the garment factory fire. Every time these people went out to shop or eat, they saw reminders of the tragedy. Not for the first time, Dean wondered if there was a connection between the tragic fire and the weird manifestations occurring all over Clayton Falls.

"Not a single body," Wild said, scanning the sidewalk,

which moments before had zombie corpses piled like cordwood. "Suppose that means less paperwork."

With the undead threat gone, people were streaming out of nearby restaurants and stores, looking around in shock and disbelief. More than a few probably decided they had imagined the whole episode. Some probably vowed to give up their drink or controlled substance of choice. The rest, no doubt, just wanted to hop in their cars and rush home.

As the coffee shop door swung open and several patrons pushed their way out, Dean held out his hands.

"Wait!" he said. "Stop them."

Since he held a handgun in one of his outstretched hands, everyone paused mid-flight.

"What?" Cerasi asked, confused.

Sam caught Dean's eyes and nodded. "He's right. We need to check them."

"For what?" Wild asked.

"Bites," Dean said.

"You can't be serious," Cerasi said. "These people just survived…"

"What?" Dean said. "You want to say it? Or should I?"

"Zombies?" Wild said as if speaking the word incurred a hefty fine. "But they're gone."

"Now," Sam said. "Two minutes ago, they were here."

Dean realized the two cops were discounting what they had witnessed, what they had participated in. They had both put down Nazi zombies a few minutes ago and were acting as if none of it mattered because the evidence had vanished.

"He's bleeding," a middle-aged woman said shrilly. "He

was fighting them with that hat rack and now he's bleeding!"

Everyone in the crowd backed away from the man she indicated.

Dean glanced down and saw blood dripping from the man's closed fist.

"Show us," Sam said grimly.

"It's nothing," the man said nervously. He had thinning hair, wore a black turtleneck under a brown suit jacket with faded jeans. Looked like a harmless college professor. No matter how innocuous he looked now, if he'd been infected, he was a danger to anyone within biting distance. "I—I cut my hand on the glass."

"Then you won't mind if we take a look."

The man hesitated.

In unison, Dean and Sam raised their handguns. At this range, between the two of them, they were guaranteed of at least one headshot.

"Wait!" Wild said. "This is crazy."

"Crazy night," Dean said.

Cerasi raised his hands. "He's not—he's not like those other things."

"Not yet," Sam said.

"You can't just shoot him!" Wild said.

"Second he goes zombie-eyed," Dean said coldly. "Watch me."

"Okay. Okay," the man said. He raised his right arm, showing them his hand, wrapped in a bloodstained white handkerchief. Slowly, he removed the cloth and exposed the wound.

Dean glanced down at the man's palm. A nasty cut crossing

from the middle of the palm to the skin above the thumb. As
the man patted the welling blood, the smooth edges of the
wound were apparent.

Dean lowered his gun. "You should have that looked at."

"Thanks," the man said and rewrapped his hand.

Everyone in the crowd visibly relaxed.

"Show of hands," Sam said.

One by one, the patrons raised their hands for inspection.
Dean made a quick visual check of all exposed skin, including
necks, arms and legs, buoyed by the fact that none of the
zombies had entered the shop. Only the people who'd stood
closest to the windows had been at risk. In the end, they
were told to go home, leaving the Winchesters with the two
bemused cops.

"You really thought somebody could have been...
infected?" Wild asked.

"Can't be too careful," Dean said.

"We don't know what we're dealing with yet," Sam added
in a more reasonable tone. "We have to view these... attacks
as potentially lethal. In any number of ways."

"The report we heard placed the zombies on Main Street,"
Dean said. "Anybody check there?"

"We followed them here," Cerasi said. "The municipal
building area is usually quiet this late at night. Though now
and then you'll find mourners leaving flowers, cards, or
stuffed animals at the memorial."

"Most pedestrian traffic ends up here later in the evening,"
Wild said. "Around the restaurants and the shops with late
hours."

"How can we be sure we got them all?" Cerasi asked.

"Any others probably disappeared with the main group," Sam said. "But De—Agent DeYoung and I will drive by before we leave to interview some other witnesses."

"Not necessary," Wild said. "That's our job. Right, Cerasi?"

Cerasi nodded.

Dean exchanged a look with Sam and saw they were in silent agreement. Now that Sam had his soul restored, they were in tune with each other again. Dean no longer had to guess at Sam's motives and ruthless—bordering on sociopathic—approach to hunting. They would continue to check the site of any manifestation even if the Clayton Falls PD thought they had everything under control.

With a quick peck on the cheek, Phil Meyerson's wife had left him sitting in his usual spot at the end of the sofa, under the light from the table lamp as he worked to finish the daily *New York Times* crossword. The puzzle was his last mental exercise of the day, something he hoped would keep his aging mind healthy. "Use it or lose it," as he often told his wife. And the last thing he wanted to lose was his mind.

Tuned to a national all-news channel, the television was muted while he worked on the puzzle. Now and then he would glance up and read the news crawl to make sure he wasn't missing anything important.

The later the hour, the more often he checked the television screen. No escaping the fact that he was old and getting older. And as much as he tried to keep his mind nimble, his body failed him more often lately and he succumbed to simple physical fatigue. He would nod off with the crossword half-finished and if he awoke before morning, he'd stubbornly pick up where he left off, plugging away. That pattern had become so familiar, his wife's calm acceptance of it came as a surprise. Soon he would have to change his habit. Tackle the puzzle earlier in the day. Or give it up altogether.

Retirement had been difficult for him to accept. In all his years at the CDC, he depended daily on his mental faculties. Puttering around the house and garden seemed like a waste of any talents and skills he had ever possessed. Where were the challenges? Where were the goals?

He'd thought about teaching at a university, if one would have him. But he hadn't kept up with the journals and research and the cutting-edge science. His eyes lacked the stamina for all the reading and he seemed to need stronger eyeglass prescriptions every six months. Lines of text would blur and his eyes would tear with the effort.

Staring at the crossword clues and the tiny boxes for an hour or more started his eyes burning. He rubbed them for the twentieth time, glanced at the news crawl text he'd read six times already, or was it seven. Political posturing, fluctuating stock prices, banking regulations, civil unrest in the Middle East… Everything seemed to merge into a monotonous string of the same old news recycled again. No exotic diseases or viral outbreaks or global influenza pandemics. Nothing to remind him of the past, when he had a purpose…

He tilted his head back against the sofa cushions and closed his eyes. For a few moments, his burning eyes experienced exquisite relief. The cooling sensation was so welcome, he decided to leave his eyes closed for a few minutes more, then he would continue…

Darkness descended from the ceiling, creeping along the wall to hover near Meyerson's head. Where the lamplight fell against the thickening shadows, it was absorbed, unable to penetrate the darkness taking shape. Unable to break apart the arm or long fingers that reached for Phil Meyerson's forehead.

Meyerson slept and the darkness began to feed.

As Dean drove slowly down Main Street, Sam pointed to the lone mourner standing near the curved wall of the garment factory memorial, head bowed.

"Should we ask if he's seen any zombies?"

"If he saw zombies," Dean said, "he'd be long gone."

"Slow down," Sam said.

"What is it?" Dean asked, but then noticed it himself.

The man was trembling, twitching where he stood. Possibly overcome with emotion, remembering a lost loved one. But Dean's gut told him something else was at work. He eased the Impala to the curb and switched off the engine.

"Could be he's infected," Dean said. "If he is…"

"Perception is reality," Sam said, nodding. "Worst case scenario. He's a goner."

"We do this," Dean said. "Kill a civilian. We've turned a corner."

"I know," Sam said grimly and stepped out of the car, gun in hand.

Soulless Sam wouldn't have a problem pulling the trigger.

Hell, he'd shoot first and ask questions later, Dean thought. This one might be on Dean. He'd have to be prepared.

Dean followed Sam, gun drawn, and together they approached the man.

"FBI," Dean said. "We'd like a word."

"Help me," the man whispered harshly.

"Excuse me?" Sam said. "Mister, are you okay?"

The man turned toward them with pained precision, as if coordinating his muscles for that simple task required extreme effort. His head rose from his chest and he stared at them with bloodshot eyes, which seemed to lack a pupil. Blood trickled from his ears, nose and mouth. An inflamed red rash covered every square inch of his exposed skin, as if all the blood in his body wanted to vacate the premises as soon as possible.

The Winchesters stopped in their tracks, stared.

The man raised a hand toward them and his fingers dripped blood.

In a voice harsh with pain, he gasped, "Help me!"

When he blinked, tears of blood streamed down his cheeks.

"Buddy, what happened to you?" Sam asked, keeping his distance.

"I need help!"

The man staggered toward them.

Sam and Dean raised their guns.

"That's far enough," Dean said.

The man stopped walking toward them, but he continued to twitch.

"He's not a zombie, Dean."

"Looks like a friggin' blood grenade."

From the opposite direction, a police cruiser approached. The light bar came on, but not the sirens. The cruiser swung across two lanes of traffic and parked on the shoulder on the opposite side of the memorial.

"It's Officer Blondie," Dean said.

"Wild," Sam said. As she approached, Sam called. "We meet again!"

"And you two with your guns on a civilian," Wild said.

"Is he?" Dean called. "One of yours?"

"Of course, he…" She stopped talking as she walked toward the man in a wide arc with her hand on the butt of her holstered sidearm. "Sir? What's your name?"

He looked at her and coughed when he tried to speak. Blood sprayed from his mouth in a fine mist. Wild backed away instinctively.

"What is this?" she asked.

"He's infected," Sam cautioned. "Something nasty. Ebola. Hemorrhagic fever. Marburg virus."

"You have to help ME!" the man cried, hysterical.

Turning back to Sam, the man lumbered toward him, arms outstretched.

FOURTEEN

Blood coursed down the infected man's face, spilling from his ears, eyes, nose, and mouth. When he was within ten feet of Sam, his body became wracked with a coughing spasm and blood sprayed from his mouth. Stiff-legged, he continued to stumble toward the brothers.

"Stop!" Sam warned him, his jaw bunching as he tightened his grip on the trigger.

"Hell with that," Dean said and fired.

The bullet struck the man above the left eye, whipping his head back. His body collapsed in a tangle of legs—and winked out of existence before reaching the pavement. All the spilled blood vanished as well.

Sam turned to Dean. "How did you know he wasn't real?"

"I didn't," Dean said. "Your rules. Perception and reality."

Wild joined them. "That could have been one of my people!"

"Either way," Sam said with a nod to Dean. "He was infected and lethal. Ninety percent mortality rate."

"Ten percent chance he could have lived," Wild countered.

"You willing to turn your town into a hot zone?" Dean asked.

"Not my call."

"Whatever this is," Sam interrupted before the argument could escalate. "Whatever creates these manifestations, I doubt it plays the percentages. You get infected, you die."

"So what are we supposed to do?"

"Shoot on sight," Dean said. "Lethal force."

As he slept at the end of the sofa, mired in a troubling dream, Phil Meyerson's hand slipped and he jabbed his thigh with his mechanical pencil. The sudden movement, more than the injury to his leg, woke him from what had started out as a break to rest his burning eyes and had turned into sound sleep. His eyes opened to darkness and he experienced a moment of disorientation. A few seconds later, the lamp flickered and winked on, followed by the television set. He assumed the house had experienced a short power loss while he'd been asleep.

Glancing down at the half-finished *New York Times* crossword, he sighed in self-disgust and slapped it down on the end table and placed the mechanical pencil on top of it.

"Damn old age," he muttered.

He leaned over the coffee table and pressed the remote button to turn off the television set. Then, with another sigh, he pushed himself from the comfortable embrace of the sofa. Six months ago, he would have battled on with the crossword. Hell, one month ago, he'd have been game to keep plugging along. But not now.

"Not tonight," he whispered in quiet surrender.

For some reason, his physical exhaustion would not be denied. Maybe he was coming down with something. A bug incubating, draining his stamina, what little he had at his age. Nothing like the exotic diseases he had studied his whole life. Just some common, garden variety virus staking its claim, challenging his immune system to a duel.

In a way, the conjecture made him feel better. Anybody could become sick, need more rest than usual. Not necessarily a sign of advanced age or deteriorating faculties. If he had to rest, he would. But was it asking too much for some dreamless sleep? As much as he missed his youth, he wouldn't mind a night's sleep without dreaming about deadly viral outbreaks.

Switching off the table lamp, he made his slow way up the stairs, hearing his joints creak and pop like rusty hinges, pressing down on the banister rail with his palm because he needed the support to make the simple trip to his bedroom and his sleeping wife.

In the dark room he left behind, a deeper darkness detached from the wall and drifted across the open space, spilling out through a keyhole and then through a small gap between the edge of the storm door and the doorjamb. Once out in the night, it floated above the rooftops in a familiar direction and paused above another house before drifting down, ready to feed again before the night was over.

* * *

Alden Webb, sitting in bed in his pajamas, yawned as he flipped through assorted internal prison documents. He turned the television to a nighttime talk show host whose monologue patter became like white noise filling the unnatural silence of the house. Thunderstorms had passed and the sirens he'd heard earlier had faded. Car accidents, downed power lines, the usual heartbeat of town emergencies in severe weather, he presumed. Nothing to concern him. But even with all those distracting sounds outside the house, he could never acclimate to the silence inside the house.

Ever since his wife divorced him and moved to San Francisco to work for her niece—who founded a company that helped corporations develop social networking strategies—he swore he could hear the clocks in the house ticking. And the sound was enough to drive him to distraction—or a psych ward. He found himself turning on the stereo or the television as soon as he returned home. Background noise. Because the silence was too loud.

What the talk show host joked about was of little interest to him, but it trumped the hollowness of ticking clocks and humming electronics. Instead, Webb flipped through the file folders filled with routine paperwork and incident reports from his deputy wardens, the food service supervisor, his corrections center manager, the director of security operations, and the building manager. The reports dealt with everything under his purview, including food preparation, counseling, treatment, health care, security issues, purchase orders, human resources matters involving prison employees, and building maintenance. Most of the reports were standard administrative matters. He looked for irregularities in the routine reports. And he paid special attention to matters involving prisoner treatment by the guards and violence or insubordination among the prisoners.

His early conversation with the young FBI agents had not been unexpected. Defending the safety of the prison had become something of a knee-jerk reaction for him. Nevertheless, he took his responsibilities as warden of a federal prison seriously. While he assured the mayor and the citizens of Clayton Falls that Falls Federal presented no threat to their welfare, any prison was a potential powder keg. One large-scale riot and all his careful assurances would be undone.

The addition of the supermax wing had been a sore point for the town, a rallying cry for all the protestors who decried the housing of the "worst of the worst" criminals minutes away from the families and children of Clayton Falls. In reality, the supermax cons were the least of Webb's concerns. They were locked down in solitary cells twenty-three hours a day. And their one free hour out of their cells was spent alone. Not much trouble for them to get into with that one hour of exercise time.

Truth be told, he had a visceral loathing of the supermax felons. In his opinion, they were beyond redemption or rehabilitation. They were marking time, lifers or awaiting lethal injection. Webb had a hard time looking them in the eye, because what he saw there struck him as inhuman. Maybe it was the total lack of compassion or conscience. Something was just... missing. The latest addition had been particularly heinous: Ragnar Bartch, a confessed cannibal with seventeen known victims and whose weapon of choice was a cleaver. Before he arrived, the worst con in supermax was Kurt Machalek, who kept a collection of human hearts in mason jars after cutting them from the chests of his victims with a serrated bowie knife. Profilers called the hearts souvenirs. Machalek called them totems and believed they gave him mystical powers. But Bartch and Machalek and their ilk weren't going anywhere.

All the other prisoners under his watch had much more potential to cause trouble. They had far less direct supervision and oversight. They mingled. They divided themselves along racial lines, us versus them. One spark, one real or imagined slight and they could cause serious injury to their fellow cons and damage to the prison. Yet even the worst-case scenario presented no threat to the town. Even a full-blown riot could be locked down. Yes, there most likely would be casualties in the prison—but the town would remain safe. Guards and prison employees would be the only civilians at risk.

Webb shuddered with a sudden draft in his bedroom. He was not poetic enough to consider the sensation a presentiment of doom. He read nothing in the reports that hinted at anything more than the expected amount of conflict within the walls of his prison. Everything was, well, routine.

Acquiescing to the frequency of his yawns, he filed the reports in their folders and stacked them on the bedside table to take to work in the morning. He picked up the television remote, trying to decide if he should turn the volume up or turn the set off. While he weighed the pros and cons, he fell asleep.

Coils of darkness unspooled from the curtains and settled above his headboard, taking shape to feed...

By the time Dean and Sam arrived at the scene of Tony Lacosta's hit and vanish, the young man's body had been taken away, and the front yard and wrecked porch had been encircled with crime scene tape. His parents stood in the driveway in their night clothes, arms wrapped around each other. While his mother sobbed, his father looked as if he'd been kicked in the gut. They had already told Chief Quinn what they'd witnessed after the initial attack twice and refused to go over it again. The Winchesters eavesdropped on the conversation as a detective that Quinn assigned to the case promised to talk to them in the morning, after they'd had a chance to process what had happened. Dean doubted their "processing" would adhere to a convenient timetable.

At the curb in front of the house, Lucy Quinn argued quietly with her father. The police chief's concern for his daughter was evident in his eyes and body language, but clearly he found her account of the attack unconvincing. In deference to the grieving parents standing less than twenty feet away, Chief Quinn and Lucy spoke in hushed but urgent tones.

"Why would I make this up?" Lucy demanded.

"You wouldn't," Chief Quinn said. "Not intentionally. I'm suggesting you didn't see what you think you saw. A car might roll down a hill unattended, but they simply don't drive themselves."

"This one did," Lucy said. "Saw it with my own eyes."

"Eyewitnesses are notoriously inaccurate," the police chief countered. "Three people witness the same crime. Later, they'll each give completely different descriptions of the perp. And they're all positive about what they saw."

"So, you're saying you don't believe it was Teddy's car?"

"Teddy's car was totaled, Lucy. You know that."

"Then it was an exact copy."

"Now we're getting somewhere. Somebody—a real person, not a ghost or an invisible driver—got hold of a similar car. Maybe even painted on the white stripe."

"What?"

"An old friend, maybe," Chief Quinn suggested. "Out for revenge."

Lucy placed her hands on her hips and stared at him. "You know how crazy that sounds?"

Chief Quinn scoffed in frustration. "Any crazier than a car driving itself around town, running down civilians?"

"You're impossible."

Dean stepped up during the awkward silence.

"Mind telling us what you saw. Or didn't see," he asked Lucy, with a quick glance at her father.

"Why bother?" Chief Quinn said. "There's a simple explanation. A tinted windshield hid the driver from view."

"The windshield was *not* tinted!" Lucy glanced at Tony's parents as she spoke, trying to keep her voice under control.

Chief Quinn threw his hands up in the air.

Lucy turned to Dean. "He's right. What's the point? I already told him what I saw. He refuses to listen."

"We—Agent Shaw and I—might be open to different possibilities."

"What's *that* supposed to mean?" Chief Quinn asked indignantly, as if Dean had called his judgment and entire law enforcement background into question.

"Have you been listening to your police reports, Chief?" Dean asked. "Giant spiders, Nazi zombies in the restaurant district, packs of hunting dinosaurs. You saw the sinkhole deep enough to hold a gymnasium."

Quinn shook his head. "Crazy talk. If I hadn't been tied up here with this terrible accident... Well, let's just say I'm now willing to believe your information about a hallucinogen was credible. Clearly, some people in Clayton Falls have been dosed. It's the only explanation for all the irrational radio chatter. As far as the sinkhole, that's all it was. Bigger than most, I'll grant, but they happen."

"Mind if we have a word with your daughter?" Sam asked in a reasonable tone. Dean always figured Sam had the better chance of making it in the world of politics.

"No, go right ahead," he said. "I love her, but her fantasy story is not helping the situation."

Chief Quinn walked brusquely to his police cruiser, climbed in and slammed the door. He brought the police radio to his mouth and spoke rapidly into it. Dean watched as the chief began to listen to more reports from his officers. Within seconds he was shaking his head in disbelief.

"Lucy, tell us what happened," Sam said gently. "Were you here when the car hit Tony?"

"No," she said. "It started before that. I had already left his house. I was walking home when the car… saw me."

"Saw you?" Sam asked.

The possessed car talk made Dean nervous. He glanced at the Impala parked at the curb, willing it to stay silent and dark. He took a breath and refocused on the conversation.

"That's what it felt like. I believe it was coming for Tony," she said. "But it saw me and decided to take a swipe at me. So, maybe it was thinking, two-for-one, right? First Lucy, then Tony."

"How so?"

"About the same time I saw the car, it drove to my side of the street, jumped the curb and tried to run me down. I froze for a moment. Kept thinking, this can't be happening. But I remembered that it *had* happened, that it got Steve."

"What did you do?"

"I snapped out of it. I was standing next to a white picket fence. Fortunately, it wasn't too high. I dove over it to get out of the way. The car hit the fence, pretty much wrecked the whole thing. I can show you if you don't believe me."

"I believe you."

Lucy smiled in relief.

Probably the first she's heard those words all night, Dean thought.

"So, the car kept driving. Back the way I had come. Toward Tony's house. Since it had already got Steve, and tried for me, I thought maybe it's going after Tony next. When I left his house, he was out on the porch. I wanted to warn him. Thought he'd be safe as long as he didn't come down to the sidewalk or try to cross the street. I had no idea it would drive up on the lawn and… and ram the porch."

Dean scanned the ruined front lawn, scored with deep tire ruts, the sagging midsection of the porch and the overturned Adirondack chairs. It had been easier to imagine the car hitting someone standing in the middle of the road. Aside from the last-second acceleration to hit Steve Bullinger, the hit and run fit the profile of an accident. This attack was... premeditated. The car had known where Tony Lacosta lived, had sought him out and used every means at its vehicular disposal to kill him.

"The car jumped the curb and struck the porch?" Dean asked.

"Yes," she said. "First it turned to face the house. Then it went right over the curb and slammed into the porch. Over and over until the porch collapsed. Tony fell onto the lawn. Once he was at ground level, the car... it crushed him." She pressed her wrist against her mouth and started to cry quietly.

Sam placed his hands gently on her shoulders and looked her in the eyes.

"Lucy, I'm sorry about your friend. I know this is hard."

She nodded quickly and a tear slipped down her cheek.

"Why is this happening?"

At the risk of losing her trust, Dean said, "Lucy, can you think of anyone who might want to hurt you and your friends? Because of Teddy's death?"

"Revenge? Like my father said?"

"I'm not saying what you saw isn't real," Dean said quickly. "But maybe somebody caused it to happen."

"We were Teddy's closest friends," Lucy said, genuinely puzzled. "His only friends in school."

"What about family?" Dean recalled Sam's reading newspaper articles about the accident. "Lived with his grandmother, right?"

Sam nodded. "Olga Kucharski."

Lucy shook her head. "Mrs. Kucharski is an old woman. Other than grocery shopping, she never leaves her house."

"You on good terms with her?"

"Not really," Lucy said. "I mean, she never really approved of us hanging around with her grandson. And she dismissed my relationship with Teddy as a crush. Thought it would pass. But she knew we were his only friends.

"After the accident, I visited her a couple times, but it was just… too much, you know. I couldn't handle her grief and my grief. Because, after Teddy died, I couldn't breathe in that house. Felt like it was crushing me. I'll never forget what happened, but it's… easier without the constant reminders. Last few months, I haven't really seen her. Or made an effort. Guess that makes me a bad person."

"Everybody handles grief in their own way," Sam said.

"I know," she said. "But I still feel guilty."

"You should go home," Sam said pointedly.

"No, I'm okay," Lucy said. She glanced toward the Lacostas, still huddled together in their driveway, whispering to each other. "Maybe I should stay with them…"

"It's not safe here," Dean said. "You're not safe here."

She looked up at Sam and then at Dean. "You think it will come back?"

Sam cleared his throat. "Definite possibility."

"We could drive you home," Dean said.

"Thanks, but—" she glanced over at her father's police cruiser—"I should go with my father."

"You're okay with that?" Sam asked.

"If I'm not safe with the chief of police, I'm not safe with anyone."

Dean frowned but said nothing. He'd feel better about her safety with her dad if the man actually believed in what was trying to kill her and had already killed her friends. The car might be a blind spot for him. Until it was too late.

Taking out one of his FBI business cards, Dean handed it to her.

"That has my cell number. If anything—and I mean *anything*—weird happens, call me."

"Okay, Agent DeYoung."

"No matter how crazy it seems. Call."

"I will," she said. "Thank you. Thank you both."

With a brief smile, she walked to the police cruiser and knocked on the passenger side window. When her father looked up at her, she opened the door. Then she hesitated and glanced back at them with a slight wave goodbye before climbing into the car. Inside, she gave her father a mild shove to disarm his stubborn frown.

Watching father and daughter, Dean cast a sidelong glance at Sam and said, "You thinking what I'm thinking."

"Yeah," Sam said. "She's next."

FIFTEEN

A few blocks east, the Winchesters approached the house with the killer tree.

"Have I told you it's good to have you back," Dean said, smiling. "The real you?"

"What?"

"Sammy with the soul inside," Dean said. "You were good with her back there."

"Lucy?"

"May seem natural to you," Dean said. "And I know you don't remember how it was—how you were, before. But it's night and day, man."

Sam nodded thoughtfully. "You're right. I don't remember being different. Hell, I don't remember being gone. Guess it's like waking from a coma. Everyone else lived through that time and I was... on pause. This part of me, I mean. But, in some ways, feels like I recovered from a serious illness. Feels good to be back."

From where Dean parked the Impala on the shoulder of

Chaney Lane, it looked as if somebody had killed the tree. The large white oak had toppled onto its side right across the street, completely uprooted, and blocking through traffic. A municipal truck with a flashing yellow light idled nearby. The driver had tied a rope around the upper trunk, preparing to tow it out of the way. A few neighbors stood in front of their houses or in doorways, silently watching the workman.

"That tree killed a man? Friggin' *Day of the Triffids*?"

"According to Jeffries," Sam said. "A branch broke through a second-story window and impaled Max Barnes."

"So they put it down?" Dean asked. "Like a rabid dog?"

"That's all I know, dude."

"Storm wasn't that bad," Dean said. "Lightning, maybe?"

"No sign of a lightning strike."

"Maybe the truck driver knows."

Before they reached the man, Dean noticed something odd. The tree had come out of the ground with its roots *intact*. Behind the cluster of roots, clods of dirt and stones trailed back to the side of the house at 109 Chaney Lane. The large hole in the ground where the roots had been reminded Dean of the ever-expanding sinkhole he'd fallen into earlier in the evening. But this hole, for now at least, remained stable. He glanced up the side of the house and saw the shattered second-story window, the edges of the glass streaked with blood.

"That's the boy's room," a middle-aged woman said to him from the neighboring yard, nibbling nervously on her thumbnail. "But it wasn't him."

"Excuse me?" Dean said.

"Are you with the police?"

"FBI," Dean said. "And you are?"

"Barb," she said. "Barb Henn."

"You know what happened here?"

"Max Barnes, the father, was killed. Some kind of freak accident."

"Freak accident?"

"Apparently he was killed by a tree branch going through the son's window. That's what I meant about it being the boy's room but the boy wasn't the one hurt."

"What happened leading up to the... accident?"

"When the storm started, I was watching TV with my daughter Nicole." She pointed back toward her house and Dean saw a teenaged girl standing in the doorway, arms folded, leaning against the doorjamb, which had a black ribbon pinned above the doorbell. When Dean's gaze fell on the girl, she gave him a little wave. Dean smiled with a slight nod of acknowledgment before turning his attention back to the mother.

"Go on."

"The wind was gusting, but I didn't think about it too much," she said. "Other than worrying we might lose power, which we did, briefly. A brownout."

"And the tree?"

"I heard it thrashing about, hitting the siding, but..." She shrugged. "Nothing unusual, considering the wind. Then I heard glass shatter."

"Did you go outside? Look out your window?"

"Not until I heard Melinda—poor Mrs. Barnes—screaming. I thought something had happened to her boy,

Daniel. That's when I looked out the side window. I knew something was off. Then it hit me. Their white oak tree was missing. I could see the entire side of their house." She shook her head in disbelief. "Of course, I went outside then and that's when I saw the tree. In the street."

"Like it is now?"

"No," she said. "It was standing! Upright. Well, at least for a moment. But then it slowly tipped over and crashed to the ground. How is that possible? Sure, a tornado could uproot a tree, but this wasn't a tornado. Other than the window, nothing was damaged—I mean, aside from Max."

"Freak storm cell, maybe."

"Something freaky," she said. "Such a shame. I can certainly sympathize with the family. I lost my husband in the factory fire."

"Sorry for your loss."

"Thank you," she said. "Nicole and I lean on each other a lot since then."

"Earlier tonight, did you happen to see the vic—Max Barnes?"

The woman shook her head. "Paramedics brought him down on a stretcher but his body was completely covered. That's when I knew he was… that poor man."

"The mother and son? Where are they now?"

"They left in one of the police cars," Tom Cuffee, the municipal worker, said to Sam over his shoulder as he walked toward the open door of his truck.

"To give a statement?"

"No," the workman said. "She did that here. She wanted the boy checked out. Mother was kind of hysterical, but the kid was worse, in a way. Robotic."

"Shock."

"Yeah," Cuffee said, shaking his head in sympathy. "Jeez, young kid like that, sees his dad killed right in his own home. Can you imagine?"

"Did you see the father's injury?"

"Not personally," Cuffee said, sitting in the driver's seat with the door ajar. "But I heard the branch went clear through his chest, back to front."

"During the storm?"

"That's what I hear."

"Is that branch still on the tree?"

"Police had it sawed off," Cuffee said. "Evidence. Of what, I don't know."

"Anything like this ever happened here in town before?"

"Are you serious? I doubt anything like this ever happened anywhere."

"Good point," Sam said. "About the tree…"

"Just moving it to the side of the road. Crew will come by in the morning with chainsaws and take care of the disposal."

"Any idea how it got in the middle of the street in the first place?"

Cuffee closed his door, but lowered the window to continue the conversation.

"As if it couldn't get any weirder, right? One of the cops said… No, I shouldn't repeat that stuff. It's in poor taste."

Sam raised an eyebrow. "Trust me, I won't be offended."

The man started the truck, put it in gear and slowly began to drag the tree toward the shoulder of Chaney Lane. Branches bent, twisted and a few cracked as the trunk neared its temporary destination. Sam walked beside the truck, casting nervous glances back at the fallen tree with its thrashing limbs. Such was the life he and Dean had led that he had no trouble accepting the possibility of a murderous tree.

With the tree parallel to the curb, occupying the shoulder of the suburban street, Cuffee shifted the truck into park and climbed out to untie the rope.

"Okay," he said to Sam. "I suppose you being FBI, you understand gallows humor in these types of lousy situations."

Sam nodded.

"One of the cops looks from the side of the house where the tree used to be to the middle of the street where it ended up and says, 'this tree committed murder then tried to flee the scene of the crime.'" Cuffee punctuated the delivery of the line with an embarrassed frown. "What I tell you? Poor taste."

Sam shook his head. "As good an explanation as any."

Dean joined them as the workman took out a utility knife and sliced the rope above the knot around the tree trunk. Then the man walked back to the truck's tow ball hitch and sliced the rope free at that end, coiled it and tossed it in the truck bed.

"What do the cops think really happened?" Dean asked.

"They talked about writing it up as a wind-related accident," Cuffee said. "But honestly? I think we all know that's bull crap."

The man climbed back into the driver's seat of the truck, closed the door and turned off the yellow warning lights that had been flashing since the Winchesters arrived on the scene.

"What's your explanation?" Dean asked.

Cuffee leaned out the window with a conspiratorial look on his face.

"Three words," he said and ticked them off on his fingers. "U-F-O."

"Really?"

"Wouldn't put it past them ETs to have a secret base up there in the Rockies. Their own version of Cheyenne Mountain."

Sam glanced at Dean. "Why would… aliens want a tree?"

"Who knows? Thumbing their noses at us."

"Fight the fairies," Dean said—just loud enough for Cuffee to hear.

"I wouldn't hazard a guess as to their sexual persuasion," he said, shrugging. "But if you got a better explanation, I'd love to hear it."

"Not at the moment, no," Sam said.

"You said FBI, right?" Cuffee said, arching an eyebrow. "You wouldn't happen to be MIB? No, wait. If you tell me, you'll have to wipe my memory. Forget I asked."

As the man drove away, Dean cast an accusatory glance at Sam.

"What?" Sam said. "He seemed rational up until the end."

"Nice boy. Always kept to himself."

"Shut up, Dean."

As they walked back toward the Impala, Sam asked, "Neighbor lady see anything?"

"Saw the tree topple in the middle of the street," Dean said. "Not how it got there. Mother and son taken to the hospital to have the kid checked out."

"Got that from the workman too," Sam said. "Kid had to have seen something."

"We'll catch him in the morning," Dean said. "Hey, you remember all those black ribbons and bows on Arcadia Boulevard?"

"Yeah. Hard to miss."

They climbed into the Impala. Dean hesitated before turning the ignition.

"Neighbor had one on her door. Lost her husband in the fire."

"You're thinking we should check out the garment factory?"

"Worth a look."

Dean started the Impala. Before he pulled away from the curb, Sam's cell phone rang. He glanced at the caller ID and said, "Clayton Falls PD again."

Sam answered.

"Agent Shaw," Officer Richard Jeffries said. "Keeping you and your partner in the loop, like you asked."

"Go ahead."

"Report on the radio of an escaped supermax inmate."

"A jailbreak?" Sam asked, incredulous. Though, at this point, nothing should have surprised him.

"Yep. Most recent addition to the zoo. Serial killer named Ragnar Bartch, better known as Butcher Bartch or the Cleaver Cannibal."

SIXTEEN

"I'm familiar with Bartch," Sam said to Jeffries, because he thought an FBI agent should be aware of "most wanted" criminals even after they were no longer at large. "Anyone heard from the warden? Alden Webb?"

"Chief's trying to reach him as we speak."

"Where was Bartch spotted?"

"303 Perry Lane," Jeffries said. "Off of Welker, near the cluster of hotels and motels. Phoned in by… Jylene Livengood."

"Got it. Thanks," Sam said, ending the call. He gave Dean the details on Bartch and the address of the eyewitness. "Perry Lane's near our motel."

Dean drove north toward Welker Street.

"Wondering if this is the real con or another manifestation."

"Either way, he's dangerous."

"That's what puzzles me about the trees."

"What?"

"This whole perception as reality theory of yours," Dean said. "People don't perceive trees as mobile, let alone murderous?"

"Not usually. No."

"That tree looked like it pulled itself out of the ground and took a stroll."

Dean caught the light at Welker and headed west. With four lanes of traffic instead of two, he pressed down on the accelerator and zipped through town.

"Before it collapsed."

"And it's still there," Dean said. "It's a real tree."

Sam nodded grimly. "Even the things that aren't real," he said. "There seem to be more of them, and they're lasting longer. Dude, whatever's causing this, it's getting stronger."

"And we're no closer to figuring out what it is."

With that sobering thought on their minds, they drove in silence until they reached Perry Lane. Sam spotted one house on the block lit up like a Christmas tree. Every light in every room on both floors was on, along with the lights on either side of the front door. Made it easy to read the address.

"That's it. Three-oh-three."

A police cruiser, light bar flashing, waited at the curb.

As Sam and Dean walked toward the house, a tall African American cop with a touch of gray at his temples and sergeant's stripes on his sleeves exited the house and walked toward his cruiser. Stopping when he spotted them, he hooked his fingers in his belt and said, "You're the gentlemen from the FBI?"

"Yes, we are," Dean said.

"Could I see some ID?"

"Sure," Sam said. After a long night, their FBI suits were looking more than a bit disreputable. Either that or the man was overly cautious.

"Agents Shaw and DeYoung," he said as they showed their laminates.

"Sergeant Cornelius Harrison," the man said, extending his hand to Sam and Dean in turn. "Good to meet you. Ms. Livengood reported a prowler."

Dean looked at Sam, then back at the sergeant.

"We heard she reported Butcher Bartch on the loose."

"She was mistaken about the ID," Harrison said. "Deputy Warden called the station. As of five minutes ago, Bartch was still in his cell."

"What about Webb?"

"No word from the warden," Harrison said. "Chief's sending a car to his home." He jerked a thumb over his shoulder at the house with the red-lined electricity usage. "She may have seen a prowler, but it wasn't Bartch. I had two more units here. Searched the grounds and the house. Nothing. I'm heading back to the station. You're welcome to talk to her. I doubt she'll be sleeping any time soon."

Harrison climbed into his cruiser and pulled away as Sam rapped on the door of the house. A moment later, the door opened a crack, revealing a security chain in place. A pale young woman with long black hair and wide gray eyes stared at them.

"Jylene Livengood?" Sam asked.

"Yes," she said. "And you are?"

"FBI," Sam said.

"FBI. Really? That was fast."

"Already in town," Dean said.

"The police were here and gone," she said. "They found nothing."

"We have a few questions," Sam said. "Won't take long."

"You got ID?"

The brothers took turns holding their FBI credentials up to the gap in the doorway. She nodded, closed the door to remove the chain, then opened it again and waved them in. Locking the deadbolt and chain after they were inside, she turned toward them and clasped her hands together.

Without preamble, she said, "I saw Ragnar Bartch. Standing right in front of my house. And he had a meat cleaver in his hands! But the police don't believe me."

Sam glanced around the living room. Neat with the exception of small stacks of various newspapers, local, regional and national, along with separate piles of weekly news magazines. In stark contrast to the abundance of news, facts and figures in her reading material, her walls were hung with an assortment of what looked like original paintings of fantasy creatures and settings, centaurs striding through forests, mermaids reposing on rock clusters at shorelines, dragons sleeping in gold-strewn caverns.

"How can you be sure it was Bartch?" Sam asked.

"I know his face," she said, nodding quickly, as if it were a nervous tic. "I was among the protesters when they added the supermax wing. I keep track of who they bring into that place. I have their names, their court photos, and a list of their crimes. Well, at least the crimes for which they were convicted. Who knows what other heinous acts they committed? It's enough to keep you up at night."

"You are up late," Dean observed.

"Storms woke me," she said. "Couldn't sleep. Came down to watch a movie on cable. Looked out the window and saw him standing there. Would you like some coffee? I've already had three. It's no problem."

"No thanks," Sam said. "Actually, I could use a cup."

She hurried into the kitchen and, after a minute of clinking ceramic and stainless steel, she returned with a tray holding three cups of coffee, a container filled with packets of sugar and other sweeteners, and a small-handled creamer.

Sam drank his coffee as quickly as its temperature permitted and continued his questioning. "Did you happen to see where this man went?"

"No. I ran to the phone. Called the police. When I looked out the window again, he was gone. I checked all the doors and windows and closets. I know he's out there."

"According to Sergeant Harrison, Bartch is in his cell."

She rubbed her arms, as if for warmth, and nodded. "Yes, he told me. But I know what I saw."

"You live alone?"

"No. Well, yes, right now," she said. "My roommate's a fantasy artist. She's at a convention in Denver. Won't be back until Monday."

That explained the dichotomy between her reading material and the subject matter of the paintings.

"If you like," Sam said, "Agent DeYoung and I could check the exterior of the house again."

"That would be awesome," she said. "Thank you!"

"No problem."

After Dean downed his coffee, the Winchesters stepped outside. Sam waited as she locked and chained the door behind them. Dean walked to the Impala and brought back a pair of flashlights.

"One more cup of coffee and she will literally climb the walls," Dean said as he slapped a flashlight in Sam's palm. "Think he might still be here?"

"She saw a manifestation," Sam said. "It's possible."

They pulled out their handguns.

Sam took the left side of the house while Dean circled around to the right.

The flashlight beam pierced the darkness, startling a cat that meowed indignantly and bolted across the lawn, climbing the nearest fence and disappearing. Toward the back of the house, a back-door light cast a wan glow that failed to extend to a padlocked tool shed at the back of the property. Sam caught movement to his right and swung the flashlight in that direction. Another flashlight answered his, momentarily blinding him.

"Dean."

"Sam."

"So far, all clear."

"Tool shed?"

"Padlocked."

"In back?"

Sam walked along the left side of the galvanized steel tool shed as Dean approached on the right. The flashlight revealed a narrow gap behind the shed. Possibly wide enough to hide a man. And this was the darkest part of the backyard.

Sam stepped away from the side of the shed, approaching the back at a wider angle, when he heard a creak of metal from above. As his gaze darted upward, he held his handgun beside the barrel of the flashlight, aiming them together.

A hulking, man-shaped silhouette rose above the roof of the shed.

A footfall creaked against protesting metal. An instant later, the large man launched himself at Sam. His flashlight beam danced across a gleaming rectangle of metal held in the man's right hand.

Alden Webb fought his way up out of a troubling dream and stared at the ceiling for a moment trying to remember the dream and why it had upset him, before the hard, repeated knocking on his front door registered on his consciousness.

The light from the television flickered across the ceiling of his bedroom, revealing an odd pattern of pulsing shadows that seemed to fade away as he became more alert. Shaking off the lethargy, he climbed out of bed and grabbed a robe from his closet.

"Just a minute," he called out but doubted the visitor could hear him.

A few moments later, he swung open the door to reveal a police officer standing there, fist raised as if he intended to knock again—on Webb's face if necessary.

"Is there a problem Officer—" he read the man's nametag—"Jarrett?"

"Chief Quinn sent me when you didn't answer your phone."

"I didn't hear it ringing," Webb said, surprised he had slept through a ringing phone long enough to prompt a personal visit from one of Quinn's men. "What's wrong?"

"We had a report that a supermax con was loose in town," Jarrett said. "Ragnar Bartch."

"That's impossible," Webb said. "Besides, I would have been notified of any incident…" *What if I missed that call as well?* "I'll call now."

"That's not necessary," Jarrett said. "It was a false alarm. The deputy warden reports Bartch is in his cell. But when you didn't answer your phone, Chief Quinn thought we should check on you."

"Of course. Thank you. But I'm fine. I was sleeping. Deeply, I imagine, to have not heard the phone."

"Have a good night, sir."

After the police officer left, Webb closed and locked his door. "False alarm," he said, shaking his head. "More like a crank call."

After all this time, he thought he'd reached an accommodation with the townspeople. He knew they disliked having the prison nearby, but its record was immaculate and, over time, he had hoped for peaceful coexistence. But that was looking like a pipe dream.

Crank calls, he supposed, would be the order of the day now, another form of passive aggressive protest from all those with the "not in my backyard" attitude.

* * *

Sam fell backward, his finger tightening against the trigger of his gun as the gleaming stainless steel blade of the meat cleaver arced toward his neck. The gun went off and the round ripped into the galvanized metal wall of the tool shed—the manifestation of Butcher Bartch had vanished an instant before the bullet left the muzzle of the gun.

Dean came around the back of the shed, sweeping the area with his gun.

"Sam?" he called. "You all right?"

"Fine," Sam said, rubbing his palm against the side of his neck. "Bartch jumped me and vanished."

"You got a good look at him?"

"Just the cleaver," Sam said as Dean helped him to his feet. "That was plenty."

"You hit him?"

"No." Sam grabbed his flashlight out of the grass. "Vanished in mid air before the bullet could hit him."

"Should we tell the lady of the house?"

"Not unless she heard the shot. Doubt he'll come back tonight."

With dawn approaching, Dean started the Impala, thought about calling it a night and heading back to their motel, which was only a few blocks away, but a missed opportunity had been nagging at him all day. He turned to Sam and said, "You up for one quick run?"

"The garment factory?"

"You got the address?"

"Should be in my browser history," Sam said. He reached

back over his seat and grabbed the laptop case, removed the computer and booted it. "From what I read, there's not much left."

"You said they debated making the factory the site of the memorial?"

"Yes."

"Which means something's there," Dean said. "It's the elephant in the room, so let's not ignore it."

Sam found the address and relayed the directions to Dean.

The Clayton Falls Apparel Company was located on the western edge of town, less than a half-mile from the site of the tarantula attack. But not much remained of the redbrick building. As Dean parked across the street from what had been the entrance to the factory, even with its exterior bathed in the cold glare of streetlights, he had the impression of darkness.

He climbed out of the Impala and stared at the factory, trying to get a sense of the place. Wrought-iron fencing outlined the perimeter of the grounds, but here and there sections had collapsed or were about to fall over. At one spot, it looked as if a bulldozer had rolled over the fencing to create a mound of debris, but the task had been abandoned. There was so much yellow police tape repeating the words DANGER and KEEP OUT zigzagging through the fencing that Dean wondered if the tape was all that held the rest of it upright.

Most of the exterior walls were intact, but crumbling away from the top down, stained black from the fire and smoke. The entire roof was missing, having collapsed into the interior. And a wall on the left side was little more than a mound of damaged bricks.

The building was dead. A bit of urban blight on the landscape. Like the physical representation of a psychic scar on the collective consciousness of Clayton Falls. Something they were unwilling to let go. But was it responsible for the strange phenomena in the town?

Slamming the trunk of the Impala, Sam joined Dean carrying an EMF meter.

"Ready?"

Dean nodded.

As they neared the building, Dean saw the freestanding wooden sign angled toward the path leading to where the front doors of the factory had been. The copper sheeting of the sign had tarnished over time, coated with a green patina, but Dean could make out the words engraved in the metal.

CLAYTON FALLS APPAREL COMPANY
EST. 1898

"Look," Sam said, pointing to the base of the sign.

Bouquets of flowers, still fresh, encircled the sign's twin posts. Dean pointed at the open entranceway, which was home to several more bouquets and a few stuffed teddy bears. Not nearly as many visitors as the official memorial, but significant.

"An alternate memorial," Dean said.

"This place is condemned, but they refuse to tear it down."

"Got anything?"

Sam turned on the EMF meter, swept it back and forth as they walked under the doorway. "Nothing... yet."

Dean looked up at the looming walls and the open sky overhead.

"Watch for falling bricks."

"What?"

"Forgot our hardhats."

The streetlights failed to penetrate the gloom inside the building. Dean found he had to keep his head down. The footing was treacherous. Loose bricks, burnt and charred joists, and partially melted or shattered industrial sewing machines littered the floor. Broken tables and the hulks of ruined cutting machines impeded their progress. A charred and crumbling staircase that was probably once attached to one of the partial walls led up to nowhere before terminating. Dean's flashlight beam startled a foraging rat, which promptly scurried away in the opposite direction. Throughout their examination of the interior, the EMF meter remained quiet.

After they completed a circuit of the factory, Dean said, "Okay. That was a whole lot of nothing."

"Worth a shot," Sam said as he switched off the meter.

SEVENTEEN

Before the fading of the night commenced, the deeper darkness continued to navigate through the town, coiling and uncoiling in puffs and wisps and streamers, in the familiar path, unaffected by the prevailing winds and the vagaries of the atmosphere. Its cycle repeated throughout the night, dipping to feed before moving on to sample another meal, and it had fed well. Its dark influence was spreading, like drops of ink in clear water.

Even humans not in direct feeding contact had begun to feel its ill effects. Anyone within the periphery of its awareness became a food source, a battery providing energy for its nocturnal presentations. And in feeding on their darkness, their fear and despair, it grew stronger, sensing more of itself and forming more of itself with each stop.

Soon it would be whole, and fear would become all they knew, death their only escape.

* * *

Once again Sam found himself underground.

Not in the root cellar. This time he was tied to a ladder-back chair in an unfamiliar, dank basement. Three narrow windows high in the concrete wall to his right provided a view of ground level, judging by the blades of grass visible above the windowsills. The windows supplied the only source of illumination, but no more than the gloom of dusk. Maybe a half-hour from nightfall.

Yet the dim light was sufficient to reveal the man standing ten feet away from him, the top of his head close to exposed pipes between joists in the low ceiling. He stood with arms crossed over his chest, a satisfied smirk on his face. In one clenched fist he held a long butcher knife, its blade pointing up, beside his jaw.

Soulless Sam.

"You again," Sam said with disgust.

"Long night?" Soulless Sam said. "Or have you been avoiding me."

"Haven't given you a second thought."

"Oh, you should," Soulless Sam said. "Because I've decided to do you a favor."

"Favor?"

"Help you become a better hunter."

"Really?" Sam said. "I thought your goal was to replace me."

"Oh, that will happen soon," Soulless Sam said. "But first, the favor. I'm taking Dean out of the equation."

"What?"

Sam's forehead had become damp.

Condensation began to bead on the concrete walls of the basement. Though Sam could see the darkening sky through the windows, he had the sensation they were descending underwater, in a chamber with faulty seals, as if somewhere nearby the increasing pressure would blow gaskets and water would flood the room. Sam would drown. But somehow Soulless Sam would have an escape route.

"You heard me," Soulless Sam said. "Addition by subtraction."

Along the walls, the clear moisture ran like tear tracks down the concrete. Slowly, the running water turned pink and then, trickle by trickle, a deeper red. At some point, Sam decided the walls were bleeding but could not understand why or how.

"You don't need Dean," Soulless Sam said. "You were a better hunter without him. Much more efficient and ruthless."

"Yeah. That worked out well," Sam said bitterly, the botched handling of the Arachne in the forefront of his mind.

"It's a marathon, Sam," Soulless Sam said, waving off the criticism. "On balance, a hunter needs ruthless efficiency. Dean gets in the way of that. Besides, I won't want him around when I take your place. So my first order of business is to take him out."

"You can't hurt Dean."

"You'd be surprised what I can do, Sammy."

"I won't let you."

Fissures formed in the damp concrete walls. Blood welled

up from the cracks and oozed down to the floor, pools of it joining together and spreading toward the center of the basement. Soon it would cover the entire floor. And begin to rise.

"I'll have the power," Soulless Sam said. "You'll be an afterthought."

"No."

Sam pulled against the rope binding his wrists to the chair behind his back. His ankles were tied to the front legs of the chair. No give in the knots. He considered throwing himself to the floor in an attempt to shatter the chair. But he'd be vulnerable for a few seconds and his doppelganger had the butcher knife.

"Face it, Sammy. You're keeping Dean away from Lisa and Ben. He'd run to them in a heartbeat if he thought you could handle yourself. But he'll never go while you're alive. We both know it. And that leaves me with one option." Soulless Sam chuckled, tapping the edge of the blade against his palm. "Actually, you should thank me. Dean's excess baggage. You'll travel faster without him. And be a better hunter for it."

"You're over," Sam said to him. "A figment of my imagination."

"Imagination is powerful," Soulless Sam said. "Especially these days, don't you think? I feel… rejuvenated."

"What's that supposed to mean?"

"You'll find out. Sooner than you think."

Sam lunged toward his doppelganger, pitching forward in the chair. He braced for the impact, determined to break free of his bonds before Soulless Sam could strike with the knife. But the impact never happened.

The basement floor opened in front of him, an expanding darkness, like the sinkhole at Mack's Qwik Mart, but instantaneous. Blood rushed over the receding edges of the hole, a macabre waterfall.

Standing clear, Soulless Sam laughed as the floor swallowed Sam whole.

Sam awoke with an involuntary jerk of the muscles in his arms and legs. In the dream, he'd been fighting against the ropes binding him to a chair. Once awake, the ropes were remnants of his imagination and his limbs flailed wildly at the sudden freedom.

The motel room was dark. They'd pulled the blinds so the morning sun wouldn't wake them before they'd logged a few hours of sleep. After two long nights in a row without much rest, the Winchester brothers were running on caffeine vapors and little else.

Wanting some fresh air to clear his head, Sam stood and walked to the foot of his bed. He stopped when he noticed the silhouette of a man across the room, back turned toward him, standing next to the other twin bed. Sam almost called Dean's name, but saw his brother was asleep on the far bed. Then Sam saw the glint of stainless steel extending from the stranger's fist.

For a moment, he thought the Butcher Bartch manifestation had somehow followed them back to their motel room, but the body type was wrong—and so was the blade. Not a cleaver—a butcher knife.

That's impossible, Sam thought. *I'm still dreaming.*

Dreams within dreams. A waking dream?

The stranger raised the butcher knife over his head, clutching the dark handle in a double-handed grip, knuckles flexing, prepared to strike.

Sam charged across the room.

He almost expected his legs to betray him, or the floor to open up beneath him again, or the carpeting to bunch and trip him. But none of that happened. And he was almost fast enough to stop the attack.

As the stranger drove the point of the butcher knife downward, Sam slammed into him and the other man's weight was as solid as his own, the impact jarring as they both fell to the floor. Before Sam saw the man's face, saw that it was in fact his own face staring back at him, he registered the man's empty hands.

The knife was missing.

Soulless Sam smiled at Sam.

"Too late!" he said.

Then vanished.

Dean Winchester, alone in the Impala, drove through a rainstorm at night with the radio turned to a classic rock station, but he heard more static than music. Over the hiss of the tires on the wet road, he heard snippets of Seger and AC/DC and Skynyrd. And no matter the song, the repetitive *thwum-thwump* of the windshield wipers kept time with the beat about as competently as an inebriated percussionist. Rising above this confused mush of sound with stark clarity, his cell phone rang. He glanced at the caller ID display: Lisa Braeden.

Shaking his head, he answered the call and said, "Ben, we're not doing this again."

"Dean!"

Lisa's voice. Hushed and frightened.

Dean tightened his grip on the steering wheel, instantly alert.

"Lisa? What's wrong?"

"It's in the house."

"What's in the house?" he said urgently. "Lisa, what's in the house?"

"He looks human," she whispered. "But he's not."

"Who—what is it?"

"Dean, he's calling for you. Says he wants you but he'll enjoy the fresh meat while he waits. He knows we're here!"

Casting aside a dozen possibilities, Dean's mind seized on one: ghoul.

"Where are you?"

"In the closet, in my bedroom. With Ben."

"Dean, you gotta hurry!" Ben's voice, smaller and somehow more distant.

"We're frightened, Dean," Lisa said and her voice sounded raw.

"Hang on, Lisa. I'm coming."

Dean floored the accelerator, staring through the muddled windshield, wipers turned to their highest setting. Visibility sucked. He could see less than fifty feet in front of the Impala's headlights before darkness swallowed his surroundings. He had yet to see one sign on the empty road, which seemed endless and unchanging no matter how long he drove. No destination ahead of him. Nothing in the rearview mirror.

"Dean, where are you?"

"I—I don't know."

"How long before you get here?"

"Soon—soon as I can."

Dean looked left and right, desperate for a street sign or a route number. Anything. Was he even driving in the correct direction? Maybe he was heading away from them.

"Dean… he's coming up the stairs," Lisa whispered frantically. "I can hear him. Tapping a knife on the banister."

Facing the inevitable, Dean asked, "Do you have any weapons? Anything you can use as a weapon?"

"I didn't have time," Lisa said. "I grabbed Ben and hid. Let's see…" Dean heard sounds of rustling movement. "I have… hangers…"

"Wire?"

"Plastic."

"Anything else?"

"Boots, shoes… Dean I didn't know I'd need weapons in my closet!"

"Call 911."

"I tried. They put me on hold. Dean, he's going to kill us…"

"No," Dean said defiantly. "That won't happen. I won't let it happen."

Her voice dropped to a whisper. "It's too late. He's in my room…"

Silence on the line.

"Lisa? Lisa, talk to me?"

A moment later, he heard her scream.

"No!" Dean yelled.

He pounded the dashboard with his fist and—

—he was standing in her house, at the bottom of the staircase.

As Dean grabbed the railing and took the first step, a dark-haired ghoul appeared at the top of the stairs whistling an unrecognizable tune. It held a blood-streaked butcher knife in one hand. The index finger of the other hand pressed casually against the tip, as if testing its sharpness. In addition to the blood on the knife, the ghoul had blood smeared around its mouth.

"About time you showed up, Winchester," the ghoul said. "Had to amuse myself while I waited. And I was feeling a bit peckish."

"You son of a bitch!"

Dean launched himself up the stairs.

The ghoul waited for him impassively. Until the last second. Then it slashed the butcher knife toward Dean's throat.

But Dean was expecting the attack, and threw his forearm into the crook of the ghoul's elbow as he drove it back and slammed it into the wall. Dean drove his right fist into the ghoul's abdomen, doubling it over. Then he placed his palm under the ghoul's jaw and shoved its head back so hard the back of its skull smashed through the drywall.

Stunned by the head blow, the ghoul failed to resist when Dean grabbed its knife-wielding hand, twisted the wrist down and forced the blade deep into its gut. The ghoul gasped and sputtered, blood foaming on its lips. Dean grabbed the back of the ghoul's neck with his right hand and its belt with the left, and ran it forward, hurling the creature down the staircase, head over heels.

Grunting in pain as the embedded knife cut through assorted internal organs, the ghoul rolled end over end, feet bursting through the railing at one point before its body veered toward the wall and crashed to the landing below. Moaning, the ghoul stirred, plucking feebly at the handle of the butcher knife.

Dean marched down the steps, pulling his gun from the holster and taking aim as he neared the last step. When Dean finally stood over the prone form, the ghoul opened its eyes and tried to focus on Dean's face, but it couldn't ignore the muzzle of the handgun.

"As last meals go…" it began.

Dean fired two quick shots into the creature's head.

Standing in a dark silence broken only by his ragged breathing, Dean steeled himself for what he would find upstairs. He holstered his gun and rubbed his palm over his face. Numbness spread from his head to his toes. He clenched and unclenched his hands, sensing that he stood on a precipice. Looking down, he would see the face of madness.

Several moments passed before he realized he heard sobbing from upstairs.

Lisa!

Dean turned back to the staircase, moved toward it,

fighting the sensation that the stairs would disappear before he could ascend them. He gripped the railing for support and it wobbled crazily beneath his grip, weakened by the balusters damaged in the ghoul's fall. With each step up, he had increased difficulty breathing. When—*if*—he made it to the top, he was certain there would be no oxygen left in the house.

One plodding step after the other he came closer to the source of the sobbing. As much as he tried to hurry, he dreaded what he would find. The staircase seemed to rear upward, making the climb steeper. He pressed onward, determined to face the consequences of his actions, the price of his inaction… the result of his absence.

At the top of the stairs, the sobbing became louder, more sporadic and—how was it possible?—even more inconsolable.

The mournful sound led him to Ben's room.

Dean stood in the open doorway. His body trembled with his inability to step forward, into the room. Lisa sat with her back toward him, hunched over—

—blood on the walls—

—blood stained the bedcovers and—

—blood on the floor, near…

Dean pressed his eyes shut before he could see—

—if he opened his eyes he *would* see—

He turned away and—

He woke up.

In the dark motel room, lying on his right side, shuddering as he held back a bottled grief that carried over from his disturbing dream. He'd collapsed on the bed without changing out of his rumpled clothing, falling asleep the moment his head hit the pillow. Now he felt as if he'd been through a spin cycle.

"Whoa," he said softly as he swung his feet over the side of the bed.

"Dean!" Sam said from behind him, undisguised relief in his voice. "You rolled over."

Dean looked over his shoulder. "What?"

"You moved—rolled away. Bad dream?"

"Doozy," Dean said. "What's wrong? Couldn't sleep?"

"Same here. Bad dream."

As Dean turned around, he saw Sam pass his hand over the edge of the bed, as if searching for something.

"You need loose change for the vending machine, just ask," Dean said, looking at his brother, puzzled.

"No—it's not that. Thought I saw a tear in the blanket. Guess I imagined it."

Dean stood up and turned to face Sam across the bed.

"This ain't no four-star hotel," he said. "But I think I would have noticed ripped bedding."

"Right."

Sam stood there for a moment, looking dazed. Then he ran his fingers through his hair and exhaled forcefully.

"It's late morning," he said. "What do you say? Coffee with an energy drink chaser?"

"Sam? Something you want to talk about?"

"No. I'm good."

"You don't look good."

Sam sighed. Dean had the impression his brother wanted

to tell him what was bothering him so he kept quiet, waiting, to let Sam work it out.

"Like I said, bad dream. More like a waking dream. I was… talking to Soulless Sam. Guess it's the unknown. He was me. But he's a stranger, in a way."

"Sure."

"Don't know, man," Sam said. "Maybe it's a psychological side effect of having this wall in my head. Wondering what it—he was like. But what can I do? Doubt I'll find any case studies on the Internet."

"You think it's cracking? The wall, I mean," Dean said. "Maybe Cass can patch it."

"No, it's not that. I'm not remembering anything about my… lost time. Or what went on in the pit with Lucifer and Michael. It's just about *him*… the not knowing."

"Make sense, I suppose" Dean said. *As if any of this makes sense.*

EIGHTEEN

By the time Dean parked the Impala across from 109 Chaney Lane, a tree service company was reducing the downed white oak to disposable pieces. One man cut off smaller branches and fed them into the wood chipper while a second man turned the trunk into manageable slices with a heavy-duty chainsaw.

Between the raucous roar of the chipper and the repetitive whine of the chainsaw, Dean felt a massive headache brewing. Lack of sleep and too much caffeine could be a crappy combination. At least he wasn't hung-over. Although, at the moment, he couldn't imagine how a hangover could possibly feel any worse.

Sam pressed the doorbell.

They waited with their FBI laminates at the ready. Melinda Barnes might assume they were with the press, intruding on a family tragedy, and slam the door in their faces. She would be more inclined to speak to someone trying to figure out what happened. But what they really needed was to speak to her son.

Nobody answered.

"Maybe the doorbell's broken," Dean said.

They certainly couldn't hear much over the tree destruction in progress twenty feet behind them. Sam rapped on the door.

A few seconds later, a young woman with puffy eyes greeted them, taking a moment to check their IDs.

"What do you want?" she asked loudly, frowning as the wood chipper shrieked in the background.

Dean wondered if the constant reminder of the tree that had killed her husband bothered her, or if she found some solace in witnessing its methodical dismemberment. Either way, Dean decided he'd defer her question to Sam.

"Just a few questions, Mrs. Barnes."

"I can't hear," she said, shaking her head. "Come inside."

She led them through the house to the kitchen, which was decorated in a country style with pink gingham wallpaper, white cabinets with glass-front doors, and a light-colored hardwood floor. The windows overlooked a backyard with an all-purpose wooden playset in the center that featured a mini fort and climbing wall, a sliding board and swings. The kid wasn't out there.

Melinda Barnes sat down at the kitchen table and motioned them toward chairs. Dean and Sam sat facing her.

"You're with the FBI?"

"Yes," Sam said. "We're sorry for the loss of your husband. We have a few questions and then we'll get out of your way."

"I talked to the police last night," she said, pressing one

hand to her quivering chin. "Don't know what else I can say."

"We're conducting a parallel investigation," Dean said.

"This was a freak accident," she said. "A horrible freak accident. That's all, right?"

"Ma'am, you may be aware of some of the other... strange incidents around town in the last few days."

"A boy killed in a hit and run."

"Two now," Dean said.

"Two?" she shook her head. "I hadn't heard. Just some crazy talk down at the hair salon about a giant alligator."

"Gila monster," Dean said. "And a giant tarantula."

"What?"

"Red-kneed."

"The point is," Sam said. "We believe there may be a connection between all these incidents."

"How could there be a connection to what happened to Max?" she asked. "It was a storm and the—the tree branch came through the window. Max was in the wrong place at the wrong time."

"Was he?"

"Yes. We talked about trimming the tree because the branches scraped against the house. They scared Daniel, my son. Max said he would cut them in—in the morning."

She clamped a hand over her mouth and squeezed her eyes shut. Tears rolled down her cheeks and she quickly wiped the tracks away.

"I'm sorry..." she choked.

"No need to apologize, ma'am," Sam said.

"He was standing by the window because of the branches

being so close… checking them, and the wind gust…"

"Is that what your son saw?"

"What? Of course, that's what he saw. That's what happened."

"Did he tell you what he saw?" Sam pressed softly.

"He's not—he's not talking about it. I told him he didn't have to talk about it," she said. "But I saw. I heard him calling me and I ran into the room seconds after it happened. There was—the window was broken and… and Max was on the floor and there was so much blood." She took a deep, shuddering breath. "I'm taking Daniel away from here for a while. I called my sister in Colorado Springs and we're going…"

"I understand how upsetting this is, Mrs. Barnes," Sam said. "It's important that we talk to Daniel—"

She shook her head violently. "No!"

"He's the only witness."

"No!" she said again. She looked down at the kitchen table, nibbling on the fingernail of her index finger, slowly shaking her head. "No. I don't want him to go through that again. To relive what happened to his father. Can you imagine how horrible that must have been? For a ten-year-old boy to see that… to see his father…"

Sam waited while she composed herself. Then he tried again.

"Ma'am, whatever caused this, whatever killed your husband, we don't believe it was a freak accident. And we believe these incidents will continue to happen until we figure out what's causing them and stop it." Sam paused for a moment, then continued, his voice gentle but firm.

"As a wife and as a mother, you wouldn't want something like this to happen to another family, to another little girl or boy."

She continued to shake her head.

"No, of course not," she said.

Finally, she looked up at Sam, met his gaze, and her eyes were wet with more unshed tears.

"But, as a mother, I can't put my son through this."

"It's okay, Mom," a small voice said from the kitchen doorway.

"Daniel?" she said, wiping her cheeks hastily again. She rushed from the table and placed her hands on his shoulders. "You're supposed to be sleeping in the guest room. What are you doing down here?"

"Couldn't sleep with all the noise outside," he said. "And I heard you talking to these men."

"They were just leaving," she said and glanced over her shoulder. "Weren't you?"

Sam glanced at Dean, who nodded, and they stood.

"You said you can stop this from happening again," Daniel Barnes said, looking around his mother's protective stance at the Winchesters. "Is that true?"

Standing there, the kid reminded Dean of Ben.

"Yes," Dean said. "That's true."

"Then I want to help."

"Daniel, you don't need to—" his mother began.

"I want to," Daniel insisted. "For Dad."

Melinda Barnes sobbed and clamped her hand over her mouth again.

"Dad would want me to be brave."

"Yes," she said. "Yes, he would."

"Then I'll do it."

The boy took his mother's place at the kitchen table and the Winchesters sat again. Melinda Barnes poured glasses of water for all of them. Dean sensed that she wanted to keep her hands busy or she would simply wrap Daniel in her arms and not let go until they left.

With a quick look at Sam, who nodded his understanding, Dean took over the questioning. "Tell us what happened, Daniel," he said.

The boy nodded. Took a sip of his water and held the glass tightly in both hands.

"The tree branches scared me," he said. "They looked like arms with long pointy fingers. I could see creepy shadows on the walls and ceiling of my room. The branches kept tapping the window when I was trying to sleep. I was afraid they wanted to grab me. But I kept telling myself 'wind and shadows' and that it was nothing to be afraid of and I fell asleep." He took another sip of water. "Then I had a nightmare about the tree."

"A nightmare," Dean said. "Must have been spooky."

Daniel nodded. "The tree was evil in my nightmare. It wanted to kill me and its branches were like arms and fingers. They tried to grab me. Reaching through my window."

"In your dream," Sam said.

"Yes," Daniel said. "And that was when the window cracked."

"The dream window?" Dean asked.

"No. The real window," Daniel said. "It cracked in real life. Woke me up." He took a deep breath. "It was like my nightmare had become real."

Sam exchanged a meaningful look with Dean, but didn't interrupt the flow of the boy's account. "Go on."

"I freaked out," Daniel said. "I called out for Mom, but Dad came instead. He was kind of mad, but I told him about the window. And that's when we found out the lights wouldn't work."

"You lost power?" Sam asked Melinda Barnes.

"Briefly," she said.

"He—my dad—was standing by the window," Daniel said. "He asked me to try my lamp, but that wouldn't work either. And that's when it happened. The wind was blowing hard and the branch came all the way through the window…"

"Daniel?" Melinda Barnes came around the kitchen island toward her son.

"I'm okay," Daniel said and took another sip of water. "The branch went through Dad. All the way from his back out through here." Daniel tapped his chest. "It was like—like it wanted to stab him. Like a sword fight with knights."

Sam nodded grimly.

The poor kid's only ten freakin' years old, Dean thought.

"But then the tree acted like it did in my nightmare…"

"What do you mean?" Dean said, leaning forward.

"It moved. The whole tree—" Daniel spread his arms to the sides and raised them together—"lifted itself up. And, it lifted Dad up, off the floor."

"Oh, my God!" Melinda whispered harshly. "Daniel…"

"Dad was still alive…" Daniel continued.

Now the boy's voice became strained with emotion. Dean could tell the kid was holding back tears, bravely trying not to cry, for his old man.

"And the tree… the tree made him… dance in front of me."

"Jesus," Dean whispered.

Melinda Barnes finally ran forward, dropping to her knees and wrapping her son in her arms, pressing her face against his chest and neck.

"Oh, God… oh, God…" she murmured.

"The branch swung him back and forth," Daniel continued even though tears ran freely down his cheeks now. "Like he was a puppet."

"Oh, honey, stop," Melinda whispered. "Please stop! Oh, God…"

"I think it wanted to scare me before it left," Daniel said, holding his palm against the back of his mother's head in an effort to comfort her. "And then the tree… scraped him off the branch… and Dad's blood smeared on the window… and he fell to the floor and I knew he was…" Sniffling, he wiped his nose on his sleeve. "It was just like my nightmare," he said. "The tree was evil."

NINETEEN

Without speaking, Sam and Dean walked past the tree service workmen, who had made a fair amount of progress in destroying the murderous tree. Sam almost regretted their having to prod the information out of Daniel Barnes, if only for the mom's sake. Talking about the incident had seemed almost cathartic for the kid. He'd been keeping that horrible incident bottled up inside. His mom, already devastated by the accident, now had to accept a whole new and horrifying reality about her husband's death. Sam wondered if Melinda Barnes could accept that a tree had willfully killed her husband. Or if she would rather convince herself that Daniel was wrong, that his version of events was informed by an already over-stimulated imagination.

Sam settled into the passenger seat of the Impala and stared numbly through the windshield.

Dean dropped into the driver's seat and hesitated before inserting the key into the ignition.

"Poor kid," he said. "Probably have nightmares for the rest of his life."

"Nightmares," Sam said. "Kid's mom never suspected."

"How could she?" Dean said. "Usually, you wake up and escape the nightmare. Kid wakes up and the nightmare comes out with him."

Sam turned to Dean. What if there was more to his waking nightmare of Soulless Sam than he'd been willing to admit to himself, something beyond psychological fallout from the wall in his brain? "Maybe that's what's happening all over town. Nightmares coming to life. Lucy said she has nightmares about the accident that killed her boyfriend. And now his car is back."

"People are sleepwalking and having nightmares. Guy jogging was dreaming of a giant tarantula? That what you're saying?"

"What if it doesn't have to be one-to-one," Sam said. "What if the nightmares of the sleeping are coming to life and attacking those who are awake?"

"So Joe Townie, safe in his bed, has a nightmare about a giant tarantula which then pops into existence near Harvey Dufford's jogging route and slurps him up?"

"Essentially."

"Whose nightmares?" Dean asked. "Everybody dreams."

"Judging by last night," Sam said. "Only the bad dreams."

Sam recalled his own nightmare about Soulless Sam. Another nightmare from last night, however brief, that seemed to intrude on reality. But that wasn't the first dream about his soulless doppelganger. He'd had a similar but normal—for him, at least—dream the night before. The second dream had been different. But after Dean woke up unscathed, Sam had convinced himself that he'd imagined the Soulless Sam manifestation. Sleep experts called it a false awakening. Dean hadn't been injured by the butcher knife. The bedcovers hadn't been sliced or punctured by the blade. Before they spoke to Daniel Barnes, Sam had no trouble attributing the brief apparition to a waking dream, probably caused by a combination of sleep deprivation and hours spent battling what they now knew were nightmare manifestations. Before that realization, he'd been unable to entertain the possibility that a dream could assume some sort of altered reality.

After hearing Daniel's account of the tree attacking his father, Sam had to reevaluate what he himself had experienced. It seemed that whatever was happening to the residents of Clayton Falls could as easily affect him and Dean. The Winchesters weren't immune.

"So we should all think happy thoughts?" Dean said. "Sam, we can't control our subconscious."

"Dude, you and I are time bombs," Sam said. "Nuclear time bombs."

"What are you saying?"

"If this can happen to anyone in town, including us, we could be the worst thing to happen to Clayton Falls." Sam shook his head, appalled by the possibility of their subconscious minds out of control. "If memories of our experiences over the past years work their way into our dreams now, Clayton Falls could be primed for a bloodbath, maybe even an apocalypse."

"If you're right," Dean said, "until we fix this, we don't sleep."

He started the Impala. The radio was playing Bowie's "Changes."

"This involves multiple dreamers," Dean said. "How the hell do we pin it down?"

"Maybe we need to figure out why it started."

They stopped at C.J.'s Diner for breakfast, as Dean said, no point trying to figure anything out on an empty stomach. Once again, the place was packed, but the morning turnover rate was impressive and they were seated in a small corner booth after only about ten minutes of waiting.

Dean ordered what he referred to as the 'heart attack special' which included fried eggs, bacon, and home fries, while Sam asked for cereal and a muffin. Before they even looked at a menu, they each ordered the bottomless cup of coffee. Their server, who introduced herself as Bobbi Jean Todd and told them how thrilled she was to meet two honest-to-goodness FBI agents, brought their plates in record time.

Around them, many of the townspeople talked in hushed and urgent voices about weird things happening in the night. Sam heard some people say that they had seen zombies, who then disappeared into thin air. A few said they'd heard about giant bugs eating people. The other side of these conversations involved those who hadn't witnessed anything bizarre and questioned the sobriety and, in some cases, sanity of those telling the strange tales.

Sam was pleasantly surprised that his laptop computer picked up a serviceable Wi-Fi signal from their corner booth. While he ate, he skimmed through news stories on Clayton Falls, using "sleep" and "dreams" and "nightmares" as keywords. He got a hit right away, brought up the story, and spun the computer around so Dean could read the screen.

"Place opened about six months ago," Sam said. "The 'Restful Sleep Center.'"

"They treat sleep disorders," Dean said before finishing his third and final egg. "Think they might be creating a few? Mad scientist at work?"

Sam sipped his coffee and shrugged. "Can't rule it out."

A portly man with thinning hair entered the diner carrying a small notebook and, rather than asking to be seated, gravitated toward the more ebullient conversations about the previous night. Sam heard the man introduce himself as Darren Nash, a reporter for the *Fremont Ledger*, a county newspaper. He then proceeded to ask pointed questions and take voluminous notes. He kept shaking his head in incredulity, but the smile on his face was that of a man who'd just discovered he held a winning lottery ticket in his hand.

"Press," Sam said.

Dean glanced at the man. "Bound to happen. But unless he's writing for the *Weekly World News*, he'll have trouble getting any of this crazy shit past an editor."

"Don't know, dude," Sam said. "Lots of witnesses."

"I'm not lining up for an interview," Dean said. "Besides, I'm done."

As he pushed his empty plate away, Bobbi Jean arrived at their table as if magically summoned.

"Anything else, agents?"

"Just the check," Dean said. "Oh, and two large coffees to go."

Sam directed Dean to the sleep center, a detached brick building that looked like a modest inn or slightly upscale motel, while lacking the quaint charm of a bed and breakfast. The sleep center stood adjacent to a row of shops in a commercial district less than a mile from their motel. The sign mounted on the front wall of the building featured a crescent moon above the words "Restful Sleep Center." A second line of text read "Sleep Diagnostics of Clayton Falls."

"So this is it?" Dean asked, sounding disappointed.

"You were expecting a creepy old mansion?"

"They could have a hunchback working reception."

The receptionist was an attractive young woman with jet-black hair styled in a pixie cut, wearing a sleeveless houndstooth dress. She sat behind a semicircular mahogany desk with a raised front panel. Laura Bronick—according to the gold nameplate on her desk—smiled broadly.

"Welcome to Restful Sleep!" she said.

"I stand corrected," Dean said.

Her smile faltered a bit. "Excuse me?"

"Not important." Dean removed his FBI credentials from his jacket pocket and showed them to her. "Agent DeYoung and Agent Shaw. Need to talk to whoever's in charge."

"Do you have an appointment?"

"We're not here to sleep," Dean said. Then he added, sotto voce, "Although a few hours' sleep sounds mighty good about now."

Sam leaned forward. "We're conducting an investigation."

"Oh, in that case..." She consulted a chart on a stand beside her computer keyboard. "We're short-staffed this time of day. I'll see if our administrative director is available."

She donned a slim headset with a tiny projecting microphone and pressed an extension button on the top of her phone console.

"Ms. Bessette, there are two gentlemen here from the FBI. No. They didn't say. Okay. Thank you."

She disconnected the call and smiled at them again.

"She'll be here in a few moments. Please have a seat while you wait."

Sam glanced over his shoulder at the luxurious tan leather sofa and bookending chairs along the wall opposite the reception desk. If anything, they looked too damn comfortable. He didn't know about Dean, but if he sat down for more than ten consecutive seconds, he'd probably fall asleep.

"Thanks. We'll stand."

Dean shot Sam a look that told him he'd had the same thought.

"Surprised you're open on a Saturday," Sam said to the receptionist.

"We have patients check in Friday night and check out Saturday," she said. "We're closed Sunday and Monday."

"So this place helps people sleep?" Sam asked.

"At Restful Sleep Center we identify and treat sleep disorders," Laura said by rote in her infallibly cheery voice. Then she shrugged and went a bit off-script. "Sleep is important. You know what they say, if you never slept, you'd go insane."

"They say that, huh?" Sam said.

Soulless Sam had gone over a year without sleep. Sam wondered if his soulless self might be considered insane. And if so, could the insanity have been caused by lack of sleep. Or was the absence of a soul—and therefore a conscience—enough to make an otherwise normal man appear insane? Because if sleeplessness was a contributing factor, wouldn't that affect Sam too? They shared a body. Could long-term sleep deprivation cause lasting effects, even after a soul restoration?

Laura chuckled. "Well, I'm no scientist. That's just something I read somewhere. If you don't sleep, you don't dream. And if you don't dream, you go cuckoo."

"Good to know," Sam responded.

A statuesque brunette wearing horn-rimmed glasses, a blood-red business suit, and impressive heels entered the lobby through the glass door behind the receptionist's desk. Her dark hair, piled high in a loose chignon, was held in place with jeweled hairpins. Sam fought a smile as Dean almost stood at attention, stepping forward to introduce himself.

"I'm Agent DeYoung," Dean said. "This is my partner, Agent Shaw."

"Pleasure to meet you," she said, offering her hand. "I'm Sophie Bessette, director of the Restful Sleep Center."

Dean shook her hand and reluctantly—or so it seemed to

Sam—stepped aside for Sam to follow suit.

"I must say, the last thing I expected when I woke up this morning was a visit from the FBI. How may I assist you?"

"It's a—uh, matter of Homeland Security," Dean said, his voice hushed. "We're investigating a series of strange incidents in Clayton Falls. You are familiar with what's been happening in town, Ms. Bessette?"

The woman glanced briefly at the receptionist, raised her eyebrows, and looked back at Dean and Sam.

"I've heard some… unusual rumors. But I didn't give them much credence. Are you saying these things are actually happening?"

"Yes, ma'am."

"We haven't had anything unusual happen here at Restful Sleep, if that's what you're checking. Have we, Laura?"

"Just the same old routine."

"Of course, our patient records are confidential," the director said. "Unless you have a warrant, I won't be able to provide access to—"

"We're not interested in patient records," Sam said. "We were more interested in… Is there somewhere we could speak in private?"

"An office," Dean said, bumbling a bit. "Your office. You do have an office, right?"

Sophie smiled indulgently at Dean.

"As a matter of fact, I do have an office. Follow me."

"With pleasure," Dean said, echoing her earlier sentiment and yet sounding decidedly lecherous for a professional environment.

As they followed the woman down the hall, Dean held out his arm to slow Sam and whispered, "Getting a definite hot-for-teacher vibe from this one."

"Really? I hadn't noticed."

"No?"

"Aside from when you tripped over your tongue."

"Oh."

"Maybe she's luring you into her trap."

They picked up their pace and fell in step behind her by the time she motioned them through a doorway into her spacious office. After they were all seated with the door closed, she asked, "Private enough?"

"We don't want to cause a panic," Sam said. "You see, we're investigating possible terrorist activity here in Clayton Falls."

"Terrorism? Here?"

"Possibly," Sam said, quickly adding, "But more as a potential testing ground for a large scale attack in a major metropolitan area."

"Okay, granting that this information is a bit alarming, I still fail to see how Restful Sleep could be involved in your investigation."

"We suspected a weaponized airborne hallucinogen," Sam continued. "But now we believe these incidents are related to sleeping."

"Ah, comes the dawn."

"Specifically, nightmares," Dean said. "And we recently discovered that you treat sleep disorders here."

"Agent... DeYoung, was it? All sleep centers treat sleep disorders."

"We thought maybe it was more than a coincidence that nightmares seem to trigger these incidents and there happens to be a sleep center in town."

She folded her hands on a daily planner in the center of her desk, a prim pose that was no doubt fueling Dean's schoolteacher fantasies.

"Sleep centers are not that uncommon," she explained. "One in fifteen Americans suffers from sleep apnea. In a town the size of Clayton Falls we could have close to a thousand patients for that disorder alone."

"You must be very busy here," Dean said.

"Unfortunately, the condition often goes undiagnosed."

"Do you treat people who have nightmares?"

"Not directly," she said, adjusting her glasses on the bridge of her nose. "We don't treat people simply because they might have nightmares. But those who have trouble sleeping may experience loss of breath and anxiety. Some of them stop breathing many times during a single night. Physiological symptoms of distress could potentially trigger bad dreams."

"But you would have no reason to cause someone to have nightmares."

"Certainly not," she said indignantly. She took a deep breath to calm herself. "Maybe I could assist your investigation better if I understood what you believe is happening."

"It's complicated," Sam said.

"Just a theory," Dean added.

"We believe that somehow nightmares are… becoming real."

"You're joking."

"We're not sure *how* this is happening," Sam said. "Initially we suspected a hallucinogen as the sole bioterrorism agent, but several people have been killed by these manifestations."

"There was something odd about the hit and run," she said. "A tragedy, certainly, but not a nightmare."

"What's 'odd' is that the car vanished after it killed each victim," Dean said.

"There was more than one?"

"A second one last night. Same car. Multiple witnesses," Sam said. "And we—Agent DeYoung and I—witnessed a few bizarre incidents personally last night."

"And you believe these are somehow connected to nightmares."

"A boy dreamed a tree outside his bedroom window wanted to kill him," Sam said. "He woke up in a panic. His father came into the room and was killed by a tree branch coming through the window."

"Again, a tragedy, but that could also be a horrible coincidence," she said. "There was a violent storm last night."

"The car involved in the hit and runs was destroyed a year ago," Dean said. "Now it's back. In mint condition."

She patted her hair, tucked a few loose strands behind her ears and shook her head slightly.

"I'm not convinced—at least nowhere near as convinced as you two seem to be—but I can offer you a quick tour of our facility to… assure you that Restful Sleep has absolutely no involvement in these so-called terrorist activities, whatever their cause."

Sam opened his mouth to decline, but Dean accepted her offer before Sam could get a word out. Resigned, Sam shut his mouth and followed behind as she led them to a few empty patient bedrooms that were orders of magnitude more luxurious than any of the motel rooms they had ever stayed in. Several times, Sam caught himself yawning, fighting the desire to curl up on one of the beds and catch a few winks while Dean and the director completed the tour without him.

"We diagnose and treat a number of common sleep disorders," Sophie Bessette said as they walked through the facility, "including obstructive sleep apnea, insomnia, narcolepsy, sleepwalking, and snoring."

"How?" Dean asked. "By watching them sleep?"

"Through polysomnograms, or sleep studies. Sleep technicians place sensors on the patient that record brain activity, breathing patterns, heart rate, and body movements. This feedback is monitored throughout the night. The results are then interpreted by our in-house physician and later sent to the patient's referring physician for a consultation. Most sleep studies are concluded in one day—well, night."

"What are the treatments?"

"The most common nonsurgical treatment is positive airway pressure therapy. The patient wears a mask that converts room air into pressurized air, which keeps the breathing passages open throughout the night. Sometimes weight loss can alleviate a condition. Or sleep position modification, using cushions or wedges to keep the patient from sleeping on his or her back."

"So you wouldn't, for instance, inject patients with experimental drugs?"

"Absolutely not!"

"Fascinating stuff, Ms. Bessette," Dean said, turning on the charm. "Wouldn't mind discussing it in detail over dinner."

"Perhaps when the crisis is past."

"Yes, of course," Dean said. "Excellent point." He patted his pockets, found one of his FBI business cards and handed it to her. "In case you think of anything that might help our investigation. Anything at all. Day or night."

Holding the card delicately at the edges between her thumbs and forefingers, she flashed Dean a provocative smile. "Certainly, Agent DeYoung."

"Good," Dean said, clearing his throat and nodding. "That's good."

"Glad I could be of assistance. Let me show you both out."

As they walked back to the Impala, Dean said. "Wouldn't mind studying her sleep." Frowning, he added, "Wait. That came out like stalker talk."

"Little bit."

"Just saying. We clicked. Nothing wrong with that," Dean said. "Unless you saw a mad scientist laboratory in there I somehow missed."

"Don't know, Dean," Sam said. "All those sensors on sleeping people. Maybe they're recording nightmares and playing them back later in town."

"You're not serious…"

Sam smirked and shook his head.

"Good one," Dean said. Then his mind drifted back to Sophie and he whistled appreciatively. "Think she lets that hair down after hours?"

"Relax, Dean," Sam said, grinning. "She was humoring you."

"She was undressing me with her eyes."

"That had 'don't call me, I'll call you' written all over it."

Dean's cell phone rang.

"A-ha! That was fast." He glanced at the display. "Crap."

"Not her?"

Dean shook his head and took the call.

"Chief Quinn? Checking in or…?"

The Winchesters climbed into the Impala. Dean waited until he finished the call before starting the engine. Putting his phone away, Dean frowned as he turned the ignition.

"What was that about?"

"Chief says we have some explaining to do."

"He's blaming *us* for this?"

"Who knows? He's in denial about most of it."

"Can you handle him alone?"

"Why? You got somewhere to be?"

"Someone I should talk to."

"You want me to guess?"

"Olga Kucharski," Sam said. "This started with the Charger. And there've been two deadly incidents involving that car."

"A car that belonged to her dead grandson."

TWENTY

Dean dropped Sam off at Olga Kuckarski's house, in the less affluent south end of Clayton Falls, where the homes were closer together on smaller lots. According to Lucy Quinn, the woman rarely left her house. Dean waited at the curb in the Impala while Sam rang the doorbell. Less than a minute later, a weary gray-haired woman in a rumpled, shapeless housedress opened the door and squinted up at Sam, who showed her his FBI laminate. She frowned, nodded and waved him inside.

Satisfied Sam wouldn't be standing around for the next hour or so waiting for the woman to return from grocery shopping, Dean drove north to Welker Street, turned left and then right onto Main. He parked in the municipal lot behind the Clayton Falls Apparel Company memorial. Cars occupied about a quarter of the lot. Considering it was a Saturday, Dean imagined many township employees were off for the weekend.

Dean walked past the curved memorial, right over the spot where he'd shot the man stricken with nightmare-Ebola. Glancing down at the sidewalk, he marveled at the complete absence of blood. Vanished without a trace. Same as the Nazi zombies. In the harsh light of day, he could almost believe everything had been a regular nightmare. But then he remembered the dissolved flesh and bones of Harvey Dufford and wondered if the paramedics had found a way to extricate his embedded remains from the asphalt. *Not without a jackhammer and a backhoe*, he thought.

In the police department lobby, he told Millie, the dispatcher, that Chief Quinn was expecting him. She nodded and buzzed him through. This time the inner sanctum was bustling with uniforms. Dean spotted at least two shift sergeants and a dozen patrol officers, conferring with each other, hacking away at computer keyboards, printing and collecting forms and photos for report binders. Wild and Cerasi spoke together in low tones, the former sparing a brief nod to Dean before returning to her conversation.

Sitting at his desk over a flurry of paperwork, Officer Jeffries belatedly covered a yawn when he saw Dean approaching.

"Crazy night, huh?" he said.

"You look like hell, Jeffries."

"Pulled a double shift yesterday," he said. "Off duty now, but something tells me I'm not getting out of here anytime soon. What about you? Sleep in that suit?"

"Sleep is for wimps," Dean said. "Chief Quinn?"

"In his office."

Dean knocked on the closed door and waited for the old man to invite him inside. The spartan office seemed more severe than it had the first time Dean saw it. Although the grim expression on the police chief's face, along with the sight of his clenched fists resting on a mound of police report folders stacked in the middle of his desk might have contributed to the chill in the room.

"Close the door," Quinn said. "Take a seat."

Dean complied. "How's your daughter?"

Quinn's eyes flickered to Lucy's graduation photo on the corner of his desk and he frowned. "Upset, naturally. She lost a good friend. Two now. But she's sticking with her ridiculous story. I'm not sure I can help her unless I get some reliable information."

"No luck finding the car?" Dean asked, even though he knew the car wouldn't exist until the next time it manifested. *Humor the man*, he reminded himself.

"None," Quinn said. "Probably under a tarp in a garage somewhere. But I've got nothing to go on."

"You wanted to see me," Dean prompted.

"You and your partner," Quinn said. "Where is he?"

"Following a lead," Dean said, reluctant to go into details. Technically, Olga Kucharski was a grieving grandmother, not a witness to any of the living nightmares. The Chief might not approve of them troubling an old woman with no apparent connection to the town's troubles. "How can I help?"

"You can start by telling me what the hell is happening to my town," Quinn said. "Half my officers out there are convinced they've seen zombies or that giant monsters are attacking residents."

"We warned you about the hallucinogen," Dean said.

"And I was disinclined to believe you at the time."

"But now?"

"Now I'm willing to concede that something is causing people to hallucinate, but something else is going on." He slapped a hand down on the top folder on his desk. "Do you know what's in here?"

"I can imagine."

"There are photos of a human being who looks like a half-melted Popsicle."

"I saw that in person. Nasty."

"Jeffries told me," Quinn said. "He also told me that two witnesses blame a giant spider for the attack."

"Yes, sir, a tarantula."

"It was *not* a tarantula."

"It wasn't?"

"Of course it wasn't a giant spider! That's just what they saw."

"Ahh…" Dean said, nodding.

"That part is the hallucinogen. I get it. What I don't get is what's *really* going on here. Samples were taken to the lab. I won't have a report anytime soon, but I'll go out on a limb and say it was some sort of acid."

"Some sort of bioterror agent," Dean said, trying to couch the seriousness of the situation in a manner the pragmatic lawman could accept.

Quinn snapped his fingers.

"Exactly. A psychotropic drug to create false impressions of what's happening. Unreliable witnesses. Damn sneaky, if you ask me."

"That's one possibility."

"What I'm grappling with here is the scope of this attack," Chief Quinn said, nodding thoughtfully. "I know you saved a child at the Qwik Mart sinkhole. Good work."

"Thank you."

"And some jackass was crushed by his own car."

"Tried to warn him."

"Some people never listen."

Dean frowned briefly, wondering if the police chief was inadvertently—or subconsciously—referring to himself. No matter what his officers told him, he was determined to find his own explanations.

"We've had a nasty storm, lost some power lines, car accidents and that awful tree accident that killed Max Barnes, none of which I can blame on terrorist activity. Well, there is the matter of the tree being relocated to the middle of the street, which makes no sense. Damn prank, if you ask me. Why would a terrorist move a tree? The sinkhole? They occur naturally and some are frighteningly large. Unless you expect me to believe in some kind of subterranean sabotage, right? A terrorist cell, embedded for years, having some hand in local construction?"

"It's possible."

Chief Quinn drummed his fingers on the mound of police reports.

"Something on your mind, Chief?"

"I told you this was a quiet town," he said. "And it has been. But this isn't over yet, is it?"

Dean shook his head. "Not until we find... whoever is responsible. No."

Quinn tugged on his earlobe, a deep frown on his face.

"I have a captain, four shift sergeants, thirty patrol officers, a couple of detectives and administrative staff at my disposal. More than enough to handle the usual level of madness. But I find my officers compromised by these... hallucinations. I've asked all of them to work double shifts until we put an end to this."

"Sounds good," Dean said. Unless Sam and he stopped whatever supernatural agent was bringing nightmares to life, the level of violence in Clayton Falls would only get worse. Until then, an all-hands-on-deck mentality would, he hoped, save some lives.

"Good," the chief echoed. "But not good enough."

"Have you considered enforcing a town-wide curfew?" Dean suggested. But the more he thought about it, the more impractical it seemed. It might stop the public violence, but it wouldn't stop people from sleeping and having nightmares. The terror would migrate to more homes, like the Barnes house.

"Not enough evidence," Quinn said. "I can't issue a curfew because of some phantom menace. Storms and sinkholes? No, we'll handle this proactively. With manpower."

"Manpower?"

"One of the reasons I asked you to check in was to let you know I have a call in to the Colorado State Patrol."

"You do?"

"Yes," Quinn said. "For backup and support. Half-dozen extra bodies arriving here tonight. Possibly more. They'll report to me, naturally. Just thought you should know."

"I appreciate that, Chief," Dean said. "Can I make a suggestion?"

"Let's hear it."

"Have them patrol in pairs."

"Why's that?"

"Because if they're alone, they might not believe what they see," Dean said. "Hesitation could be fatal. A second set of eyes could make all the difference."

Quinn nodded. "Good point, since I don't even believe what they saw. Suppose the hallucinogenic effect might vary between them."

"That, too," Dean said reluctantly. *Whatever gets the job done*, he reasoned. "Anything else?"

"That's all for now," Quinn said. "We'll talk soon."

"Okay," Dean said, rising to leave. He paused at the door. "About Lucy."

"What about her?"

"Is she being careful?"

"She has a shift at C.J.'s," Quinn said. "I told her to go straight home after. And stay there."

"Good," Dean said. He paused again, halfway through the doorway. "Will she listen?"

"Truthfully? I don't know. Maybe. I hope so."

"Me too," Dean said. If the Charger returned for a third night, he had no doubt she would be its target.

Dean closed Quinn's door on the way out and was about to navigate a path through the gathered police officers, when Jeffries called him over. A young policewoman had turned a chair around to face Jeffries' desk and had two folders open, side by side. A quick glance revealed they were the case files for the Gila monster and tarantula attacks.

"Jeffries?" Dean said.

"Chief tell you he's calling in the State Patrol?"

"No offense," Dean said. "But you'll need all the help you can get."

"None taken."

The police woman stood and faced Dean.

Jeffries made introductions. "Agent DeYoung, Senior Patrol Officer Carleen Phillips."

Dean shook her offered hand.

"You're looking at terrorists for this?" she asked with a nod toward the file folders on the desk.

"That's our working theory."

She picked up the two monster attack folders, stared at them and shook her head in disbelief. "Weird, you know? Like something out of *Nightmare Theater*."

For a moment, Dean wondered if she had somehow stumbled onto the Winchesters' actual theory and not their cover story. *Not possible*, he thought. Even the people they told outright couldn't accept it. And by 'people' he was thinking about Sophie Bessette. A few moments passed before he realized his mind had wandered and both Jeffries and Phillips were looking at him as if they expected some kind of coherent response.

"A bioterrorism agent affecting the subconscious might be involved," Dean said and hoped it sounded plausible, even though it was a bunch of bull. Sam would have had better luck selling that line. Dean cleared his throat. "How's the coffee here?"

Phillips grinned. "An acquired taste."

"Three parts battery acid, one part roofing tar," Jeffries said.

"Beggars can't be choosers," Dean said. "Lead the way."

Entering Olga Kuckarski's house, Sam's first impression was of musty gloom. Dark curtains and blinds obstructed most of the light that attempted to enter through the windows. Dark paneling encased the bottom half of the walls; dingy wallpaper with designs too faded to distinguish covered the top. But most of the walls were fronted with dark wooden bookshelves packed with old hardbound books steeped in dust and mildew, and bulky hutches filled with worthless bric-a-brac—collections of snow globes, ceramic fish and frogs and turtles, tiny bottles filled with multi-colored sand, oriental fans. The glass doors on the hutches kept the dust away from the interior shelves, but every other surface looked as if it hadn't been cleaned in a long time.

Sam wasn't surprised by the old woman's inattention to house cleaning. She walked with difficulty, hunched over with labored breathing, her arms trembling. As she led him down a cramped hallway to the kitchen, Sam's gaze wandered to a framed portrait of Lech Walesa. A small bronze plate bolted to the bottom of the frame listed the dates Walesa served as Poland's president. Paired with the portrait in a matching frame was a map of Poland. A freestanding bookshelf on the opposite wall displayed books that—unlike those in the towering monuments of mildew he passed earlier—looked as if they had actually been read or perused in the last decade. These books covered a wide variety of topics, all dealing with Poland: multiple volumes on the history of the country, volumes on life during wartime, the changing face of politics, the legends and folklore, famous people, tourism, music, literature, sports, geography and demographics, even several cookbooks. The woman had access to anything she'd ever want to know about her country of origin.

In the small kitchen, which had enough floor space for a table and four chairs but not much else, she opened a cabinet above her head and reached for two glasses. When Sam saw her hands trembling, he stepped forward and said, "Allow me."

"I'm not helpless, you know?" she responded sharply.

"I'm a guest in your house," Sam said. "I want to help."

"Don't have any fancy bottled water."

"Tap's fine," Sam said.

He filled two glasses and set them on opposite sides of the table. When he reached to pull back a chair for her, she smacked his hand away.

"Enough of the Boy Scout crap," she said. "State your business, young man."

Sam waited as she fumbled with the chair, pushing it back with the edge of a curled fist before plopping down in apparent exhaustion. When she was settled with her ragged breathing under control, he sat down and took a sip of water.

The center of the table held a framed photo and a vase of flowers a few days past fresh.

"I'm sorry to trouble you, Mrs. Kucharski," Sam said. "I was hoping you could answer a few questions for me about your grandson."

"Teodor? You're here about Teodor? Little late, aren't you?" she said bitterly. "They let him die a year ago."

"Who let him die?"

"Sad excuses for friends, that's who," she said. "Let him drive after he'd been drinking. And that girl. Chief's kid. Teddy was too good for her."

"They were all in the car with him when he crashed."

"Of course they were," she said, her voice rising. "But only my boy died! Teodor was a good Polish boy. He deserved better." Her hand trembled as she raised the glass to her lips, water nearly sloshing over the rim before she took a sip. "He was the only family I had left. If they were real friends, they would have kept him out of that car…"

"I'm sorry for your loss."

She was quiet for a time and Sam debated excusing himself, but just as he was about to stand, she began to speak again.

"He loved that car," she said. "That's all his father had to leave him. When Piotr, my son, bought that car, I thought it was a waste of money. But he rebuilt it, piece by piece. Took him years. A labor of love. And Teodor took real good care of it until…"

"It was a horrible accident."

"Horrible for Teodor," she said. "His so-called friends walked away from it."

"I understand they were all injured."

She scoffed with a dismissive wave of her hand.

"Injuries? More like inconveniences. And they got off with a slap on the wrist. That girl, she has connections. Father's the police chief. Special treatment for her. And for those boys—"

"You are aware that Steve Bullinger and Tony Lacosta are both dead?"

"What? Dead?" She frowned at him. "How should I know? I don't read the papers and the TV news is too depressing. Why should I watch?"

"They were both killed by a hit-and-run driver."

"Ha! Imagine that," she said, shaking her head. "Like that old movie, *The Postman Always Rings Twice*. Maybe they should have died in the accident that killed my Teodor. What's that they say? Living on borrowed time."

"The same car hit both of them. Tony last night. Steve the night before."

"What? You think I did it? I don't drive no more. Take the bus or bum a ride."

Sam leaned forward. "The odd thing is," he said and watched her reaction. "The car that hit them was a '68 Charger. Red with a white stripe down the hood."

She looked puzzled, frowning again. "Teodor's car?"

"Identical."

"Impossible," she said. "The car was wrecked. Dumped in a junkyard. Saw it with my own two eyes. I went down there, to claim it... but it was a mess. There's no one to rebuild it anymore."

"Can you think of anyone who would want revenge?"

"I was his only family," she said. "And I'm in no condition to run down a bunch of teenaged hooligans."

"Other friends?"

"He had a blind spot for those three. Wasn't anybody else," she said. "I'm the only one who cares that Teodor's gone."

"Lucy Quinn cared for him a great deal."

"I'm sure that's what she tells everyone," the old woman said dismissively. "It's all about sympathy for her."

A coughing fit seized her, turning her pale, lined face beet red.

As Sam started to rise, she waved him off and drank some water.

Sam lowered himself in the chair. He reached for the framed photo on the table, turned it toward him and looked closer: A smiling woman with graying hair stood next to a teenaged boy in a shirt and tie in front of a church.

"Is this you with Teodor?" Sam asked, startled.

"Of course it is."

"When was this picture taken?"

"About… eighteen months ago," she said. "That girl took it, after she came to church with us. Kissing up, was all that was. But it's a good picture of Teodor."

"Yes," Sam said slowly, setting it down. "Yes, it is…"

The woman in the photo was hardly recognizable as the person sitting across from him. Tragedy and illness and stress had a way of aging people beyond their years, but the effect in this case was extreme. In eighteen months, Olga Kucharski looked as if she'd aged twenty-five years.

Something occurred to Sam, but he'd have to approach it delicately.

"How was your relationship with Teodor?"

"Fine," she said proudly. "We were family. The only family each of us had. We took care of each other."

"You'd make sure he went to school, did his schoolwork, got plenty of sleep."

"Of course."

"And he'd make sure you were taking care of yourself."

"Naturally," she said. "I'm sometimes forgetful. He'd remind me to take my medicine."

"Exactly," Sam said. "Family taking care of family."

"That's how it is," she said, nodding. "You have any family?"

"A brother."

"Then you know."

Sam nodded. "So Teodor would make sure you had regular checkups."

"Of course," she said. "He would drive me wherever I needed to go."

"But now you have to remember all that stuff on your own," Sam said. "For instance, when was the last time you saw your doctor."

"I stopped going to the doctor," she said with a bitter laugh. "When I lost Teddy, it didn't matter no more. Who cares what happens to a lonely old woman?"

"You must have friends here. Neighbors."

"It's not the same," she said with another flick of her hand. "Besides, the only doctor I need, I see every night."

"I'm sorry?"

"Heh! All right, c'mon, I'll show you."

As she painfully pushed herself up out of her chair, Sam rose to help her. But again she refused any assistance. Once on her feet, she paused to catch her breath and took another quick sip of water. Breathing audibly, almost with a wheeze, she walked back down the narrow hallway. Instead of heading to the door, she turned right into a dark living room with a twenty-seven inch television, a threadbare green-checked sofa behind a small coffee table, and a worn recliner with an antimacassar draped over the headrest. Beside the recliner, which was pointed toward the television set, a small table held a lamp, a remote control, and a folded newspaper TV schedule.

"I don't sleep good," she said. "Not since Teodor's passing. Toss and turn in my bed, so I come down and watch television until I nod off. He's on late at night, when I can't sleep."

As Olga Kucharski approached the TV, Sam's gaze drifted across the walls and discovered more than two dozen photos of Teodor Kucharski. From baby photos through high school, it was possible to trace the growth and development of the woman's grandson. He imagined that most of the photos had gone up on the walls after the boy's death, making the room a shrine, each age in each photo a memory trigger for her to recall a different time in Teodor's life. On top of the television, a more recent photo was bracketed by two glass vases filled with flowers about as fresh as the bouquet in the kitchen.

She probably brings home fresh flowers from the supermarket each week, he thought. He was reminded of the garment factory fire memorial, a communal mourning, shared by the whole town. But here, in this house, Olga Kucharski battled her grief alone.

"Started watching him every night. A habit. Now he's like an old friend. And he's from Clayton Falls. Met him once, at the movie rental place over in the strip mall downtown. That's where I got this," she said, pointing to a spot on the wall above the television. Or, more specifically, a framed eight-by-ten photo. The only picture in the room not of her grandson.

Sam stepped forward to examine the subject in the glossy publicity photo: a man theatrically costumed as a mad scientist. Probably in his mid-sixties—though his zombie makeup made his true age hard to guess—the man had a shock of white hair and startled-wide eyes. He wore a long white PVC lab coat smeared with stage blood. In one hand he held an Erlenmeyer flask filled with neon-green fluid emitting tendrils of white smoke. The other hand gestured at the improbable concoction as if to announce to the world that he'd finally made his deranged breakthrough, a B-movie lunatic's eureka moment.

"He's Polish, too," Mrs. Kucharski said as Sam examined the photo. "I had him sign his real name: Jozef Wieczorek. I knew it because of an article in the paper. Most people just know him by his TV name. Since Teodor died, he's the only 'doctor' I need."

Sam looked at the bottom of the photo, where the guy's character name was preprinted in dripping blood-red script letters.

TWENTY-ONE

"Dr. Gruesome?" Dean asked. "Seriously?"

"Well, that's not his real name," Senior Officer Carleen Phillips said.

She stood next to Dean in the small break room, on the other side of the coffee station, sipping her steaming mug o' joe as if it wasn't also burning a hole through her stomach lining. Dean wasn't so fortunate. The stuff was foul.

"Read it once. Hard to remember or pronounce."

Jeffries smiled. "And Dr. Gruesome rolls off the tongue."

"This *Nightmare Theater* is real?"

"Sure," Jeffries said. "On the air a couple years now. Late-night horror movies. Mostly old stuff. Dr. Gruesome comments during the commercial breaks."

"And he lives here in town?"

"Yeah, but you might not recognize him without the mad scientist getup and zombie makeup."

Dean glanced up at the TV mounted on an adjustable

metal arm in the corner of the break room.

"You have a guide for that?" he asked.

"Sure," Phillips said. "There it is. On top of the microwave. But the show's not on now."

Dean grabbed the thin newsprint *TV Weekly* magazine and flipped to the listing for the previous night, then the night before, working his way back to the start of the week.

"I'll be damned," he whispered. He looked up at the two cops. "I need to talk to this guy."

"You know who you should ask?" Phillips said. "Millie, our dispatcher. Dr. Gruesome's her cousin."

"That's right," Jeffries said. "She'll have his address or phone number."

Dean tossed the magazine on the table and hurried toward the lobby exit.

Jeffries called after him.

"You don't think he's a terrorist, do you?"

Hurrying across Main Street toward the Impala parked in the municipal lot, Dean called Sam on his cell phone.

"Sam, I got something."

"Me too," Sam said. "Pick me up at Olga Kuchkarski's."

Dean retraced his route and found Sam standing impatiently at the curb.

Once Sam was inside the car, he said, "She's not directly involved. Seemed genuinely surprised Bullinger and Lacosta were dead. But she has a connection to somebody who may be behind this. Even has a photo of him in the middle of dozens of her grandson."

"Let me guess," Dean said. "Dr. Gruesome."

"What? How did you—?"

"TV host for a show called—"

"*Nightmare Theater.*"

"Right. I flipped through the TV listings for the week," Dean said. "Know what I found?"

"Movies this week featured a headless horseman, a giant Gila monster and a giant tarantula." Off Dean's surprised look, Sam added, "Mrs. Kucharski's a big fan of the show. I checked her guide."

"I got us one thing, you didn't," Dean said with a wry smile.

"What's that?"

"An appointment," Dean said. "Of sorts."

"How?"

"Talked to Cousin Millie."

Dean glanced at the address Millie had written on a sticky note.

"Should be right up ahead," Dean said. "Dr. Gruesome, a.k.a. Jozef Wieczorek, rents studio time here."

He parked the Impala in the lot behind a long redbrick building that—according to the sign in the front lawn—housed the headquarters of the local cable company. The Winchester brothers approached the rear door which was protected by an overhang the width of an umbrella. Though the door had a keypad and card reader, Dean gave the handle a tug. Locked.

"State your business," a voice squawked from a speaker above the keypad.

Sam noticed a security camera mounted above the door. He took out his FBI credentials and held them close to the camera lens.

Dean pressed a black button above the speaker.

"FBI. Agents DeYoung and Shaw. We have an appointment to see Jozef—Dr. Gruesome."

A moment later the door buzzed.

Dean grabbed the handle and pulled it open.

They entered a battleship-gray lobby with a scuffed gray linoleum floor. Several molded gray plastic chairs lined the near wall, positioned on either side of a small gray table piled with jumbled newspapers Dean had the impression that all color had suddenly been leached out of the world. On the far side of the lobby, a security guard with droopy eyes, bushy sideburns and a noticeable beer gut sat inside what looked like a bulletproof glass booth.

"Guarding the crown jewels in here?" Dean said in an undertone to Sam.

The guard leaned forward and spoke into a microphone. His gravelly voice came through speakers mounted at the top of the glass booth.

"Down the hall, first right. Studio's second door on your left. If the red light is on above the door, wait until it goes off."

After those terse instructions, the guard pressed a button on his console. The inner door, adjacent to the guard booth, buzzed. Dean stepped forward and opened it.

"Have a wonderful day," Dean said before letting the door close behind him and Sam. Guy gave good directions, Dean thought. In a few moments, they reached the studio door where a red light mounted atop it was indeed aglow.

Beneath the light, with her back pressed to the door, stood a frazzled-looking woman in her mid-thirties holding a clipboard in her crossed arms. As they approached, she turned her head toward them.

"Agents DeYoung and Shaw," Dean said.

"Just a minute or two," she said.

"Dr. Gruesome in there?" Sam asked.

"Redoing a few prerecorded bits. Perfectionist."

"And you are?" Sam asked.

"Sandy DeSio, his producer, technical director, sometimes scriptwriter, and occasional director. Most of us juggle multiple crew positions."

"Is the show national?" Sam asked.

"He's national," she said, "If you get NMC in your cable or satellite package."

"No offense," Sam said. "But I've never heard of Dr. Gruesome or *Nightmare Theater*."

"*Nightmare Theater* isn't a show, per se," she said. "NMC's a twenty-four hour movie channel. They were airing old horror movies late night and decided they needed to add some, I don't know, pizzazz. Joe—Jozef—has a friend at NMC. Found out what they were looking for, sent an audition tape and got the job. We prescreen the movies and record a series of interstitials that play during commercial breaks."

"Interstitials?" Dean asked.

"Basically, short commentaries on what's happening in the movie as we go into and come out of commercial breaks. We tape fifteen to twenty bits for each movie, about twenty to thirty minutes of material, depending on the runtime of the movie."

"So it's like the viewer is watching the movie with Dr. Gruesome," Sam said.

"Exactly," Sandy said. "Technically, Dr. Gruesome is presenting the movie. Then he makes comments on it throughout. With a mad zombie scientist as your host, it's obviously cheesy and campy, but the ratings improved about twenty percent with the segments."

Sam turned to Dean. "Olga Kucharski said Dr. Gruesome had become like a friend."

"That's especially true of his fans in Clayton Falls," Sandy said. "Home town celebrity. Local pride."

"Mad scientist next door," Dean said.

"Right," Sandy said, forcing a smile. "All in fun."

"You have no idea."

Off her confused look, Dean pointed above her head to where the red light bulb had gone dark.

"Oh, right," she said with a quick smile. "Cute. Let's go."

They followed her inside the studio. A control room behind glass on their right faced three cameras on wheeled tripods focused on the mad scientist laboratory set, which consisted of a single three-walled room. The walls were covered with a faux stone texture. The broad side of a lab table occupied the foreground, its surface covered with various beakers and flasks and test tubes filled with multi-colored liquids, and a Bunsen burner. Mounted to the walls was a steampunk-inspired network of glass tubes and meters attached to polished brass and iron piping, wheels, gears and levers. In keeping with the intent of a show called *Nightmare Theater*, the sprawling contraption looked functional and slightly ominous. But everything that looked metallic was, in all likelihood, painted plastic.

Two camera operators huddled around a short bald man wearing a headset.

"Al Dornfeld, our floor director," Sandy said as she led them toward the man in zombie makeup wearing smudged goggles pushed up on his forehead, a white PVC lab coat and black gloves that extended to his elbows. "And this… is our star, Dr. Gruesome."

The man pulled off his gloves and offered his hand.

"Call me Joe," he said with a pleasant smile that ruined the zombie effect. "I'm only a mad scientist returned from the dead by his own diabolical experiments while the cameras are on."

"Agents DeYoung and Shaw," Dean said.

"Right," Wieczorek said, "FBI. I can't imagine why, but Millie said you had some questions for me."

"Hold that thought for a second," Sandy said. "Joe, I'll need to talk to you about scheduling when you're through with these gentlemen." She patted him on the shoulder before walking to the control room.

"Sure, Sandy," Wieczorek called after her. Then he whispered to the Winchesters, "I know I drive her crazy sometimes. But it's my reputation on the air. My brand."

"Mr. Wiec—Joe," Sam said, "Are you aware of what's happening in town?"

"This show keeps me busy," Wieczorek said. "We're on

every night. So I don't often catch the news or read the paper. But I heard something about storm damage, power outages, and a big sinkhole at a convenience store—the Qwik Mart. And a hit and run. Two in two days. Awful. Oh, and somebody said a man died falling out of a tree."

"The man was killed by the tree," Dean said.

"Not the fall? I'm afraid I don't understand."

"The tree stabbed the man."

"My hearing's not what it was," he said. "Did you just say a 'tree stabbed a man?'"

"With a branch," Dean said. "But that's not why we're here."

"Thank heavens," he said. "Why are you here?"

"Several police officers, Agent DeYoung and I witnessed other incidents last night that have a connection to your show," Sam said. "A man was killed by a giant tarantula. The night before, another man was attacked by a giant Gila monster. That same night, three teens were chased by a headless horseman."

As Sam spoke, Wieczorek's smile faltered and faded, but then his eyes widened and he chuckled, clapping his hands together in delight.

"Okay, this is somebody's idea of a joke, right? Hidden camera. It's Sandy getting payback, right?"

"No joke," Dean said. "Two local men witnessed the tarantula attack."

Again, Wieczorek's smiled faded by degrees, a bit faster this time. He looked from Dean to Sam and back again.

"Either you have the best poker faces I've ever seen or... You *are* serious."

He reached a hand out sideways and grabbed the edge of the laboratory table for support, then took a deep breath.

"These are popcorn movies, harmless entertainment..." he said. "I don't understand. This stuff isn't real. It can't be real. It's pure fantasy."

"Something is making it become real," Sam said.

"And we need to know if that something is you," Dean added.

"Me? How could I...? How could anyone...?"

"Have you met anyone unusual lately?" Sam asked. "Found a strange old coin? Come across a peculiar antique? Received an odd inheritance?"

"What? No. Nothing like that. This is a daily routine for me. Screen the movies, work up the script for the interstitials, makeup and props, rehearse, record, edit. On television it may all look strange and surreal, but for us it's... routine. Mundane, even."

Dean looked at Sam. "You got any ideas?"

Sam nodded, turned to Wieczorek. "Do you remember a woman name Olga Kucharski?"

"Olga... Olga Kucharski? No. Should I...?" He snapped his fingers. "Wait—Olga—is she an older woman? Ha! Look who's talking? No spring chicken myself. But I do remember a woman from one of my personal appearances. Very much into her Polish heritage. Seemed delighted to learn I was Polish too. Had me sign my full name on a publicity photo. Said it would have a place of honor in her home."

"That would be the lady," Sam said. "Have you had any other dealings with her?"

"Dealings? No, nothing. She's a fan of the show. Said she watches every night." He shrugged. "I believe that appearance was the one and only time I ever met her. But she did leave an impression."

Dean looked at Sam, who gave him a barely perceptible shrug. They were both stumped.

"Just out of curiosity, Doc," Dean said. "What movie are you working on now?"

Wieczorek beamed. "Ah, a wonderfully cheesy, space invasion flick. About aliens with lobster-claw hands that crack open human skulls and suck out the brains with their tentacle-like proboscis."

"You gotta be kidding me," Dean said.

"How do we kill them?" Sam asked.

"If I tell you, it will spoil the movie."

Dean rolled his eyes. "We don't care about the friggin' movie!"

"Oh, of course," Wieczorek said and frowned. "They're bulletproof, because of their exoskeletons. So the National Guard kills them with flamethrowers. Cooks them, actually. Ends with a joke about lobster bibs."

Dean turned to Sam. "Dude, we've got zero flamethrowers in the Impala."

"We'll improvise," Sam said. "Aerosol cans and cigarette lighters."

"Wait," Wieczorek said, catching Sam's arm. "How do you believe these movie creations become real?"

"People have nightmares," Sam said. "The nightmares manifest in town somewhere."

Wieczorek looked as if he wanted to request a thorough examination of their FBI credentials, but then decided against it.

"Even if that is somehow possible, the aliens won't be a problem."

"How so?" Dean asked.

"We tape our interstitials a week ahead," he explained. "Nobody will see this movie until next Saturday."

"Good," Sam said. "One less nightmare scenario to worry about."

"Unless, of course, somebody in my crew has a nightmare about it."

"Great," Dean said.

"I wouldn't worry. We watch the movies so many times while working on our scripts that they lose any shock value they might have," Wieczorek said. "If anybody here has a nightmare, it would be about working overtime or not making a deadline."

"Thanks for your help," Sam said. "Wait. What's tonight's feature?"

"Oh, yes! Wolves."

"Werewolves?" Dean asked apprehensively.

"No, regular wolves," Wieczorek said. "Maybe a bit large. And there's a pack of them. And… they're all rabid. They invade a small town and rip…"

"We get the idea," Dean said. "Thanks."

As the Winchesters walked toward the studio door, Wieczorek called out for them to wait. They stopped and turned back.

"Listen, I can't help but think how crazy this all sounds," he said. "And I promise you we have not changed our routine at all. I can't imagine a scenario where what you say is even possible…"

"Your point?" Dean asked.

"If what you say is true, and I have no reason to doubt you, I can't ignore the fact that something unexplainable is happening and that it is somehow connected to my show. A man attacked by a giant tarantula…"

"Want to see police report photos of the half-eaten victim?"

"That's quite all right," Wieczorek said. "I'm trying to say that I feel partly responsible for whatever is happening here. I want to help, but…" He raised his shoulders, hands spread. "I'm not sure what I can do."

"You want to help?" Dean said. "Convince NMC not to run the wolf movie."

"Not run it?"

"Preempt it," Sam said. "With *Lassie Come Home* or something?"

Wieczorek pursed his lips. "I'll try. But I don't know if they'll believe me. Or listen. Maybe they can black out this market."

"Do what you can," Dean said.

"I will," he said. "But the nature of nightmares is that they linger."

"We know," Sam said.

"Oh, and I'll talk to Millie," Wieczorek said. "She'll have a record of all the emergency calls. Maybe that will help."

"Knock yourself out," Dean said.

His mind had already leapt ahead, considering the likelihood that he and Sam would be shooting rabid wolves in several hours. At least wolves—unlike lobster-clawed aliens—weren't immune to bullets. As they exited the studio, Dean looked back and saw Sandy rejoin Wieczorek, handing him a towel to begin removing his makeup. The old man stared after the Winchesters, but his gaze seemed unfocused, lost in thought, a pensive zombie.

Dean and Sam retraced their steps to the lobby.

"You got anything?" Dean asked. "'Cause I got nothing."

"Whatever is happening, it's connected to Dr. Gruesome's show and Olga Kucharski," Sam said. "The Gila monster, the headless horseman, and the Charger started this. If those two are not directly involved, something is using them."

"What about the Raptors? And the sinkhole. And Nazi zombies?"

"Like he said, nightmares linger," Sam said. "We only checked one week of TV listings. Maybe movies about that stuff aired two weeks ago. Or… maybe not. I don't know."

Exiting the building proved much simpler than entering. The droopy-eyed security guard barely looked up as they passed through the lobby and stepped outside. Sam paused and looked at Dean over the roof of the Impala.

"I've got an idea."

"All ears, Sammy."

"Let's go with the premise that Olga Kucharski is patient zero."

"Okay."

"The most significant event in her life is the death of her grandson," Sam said. "And two of the people who were with him when he died have been killed by the nightmare car."

"Right," Dean said. "So we're back to her?"

Sam shook his head. "Not directly. But something triggered this. Something about that accident. But I'm missing something."

"Sounds like research dead ahead."

"I'll call Bobby. Get him working the nightmare angle."

"Good."

"Then I need you to drop me off at the *Fremont Ledger*," Sam said. "The online archives are a bit thin. I want to check back issues in their morgue, dating back to the accident."

"Watch out for that reporter—Nash," Dean said. "Last thing we need is our pictures all over the paper."

"Right."

"While you're at the *Ledger*, I have something to check out."

"What's that?"

"Last survivor of that car accident," Dean said. "Lucy Quinn. Way I see it, she has a big honkin' bull's eye on her back."

TWENTY-TWO

"I'm surprised you asked me here."

"I'm surprised you came," Dean said, smiling.

"Is this the early bird special?" Sophie Bessette said after taking a cursory glance at the laminated C.J.'s menu she'd plucked from the wire holder next to the paper napkin dispenser.

"I missed lunch," Dean said.

"Don't FBI agents have expense accounts?"

"You know how it is. Budget cutbacks," Dean said. "Besides, I wasn't sure if this was business or pleasure."

"Oh," Sophie said. "Definitely business."

"Too bad," Dean said. "But they have great cheeseburgers here."

"So I've heard," Sophie said. "And yet I've managed to avoid the temptation."

"We're still talking cheeseburgers, right?"

She smiled winsomely. "So far. Yes."

"Good."

"I'm assuming the crisis is not yet past?"

"Unfortunately, no."

Lucy Quinn approached their booth in her C.J.'s Diner navy blue vest with the red buttons, carrying two glasses of water, which she placed in front of them.

"Hello again, Agent DeYoung. Are you both ready to order?"

Sophie cleared her throat. "You serve salads?"

"House salad," Lucy said with a slight shrug. "It's okay. Nothing to write home about."

"That will be fine," Sophie said. "Vinaigrette. On the side."

"Cheeseburger and fries," Dean said. "Lady doesn't know what she's missing."

Lucy smiled, pulled a pen and order pad from a side pocket in her vest and scrawled down their order quickly.

"Any appetizers?" she asked. When they declined, she said, "Okay. That'll be a few minutes. Or do you want the salad brought out right away?"

"Together is fine," Sophie said.

After Lucy left the booth, Dean said, "She look familiar?"

"Yes," Sophie said. "I believe she's the daughter of the chief of police."

"Know her any other way?"

"No," Sophie said, eyeing him suspiciously. "What are you suggesting?"

Dean reached into the inside pocket of his jacket and pulled out a list of names he'd written down while waiting for her to show up at the diner. Unfolding the paper, he placed it on the table, flattened the creases and turned it so she could read the names.

"Is this a list of terror suspects?" she asked him, intrigued.

"No. I mean, probably not."

"Then what?"

"Look, I know you're worried about patient confidentiality, so I want you to look at those names and let me know if any are familiar."

"I can't say I'm comfortable with this."

"Read the list," Dean said. "If you don't know any of the names, fine."

"And if any of them *are* familiar?"

"I could get a court order," Dean said. "But let's cross that bridge when it's time to blow it up."

She sighed. "You realize I don't treat patients personally? Half of these people could have been patients at Restful Sleep and I'd be oblivious."

"I find that hard to believe."

"Believe what you want," she said, but she examined the names, running her manicured index finger down the list slowly enough that Dean knew she was making an honest effort. He watched that finger closely, looking for any telltale pauses beside any particular name, but each one received equal treatment. "No," she said, eventually. "None of these names are familiar."

"Worth a shot."

"Who are they?"

"Witnesses and victims," Dean said. Lucy Quinn was the only name he'd left off the list. All along, he'd planned on watching Sophie's reaction to Lucy in person. But her reaction—or non-reaction—had told him nothing.

After Lucy had set down their plates and walked away, Dean said, "Guess this is pleasure after all."

"You wish," Sophie said, but smiled affably as she picked at her lettuce.

Hoping Sam was having better luck with newspaper research, Dean tore into his cheeseburger with gusto. *She really doesn't know what she's missing,* he thought. And he was still referring to the cheeseburger.

Appropriately enough, the morgue of the *Fremont Ledger* was located in the basement of the newspaper office building. A clerk helped Sam locate the year-old issues of the newspaper, which had been converted to microfiche. Sam started two weeks before the accident that killed Teodor Kucharski, in case anything unusual had precipitated the crash. But there we no mentions of the boy or his grandmother in any of the local stories.

The day after the accident, the coverage was minimal. Police blotter details. Nothing more. In the days that followed, a few human interest stories appeared, some with reprinted photos of Olga Kucharski and her grandson. Again, Sam marveled that he was looking at photos of the same feeble and sickly woman he'd interviewed a couple of hours ago. The Olga Kucharski in the newspaper photos looked young enough to be her daughter. A sympathetic reporter had interviewed her after the accident to delve into Teodor's character and personality, and she referred to him as a "good Polish boy" more than once in the interview. The reporter had commented on the pride she had in her Polish heritage and how she'd lost her husband to illness before immigrating to the United States.

Photos at the crash scene showed the totaled Charger, crumpled like an accordion. Looking at the wreck, Sam shook his head. Hard to believe the other three teens had survived the crash.

Other newspaper stories dealt with the issue of driving while intoxicated and underage alcohol consumption, drifting from human interest to op-ed. Teodor had become a grim cautionary tale for the youth of Clayton Falls. Less than two weeks after the accident, however, the press coverage ended. Sam skimmed through a month's worth of microfiche after the last article and found nothing else about Olga or her grandson. Seemed like Teodor Kucharski had been dismissed from the public consciousness.

The microfiche archive began six months back. According to the clerk, anything more recent would be converted to digital records in parallel with microfiche but neither was available yet.

Sam pulled hard copies from the time of the Clayton Falls Apparel Company fire. Almost three dozen employees had died in the fire. The press coverage was extensive. Front-page stories about the explosion that led to the fire, the malfunction of the sprinkler system, the investigation into the cause and culpability of the fire, inspection records, capsule biographies of all the victims. Days and weeks after the fire, longer human interest pieces, detailed profiles of the victims, basically mini biographies covering the entire span of their lives.

Sam skipped forward weeks and months and found more human interest articles. How families continued to cope with the loss, how they had changed their lives in the wake of the deaths, changed priorities, sons and daughters returned home from college, or changed courses of study, volunteered to help with burn victims, and one high school senior had decided to become a doctor. These articles turned into calls for a memorial, public debate on the memorial's location and design and when it would be constructed and dedicated, and whether the ruins of the factory would be razed or preserved or rebuilt as a church or a community center.

During this last batch of articles Sam caught up to the online archive he'd reviewed before he and Dean arrived in town. He returned the hard copies to their shelves and left the building, thanking the helpful clerk on his way out.

If he looked at the town's reaction to the two tragedies from Olga Kucharski's perspective, Sam could understand how she'd feel Teodor had been forgotten. For the last six months, the town had shared a communal grief that excluded her because her personal grief had become too isolating.

The living nightmares had begun on the one-year anniversary of her grandson's death. An anniversary forgotten or ignored by everyone but Olga Kucharski. At least that's how it would seem to the old woman. The living nightmares, however, could not be ignored. They would continue to grab and hold the town's attention. And that's why Sam kept returning to her, his patient zero. But if Olga had triggered the living nightmares, he was pretty sure she'd done so unintentionally—or subconsciously.

Two things had been the focus of her life. Her grandson and her heritage. The *Fremont Ledger* reporter had noticed it, as had Sam, from the moment he entered her house and saw the Lech Walesa portrait, the map of Poland and the entire bookcase of volumes on…

Cell phone in hand, Sam stopped at the bottom of the stairs of the *Fremont Ledger* building.

Across the street was the Clayton Falls Public Library.

Pocketing his cell, he crossed the street to the single-story white stone building. As he walked up to the entrance, he saw a brunette in a gray business suit standing with her back to him at the door. He heard a metallic click and realized two things simultaneously: she was the librarian and she'd just locked up for the day.

She dropped her keys in her pocketbook, turned around and emitted a startled squeal when she saw him standing there.

"You scared me!" she cried.

"Sorry," Sam said. "Bad timing. I need to get in there."

"Really bad timing," she said. "We closed an hour ago. I was cleaning up after everyone left."

Sam pulled out his FBI credentials. "It's a matter of life and death."

The woman smiled. "Has that line ever been used in the history of law enforcement in reference to a library?"

Sam shrugged. "First time for everything."

"If nothing else, this will make a great article for the library newsletter," she said as she plucked her keys out and unlocked the door. She held it open for him and followed him inside. "How can I help?"

"Do you have any books on Poland?" Sam said. "More specifically, Polish legends and folklore?"

"We have a few books on Poland, some related to World War II," she said, leading him through the aisles and pointing to the appropriate sections as she spoke. "Any books on myths, folklore, and legend would be in a different section."

Sam pulled four volumes on world folklore and legend from the shelves—one title matched a book he'd seen on Olga Kucharski's bookcase—and carried them back to a long table in front of the checkout counter with a row of four computers connected to the internet.

The librarian grabbed the chair at the end of the table and turned it to face him. She sat down with her legs crossed, chin on her palm.

"Sir, as a librarian I am very curious how these books have the ability to save lives. I'm Vickie Steuber, by the way, branch manager."

Sam spoke absently as he checked the index of each of the books.

"My partner and I are investigating the unusual incidents happening in town," he said. "We believe something... unnatural is responsible."

"Unnatural? As in supernatural?"

"Yes." Sam flipped to pages referenced in the indexes, finding some spotty information, but enough to convince him he was on the right track.

"Interesting," she said. "I've heard some admittedly strange stories about last night. Didn't give them much credence.

"You should."

"Are you saying it's going to happen again?"

"Unless we figure out how to stop it," Sam said. "Tonight will be worse."

The librarian's casually curious attitude evaporated. "How much worse?"

"Go home," Sam said. "Lock your doors and windows until morning."

"Oh…"

Sam tapped the keyboard of the nearest computer. A login screen appeared.

"How do I…?" he began.

"Login as guest," she said. "Password is also guest. All lowercase."

Sam logged in and opened a web browser to run a search. He selected blocks of text and sent them to the printer at the end of the table. Frowning, he closed the browser, stood up, and pulled out his cell phone to dial Dean.

When Dean picked up, he said, "I know what we're up against. Pick me up at the library. Across the street from the *Ledger*."

To afford Sam privacy while he made his call, Vickie Steuber had wandered toward the front of the library. Staring through the floor-to-ceiling windows, she crossed her arms and shuddered. Sam walked up beside her.

"It will be dark soon," she said.

"Do you have a ride?"

"The ten-year-old white Corolla in the parking lot is mine," she said. "Very reliable."

"Good," Sam said. "Remember what I said and you should be safe."

"Even as a child," she said, "I was never afraid of the dark."

"Not too late to start."

TWENTY-THREE

Pausing at the passenger door of the Impala, Sam nodded to Vickie Steuber as she pulled out of the library lot in her Corolla. Judging by her pale face and wide eyes, Sam was confident she'd make a beeline for home. Other than leaving town, the next safest option for her should be inside her own home. Although that hadn't helped Max Barnes.

"Find something in the *Ledger*'s morgue?" Dean asked.

"More like what I didn't find," Sam said. "Brief coverage of Teddy's accident a year ago. Nothing since. But the garment factory fire is still the subject of stories six months later. In Olga's eyes, everyone has forgotten about her grandson."

"So patient zero is a suspect again."

"Not intentionally," Sam said. "Not consciously. It's more complicated than that. I think she… called it. Subconsciously. In her own nightmares."

"Called what?"

"Nocnitsa," Sam said. "The night hag in Polish mythology.

A nightmare spirit. It's known for tormenting children."

"Like the Barnes kid."

Sam nodded. "Dean, it drains life energy. Looking at pictures of Olga from a year ago compared to how she looks now. Like the thing has aged her twenty-five years."

"So it's feeding off her and creating these living nightmares."

"Who knows? Maybe Eve used something like nocnitsa to generate some of the monsters that hunters have been killing for hundreds, maybe thousands of years."

"A mobile monster factory."

"And it feeds off of emotional darkness," Sam said. "Depression and sadness make it stronger, more powerful."

"This town must be like a friggin' smorgasbord."

"A vicious circle," Sam said. "More death and destruction, more negative emotions to feed it."

"Perfect storm," Dean said, nodding. "How do we recognize it?"

"It's made of shadows, with glowing red eyes."

"Shadows? How do we gank it?"

"Supposedly not fond of iron."

"So we attack random shadows with iron? Hope for the best?"

"Sorry, Dean," Sam said. "That's all I could find in the library and online. Soon as I figured out the nocnitsa was involved, I called Bobby again. He'd already locked onto the night hag as a possibility but has no new information. Promised he'd keep looking."

"Dude, it's almost evening. We're running short on time here."

"While we're waiting, I know where we can get our hands on some iron."

The shadows stretched long and had begun to fade as Dean hacksawed another wrought-iron post from the collapsed fence around the hulking remains of the Clayton Falls Apparel Company. Once the posts were freed from the panel, they cut them in half, about the length of a sawed-off shotgun. Since the posts had ornamental points that resembled spearheads, they made serviceable stabbing weapons.

"This site is responsible for most of the negative emotions feeding the nocnitsa," Sam said. "These fence posts might turn that negative energy against it."

Dean hefted one of the posts, practiced thrusting it forward with one hand and then both hands.

"Olga called this thing in her sleep?" he asked.

"Maybe that's the only way somebody can call it," Sam said. "It speaks nightmares. Olga has bottled-up rage, an unspoken desire for revenge, and sees only injustice where her grandson's friends are concerned. Subconsciously, I think she... vented. She wanted them punished. She's read all those books on the history and folklore of Poland, probably multiple times."

"So subconsciously, she hired a monster hit man—hit woman? This night hag?"

They returned to the Impala, each holding a pointed half-post.

"Maybe that's how it works," Sam said. "That's its currency. You feed it, and it does the dirty work."

"Came for the cake, stayed for the negative emotion party."

"She's a stubborn old woman," Sam said. "But on a conscious level, she has no idea what's happening. She's sickly and blames aging. Bitter but blames karma for what happened to Bullinger and Lacosta."

Dean tossed the hacksaw in the trunk of the Impala, slammed the lid shut.

Sam's cell phone rang.

"Bobby," Sam said after checking the display. He put the call on speaker and walked toward Dean. "Bobby, you find anything?"

"Lore's a little light on this one, boys."

Dean frowned. "You called to tell us you got nothing?"

"No, ya idjit," Bobby said. "Of course I got something."

"Let's hear it," Sam said.

"Everything I found says this nocnitsa is made of shadows…"

Dean mouthed the word "nothing" and Sam shook him off.

"But I found a pattern," Bobby said. "If two cases make a pattern."

"What is it?"

"Both times a hunter went up against a nocnitsa, the thing was feeding."

"She takes solid form to feed?"

"Best guess," Bobby said. "And she only feeds when her victim is sleeping."

"We gotta gank her red-handed?" Dean said.

"Job was easy, boy, everybody'd do it."

"Doubt that, Bobby," Dean said.

"Quit yer bitchin' and listen."

"You got more?" Sam asked.

"What I gather, if you don't end this thing, the nightmare manifestations will outlast the nightmares that spawned them, take on a life of their own. Phrase 'eternal night' keeps popping up. And not like it's a good thing."

"How much longer before that happens?"

"Rate this thing is powering up? Better kill her tonight or there won't be a town left to save."

With Dean driving east along Welker, Sam said, "Our best chance—maybe our only chance—at catching this thing feeding is at Olga Kucharski's house."

"Why there?"

"She starts there," Sam said. "Hasn't finished her original mission."

"Lucy Quinn."

"Last one left," Sam said. "After that, the night hag could go anywhere."

"We can't kill it unless it's feeding," Dean said. "By the time that happens, the Charger will be back, gunning for Lucy."

Sam nodded. "She'll be a sitting duck."

"We split up," Dean said. "I bodyguard Lucy, you wait at Olga's for feeding time."

Dean dropped Sam off near the Kucharski residence and then drove to C.J.'s Diner to keep an eye on Lucy Quinn. When he'd left to pick up Sam at the library, Sophie Bessette left as well. Dean had advised her to go home, but

she flashed a mysterious smile and gave him a little wave
goodbye without revealing her intentions. Lucy, however,
hadn't finished her shift and had promised to hang around
until Dean gave the all-clear.

He pulled into the diner's crowded parking lot and hurried
inside. Betsy had taken over Lucy's section and navigated
the booths and tables with practiced fluidity. A buzz of
excited conversation filled the air and Dean heard the word
"nightmare" several times as neighbors and acquaintances
compared notes. Dean intercepted Betsy when she returned
to the counter to pick up an order.

"Lucy in the break room?"

"She was," Betsy said. "Got fidgety. Went outside for some
fresh air."

"Crap," Dean said under his breath. He hadn't seen anyone
outside when he parked the Impala. "If she comes back, tell
her to wait here."

"Sure thing, Agent DeYoung," Betsy said and slipped
past him, balancing a large round metal tray filled with
several entrees.

Dusk had transitioned quietly, dangerously, into evening.

When Dean stepped outside, the streetlights were on
and all the passing cars had turned on their headlights.
He walked a circuit around the diner to no avail. At any
minute, anywhere in town, lethal nightmares could be
forming. One of the first ones would be a '68 Dodge
Charger lining up Lucy Quinn in its high beams. And she
was nowhere to be found.

* * *

Sam couldn't take the chance that Olga Kucharski would let him wait in the house while she turned in for the night. She was sick, feeble, and slept fitfully at odd hours. Now that night had fallen, the chances of her falling asleep had increased. And the night hag would be ready. Even if the old woman were amenable, the thought of having a stranger in her home might prevent her from falling asleep. And if she stayed awake, would the nocnitsa wait around? Or move on to another, random, house to feed off a different dreamer? A stealthy approach provided his best chance at catching the night hag feeding. With that in mind he'd brought along a set of lock picks.

Checking the street for pedestrian traffic, Sam slipped along the side of the house and peered through a living-room window. A gap in the blinds revealed a glimpse of Olga Kucharski in her recliner, the TV remote control dangling from her hand at the end of the armrest. The television was on with the sound turned too low to hear through the closed window. Another peek revealed that Olga's eyes were closed. The lamp on the table beside her chair began to flicker. Sam worried the stuttering light would rouse her, but she seemed too tired to react to the shifting shadows. As he watched, a deeper shadow slid down the wall, a shadow whose impenetrable darkness defied the arc of light that intermittently flashed across it. A moment later, the lamp winked off and the ambient light cast from the television set vanished. The room plunged into darkness. At the same moment, the streetlight in front of the house seemed to burn out.

Sam crept back to the front door, knelt in front of the lock and placed his wrought-iron short-spear on the welcome mat, freeing his hands. First he tucked a thin Maglite between his chin and shoulder to illuminate the lock, but the flashlight immediately dimmed until it provided no light. *The night hag*, he guessed, *it's knocked out all electric light*. He'd have to work the lock by feel alone.

Inserting the tension bar in the lock, he applied torque to the cylinder while working the pick to set the pins. He'd had years of practice picking locks. The skill relied on touch and hearing more than sight anyway. In a few seconds, the pins were set and he slowly turned the cylinder, releasing the deadbolt and unlocking the door.

After tucking his lock-pick set in his jacket, he scooped up the short-spear and eased the door inward. If he'd timed it well, Olga was sleeping and the nocnitsa was feeding. But that meant that the phantom Charger would be hunting Lucy.

After pacing in the diner's break room, Lucy Quinn had walked around the parking lot waiting for DeYoung, the shorter FBI agent, to show up. Unable to sit still for more than a couple of minutes, she thought a brisk walk would burn off her nervous energy. But she had walked farther than she intended. As dusk slid into nightfall, she looked up and saw C.J.'s several blocks distant.

Her first thought was to call Agent DeYoung and tell him she'd be there in a couple of minutes, but her cell phone signal strength kept dropping from three bars to none, and each time the display flashed the "no signal" icon, the call disconnected. As she hurried back toward the diner's neon sign, white mist swirled around her shoes, immediately reminding her of the headless horseman in Founders Park and the—

Behind her a car motor revved.

Headlights flipped on, casting her shadow forward.

She looked over her shoulder and recognized the muscle car rumbling in the middle of the road. The car had inhabited her dreams and nightmares for the past year. And she'd watched helplessly as it crushed her friend against his house.

Stunned, she stared at it now and imagined the cherry-red paint had transformed into blood. From what she could tell in the relative darkness, with the headlights glaring at her, the damage Tony's father had inflicted on the Charger was gone, as if the car reset itself each time it appeared. And that made as much sense as the wrecked car returning from the junkyard in pristine condition.

The Charger inched forward. The tires angled toward the sidewalk. Like a predator ready to pounce on overmatched prey.

Keeping her head turned over her shoulder, Lucy began to jog away from the car on a course leading her toward the diner. She should have stayed in the break room and not let anxiety drive her into the night.

Suddenly, the car's tires squealed and the Charger lurched forward with a full-throated roar of its engine. With a shower of sparks, the car jumped the curb and veered toward her.

Lucy sprinted across the street and ducked behind a parked blue Ford Fiesta. But her logic was flawed. Treating the car as if it were directed by a human driver who needed to see her to hit her made no sense. The Charger had appeared out of thin air behind her. It couldn't *see* her. Didn't need to see her. It *knew* where she was.

The engine roared again becoming unbearably loud.

Almost too late, she realized what was about to happen.

Rising from her crouch, she ran alongside the Fiesta a split second before the Charger rammed into the opposite side of it, shoving the smaller car onto the sidewalk as if it had been struck by a jet-powered bulldozer.

Reversing, the Charger spun out into the middle of the street, its grill crushed, both headlights shattered. Shifting into drive again, the Charger raced toward her, angling again for the curb. Lucy screamed and sprinted toward the diner, knowing she was too far away to make it before the Charger struck again.

A shadow darted past her, bright light bobbing at his side. *Agent DeYoung!* she realized.

He heaved his arm forward, throwing something in a blur of golden, flickering light. Glass shattered against the windshield of the Charger, followed by a *whoosh* of sound, and the hood of the car was suddenly awash in flame.

DeYoung spun around, caught her hand and tugged her so hard she almost fell. But she caught her balance and together they raced toward the diner.

"What was that?" she breathed.

"Molotov cocktail," he replied. "When I couldn't find you, thought I should have something prepared."

"Won't help," she said panting.

"What?"

"No driver," she said. "Doesn't need to see."

He looked back and she followed his gaze.

The Charger was burning but continued its relentless pursuit. It veered toward the curb and the tires on the right side lurched over it. Lucy heard a crumpled wheel well rubbing against one of the front tires. Damage sustained from the powerful collision slowed the car's acceleration, buying them a few extra seconds.

But the Charger was gaining fast.

TWENTY-FOUR

Sam closed the door softly behind him.

While feeding off the life energy of Olga Kucharski and generating living nightmares in town, the nocnitsa might not notice his approach, but that was no excuse for carelessness. He might have one chance to kill the night hag. Once it left Olga's house, it could go anywhere and elude Dean and him until dawn, growing more powerful with each passing hour.

Pressed against the wall, he eased forward, the living room through the entranceway on his left. Olga sat on the opposite side of the wall, feeding the monster that was exacting the old woman's revenge, while terrorizing the entire town. Raising his wrought-iron short-spear in a double overhand grip, Sam stepped away from the wall. Though he stood in relative darkness, he remembered the layout of the room, imagined the exact position of the ratty recliner, picturing the table and lamp beside it, the ivory-colored antimacassar on the headrest.

Taking a deep breath, he rushed through the entranceway and struck out with the short-spear, aiming the tip about a foot above the headrest. He overbalanced when the spear tip whistled through the air and took a divot out of the drywall.

Other than the ambient light coming through the edges of the blinds, the only illumination in the living room came from the glowing red eyes of the nocnitsa, from where the monster perched on the left armrest of the recliner, staring at him.

"Too late, hunter," the nocnitsa rasped, like wind given voice.

The monster's body was a deeper black than the darkness she inhabited, presenting a sinuous, three-dimensional silhouette Sam could track, her torso and limbs little more than muscle stretched over a narrow skeleton, with overly long fingers and toes. Though she had stopped feeding, she remained solid, at least for the moment.

"Feeding off a harmless old woman," Sam said, subtly altering his stance to allow for a second quick strike with the iron rod. "Not impressed."

"The choice was hers," the night hag said. As she talked, she moved her hands, fingers hypnotically curling and uncurling like a magician preparing for a demonstration of sleight of hand. "She wanted revenge, prayed for it, *dreamt* about it. That's why I was drawn to her. And what a feast of fearful images she provided!" A long sigh of pleasure escaped the nocnitsa's elongated maw. "But she's dead now."

As if to punctuate those words, the TV remote control slipped from Olga Kucharski's fingers and struck the floor.

The twin burning embers of the nocnitsa's eyes seemed to track the downward movement.

Sam lunged forward, roaring as he swept the point of the wrought-iron short-spear through the night hag's torso. With a sharp hiss, the monster rose toward the ceiling, dissolving into loose shadows like dissipating coils of black smoke. For a moment, Sam thought he'd pierced its solid form, but the monster's head and glowing eyes drifted away from him and it spoke once more.

"I will gorge on this town's darkness. I will feed until no one is left. And there is nothing you or any hunter can do to stop me."

Sam darted around the recliner and swung the short-spear over his head, as if striking a piñata, aiming for the spot between the two glowing red eyes, the last solid remnant of the night hag's body. A desperation move. One he didn't expect to succeed and in that he wasn't surprised.

The burning eyes faded away before the wrought-iron got close.

Sam stumbled forward but caught himself before he crashed into the street-facing window. He turned around as the table lamp and the television came back on. Despite expecting the worst, he was startled by what he saw.

Olga Kucharski's body had been reduced to a desiccated husk with papery, liver-spotted skin stretched taut over her arthritic bones, her head little more than a skull with wisps of gray hair clinging to the sides. Sam feared that if he touched her, she would crumble to dust.

He reached into his jacket for his cell phone.

* * *

Dean was running for his life.

Technically he was running for Lucy Quinn's life, but he had his hand wrapped around hers and if the Charger caught them, it would run them both down. When his Impala had been possessed, it hadn't ended well. Dean was determined to avoid a similar outcome. He looked up and smiled.

"Thank you!"

"What?" Lucy said.

"Get behind that monster," Dean said. "But not too close—and watch out."

Gleaming under a streetlight, a parked mustard-yellow Hummer H2 awaited them.

Lucy ran alongside the formidable SUV and ducked behind it. Dean leapt onto the hood, scrambling up onto the roof, dropping flat as he grabbed the luggage rack and spun himself around to face forward. He whipped out his automatic and fired several shots at the onrushing Charger. The second shot blew out the front passenger tire and the fifth ruptured the driver's side tire.

The Charger's windshield wipers continued to burn, but the flames on the white-striped hood and the windshield itself had burned themselves out. Fortunately, some of the gasoline from the Molotov cocktail had leaked through the gaps in the crumpled hood and smoke billowed out from both sides. The engine was burning.

The racing car chewed through its damaged wheels and surged forward on the rims, striking sparks from the asphalt. Dean braced for impact.

The Charger slammed into the frame-mounted bumper of the Hummer, rocking the much larger car backward but not by much. Nevertheless, the impact hurled Dean forward, wrenching his arm in its socket as he tumbled onto the Hummer's windshield. His grip held and he stared down at the Charger as it reversed a short distance then rammed the Hummer a second time. Flames were spreading under the muscle car and Dean had a bad feeling about the next few seconds.

Pulling himself back to the roof of the Hummer, he raced toward the rear of the SUV and leapt into the darkness, spotting Lucy crouched below as he sailed over her.

He hit the ground on his shoulder and rolled with the impact.

Behind him a concussive roar presaged a blast of open-furnace heat that washed over him as a fireball spread outward and lit the night sky. Metal debris rained down around him, rattling across the road, trailing smoke and—

—vanished in the blink of an eye.

The fiery light winked out and with it the heat was abruptly gone.

Dean's cell phone rang.

Brushing himself off, Dean stood and massaged his sore neck with his free hand as he answered the call. "Sam?"

"Olga's dead," Sam said, his voice dejected.

"The nocnitsa? Tell me you got it."

"Wish I could."

"Son of a bitch," Dean said. "What now?"

"Dean, she's going to kill them all."

"Be there in five minutes," Dean said. "We need a plan."

As Dean and Lucy hurried back to the diner, thunder rumbled ominously and rain began to fall. Dean glanced upward as lightning speared the night sky, leaving stark afterimages on his retinas.

The storm was coming.

As was his custom, Lou Santulli stayed after hours to file paperwork at Santulli Auto Sales, his used car dealership. When he was done, he walked through the place in the dim lighting and checked the desks of his salesman and receptionist, making sure they hadn't left a mess for the morning. Anything to keep himself busy. The longer he stayed at work, the less time he had to listen to his wife's grousing and her never-ending honey-do list. After hours, the dealership was a calm oasis for him to unwind.

Before heading home, he'd play online poker for an hour or two, mostly losing but he kept the losses manageable. The poker was another excuse to stay away from home. Hadn't always been that way, but business had been slow the last couple of years as the economy tanked. When it came to cars, people wanted to squeeze blood from a stone. More of them accepted used car purchases but his margins kept getting shaved by the new frugality. But God forbid the Santullis had to tighten their belt. And yet that's what it had come to and he had to listen to the complaining as if it was on a tape loop.

As he lost another hand of Texas Hold 'em, his third in a row, the intensity of the rain pounding the roof caught his attention. Second night in a row with bad storms. Torrential downpours and flash flooding made for a lousy commute. He read that power lines had been downed by the previous night's storm, not too far from his home but, fortunately, not affecting the Santulli household or she would have had one more damn thing to complain about.

With a heavy sigh, he ran his palm over his balding pate and leaned back in his leather desk chair. He ended his gambling session and shut down his computer. If the dealership lost power or was hit by a power spike, the machines could suffer damage and the thought of replacing a bunch of computers set his ulcer percolating. He walked through the dim interior of the building and shook off the screensavers so he could power off each workstation. As extra precaution, he pulled the plugs from the outlets.

The wind roared outside the broad plate-glass windows, rain lashing against them almost horizontally. He walked to the locked door and looked out at the car lot. The multicolored pennant flags that outlined the perimeter near the top of the streetlights whipped crazily for a few seconds before the line snapped. Somebody's screen door cartwheeled down the street before sailing off into the night. The floor seemed to vibrate beneath him. A wooden fence slat slammed into the window next to him causing him to jump backward, heart pounding.

Across the street, he saw the funnel shape forming, behind the squat white wooden building with "Jake's Snack Shop" painted on the front wall. Lou often ran over to Jake's for a quick lunch, a burger or hot dog, and some fries, when he couldn't afford time away from his own business. Now, he watched in horror as the funnel cloud barreled through the center of the building, ripping it to shreds, as if it had been stuffed into the bottom of a massive blender. Wooden debris blasted away in all directions.

Lou stood mesmerized as the tornado swirled and pounded its way through the restaurant on a collision course with his parking lot. The funnel cloud expanded, so wide he could no longer see the telltale shape without looking up and then that was insufficient as it bore down on him. Belatedly, he realized he should seek cover. His business was housed in a split-level building, with the offices in back, up a few steps. No basement in which to seek shelter. His best bet was an interior office or closet with no windows.

The roar became so loud he couldn't think straight.

As he watched in horror, the white-striped blue Mini Cooper at the corner of the lot lifted upward and flipped back toward the front windows. He ducked a second before it crashed through the plate-glass window and demolished a desk.

If he thought the roar of the tornado was loud before, nothing prepared him for the terrific noise that assailed his ears. The swirling winds reached into the building and whipped papers and mugs and desk planners into the maelstrom.

He backed away, his jaw dropping as a red Mustang blew past the window, its bumper scraping along the asphalt before it rammed a silver Kia Sportage. One after another, the cars on his lot flipped over, rolled past, or soared overhead.

Fierce winds buffeted him through the gap in the window and almost swept him off his feet several times.

He clenched his jaw so tight his teeth began to ache.

When a black Toyota Corolla rolled through the broken window and smashed into the Mini Cooper, Lou scrambled backward, feeling his body become buoyant in the air, as if he had no more substance than a paper bag. In seconds the tornado would sweep him up into the vortex and hurl him into the night. He clawed his way along the wall, crawled up the steps to the upper level and pried open the door to the storage closet in the middle of the building. He squeezed into the small room and the door slammed shut behind him so hard it rattled against its hinges.

Squatting on the floor, hands wrapped around his knees, Lou Santulli prayed softly, almost incoherently, a rambling jumble of sibilant words. If only he'd skipped the online poker and driven home at the start of the storm. If only he'd waited until morning to tidy the office…

More thunderous crashes and jarring bangs shook the walls of the building. The light in the closet winked out, plunging him in darkness. The roaring filled his ears, became his world. As the walls around him creaked and groaned, he fumbled in his pocket for his cell phone, to call his wife, to apologize for avoiding her, to tell her he still loved her, despite all the pointless bickering.

The phone display seemed unnaturally bright in the closet, revealing the shelves of notepads, folders and cleaning supplies—and the blood dripping from his forehead. He must have been struck by debris and, in his panic, hadn't even noticed. Unfortunately, the cell phone had no signal. He held down the speed dial key for home to no effect, pressed disconnect, speed-dialed again, pressed disconnect, speed-dialed…

Something massive burst through the closet wall.

Before his brain could register what the object was, it struck the front of his head with the force of a sledgehammer, pulping his eyes, smashing the bone and cartilage of his nose into his brain and crushing his skull—

In the second or two before his cell phone shattered against an exposed two-by-four, a woman's voice spoke through its tiny speaker, "Hello? Lou…?"

Roman Messerly woke up with someone shaking his shoulder.

"Dude, wake up!"

"What…?"

"You gotta go to work, man!"

Roman sat up and looked around the basement room. He was sprawled on a sofa facing a wide flat-screen TV. A game controller fell from his lap and clunked on the floor. Took him a few seconds to remember he'd stopped at his friend's house to pass some time before his shift. In Gavin's man cave.

"Gavin, weren't we…?"

"Dude, you fell asleep in the middle of Halo," Gavin said. "Ever hear of an energy drink? What's up with you? Forget your multivitamins? You look like shit, man."

"Trouble sleeping lately."

"I left for a Coke, but we lost power down here, so I figured I'd let you sleep until you had to leave—which is *now*, dude."

"Thanks, man, don't want to be late."

Roman pushed himself up from the sofa. Lately, he'd been wiped out. Kept thinking he was on the verge of a nasty virus, but so far exhaustion was his only symptom. As he lumbered up the stairs and through the front door, he fought another jaw-cracking yawn and ran into a torrential downpour.

His old black-and-tan Subaru Outback seemed a mile away. By the time he ran to the curb and fumbled his key into the lock, he was thoroughly soaked. As he started the engine, water dripping off his face and hands, he thought about putting in for a week's vacation. He'd sleep for five of the seven days. Make that six. He'd save the seventh for a day trip somewhere.

Pulling away from the curb, he felt a wave of exhaustion wash over him and he became hypnotized by the fierce metronome of the windshield wipers on their highest setting. For a moment, he thought his vision had dimmed, but darkness had come inside the car and swelled around him. The dashboard lights faded away and a raspy woman's voice seemed to whisper in his ear.

"Not done with you yet."

When the engine died and the Outback's momentum carried it down the side of the road, along a grassy embankment, Roman was already unconscious, his breathing labored.

"That's a freakin' tornado," Dean said moments after Sam climbed into the Impala, dripping wet.

Biting her nails nervously, Lucy Quinn leaned forward from the backseat.

"This is totally crazy," she whispered.

"Crazy's coming," Dean said. "But it hasn't reached the station yet."

"I had it, Dean," Sam said, furious with himself. "Close enough to hurt it. Just not bad enough."

"We'll gank it, Sam," Dean said with more confidence than he felt.

Through the frenetic slashing arc of the wipers clearing the windshield in split-second intervals, they watched the massive funnel cloud—a wedge of darkness against the evening sky—churn its way across the western edge of town.

Dean drove west along Welker, proceeding with caution because he had no plan once he reached the tornado. Like catching a tiger by the tail. As if to confirm the foolhardy nature of his direction of travel, every other car on the road was racing in the opposite direction. They were a mile away from the tornado when it ripped the roof off a house and flung it into the night like a kite with a severed string.

"Plus side," Dean said grimly, "don't see any flying cows."

When they were within a half-mile, the funnel cloud swept across the parking lot of a gas station, veering toward the pumps. One of the supports holding a canopy over the gas station lot buckled and the roof toppled over, metal screeching and scraping along the asphalt, trailing sparks.

Two blocks away, Dean jammed the brake pedal, skidding to a stop on the slick road.

The explosion blossomed in front of them and the concussive blast rocked the Impala's suspension. Bits of glass and flaming metal debris pelted the ground around them. A charred piece of a gas pump housing plunked the hood of the Impala and ricocheted across two lanes of traffic before slamming into a curb.

"Dean, it's gone," Sam said.

At first, Dean thought his brother was referring to the gas station explosion which, unlike the exploding phantom Charger, had definitely not vanished. Flames continued to burn, smoke continued to billow into the night, and wreckage continued to clink and clatter around them. The gas station was real, not a living nightmare. Its destruction was a reality. But then, Dean noticed the absence of the fierce wind that had buffeted the Impala as they had approached the tornado. Looking left and right, and then leaning out the window for a better view, he confirmed that the twister was gone.

"Small favors," he mumbled.

Dean made a looping turn on the empty road and headed east, back toward C.J.'s Diner, but they had traveled less than a mile when the Impala trembled slightly. A moment later, it rocked to the right and shimmied. Thinking the car had taken some damage, Dean pulled to the side of the road for a quick inspection.

The moment he stepped out of the car, the ground trembled. Along the street, parked cars began to wail as their theft alarms were triggered. Windows in a nearby building cracked and shattered. In the spread of the Impala's headlights on the asphalt, Dean saw cracks forming.

"Great, tornadoes and now an earthquake," he muttered

He jumped back in the car, shifted into drive and sped toward the diner.

"Dean! Look out!" Sam yelled.

He saw it in time, a fissure opening diagonally across Welker Street, spreading wide enough to accommodate a car tire and break an axle. He swerved away from the worst of it, but felt the Impala lurch over a gap when he gunned the engine.

A Colorado State Patrol cruiser coming from the opposite direction wasn't as fortunate. As the fissure continued to widen, the front wheels of the speeding cruiser dropped into the gap and the front bumper smashed into the opposite edge. The vehicle tilted forward, slipping into the abyss. The doors of the cruiser swung open and two uniformed troopers jumped out and scrambled away from the car a second before it lurched down into the crack. Only the trunk remained above ground.

Dean slowed, waiting to see if the men needed help, but another State Patrol cruiser, which had been following the first, managed to stop before plowing into the lead car. The two stranded troopers scurried back to the second car and climbed into the back.

At the end of Roman Messerly's life, when he had no more left to give her, a spasm wracked his body so violently his collarbone shattered. When the nocnitsa released her grip on his forehead, the husk of his body fell forward, dangling against the support of the shoulder strap. He had worried about potential tragedies and emergencies his whole life, despite actions and training he'd taken to prepare himself to face them. He'd never have to worry about them again, but she'd made his fears a reality and, in his own way, Roman had left his mark on the town.

The nocnitsa shed her substance and spiraled up into the night air, potent with energy she'd culled from her first victims. With her glowing red eyes she gazed upon the town and the spreading chaos and roared with pleasure, a sound like shrill wind whistling through confined spaces. She could feel the town as a whole, from edge to edge, a busy little hive of fear and uncertainty, doubt and grief. For a few moments, before flying down to her next victim, she rippled outward, a flash of darkness that would infect every mind within miles. Those awake would feel a cold chill race up their spine and experience an unexplained feeling of dread, while those asleep... ah, those asleep spoke her natural language, and she spoke to them, deep in their minds, summoning the deepest darkness to the place where it could live...

TWENTY-FIVE

Kurt Machalek had collected hearts in mason jars because hearts were totems. They imparted mystical powers to the one who claimed them. But for that power to pass to him, he'd had to seize them from living sacrifices. His so-called victims never understood their higher purpose in his apotheosis, so he explained it to them in detail before carving the still-beating organ from their chests. To become invulnerable and immortal, he'd needed to collect a dozen hearts. Unfortunately, the FBI caught him after his seventh acquisition and took the hearts from him. Unenlightened, they didn't understand. As a result, when he escaped from his solitary cell, he would have to begin his collection all over again. He'd lost his accumulated mystical powers when they captured him and removed his totems. Locked away in his cell in the supermax wing of Falls Federal, he slept and dreamed of the day when he could restore his mystical energies. Once he got his dozen, he would show them true power.

In his dreams he saw his victims again, every one of them, and he would smile at the fond memories of those early acquisitions. They would scream as the power left their bodies, propelled into their hearts for him to capture. By the time they were still, their power was his to wield and it electrified him with his growing potential.

While he would have preferred to dream and fantasize about future sacrifices to his glorification, he had no control over his subconscious. Not that it mattered. Reliving his so-called crimes was a pleasurable experience, a brief mental vacation. He never had nightmares because he feared nobody and nothing…

But suddenly, his dream became troubling. He'd been toiling over his fourth victim—a young soccer mom who begged him to let her go, saying she wouldn't tell if he just let her go—when he noticed people standing around him in a circle. That was wrong. Each sacrifice demanded his complete focus to channel the heart energy at the moment of death. He never allowed witnesses to his sacred rite. But for some reason, while he could sense people closing around him in a tightening circle, he couldn't see them. He plunged the bowie knife into the soccer mom's chest, delighting in the brief scream of primal power as he sliced his way to the pulsing heart and—

—woke up in his bunk in the dim lighting of his solitary cell.

But he was not alone. Others stood in his cell, in a semicircle around him, their clothes stained with dried blood, smeared and clumped with the dirt of their shallow graves. All except for the young soccer mom standing in the middle of the seven. Her torn blouse was wet with fresh blood, the gaping hole in her chest dripping crimson droplets onto the floor of his cell.

"No," he said. "You can't be here. None of you. I took your power."

En masse, they stepped forward, their eyes wide with fury, teeth bared, spittle and flecks of blood on their chins. As one, they raised their arms, each holding a butcher knife.

"No! This isn't right," he said. "It's personal and sacred!"

The soccer mom stabbed his thigh, the butcher knife sinking deep enough to scrape bone.

He roared in pain and shoved her back. She smiled a wicked little smile and spat in his face.

As if that was their cue, the other six surged forward, knives rising and falling, plunging into his flesh, slicing his arms and legs, sinking into the meat behind his collarbone, puncturing a lung. Though he was physically strong, they overwhelmed him. Every push and shove, every punch and kick, was met with the bite of steel ripping into his flesh. They swarmed over him, knocking him from his bunk.

He curled into a fetal position, arms over his face and head, but they aimed lower, cutting through his abdomen with single-minded ferocity. Then, one by one, they reached their grave-cold hands inside his body, and their clawing fingers ripped out his organs and crushed them in their fists.

They saved his heart for last.

In the break room of Taco Terrace, located at the southern edge of town, Mike Keoghan leaned his chair back against the wall, put his feet up on the table, crossed at the ankles, and shoved earbuds into his ears with the iPod's volume turned up loud enough to drown out the usual commotion at the front of the fast-food restaurant. He was determined to get maximum value out of his fifteen-minute break. The previous night he'd been up until nearly dawn, talking on the phone with his girlfriend, who'd had a big fight with her parents about breaking curfew.

After a long day, he was tired, his feet ached and his eyes burned. He crossed his arms over his chest and closed his eyes, drifting into a nap while Johnny Cash sung about his "Ring of Fire."

He dreamed of black smoke rising from a fire but when he looked for the flames, all he saw was the smoke, hanging overhead like poisoned clouds. Something was wrong about the black clouds, but the reason escaped him. Slowly, he became aware of someone tugging at his brown polyester Taco Terrace shirt.

"Couple more minutes," he mumbled.

The tugging continued.

Irritably, he moved his arm to brush away the person's hand but something wasn't right. Instead of touching clothes or skin, he felt fur beneath his fingers. Rising to groggy consciousness, he experienced the tugging and pulling from both sides of his body. Something pushed at his chest and arms, even his legs. When he shoved against the weight on his left arm, he yelped, jerking his hand away. Something had bit him.

"What the hell—?"

Opening his eyes, he saw dozens of beady black eyes

staring back at him. Rats—crawling all over his body. They waddled up his torso, pink noses twitching, sharp teeth flashing at him.

Yelling, he kicked convulsively, causing the tilted chair to slide down and drop him hard. The back of his head struck the linoleum floor and lights flashed in his skull.

In a moment, the rats swarmed over him.

Frantically, he looked to the left and right and saw hundreds of them flowing across the floor, a pulsing tide of grimy fur. He rolled onto hands and knees, crushing some rats beneath him, while dozens more bit his hands, neck and ears. As he lunged upright and staggered toward the door, they covered his body like a living fur coat, continually biting his exposed flesh. Three climbed up the back of his scalp while another ducked its head inside his mouth and, when he tried to scream, gnawed his tongue.

Furious, he bit its head off and spit it out like a bloody wad of chewing tobacco and slammed his body against the door. Several rats were dislodged from his clothing, but others scrambled up his sneakers and under the cuffs of his trousers, clawing his shins and biting the meaty back of his calves.

He fumbled with the doorknob while rats gnawed the back of his hand, tearing away his flesh, bit by bit. His own blood made the doorknob slippery but he finally managed to turn it and push his way through into the cooking area.

The customers lined up to order their meals saw him draped with hungry rats before his coworkers noticed. Uniformly, the customers screamed and ran for the exits.

One teenaged girl held up her cell phone and recorded some video as she backed out of the restaurant. But when Mike had opened the door to the break room, all the rats that hadn't climbed on him, rushed through the doorway into the restaurant's seating area. The screams became shrieks and the people who hadn't already left shoved each other aside and struggled through the doors. Some fell and were trampled by those behind them, then were attacked by the rats themselves.

Mike's coworkers reacted seconds after the customers. Gail had just lifted a metal basket filled with fries out of the deep fryer. When she saw him, she screamed and hurled the basket at him. The hot grease dripping from the basket burned his face, but dislodged the two rats that had been chewing through his cheeks and another that had crossed over his ear to gnaw on his right eye.

"Help me!" Mike cried.

Jimmy, who ran on the high school track team, jumped over the counter, his legs swinging to the side and knocking over a condiment stand before landing on all fours in front of the soft drink refill station. Rats covered the floor like a living carpet and when Jimmy landed on them, they swarmed up his arms and legs.

Gail, who was naturally thin, backed away and tried to climb through the drive-through window. Snakelike, she wriggled her way through the narrow gap, but her hips got caught when she bumped the lever that worked the window. Hanging in space, half in and half out of the restaurant, she began to scream in terror.

Albert, the night manager, backed away from Mike, a look of incomprehensible horror on his face. He stumbled backward and reached out to catch himself, inadvertently pressing his palms on the hot grill. Yelping in pain, he lurched in the opposite direction. He grabbed the phone off the hook with his tender hands and dialed 911, all the while backing away from Mike and completely ignoring Gail's helpless screams. His heel mushed a jumble of fries strewn on the floor and he slipped, cracking his forehead against the edge of the counter. By the time the 911 operator asked him to state the nature of his emergency, Albert was unconscious. As she repeated the question a second time, the rats swarming along the floor ignored the plentiful fries and chewed ravenously on Albert's face.

Watching Albert accidentally burn his hands had given Mike an idea.

He slammed his fur-covered forearms on the grill and burned at least seven rats, enjoying their pitiful squeals as they sizzled against the hot metal. With his arms free, he stumbled past Albert and kicked running rats away from his feet. He squeezed one eyelid shut to ward off a rat nipping at the tender flesh there and managed to swat it away before it sank its fangs into his eyeball.

Gail was kicking her legs frantically while she screamed, even though the rats hadn't worked their way up to the counter yet and none were attacking her. Catching her legs in his arms to still them, Mike twisted her hips and pushed her through the window. She fell awkwardly outside, with a yelp and a curse, but she had escaped. Since Gail never went anywhere without her cell phone, Mike prayed she would call for help—soon as she stopped freaking out.

He tried to call to her, but his voice came out as a gurgle. Two rats were ripping into his throat and blood had washed down the front of his uniform shirt. Too much blood. He felt lightheaded and his balance was iffy. Seeing the phone dangling from its cord, he staggered toward it and dropped to his knees. He cradled the receiver in his hands but his fingers were numb, useless. He leaned over and tried to call for help, but no words escaped his lips. Everything had become darker, as if the restaurant lights were dying, and the floor spun beneath him and then his cheek was pressed to the linoleum, sticky with warm blood.

Far away, too far to matter to him anymore, sirens wailed in the night.

Rat tails slithered along his neck. A cold nose poked into his bloody ear.

Darkness swept over him and he remembered the darkness in his dream of the poisoned clouds...

TWENTY-SIX

For the past two days, Bryn Gunning had felt a tickle in her throat, a sure sign she was coming down with a head cold or some kind of virus she had probably picked up from one of her fifth-grade students. During the school year, somebody was always sick and the viruses survived by tag team propagation, as she called it. Sometimes it seemed as if schools were just incubators for the evolution of the super flu that would one day create an extinction event for the human race. Or, maybe she was feeling sorry for herself at the thought of yet another illness wracking her body for the next three to six weeks.

She'd been getting plenty of rest and taking echinacea, zinc and mega-doses of vitamin C since the first sign of the cold, hoping to nip it in its viral bud, but that strategy always amounted to little more than hopeless optimism. At least, she reasoned, she'd go down swinging.

Thunderstorms jarred her from sleep and the

uncomfortable dream she'd been having about difficulty swallowing. Tangled up in her bed sheets, she wrestled her way out of bed and stumbled toward the bathroom in her fuzzy bunny slippers. Without warning, she began coughing and couldn't stop. It was a dry cough and soon she was wheezing, unable to catch her breath. Flicking on the bathroom light, she grabbed a cup and tried to fill it with tap water while her body was wracked with spasms.

She managed to get a mouthful into the cup and half of that into her mouth, then sprayed it across the mirror as another round of coughing doubled her over. Hacking, she had the sensation that something was caught in her throat— and it was trying to get out!

With trembling fingers she reached into her mouth and grabbed something hard and pulled. The size of a large button, it had thin, twitching legs. Disgusted, she flung it into the sink and it crawled around the basin—a cockroach. Backing away from the sink, she bumped against the door and wiped her saliva-sticky hands against her oversized nightshirt, panting. Then the panting degraded into more coughing.

She spat three more wiggling cockroaches out of her mouth.

Weeping and shaking in revulsion, she gagged as she imagined them swarming in her stomach and crawling up her throat. On hands and knees, she crossed to the toilet, flung up the lid and gripped the edge of the bowl a moment before the torrent of vomit surged up her esophagus. Clear fluid, streaked with blood and riddled with squirming cockroaches, centipedes and spiders spilled out of her and flowed down the side of the toilet bowl. Desperately, she reached for the handle to flush the chitinous mass down the drain, but many of the bugs scrambled up the porcelain and dropped to her tile flooring. They wriggled and twitched and scuttled toward her legs.

Screaming between coughing fits, she scrambled out of the bathroom in a frantic crabwalk, rolled over and ran toward her bedside telephone. She lifted the receiver and punched in 911. Her stomach rumbled alarmingly. The operator answered but when Bryn tried to explain what was happening, she could only cough and hack, and she spit up more bugs. Several landed moistly on her forearm and skittered toward the hand holding the phone, while others scrambled up her arm, under the loose sleeve of her nightshirt. Dropping the phone in disgust, she swatted at the bugs nestling in her armpit or crossing over the swell of her breasts.

At some point, she'd lost her fuzzy slippers and, as she backed away from the phone, bugs on the floor squished between her toes. She gasped for air and coughed again, hacking out a wiggling centipede before she ran from her bedroom in a blind panic and stumbled down the stairs, catching herself on the railing a moment before she would have plunged headfirst to the landing. In sparing herself from a nasty fall, she'd twisted her right wrist hard enough that she thought something had broken.

Cradling her throbbing wrist against her rumbling stomach, she flung open her front door and ran into the street, grateful that the stormy night had brought cleansing rain to wash away the live bugs crawling on her body and the bits of dead bugs tangled in her hair or clinging to her face, arms and legs.

She lived behind the school where she worked, in the eastern suburbs of Clayton Falls and had always loved that when the weather was pleasant she could walk to work. Now she ran toward the sprawling elementary school building as if it were a sanctuary for her.

By the time she realized she should have stayed close to home after placing the incoherent emergency call, her stomach was protruding painfully beneath her nightshirt. She pressed her hands to her abdomen and felt her flesh rippling under her fingers. With each painful step, she coughed up more blood with the bugs. No matter how many of them she expelled, more remained inside her and they were impatient to get out. From the sharp pains telegraphing from her abdomen, she knew they were eating their way out of her body.

She ran as far as the playground equipment before collapsing to her hands and knees. Sobbing, she couldn't find the energy to rise again. Wood chips bit into her palms and bare knees. Gagging, she coughed up a wolf spider large enough to fill her palm. As it dropped to the ground she smashed it with her fist.

A stabbing pain took her breath away.

She flopped on her back and moaned in agony.

Clutching at the bottom of her nightshirt, she pulled it up to expose her engorged abdomen. As she watched, golf-ball-sized lumps moved under her bruised skin. She clamped her fingers against the shifting mass and her broken fingernails cut into her skin. Blood welled up and the rain washed it away. Then, through one of the cuts, something dark brown edged upward, with twitching antenna and tiny barbed legs. The submerged mass gravitated toward the breach, pushing, surging—

—and Bryn screamed as her flesh tore open and released hundreds, thousands of roaches, beetles, centipedes, crickets, and spiders. Blood gushed out of her ruptured stomach, running down her sides and soaking into the bed of wet wood chips. But the bugs clung to her. They swarmed over her skin, biting and burrowing back into the flesh they had so recently escaped.

Always tired because sleep was no longer restful for her, Carla Battie would nod off in unconventional locations. Often she fell asleep on the sofa or an easy chair at home, rather than in her own bed. On several occasions, while sitting in one of the rear pews at United Methodist, she'd dozed off during the long sermons. Two weeks in a row, the Clayton Falls librarian had to wake her up after she'd spent too much time debating which *New York Times* bestseller to check out. And once, unfortunately, she'd fallen asleep while sitting in bumper-to-bumper traffic on I-80.

Although she often awoke from these impromptu naps with a bloodcurdling scream before regaining her senses and her sense of decorum, her neighbors were nothing short of sympathetic. Because they knew her as one of the few survivors of the Clayton Falls Apparel Company fire. Her car insurance company, on the other hand, had been less understanding about the fender-bender that had jarred her back to consciousness on the interstate.

For a while, she took the prescribed sleeping pills so she

could sleep at night—through the night—but the pills made it harder to awaken from the nightmares which then became even more terrifying. After a week or so, she set the pills aside.

Six months had passed since the factory fire but Carla continued to have vivid nightmares about the raging flames and suffocating smoke that had taken the lives of her coworkers, many of whom had become close friends. Long after her doctor removed the plaster cast from the ankle she broke after jumping from the second-story factory window to escape the blaze, the psychological wounds refused to heal. She'd tried counseling for a while, learned about survivor's guilt and post-traumatic stress, but none of the rationalizations or medications stopped the nightmares.

Each night she relived those minutes of stark terror before she had managed to escape the inferno. She hadn't worked on the factory floor. She'd been a bookkeeper, leveraging her associate's degree in accounting to earn an income that impressed no one. With what she always described as dumb luck, she'd taken a break from her tedious bank reconciliations to restock her desk drawers when the fire overwhelmed the factory. In the second-floor supply room, clutching several rolls of adding-machine tape, a few pens and telephone message pads, she staggered when she heard—and felt—the gas explosion. At the time, she imagined a tractor-trailer had jumped the curb outside and plowed into one of the building's walls—only later, after she escaped, did she learn the cause of the destruction.

Seconds after the explosion, the heat became unbearable. Scattered supplies forgotten at her feet, she edged out of the second-floor room into what felt like the heart of a furnace, sinuous flames flowing up every surface, charring wood, leaping from point to point, devouring the old factory with incredible alacrity. Soon the billowing black smoke became overwhelming. She heard the screams, but the burning bodies—her choking friends and coworkers—suffered and died beneath the turbulent shroud of impenetrable smoke.

Almost every night, Carla relived the fear and hopelessness of that moment, the certainty that she would die with the others. She always woke from the nightmare version of those events before she noticed the beacon of light at the end of the catwalk, before she sprinted to that recalcitrant window in its warped frame, before she smashed it open with her jacketed elbow, scrambled through while sustaining multiple lacerations and dropped to the cement courtyard below, grateful for the stabbing pain in her leg because it meant she was alive, that she had miraculously survived. The nightmare always ended on the high note of her fear, not on the glimmer of hope, as if she had never escaped...

Once again the fullness of the nightmare seared through her subconscious, striking the nerve-jangling chord of fear at the penultimate moment, rousing her in that familiar, heart-stopping instant to stark consciousness, gasping for air. But strangely, she found herself in her own bed. For the briefest time, drenched with perspiration, she marveled that she had managed to reach her bed before passing out from chronic exhaustion. Despite the recurrence of the nightmare, she entertained the idea that she had made progress. Maybe she wouldn't need to move from Clayton Falls to free herself from reliving the horror. She'd been saving her money to move away from town and its constant reminders, but… No, she would move, to the west coast maybe, start over, make new friends and—

She coughed.

The acrid tang of smoke filled her mouth.

Suddenly, her smoke alarms wailed.

"No!"

An orange glow flared down the hall as a coughing spasm wracked her body. She stumbled out of bed, doubled over as black smoke swirled around her, as if she were the center of a vortex. Dropping to her knees, she fought for breath, her tears etching soot-streaked tracks on her cheeks as she cast about frantically for an escape route. In seconds, the walls surrounding her were engulfed in flames and the suffocating layer of smoke bore down on her. Face down on the beige carpet, she watched in horror as tongues of flame detached from the burning walls and darted toward her.

When her nightgown ignited, she screamed—but only for a second. Another coughing spasm curled her into a fetal position, blotting out her vision. She swatted at the flames searing her legs until the palms of her hands were no more than raw, shrieking nerve endings. But before she blacked out, in the moments before pain trumped everything else, her earlier thought returned.

She had never really escaped the fire.

The nocnitsa reveled in the darkness her effort had created, but reaching so far beyond her unformed body had drained her energy. She floated through the night sky and drifted downward, slipping into a house, creeping toward her victim in her guise of shadows and found him ready for her influence. A small pulse of her power and he drifted into sleep, a ready conduit.

Ehrich Vogel made a call earlier in the day to see his doctor, but reached his answering service instead. Apparently Doc Bennett didn't have weekend hours, so Ehrich had to wait until Monday. Unless it was an emergency, in which case the service directed him to the Critical Care facility. For a man like Vogel—who had survived two car crashes, a fall on his noggin from a two-story ledge while hanging shutters, and the cave-in at Croyden Creek, which had left him with one good hand—extreme exhaustion hardly qualified as an emergency.

He suspected his heart might not be pumping at maximum efficiency. Hell, he'd be surprised if the needle hovered in the seventy-percent range most of the time. Of course, it could be his lungs. Lung cancer was not out of the realm of possibility for a former miner, not by a long shot. But he was exhausted, not short of breath.

And though he was bone-tired, sleep was elusive during the worst of the thunderstorm. He'd turned on the local news and heard there'd been a tornado sighting at the western edge of town, but that crisis seemed to have passed. Listening to the rest of the world's troubles didn't seem like a remedy for sleeplessness, so he switched off the old television set and picked up a book about John Adams he'd been meaning to read for the past few weeks.

Five pages further into the legacy of the second president of the United States, his eyes gave out, his drooping eyelids finally closed and his head bowed forward in sleep.

A curtain of darkness slid down the surface of the wall and began to coalesce above him. The lamp on the table at his side flickered off and on several times before winking out. Glowing red eyes appeared in the new darkness and a dark hand with elongated fingers closed over the old man's forehead.

TWENTY-SEVEN

The storm had ended, but the night was far from over. They'd stopped at C.J.'s—a relatively safe place to drop off Lucy—for a breather, and a fresh round of coffee. Despite the deleterious effects of prolonged lack of sleep and too much caffeine, Dean and Sam couldn't risk nodding off while the nocnitsa was alive. Their subconscious minds would be negative energy gold mines. Though Dean's head throbbed in a slow drumbeat of pain and his vision lacked focus no matter where he looked, he ordered another large coffee. Appearing as ragged as Dean felt, Sam seconded the order.

Sipping from their steaming cups, Dean, Sam, and Lucy Quinn sat in a booth in the crowded diner thankful that the weather had calmed. Sam ended a call with Officer Jeffries.

"Earthquake activity stopped," Sam said. "Not even an aftershock."

"Night hag burned through another Happy Meal?" Dean said.

Sam glanced at Lucy. "They found a paramedic dead in his car, on the side of the road," he said. "I'm sorry, Lucy. It was Roman Messerly."

"Oh, no," Lucy said, clamping a hand over her mouth. "Roman? A car accident?"

"No other car involved," Sam said. "From the description, sounds like another... husk."

Lucy slipped out of the booth and ran to the restroom.

"Before, she said he was always nervous about the job," Dean said. "Nervous enough to have nightmares about emergencies and natural disasters?"

Sam nodded. "Another victim was found by teenagers on the grounds of the elementary school. Abdomen ripped open. From the inside."

"What the hell?"

"Teacher. Her body was crawling with bugs."

"Bugs went *Alien* chest-burster on her?"

"Looks like," Sam said. "But, Dean, the bugs were still alive."

"Why wouldn't—? Oh, *nightmare* bugs. And they didn't vanish when she died? So, it's true. The night hag is getting more powerful."

"Maybe the bugs were somebody else's nightmare."

"But they appeared inside this woman," Dean said, shaking his head. "That's too... personal."

"Either way," Sam said. "Can't be good."

"So what now? We don't know where the night hag will feed. Drive around and wait for a nightmare to appear?"

Dean's cell phone rang. The display read "J. Wieczorek."

"Dr. Gruesome," Dean said. "Good news, I hope."

"Sorry, Agent DeYoung," Wieczorek said. "I begged them to black out *Wicked Wolf Weekend*, but they thought it was some kind of passive aggressive strategy for a contract renegotiation. Threatened to quit, but they said they'd have a dozen people lined up to replace me before my taped shows ran out."

Dean looked at Sam. "We could be looking at a rabid wolf pack tonight."

"Yes—no—I mean, I don't know. If that's how this… thing works. I wanted to warn you," Wieczorek said.

"Thanks, Doc."

Dean was about to disconnect when Wieczorek continued.

"I'm here with my cousin, Millie," he said. "We have pages and pages of incidents compiled from emergency calls. Maybe they can help."

"We're at C.J.'s Diner," Dean said. "We'll use this as a base of operation. If we're gone when you get here, wait for us."

Dean disconnected and told Sam that they would soon have their hands on a list of emergency calls since the nocnitsa incidents had begun.

"Not sure what good it is," Dean said, taking a large gulp of coffee. "Guess it can't hurt."

"What can't hurt?" Lucy asked as she rejoined them.

"Information overload."

"Emergency call details," Sam said.

Betsy, their server, smiled as she refilled their coffee cups and asked if they wanted anything else.

"Not right now, thanks," Sam said.

"Give a holler," she said. At last her smile faltered, revealing a layer of unease she'd been hiding from her customers. "I'm not really sure what's happening. But I'm scared—frankly, we're all scared. So we're counting on you guys. Half the people in town will need a psychiatrist before the week is over."

"We've been through worse," Sam said in a clear attempt to reassure her. "We'll do whatever it takes."

Dean's cell phone rang again as Betsy thanked them and walked away.

Not the best timing, but Dean was pleasantly surprised when he saw "S. Bessette" on the caller ID display.

"Good to hear from you, Sophie," he said. "Before you ask, the crisis isn't over."

"I know," she said, her voice tense. "It's here."

Dean sat up straighter. "What's wrong?"

"It's falling apart!"

"What?"

"Everything! It's all falling apart."

"I'll be right there. Wait—where do you live?"

He scribbled the address on a paper napkin.

Through the phone's speaker, Dean heard a resounding crash in the background. Sophie shrieked.

"Sophie, hold tight. I'll be there in a couple minutes," he said and ended the call. "Let's go."

Lucy rose with him and Sam, but Dean put a hand on her shoulder. "Need you to stay here."

"Why?"

"Doc Gruesome and his cousin are meeting us here," Dean

said, though his real reason was to keep the young woman out of harm's way. "Tell them to sit tight until we get back."

Dean crossed Main Street and turned left on Bell, swerving between cars as he raced to Sophie Bessette's house. With the severe storm past, traffic had begun to pick up to what Dean assumed was typical for a Saturday night in Clayton Falls. Big mistake. This Saturday night would be anything but typical.

Although Dean had only met Sophie mere hours ago, he felt responsible for her current crisis. Maybe not in a direct cause and effect way. But in the sense that he may have put her on the night hag's radar. He and Sam had been trying to thwart the effects of the living nightmares, and now they had attacked the monster directly, if unsuccessfully. Supernatural creatures tended to notice the hunters trying to gank them. So it was possible that Sophie had become a target merely by her association with him and Sam. And judging by the previously calm and collected woman's state of panic on the phone, Dean couldn't get there soon enough.

"What's going on?" Sam asked, braced in the passenger seat as Dean pushed the Impala thirty miles per hour over the speed limit while zigzagging in out and out of oncoming traffic lanes.

"She said everything was falling apart," Dean said. "I heard a loud crash in the background."

"Another earthquake?"

"Don't know," Dean said. He'd heard raw terror in Sophie's voice. "Something big." A few moments later, he pointed to a green-and-beige wooden sign ahead on the right. "That's her development. Eagle Crest."

He turned right at the sign and took the first left.

"Dean! Look out!"

Something dark plummeted out of the sky in front of them—flashing through the headlight beams—and struck the asphalt, shattering into several pieces. Dean swerved to avoid the mess. He glanced out the side window.

"Rocks... and clumps of dirt."

Seconds later, more rocks fell from the sky, striking the road, the sidewalks and parked cars, breaking windows, spider-webbing windshields. Car alarms began to wail. Smaller stones pinged off the hood and roof of the Impala, while others rattled around in the wheel wells. As Dean took the second right he slammed on the brakes. The Impala pulled up several feet in front of a huge sinkhole blocking both lanes of residential traffic. A gray Ford minivan had rolled onto its side in the hole.

Shifting into reverse, Dean backed up a hundred feet, and swerved under the protective canopy of a large tree. Considering the fate of Max Barnes, he hoped it was a safe location.

"It's not far," he said. "Gotta hoof it."

"You bring hardhats this time?"

"Something better," Dean said as he climbed out of the Impala. With his forearm shielding his head, he jogged up a curved driveway to a two-door garage and took the molded plastic lids off two trashcans. As he handed the spare to Sam, he received a skeptical look in return.

"Better than hardhats?"

"More coverage," Dean said.

"If you say so."

With the makeshift shields over their heads, they ran along the sidewalk past the large sinkhole. Rocks occasionally thudded against the plastic lids which, for the most part, protected them from what would have been nasty scalp lacerations, if not fractured skulls. The lids weren't foolproof, though. One rock hit Sam's shoulder and another clipped Dean's knee.

Dean took the first left and halted so suddenly Sam almost bowled him over. Stunned, they stared at the extent of the damage without comment. Two of the houses on adjoining one acre lots looked as if a wrecking ball had been hammering them all day. Porticos toppled, front walls destroyed, chimneys crumbled in ruins, interior rooms exposed to the night, walls leaning at untenable angles, on the verge of collapse. Dean might have blamed the tornado or earthquake activity, but the sinkhole they'd almost fallen into had the signature of one particular dreamer.

In nearby houses, neighbors pressed frightened faces to their windows but stayed indoors to avoid the falling rocks. Their houses were havens, but for how long? If the sinkholes spread, the police would need to evacuate the whole development. Scratch that. They'd better evacuate everyone regardless.

"Which one's Sophie's house?" Sam asked.

"The one on the left," Dean said.

As he spoke, he heard a woman's voice calling for help.

TWENTY-EIGHT

Dean ran across the street with Sam on his heels. The house on the right creaked and groaned, shifting toward the left, minutes from collapsing. From behind that house, a father, mother and two young children emerged. They were all in pajamas, the children, a boy and a girl, crying softly as their parents held them close.

"That's Sophie Bessette's house," the mother said pointing. "She's trapped inside."

"I know," Dean said. He handed the woman his trashcan lid while Sam passed his to the father. "Use those. Find cover. Under a tree. Or inside a neighbor's house."

As if to emphasize Dean's warning, a series of rocks pelted the second-story roof of the family's house, bounced and dropped with thuds onto the front lawn. Looking as if they were trying to evade sniper fire, the family sprinted for the nearest tree.

Edging past the collapsed portico, Dean tried the front

door of Sophie's house, but it was jammed in the twisted frame. First-floor windows to the right had shattered, looking like hungry maws with crystal teeth. Dean took out his handgun and ran the barrel along the edges of the window frame, clearing away the jagged glass.

Entering the development from the side opposite the sinkhole, a police cruiser rolled up, lights flashing. Senior Patrol Officer Carleen Phillips jogged across the front lawn, holding up a hand.

"Wait! I've called for fire and rescue units."

Another patrol officer Dean hadn't met joined her, hand poised on the hilt of his gun, as if he thought shooting someone might improve the situation.

The house on the right creaked again. Then a boom sounded, as if a joist had split in half.

The creaking intensified.

"No time," Dean said. "Woman trapped inside."

"We have gas lines here," Phillips said. "These houses could blow."

"This whole block's in danger," Sam said. "You need to evacuate everyone."

"Probably a good idea," Phillips said. She flinched as a rock dropped inches from her face. "C'mon, Callahan. Let's go knock on some doors."

Dean ducked through the window and found himself inside a house that looked as if a giant's hand was in the process of crushing it. The walls were split, wood bursting through drywall. The hardwood floor had buckled upward in some places, sagged in others. In the middle of the living room, a hole had opened up and swallowed a coffee table and an entertainment center.

"Sophie!" he shouted.

"Upstairs," she yelled. "I'm stuck."

Dean mounted the staircase carefully. The banister railing was split in two places and several steps and risers had shattered from lateral pressure. He skipped those that looked unable to bear any weight.

Sam climbed through the window after him and looked around.

The house trembled and support beams groaned. The ceiling above the living room had sagged, raining bits of debris down in a hazy dust cloud that made breathing difficult.

"Dean, this place is right over a sinkhole," Sam said.

"I noticed," Dean said. "Warn me if anything... bad happens."

"Like a natural gas explosion?"

"Yeah. Like that."

"You'll be the first to know."

If the downstairs looked bad, the upstairs was worse. Dean found Sophie lying on her side in a doorway. The door had shattered into several pieces and was wedged into the collapsing doorjamb, pinning Sophie's ankle even as it propped up the weight that would otherwise come crashing down on top of her.

"You came," she said, the look of relief on her face palpable.

"You called," Dean said. Her white blouse was smeared with dust and dirt but not blood. "Hurt anywhere? Besides the ankle."

"Don't think so," she said. "Are you here to amputate my foot?"

"I'd like to avoid that if possible."

"Makes two of us."

"But we don't have time to wait for the Jaws of Life to pry you out of there."

"Suppose not."

"Do you have a golf club?"

"No."

Dean called down the stairs. "Sam, we need a crowbar!"

"I have a baseball bat," Sophie said.

"Baseball?"

"For protection," she said. "I dislike guns."

"Might work," Dean said.

A few seconds later he'd navigated the distorted perspective of her twisted bedroom and retrieved the baseball bat from her closet. He worked the thin end of the bat under a gap near where her ankle was trapped.

"On three, I want you to pull your foot out. Move as far from this doorway as you can. And cover your face."

"Pull, move, cover," she said. "Got it."

"One... two... *three!*"

Dean pressed upward, pushing a section of the doorway up. For a second, the pressure on Sophie's bloody ankle was released and she scrambled out of the way. Pieces of the shattered door cracked and split and vanished under the collapsing wall. A loud rumble filled the house and the wall continued to twist and fall. The floor beneath them began to heave like the deck of a storm-tossed ship.

"We gotta move!" Dean cried.

He grabbed Sophie's hand, pulled her up, and helped her to the top of the stairs. The banister railing was gone and the stairs had tilted at a thirty-degree angle. All around them wood cracked and split, window glass crashed, drywall broke and shattered, creating more plumes of suffocating dust.

"C'mon!" Dean encouraged Sophie.

Dean helped support the limping Sophie along the twisting staircase. It was like running along a rotating balance beam. The living-room sofa had fallen lengthwise into the expanding sinkhole. A series of crashes sounded from the back of the house. Dean guessed the kitchen cabinets had opened and disgorged their contents. They both fell on the stairs, but continued to scramble down, on hands and knees, and finally reached the bottom where Sam waited, holding a crowbar. Dean was about to help Sophie through the slowly collapsing broken window, when Sam caught his arm.

"Wait," he said and wedged the crowbar in the window. "This should buy us a few seconds."

Sophie slipped through first, then Dean, and finally Sam. He yanked the crowbar out and jumped back as the window frame disintegrated under the weight of the wall. They raced away from the ruined house, Sophie favoring her ankle.

"Looks like the rocks have stopped falling," Sam commented.

Lights flashing, a fire truck arrived, tooting its horn. A steady stream of cars flowed around the emergency vehicles as Phillips and Callahan routed them away from the huge sinkhole.

The house next to Sophie's shifted too far off center and
large sections splintered and broke away, until the left side
was a shattered ruin. Light flashed and an explosion roared,
engulfing both homes. The concussion wave shattered
windows in adjacent houses and blasted debris into the
street, pelting cars and emergency vehicles. Callahan and
Phillips dropped to the ground defensively.

Dean, Sam, and Sophie staggered from the force of
the explosion. Waves of heat flashed over them, instantly
evaporating perspiration. Chunks of burning wood and
charred bricks and siding fell much too close for comfort.
As they jogged to the Impala, Dean's ears were ringing. Felt
like he had earplugs stuffed in both ears. In the distance,
another explosion lit the night sky and the ground trembled.

The tree above the Impala was leaning over the street,
some of its branches low enough to brush the roof of the
car. Roots on the far side of the tree had risen up between
broken slabs of sidewalk. They jumped in the car and Dean
swung it around in a sweeping 180-degree turn to exit the
development before the rest of the street dropped out from
under them.

"My house," Sophie said from the backseat, her voice a
soft monotone. "My home… is gone."

"You're alive," Dean said.

"Am I? This feels like a dream."

"It's somebody's dream," Sam said. "But not yours."

Sam's cell phone rang.

"Jeffries," he told Dean and took the call. "Okay. We're on
our way."

"What now?" Dean asked after Sam ended the call.

"Nazi zombies are back."

The one who dreamed of the collapsing underground would never dream again.

Old before she first claimed him, he had little more to give her. She left his withered remains and moved to the next victim in her familiar path. This one was young, with enough vital energy to feed her for days before expiring. She slipped into his home, as insubstantial as an errant breeze, and flowed into his room, nudging him toward sleep so she could slip into his fertile subconscious...

Trevor Deetz hunched over the student desk in his bedroom. His mom had warned him not to wait until the last minute again to work on his latest project, a World War II book report due Monday morning. Peeved, he had retreated to his bedroom and slammed his door. Fine. He would finish the damn thing before Sunday morning even if he stayed awake all night to complete it. Then maybe she'd get off his freakin' case for once.

Unfortunately, the reading assignment was a boring book written by some old geezer with a fondness for dates and statistics that made Trevor roll his eyes. Instead of finishing the book, he sat hunched over his desk reading the end of the *Hitler's Zombie Force* graphic novel. Now this guy knew how to tell a story. The Allies were winning the war, so a desperate Hitler decided to zombify his entire army. Any soldier unwilling to make the undead sacrifice for the Fatherland was summarily shot.

More Nazi zombies than ever, he thought. *How cool is that?*

Despite the rising excitement in the final pages of the graphic novel, Trevor couldn't help yawning. He closed his eyes and rested his head on the desk, falling asleep in seconds.

TWENTY-NINE

Dean followed Bell Street eastward with a sense of déjà vu, passing the intersection where they'd witnessed a pack of Velociraptors hunt a Honda Civic driven by Paul Hanes. The downed utility pole had been patched to restore the lines but was still a repair in progress. And when Dean turned onto Arcadia Boulevard, he once again saw police cars in the middle of the street and Nazi zombies looking for meals on legs. A full block short of the nearest zombie, Dean swung the Impala onto the shoulder of the road to allow enough time to raid the trunk of the car for extra ammo.

Twisting around to face Sophie in the back seat, Dean said, "Stay in the car. Lock the doors."

"My ankle has swelled like a balloon," she said. "Don't think I'm going anywhere under my own power."

"Just as well," Sam said. "This will get messy."

As Dean and Sam circled to the back of the Impala, Sophie double-checked the locks. Inside the trunk, Dean opened a case with spare magazines for their guns and handed two to Sam, taking two more for himself. In the distance, he heard the staccato pops of gunshots mingled with hysterical screams.

They ran south along Arcadia. Dean tracked left and right for concealed zombies. He didn't want a repeat of his last close encounter. Behind a chalk-smeared sandwich board, a young Nazi officer in a white summer tunic turned toward them, staggering into their path. A loop of intestines dangled from a nasty abdominal wound. Dean raised his arm, braced his hand and put a round through the zombie's forehead.

Adding to the chaos, several people slipped out of stores and restaurants, yelling and screaming as they raced away from the undead abominations. A shrieking woman picked up her young, crying daughter and lumbered awkwardly down the street on a broken heel. An overweight man wearing a business suit and gripping a briefcase in both hands tripped and fell, breaking the briefcase and barely managing to escape from a zombie soldier's clutching fingers. The man scrambled away on hands and knees until he could regain his feet and flee. Papers fluttered in his wake.

In the middle of the street, an older field marshal in a full-length leather trench coat spotted them and lumbered into their path. Sam drilled a round through his eye.

"Dean," Sam said. "These aren't just Nazi zombies…"

Dean nodded. "They're the same Nazi zombies we already killed."

"Regenerated," Sam said. "Like the Charger each night."

"Night hag's playing her golden oldies."

"Until she burns out the dreamer."

Three soldiers in green helmets and uniforms rose from behind the cover of an open police-cruiser door with blood and gobbets of flesh dripping from their cracked and jagged teeth. Dean shot one under the chin. Sam caught the other two with headshots. As they passed the police cruiser, they stopped. The zombies hadn't taken cover behind the cruiser. They had been feeding.

The ravaged body of Darren Nash, the portly *Fremont Ledger* reporter who'd been interviewing people in C.J.'s Diner, lay sprawled on the ground, missing half his throat and large portions of his upper arms and thighs. One of his eyes was missing, along with part of his cheek. The other eye stared lifelessly into the night sky. His notebook, now spattered with drops of blood, was clutched in his hand. Several pages flapped in the breeze, flashing the details of a story he hadn't lived to tell.

"I did not need to see that," Dean said and turned away from the corpse.

"Wait a minute, Dean," Sam said, catching his brother's arm.

Dean looked back. "What—?"

Then he saw.

The fingers of the empty hand twitched. Then the head lolled to the side. The remaining eye moved slowly in its socket until it located them. Moaning, the reporter pushed himself up with his bloody arms and slowly climbed to his feet. His head hung to the side from his ruined throat. Uttering a wet grunt, he staggered one step toward Dean, then another, reaching out with straining fingers.

"Seriously?"

"Perception is—"

"Reality," Dean said. "Yeah, I know."

He aimed his gun, the end of the barrel less than a yard from the man's forehead. Without a second thought, he pulled the trigger, blasting half the reporter's brain and the back of his skull from his head.

"Hey! They shot Nash!" a voice called.

Dean turned.

A Hispanic Colorado State Patrol officer pointed from him to Sam with the barrel of his gun.

"Drop your weapons!" he commanded.

"They're FBI, Valdez," Officer Wild said. "Watch—!"

"Look out!" Sam called.

Valdez turned around and stood face to face with a ravenous SS officer in a black uniform, peaked cap, and swastika armband. They stood too close together for the others to take a clear shot. The state cop shoved his firearm into the gut of the Nazi zombie and fired round after round to no effect. The zombie ignored the abdominal wounds and ripped a chunk out of Valdez's throat. Blood sprayed from a torn artery but Valdez continued firing until he exhausted his magazine. The zombie clutched Valdez by the shoulders and continued to tear into his flesh, even as his own midsection separated above his hips, his legs falling sideways. The upper torso of the zombie rode the state cop to the ground, continuing to eat long after the light had faded from Valdez's eyes.

Officer Cerasi, gun drawn, ran up beside Wild and looked down.

"Oh, God…"

Spinning away he bent over and vomited.

Wild walked up to the feeding zombie, aimed her weapon at the back of his head, but averted her gaze from Valdez's remains as she pulled the trigger.

Dean and Sam joined the cops.

"Now, Valdez," Dean said. "Or he'll come back as one of them."

"I—I can't…" she said and turned away from them.

Dean looked down at the bloody state cop, lying beneath the truly dead zombie's torso. His eyes were wide open and unblinking.

"Poor bastard," Dean said and took the shot.

More screams sounded, coming from a nearby Italian restaurant, one they had already passed, Mama Ferracci's. Sam cast a grim look at Dean.

"The zombies are inside!" he called, running toward the restaurant.

Two bodies crashed through the plate-glass window, a Clayton Falls man, wrestling with a Nazi soldier whose jaw snapped repeatedly so hard they could hear the teeth striking each other from fifteen feet away. The soldier's hand had clawed the man's face, but so far he'd managed to hold the snapping teeth at bay with a firm grip on the soldier's hair. If the soldier noticed or cared that his scalp was slowly tearing away, he showed no sign of it.

Sam strode forward and swung his booted foot at the soldier's head, connecting just under the jaw and elevating the zombie's torso enough to get off a clean shot through his temple. He looked down at the relieved restaurant patron.

"Were you bit?" he demanded.

The man climbed hastily to his feet, ran his hands over his arms, and gingerly touched his face and neck.

"No. No, I don't think so. Scratched. Not bit."

"You're lucky," Dean said. "Now go home."

"My wife," the man said. "She went to the restroom before those... those things appeared out of nowhere. She's still in the restaurant."

"We'll handle it," Sam said.

When Dean and Sam entered Mama Ferracci's, they saw the problem. A dozen patrons were trapped in the back corner of the place, surrounded by at least as many zombies. Some civilians cowered against the wall, backs turned, whimpering in fear while another yelled hysterically for somebody to please God do something. But a few diners held chairs up, like lion tamers in a circus, jabbing the chair legs at the zombies each time they tried to grab somebody. Because the zombies were impervious to pain, they took the abuse and continued to edge closer to their intended victims.

Wild and a few other cops entered the restaurant behind the Winchesters and took in the situation.

"More than last time," Wild observed.

"Head shots," Dean said for the benefit of the new cops.

"Not as easy as it sounds," Sam said softly to Dean.

The difficulty was that the restaurant patrons were behind the zombies. One miss or a through-and-through shot and they would kill or maim innocent people.

"Guess we get up close and personal," Dean said.

He crossed the restaurant with Sam beside him. The cops

followed, spreading out to avoid friendly fire, and seemingly reluctant to tangle with zombies.

Dean grabbed the first zombie soldier by the collar and yanked him backward. At his side, Sam had a clean line of fire and took it, splattering zombie brains over a watercolor map of Italy. Then Sam pulled back the zombie closest to him, and Dean took the shot from the opposite direction.

When Dean killed a third soldier, he saw a young officer in a white tunic. Dean spun the man around.

"No!"

Sam saw it too.

The loop of intestine hanging from the abdominal wound.

"Same damn zombie we killed outside!"

Dean shoved the white-clad officer onto a round table draped in a red-and-white checkered tablecloth, and shot him in the brain stem.

"You know what this means," Sam said.

"Running on a friggin' treadmill," Dean responded.

The Winchesters backed away from the zombies. Dean turned to Officer Wild.

"You know what to do?"

She nodded. But instead of grabbing a zombie, she removed the extendible baton from her belt and snapped it open. Stepping forward, she whipped it across the head of the nearest zombie, the graying field marshal with the full-length leather trench coat. The old man staggered sideways, but she'd commanded his attention. Turning to face her, he bore down on her, arms raised to grab her even as he opened his hungry maw to bite.

Cerasi moved to the side, mirroring the Winchesters' technique, and blew the field marshal's brains out. The other cops took out their batons and joined the fight. With the situation basically in hand, the Winchesters retreated to the front of the restaurant.

"They're regenerating minutes after we kill them," Dean said.. "She's playing with us."

"We waste time attacking the symptoms," Sam added, "not the cause."

They heard more screaming outside and ran back into the street. Dean looked south and north for the source of the cry. His eyes locked on a black-clad Nazi SS officer standing hunched over beside the Impala.

"No!" Dean yelled and sprinted to his car. *"No!"*

I'm too late, he realized with horror. *Too late.*

Sophie Bessette had been pulled through the broken side window and was thrashing in the SS officer's arms, one of which looked broken in several places from punching it through the window. Behind the black-clad Nazi zombie, Sophie's body was obscured. Dean hesitated, holding his gun extended at eye level, to make sure Sophie wouldn't be in the line of fire. When he saw her head flop down near the zombie's elbow, he fired a high shot, catching the undead officer in the back, between his hunched shoulder blades. The zombie straightened, twisted his head around to look back over his shoulder. Seeing the satisfied grin on the zombie's face, with fresh blood staining his jagged teeth and dripping from his chin, Dean lost it.

Roaring in anger, Dean emptied his magazine, firing round

after round into the zombie's face until his magazine was empty. He ejected the spent magazine, slammed another into the grip, released the slide and continued to fire, so he could blast that evil grin all the way to hell.

With nothing much left above the stump of his neck, the zombie SS officer released his victim and swayed side to side. Lunging forward, Dean kicked the zombie in the chest, knocking him clear of Sophie's prostrate form.

"No, no, no," Dean whispered as he knelt beside her.

Gently, he turned her over—and flinched when he saw her white blouse soaked with blood. Her throat had been torn open, much of the flesh gone. Above and below her collarbone, chunks of flesh had been ripped out with such force that the clavicle itself was fractured in two places. Her dark, tousled hair was sticky and matted with blood. And her eyes were wide open, seemingly caught in a moment of terror or disbelief.

"Sophie, I'm…" Dean looked away, unable to face that accusatory stare. "I'm so sorry."

Dean eased her body to the ground, stood up and backed away.

"Dean…" Sam was beside him.

"Sammy, I can't… I can't, man."

Dean turned his back.

Sam understood. Dean heard his boot scuff against the asphalt as he took a step toward Sophie's body. Squeezing his eyes shut, Dean waited for the sound, anticipated the sound, but the sudden crack still felt like a body blow.

"It's done," Sam said.

His hand fell on Dean's shoulder and he squeezed.

"Dean, we will kill this night hag bitch," Sam said. "Promise."

Dean nodded. He took a tarp from the trunk and laid it over her body, while steadfastly averting his gaze from her face. When he returned to the driver's side of the Impala, he heard a low menacing growl. Stepping to the side, he spotted the large gray wolf crouched behind the car, its snout curled back to reveal impressive fangs in a foaming mouth.

"Don't even think about it," Dean muttered. He pulled his gun and fired a round right between its glowing amber eyes. The wolf dropped to the ground and vanished. Other wolves approached from the left and right, slinking out from the shadows between the commercial buildings on Arcadia.

With Sam covering the west side of the street and Dean taking the east, they brought down the wolves, one after another. To kill the wolves head shots were a luxury not a necessity. But Dean had the idea that a wounded and incapacitated rabid wolf might be better than a dead one.

"If they're not dead, maybe they won't regenerate," he pointed out.

The dead ones vanished. But tonight, the truly dead zombie corpses weren't disappearing as they had the previous night. The zombie manifestations were stronger somehow, having a permanence the wolves lacked. So far.

When an ambulance rushed down the street, Dean flagged the driver down by waving his FBI credentials and led one of the paramedics to Sophie's body.

"Take care of her," he instructed.

"But she's already…"

Sam caught the man's arm and whispered fiercely, "Get her out of the street before the wolves get her."

The man looked down at Sam's hand gripping his arm, and the gun held in a white-knuckled grip in the other and nodded. "Sure. No problem."

"Good," Sam said.

Dean drove in silence back to the diner, jaw clenched, hands tight on the steering wheel.

No more chasing symptoms, he thought. *We will find you and end you.*

THIRTY

The life energy of the fourteen-year-old boy flowed into the nocnitsa.

While Trevor Deetz slept hunched over his desk, she perched on his back and shoulders, like a bird of prey. But instead of plucking his eyes from their sockets, she wrapped the elongated fingers of her hands around his forehead and snatched the nightmare images from his mind and gave them shape in the real world. And all the while, his energy flowed into her, giving her shadowy body form and substance and heightening her powers. Those within her sphere of influence, which encompassed the whole town, bled fear into the air. Their night terror would take shape and plague them, a vicious circle of darkness from which none would escape. Soon she wouldn't need to feed directly from them to become more powerful. She would reach into any mind she chose and unspool the darkness within. Their power would flow to her, first one-to-one and then many-to-one, until only shriveled husks remained.

As she absorbed more power from the boy, his body trembled beneath her gripping hands and feet, resisting the draw—and failing. In a few moments his legs jittered up and down and his head bucked, thumping repeatedly against the books and papers piled on his desk. His mind was attempting to throw off the psychic yoke, to rouse him from the dream state which fed her, but she was too powerful now and the energy was so delicious…

Sam watched Dean behind the wheel out of the corner of his eye. His brother hadn't known Sophie Bessette long, but he was taking her loss hard. He knew that Dean felt guilty, that he felt he'd broken his promise to keep her safe. Couple that with abandoning the zombie battle and having no idea how to locate the nocnitsa and the night was adding up to one big loss. But they had no choice but to leave. The battle couldn't be won because the deck was stacked against them. Sooner or later they would fall to the regenerating zombies and the war would be lost as well. The only way to win the night was to attack the night hag directly.

As they neared the diner, several fire trucks roared past, horns blaring and emergency lights pulsing, followed by two ambulances with wailing sirens. Judging from the names on the sides of the emergency vehicles, assistance was arriving from nearby towns. No matter which direction Sam looked, he could spot one or two house fires burning. In light of the garment factory tragedy and its human cost, Sam imagined a lot of the town's residents had nightmares about fire.

The parking lot of C.J.'s Diner was at half capacity. Alarmed faces stared out the windows rather than at their plates or dining companions. Parked in the walking lane near the diner's entrance was the police chief's cruiser. Sam guessed the man was checking on his daughter and couldn't blame him. The rhythmic thumping of helicopters reached a crescendo overhead then faded as they angled toward distant fires and their blinking lights receded in the night sky.

"Medical choppers," Sam noted.

"Or press," Dean said cynically.

Dean paused on the metal stairs leading up to the diner's front entrance and pointed downward. Sam looked and saw the spots. *Blood.*

They entered the diner and angled toward the booth where they'd left Lucy Quinn. Sitting opposite her was Millie, the police receptionist and a distinguished-looking man with silvering hair, wearing a white dress shirt under a charcoal-gray suit jacket.

"Is that...?"

"Dr. Gruesome," Dean said. "Cleans up well."

Standing in front of the booth, cradling his left arm, Chief Quinn was talking urgently to his daughter. When Sam reached the man's side, he saw the problem with his arm and indicated the wound to Dean with a slight nod of his head.

The dark sleeve of the chief's uniform shirt was torn to shreds at the forearm and soaked with blood. Through the gaps in the cloth, Sam saw the man's flesh had been ravaged by deep, jagged lacerations.

Bite wounds.

"What happened?" Sam asked.

From the dark look Dean gave him, Sam knew he was wondering which of them would have to put the chief down before he became one of the undead.

"Wolf bit me," Quinn said. "Right outside the municipal building. I put it down, but not before he took a chunk out of my arm and nearly knocked me senseless."

"You'll need rabies shots," Dean said, relief in his voice.

"I'll have its brain tissue tested."

"Did you wound it or kill it?"

"Gut shot," Quinn said. "If it wasn't dead when I left, it is now."

"The dead wolves vanish," Dean said. "Nothing to test. Besides, testing would be a waste of time. They're all rabid."

"You've seen more of these wolves?"

"Killed or maimed seven on Arcadia," Sam said. "All rabid."

"How can you know?"

"Because," Jozef Wieczorek said, "I've seen the movie."

"You too?" Chief Quinn asked Wieczorek, shaking his head in disbelief.

"Dad, whether you want to believe it or not," Lucy said, impatiently. "Weird stuff is *really happening*."

"I don't *know* how any of this is happening," Quinn said. "But I know when I need help. I've asked the governor to mobilize the National Guard."

"How long?" Sam asked.

"Day. Maybe two."

Sam exchanged a look with Dean. Not soon enough.

Quinn squeezed Lucy's shoulder with his good hand and kissed her on the cheek.

"Stay here," he said. "You need an escort home, call me."

"Okay, Dad. Be careful."

Chief Quinn nodded gravely to Sam and Dean, almost as if he were putting his daughter in their care, and walked toward the exit.

"Rabies shots!" Dean called after him.

Quinn nodded before he left. One way or another, the man would get treated for rabies. If the animal isn't caught and tested, you get the shots as soon as possible, because the prospect of contracting rabies is too terrible. Assuming he survived the night. Assuming the town survived the night. At the moment, the odds weren't looking good.

THIRTY-ONE

"Okay," Dean said. "What have you got?"

Lucy slid across the booth, making room for Dean and Sam to sit.

A large map of Clayton Falls covered the table. Red X marks with scribbled notations were scattered in a dozen locations. Millie had a stack of papers under her arm. Details of the emergency calls placed over the last two nights, Sam assumed.

"We went through Millie's logs and put an X wherever something was reported," Wieczorek said.

Millie nodded. "Plus, Wanda, the overnight dispatcher, has been calling us whenever she has a free minute with information on the calls coming in tonight."

"What about the names next to the X marks and incident descriptions?" Sam asked.

"That's who called in the incident," Lucy said.

Dean saw the problem. "We have the nightmares and

the witnesses, but we don't know who is having each nightmare."

"That's simple," Betsy, the smiling server said as she stepped up to the table with a coffee pot in one hand and two mugs dangling from the other. Her ubiquitous smile had become frayed, more habit now than anything else, and her hands trembled. "Everybody's having nightmares. That's all anyone is talking about." She placed the mugs down at the edge of the table, next to the map. "Normally, I'd offer decaff, but under the circumstances…"

"You *know* who is having nightmares?" Sam asked.

"Yes, mostly," she said, slightly taken aback by Sam's intensity.

"The type of nightmares?"

"If I haven't heard directly, Clara or Paige from the morning shift or Jesse—"

"Grab a chair," Sam said.

Betsy pursed her lips and shook her head. "I'm on duty."

"C.J. won't mind," Dean said.

Lucy smiled. "There is no C.J. Those initials are from *Charles* Clayton and *Jeremiah* Falls, the town founders."

"Whoever, then," Dean said. "This is important."

"Okay," Betsy said. "I'll do what I can."

While she returned the coffee pot to the coffee station and grabbed a chair to bring to the table, Sam picked up the red marker.

"Let's start with what we know." He found Olga Kucharski's house in the south section of town and circled it. "Olga Kucharski had dreams about the Charger and the *Nightmare Theater* monsters."

"Others are watching Doc's show," Dean said. "We got wolves after she was drained."

"But the night hag fed *directly* off Olga."

"Fed? Eww," Lucy said, tucking her chin down with a visible shudder.

"This night hag—a *real* monster—it's bringing the nightmares to life?" Wieczorek asked.

"Yes," Sam said. "I've seen it."

"Incredible," he said, shaking his head grimly.

"Goodness," Millie said, her face pale with fright. "Real monsters…"

"Just one," Dean said. This time. He turned to Sam. "Some of the manifestations are sticking around, even after death. Wolves vanished. Zombies didn't."

"She's growing stronger," Sam said. "Makes sense that manifestations created through direct feeding would be the first to have permanence."

"Daniel Barnes," Dean said, tapping the map. "Killer tree dreams."

Sam circled the Barnes address. Betsy sat down facing the table and looked at the map.

"Roman Messerly had the natural disaster dreams. Lucy, what's his address?"

She examined the map and pointed. Sam circled the location.

"But he wasn't there tonight," she said. "He was at his friend's house. Here. And… this is where Rich—Officer Jeffries—told me they found him in his car."

"What about the sinkholes? Falling rocks," Dean said.

Betsy raised her hand slightly, as if requesting permission to speak.

"Ehrich Vogel," she said.

"How do you know?" Sam asked.

"He's a retired miner. Lived through the Croyden Creek cave-in. Crushed his right hand. Told me he still dreams about it, but lately they've been... vivid."

"Got an address?"

Millie leaned forward and tapped her index finger on the map at a location to the northeast of the Kucharski house. Sam marked it.

"Ebola guy," Dean said. "Gotta be the CDC old-timer we met in here."

"Yes," Betsy said. "Phil Meyerson said he never saw someone with hem—hemorrhagic fever but dreamt about one last night. He lives... here."

She indicated an address in the northeast of Clayton Falls.

"The escaped serial killer," Sam said. He had a momentary flash of Ragnar Bartch jumping toward him from the utility shed wielding a meat cleaver. "Must be that woman we met, with the fantasy artist roommate... Jylene something?"

Lucy cleared her throat. "That might be Alden."

"Alden Webb? The warden?"

Lucy leaned forward conspiratorially.

"Hope I don't get in trouble for this. Dad told me something. Alden—Warden Webb—said once that while he believes in the security at Falls Federal, he always worries about what would happen if..."

"If they escaped," Sam finished.

She nodded. "Said it kept him on his toes. Eternal vigilance."

"Then that would be his nightmare scenario," Sam said, nodding. "Where's he live?"

Lucy pointed out his address and Sam dutifully circled it.

"We're forgetting about the zombies," Dean said.

"Betsy?" Sam asked. "Anybody having zombie nightmares?"

She frowned. "No nightmares, but…"

"What?"

"Well, Linda Deetz is always going on about how her son is crazy about zombies but she won't let him watch any of the movies because they're so violent and gory."

"Address?" Sam asked. But nobody knew. "Phone book?"

Betsy shook her head. "Unlisted. She's a single mom. Changed her number when her deadbeat ex kept calling at all hours of the night."

"Jeffries can find it for us," Sam said. "Lucy, you have his number?"

"Yeah, Dad treats him like the son he never had."

Sam asked her to call for an address.

The dreamers they had identified lived along the perimeter of the town. But it wasn't enough. They needed to know not only where the night hag was, but where she would go next. Of course, her feeding schedule could be totally random.

"What am I missing?" Sam asked rhetorically. "This thing feeds off negative energy…"

"Negative energy? Like the brownouts?" Betsy asked.

"What brownouts?" Dean asked.

"The people who've told me about their nightmares

experienced brownouts. When they woke up, their electricity was out for a few seconds before coming back on. They thought maybe the flickering lights woke them."

"When she fed on Olga," Sam said, seeing the connection. "The lights inside the house, along with the streetlight out front, lost power temporarily." Sam glanced down at the marked-up map again, crosschecking the times of the emergency calls—each living nightmare—with the person who had the nightmare. "That's it. Negative energy."

"Whatcha got, Sam?"

"The order of the nightmares." Sam traced a semicircular path with his index finger, starting with Olga Kucharski's house then moving to the northeast before coming back toward the north. "Widdershins."

"Widder—what now?" Dean asked.

"Widdershins," Sam repeated. "Counter clockwise movement. In witchcraft, some believe the use of widdershins movement creates negative magic or—"

"Negative energy."

"And that's more negative energy to feed her," Sam said. "She's feeding along the perimeter while most of the manifestations happen inside her negative energy circle."

"We know she's feeding in a counter clockwise pattern," Dean said. "And she causes mini blackouts when she feeds." He turned to Lucy, who was wrapping up her cell call to Jeffries. "Anything?"

"Rich's got his hands full," she said. "I heard a lot of gunfire in the background. Said he'll look it up and call us as soon as possible."

"Good," Dean said. "What's the highest point in town?"

"Easy," Lucy said. "The clock tower over the municipal building. Dad would take me up there when I was a kid. But why's that important?"

"We'll need spotters," Dean said.

Her phone rang. "It's Rich again." She listened for a moment and hung up. "He's on his way. Be here in two minutes."

Out of the corner of his eye, Sam noticed unusual movement. He turned to look out the window at their booth and saw what had caught his attention, the familiar shambling movement.

"Dean," Sam said. "We have a more immediate problem."

Dean followed Sam's gaze.

"They're here."

Nazi zombies. Well, at least one had made his way to the diner. The young officer with the exposed loop of intestine wearing the white tunic, which almost glowed under the streetlamps as he shuffled across the dark parking lot.

Other diner patrons started to notice the zombie with pointing and excited chatter. Three booths away, a woman screamed. People on the other side of the diner left their tables for a closer look at the source of the commotion. Several grabbed hats and jackets and rushed toward the exit.

If they all run out there now, they'll be dragged down and killed, Sam thought. *Then reanimate as zombies themselves, adding to the death toll and chaos.* Hoping to avoid mass hysteria, Sam stood and held up his FBI credentials.

"Everybody, listen! A terrorist cell is using an airborne hallucinogen to prey on your fears, to make you see and experience horrible things. They want you out there, in the night, panicking. You can fight this. The safest place is inside. Stay here. Lock the doors." If they stayed calm, kept control of their fears, they'd deprive the night hag of some negative energy. "My partner, Agent DeYoung, and I are trained to deal with this. Just… stay here. All of you. For your own protection."

Relieved to have somebody willing to handle the unimaginable, people began nodding. Those standing by the door returned to their former booths and tables.

Millie leaned across the table and whispered to Dean, "Shouldn't you tell them about the… monster?"

"They're close to panic." Dean spoke in hushed tones. "We'd rather not push them over the edge. They need to believe this is manageable. Dangerous, yes, but manageable. And it is. This is what we do."

Sam looked to Dean and together, after instructing Betsy to lock the door behind them, they went outside.

THIRTY-TWO

Linda Deetz wasn't surprised when the lights went out. She'd heard reports of the strong storms and lightning causing outages. No reason to think her house would escape the inconvenience. She'd stocked up on batteries and candles earlier in the day, just in case.

When the lights dimmed and then died, she took out a flashlight and spread lit candles around downstairs. What surprised her was that Trevor hadn't come down or complained when the power died. Either he was still sulking, or listening to his iPod, or maybe he'd fallen asleep and hadn't noticed. One less thing for her to deal with.

She poured herself a glass of Piccini Chianti and sat down in her favorite living-room chair to relax until power was restored. By the time she finished the glass and thought about having another, she heard banging from upstairs. She called out to Trevor but received no reply.

Within seconds, she began to worry. Deep-seated fears

began to surface. As a single mom, she feared being a target for home invasion or worse. Setting her glass down softly on the coffee table, she hurried to the kitchen and picked up the telephone. When she heard only silence, no dial tone, her fears began to magnify. She grabbed her purse by the front door and took out her cell phone. For a brief moment, she saw she had no signal bars and then the display died.

Her heart raced as she fought to suppress the panic rising inside her. Trevor was upstairs but not answering her calls, possibly in danger from an intruder. Hurrying back to the kitchen, she looked around for a weapon and grabbed the first thing she saw: a cast-iron skillet. She climbed the stairs as quietly as she could, counting on surprise and her familiarity with the layout of her home to help overcome an intruder who was likely stronger and possibly better armed.

Easing open Trevor's bedroom door, she almost gasped at what she saw by the moonlight streaming through his window. Somebody dressed in black, with his back to her, stood over her son in his chair. And Trevor was thrashing, as if the person was pinning him down—hurting him—but unable to cry out for help.

Anger taking over, she charged into the room, swinging the cast-iron skillet.

"Leave my son alone!" she screamed.

The base of the skillet connected with something… softer than she anticipated. And the intruder screeched—an inhuman sound—as the blow struck him. The dark shape whirled around and Linda felt weak-kneed at the flash of glowing red eyes she glimpsed before the intruder… dissolved.

Confused at what she had witnessed and unable to comprehend how the intruder had simply disappeared, she rushed to her son and shook him, her fear transformed into worry.

Groggy, Trevor slowly came to.

"What happened?" he mumbled.

"You're okay," she said, hugging him tightly. "You're okay now."

Moments later, when the lights came back on, she saw two streaks of gray in his hair, one on each side of his forehead running all the way to the nape of his neck.

Three zombies had shambled their way to C.J.'s Diner. Dean and Sam put them down efficiently with one head shot each from close range.

"Diner's no longer safe," Dean said.

"If it ever was."

Lights flashing, a police cruiser swung into the parking lot and stopped in front of them. Jeffries stepped out from the driver's side. He had a state cop riding shotgun. Noticing the dead zombies in the parking lot, Jeffries frowned.

"Damn. They're spreading," he said.

"You got info on Linda Deetz?" Dean asked.

Jeffries nodded. "Her phone and electric were dead. Just got through. Says she chased an intruder out of her son's room."

Dean exchanged a look with Sam. "She get a look?"

"It was dark," Jeffries said. "Said he wore black. Red eyes. Goggles? She hit him with a skillet and he disappeared somehow. She was a bit hysterical, so…"

"Disappeared sounds about right," Sam said. "If she moved on, maybe that ends the zombie manifestations."

"Don't know," Dean said, striking the toe of his boot against white-tunic zombie. "Still solid. Maybe they're not over until the current batch is all dead."

Behind them, the diner's front door deadbolt turned. Lucy, Millie, and Jozef Wieczorek came down the stairs.

"I told everyone inside we had information for you," Lucy explained. "What now?"

"That depends," Dean said and turned to Jeffries. "Can you get us binoculars, some spare two-way radios and access to the clock tower?"

"Yes, to all three."

"Good," Dean said. "Then here's the plan…"

Once Lucy explained that climbing a series of narrow switchback staircases was the only way to ascend the clock tower, Millie elected to remain at the diner. That left Jozef Wieczorek and Lucy in the role of spotters. With the state cop staying behind to temporarily guard the diner alone, the others drove to the municipal building.

Once there, Jeffries gave Lucy and Wieczorek a two-way radio, binoculars, and a key to the clock tower entrance. After handing Dean and Sam two-way radios, Jeffries rejoined his temporary partner. Together they would defend the diner while Dean and Sam took positions to ambush the night hag.

Dean glanced at the map, double-checking the warden's address.

The radio Sam held squawked. Lucy's voice. "We're

in position. Three-sixty view. Six… seven fires burning. Some existing power outages. But not in… Whoa! Looking northeast, it's—it's moving."

Sam spoke into the radio. "What's moving?"

"You said it was getting stronger… it's like a black veil moving over the houses. The lights, they're blotted out for a few moments as it moves over them. It's moving counter-clockwise, like you said, circling northwest."

"If it's moving," Dean said, "it's not feeding. Yet."

"Good. We need to be in position," Sam said.

Dean stared ahead as he drove north and felt himself zoning out, as if he'd been driving for hours, hypnotized by endless miles of road. Probably lack of sleep causing loss of focus. He tried to shake himself out of it, but then he glimpsed her, in his rearview mirror, running diagonally across the street, Ben beside her. One of the rabid wolves stalked them, ready to pounce.

Dean hit the brakes.

"Lisa!" Dean cried as he swung the Impala around. "Here with Ben. They're in trouble, Sam."

Sam looked over his shoulder.

"They're not real, Dean. Can't be. The real Lisa and Ben are at home. Safe. It's the night hag. She's using your fear against you."

"How? I'm not asleep."

"When you're exhausted, your mind wanders. You're having a waking nightmare. She's stronger now. Maybe that's all she needs to find a way into your subconscious."

"Gotta help them, Sam. If I don't—"

Sam grabbed his arm. "I saw something too, Dean. Yesterday. Something that wasn't real. It's all mind games. Your fears fuel her. If you give in now, she wins."

"Damn!" Hitting the brakes again, Dean took a deep breath. He'd failed to protect Sophie. And he always worried that his being a hunter would bring danger to Lisa and Ben. With nightmares to prove it. Now the night hag's psychic influence was jumbling his failure with his fears to mess with his mind. "You're right. It's not real. Lisa and Ben wouldn't be here… Can't believe I almost fell for it."

Shaking his head, Dean resumed his original course and dropped Sam off near the warden's house with his iron short-spear and lock picks. Then he drove to the home of Phil Meyerson, CDC retiree and parked half a block away. He didn't need Lucy's report over the radio to tell him when the night hag arrived and began to feed. The house and half the streetlights on the block went dark all at once.

"Going silent," Dean said into the radio before turning the volume off. Sooner or later the radio would lose power, but he couldn't know when. One ill-timed squawk from the speaker and he'd lose the element of surprise.

He sprinted up the block and hurried around the house along a bricked backyard patio to the rear door. Kneeling, he worked by sound and feel and had the lock picked within a minute.

Once inside the house, he waited quietly for a couple minutes more, long enough for the nocnitsa to assume solid form and begin feeding. But not too long. For all he knew, Meyerson's subconscious was already creating an outbreak of bubonic plague in Clayton Falls.

Iron short-spear at the ready, Dean crept through the house.

One moment Jeffries was talking to Baumbach—his temporary state cop partner who was still freaked out about what he'd seen in Clayton Falls—and the next moment he saw them wink into existence at the entrance to the parking lot over a thin bed of white mist. Even though DeYoung and Shaw warned them what type of living nightmare they might see next, Jeffries wasn't sure he would have fired so readily at seemingly ill people if he hadn't seen their eerie appearing-out-of-thin-air act himself. Baumbach stared in shocked dismay as Jeffries shot two of the hemorrhagic fever victims stumbling toward the diner.

"What the hell?" he whispered.

"They're not real people, Baumbach," Jeffries responded. "But their disease *is* contagious."

Seven more appeared at various points around the diner, lurching forward, begging for help as blood ran from their ears, eyes, noses, and mouths, their voices choking on it as they moaned.

"Help! Help us! Please!"

As they came close enough to shoot, five more appeared behind them. Soon they would be overwhelmed by sheer numbers. Jeffries took aim, but saw out of the corner of his eye that Baumbach was paralyzed by dismay.

"Baumbach! Shoot!" he commanded urgently.

The state cop nodded abruptly. "O—okay."

They fired together, Baumbach clearing the left side of the

entrance, Jeffries taking the right. Jeffries wondered what the people inside the diner thought about them mowing down apparent civilians in distress, but shook it off. A moment later all the approaching bleeders—as he had begun to think of them to disassociate them from real human beings— disappeared. Even the ones on the ground vanished.

He got on the radio.

"DeYoung? Shaw? Is it over?"

After a few moments, DeYoung answered, his voice bitter with disappointment.

"No. Meyerson is dead."

Wieczorek came on the channel.

"The creature is on the move."

By the time Dean reached Meyerson, sitting on a sofa by a table lamp with a crossword puzzle in his lap, the man was dead and the night hag was gone. When he examined the body, he discovered that Meyerson hadn't been reduced to a husk. He was wrinkled and old but not withered to skin and bones. *The strain of the feeding must have killed him*, Dean thought. Either a heart attack or a stroke. He turned on the radio to report his findings and to warn Sam he was up next.

The stairs creaked.

Dean glanced up and saw an old woman in a long nightgown staring at him.

"Who are you? Why are you in—what have you done to my husband," she demanded as she took in the scene below her.

"FBI," Dean said quickly, scrambling to produce his ID while keeping his iron short-spear beside his leg out of view before Mrs. Meyerson had a heart attack of her own. "I'm afraid your husband has passed."

"No... no," she said, her eyes wet with brimming tears as she brushed by Dean and bent down to grab her husband's shoulders. "Phil! Phil, my God, no. Philip! Please, no..." She turned to Dean with an accusatory look. "What happened? Why are you here?"

"My partner and I are investigating strange incidents in town," Dean said. "I—I thought your husband could help. I had questions. But... I think he had a heart attack."

Dean guessed she heard only about half of what he'd blurted out. She sat beside her deceased husband and rested her head against his chest, crying silent tears.

Good luck, Sam, Dean thought. *Kill this damn thing already.*

When darkness blanketed the warden's house and extinguished nearby streetlights, Sam slipped around to the back door and picked the lock, allowing enough time for the night hag to settle in and begin feeding. Webb was younger than Meyerson, so she should have time to feed. If Sam acted too soon and the nocnitsa fled, they would be back to square one, not knowing where she'd strike next, with dawn two hours away.

This was it. All or nothing. Clayton Falls wouldn't last another night.

THIRTY-THREE

On the western outskirts of town, inside the Falls Federal Prison compound, the walls of the supermax wing began to tremble. Fissures appeared in the concrete and raced upward, forking and spreading in all directions. Large chunks of the walls fell away like a calving glacier.

While the walls crumbled, the electrical systems shorted out, rendering motion detectors and closed-circuit cameras blind. Inside the solitary cells of poured concrete, the prison's most dangerous inmates took notice. Lights flickered and dimmed. Cell doors creaked in their housings. Cracks spread across the walls of cells that were de facto sensory deprivations chambers, with the exception of narrow window slots that revealed only a slice of sky and nothing more. Supermax inmates spent twenty-three hours of every day alone in these cells, known as "special housing units" or "SHU." They were granted one hour per day to exercise, alone, in what amounted to an empty swimming pool. When the walls began to crack, some of the inmates imagined that the heavy concrete slabs would crush them, unlamented victims of a natural disaster.

But all of them considered the possibility of escape.

Ragnar Bartch jumped up from his bunk and watched in awe as two long cracks rose from opposite sides of the wall across from his cell door and formed an inverted V. Walking forward, he pressed his hands to the block of stone and marveled as the section scraped and slid away, opening a gap in the previously impenetrable wall. A gleam of reflected starlight on his bunk caught his attention. When he saw the familiar rectangular shape lying there, beckoning to him, he smiled for the first time since he'd come to Falls Federal. He grabbed the handle of the shiny new meat cleaver and ran through the breached wall, eager to claim the destiny that had been granted him.

Jasper Dearborn, Deputy Warden in charge of security at Falls Federal ran his hand through his thinning gray hair, convinced he was a cursed man. Alden Webb, his boss, had placed Dearborn in charge after leaving early for the day. Said he felt "wiped out." Thought he might be coming down with a nasty virus or something. Surely Dearborn could handle things for a day or two. Most days passed without incident. Dealing with administrative red tape was the biggest headache. But routine led to complacency. And Dearborn never accepted complacency in himself or others. The previous night's false report of an escaped inmate had even provided a bit of a wake-up call for his staff.

Dearborn's internal alert level went up a notch when he'd received reports of a tornado touching down a few miles from the prison. But that was nothing compared to the report Ray Strawder, his security operations director brought him a few hours ago. Somehow, Kurt Machalek, one of their most notorious supermax cons, had managed to thoroughly and completely disembowel himself while under closed-circuit camera surveillance. Corporal Urbino, the guard monitoring the feeds, noticed static on the monitor. By the time he thought to report it, the image cleared and Machalek was lying in blood-strewn pieces all over his cell.

Dearborn thought it unlikely a man could commit an act of such grievous violence on himself. The logical conclusion was that he'd had help. No prisoners had access to that cell. Only Dearborn's men. He was determined to find whoever had decided to mete out his own idea of justice—a brutal execution. And if there was a conspiracy in Dearborn's ranks, he wanted to root it out before he told Webb of his failure. The situation was contained. Urbino had been relieved of duty and awaited interrogation. Dearborn planned to interview anyone who had access to the supermax wing, and anyone who could not account for his time. Even if it took all night.

Lost in thought, Dearborn stared at his desk when it began to vibrate beneath his hands. Picking up the phone, he called Ray Strawder.

"Strawder, what the hell—?"

"The supermax wing, boss," his security operations director said. "It's crumbling."

"What?"

"The walls are literally falling apart!"

"How? Earthquake?"

"Only supermax is affected. All electronic surveillance is down. We're blind, but I'm getting reports some of the prisoners are outside the walls. I've sent men and guard dogs out—hold on a minute."

Strawder must have cupped the receiver. Dearborn heard rushed and maddeningly muddled conversation before Strawder came back on the line.

"Boss, the prisoners are armed!"

"How the hell is that possible!"

"Don't know, boss," Strawder said, his voice piano-wire taut. "We're taking casualties. Bartch is out, with a damn cleaver. Killed two guards."

Dearborn almost dropped the phone. His hands were numb.

"Gets worse, boss," Strawder said. "Stun fences are offline. Tower guards are reporting physical gaps in the fences. Boss, this is some kind of coordinated mass escape."

"This is a nightmare, Strawder," Dearborn said. "Have the tower guards shoot them all. Shoot to kill. Nobody escapes!"

Not on my watch, Dearborn thought. *I won't let this happen.*

He needed to alert the Clayton Falls police chief, but first he had no choice. Time to notify his boss that everything had gone to hell while the old man caught the sniffles. With a heavy sigh, he picked up the phone and dialed Webb's number—

—but the call wouldn't go through.

* * *

Ragnar Bartch sprinted across the prison yard in a state of pure exhilaration. Ignoring the blaring sirens and the blinding watchtower spotlights that swept back and forth, he swung his bloodied cleaver with lethal accuracy at anyone who came within arm's reach, whether fellow inmate or prison guard. He'd even decapitated one of the German shepherds they'd sent after him without suffering a bite or a single scratch. Handgun bullets whizzed by his ears. Rifle bullets rained down from the watchtowers.

Two cons running on either side of him dropped seconds apart, but he continued unscathed. Once he spotted the gap in the inner fence, he embraced his destiny. Freedom. Through the opening in the first barrier, he hardly had to alter his course to duck through the gap in the second fence. With fresh blood dripping from his cleaver, the night welcomed him and the lights of the town beckoned.

Alden Webb, warden of Falls Federal Prison, thrashed in his sleep, unable to wake up from his worst nightmare. Crouched on his chest, elongated fingers of both hands wrapped around his damp forehead, the solidified darkness of the nocnitsa hissed and sighed with delight as she drained the life energy from his body, mining his nightmare for images of fear and darkness to unleash upon the hapless town. She had grown too strong for the man to free himself from her feeding. She ravaged his subconscious mind with limitless abandon. She would ride out his feeble psychic resistance until his body and his mind succumbed to her will. Only when he had been reduced to a lifeless husk would she move on. No need for half measures now. With total focus, she slowly snuffed him out…

Sam had one shot at ridding the world of the night hag.

When he slipped into Alden Webb's bedroom, the man was convulsing on his bed, the predatory monster crouched on his chest, cupping his head in her inhuman hands. Between the warden's thrashing and the nocnitsa's discordant hissing, Sam's approach was masked, allowing him to reach striking distance.

Without hesitation, Sam thrust the iron short-spear forward in a two-handed grip, the point directed at the center of the night hag's back—

—the same moment Webb's heart gave out and he fell still.

Perhaps the creature heard Sam's short exhalation as he struck.

Whatever gave him away, she spun toward him and the blow pierced her left arm instead of her back. The arm shriveled up instantly and withered away. The night hag shrieked and bounded toward Sam with remarkable speed, knocking him on his back, the short-spear clattering on the floor just out of reach.

Pushing himself back on his heels, he caught the short-spear in his hand—and froze as the night hag landed on his chest. She lashed out with her remaining hand and the solidified darkness of her fingers reached out to his forehead and through his skull, probing his mind.

Sam stared at the dark face with its glowing red eyes, long

crooked nose, and wide mouth filled with sharp, obsidian teeth, and he couldn't move a muscle. She'd forced him into a state of sleep paralysis. While his mind was aware and his consciousness raged, he couldn't lift a finger against her.

"Ahh…" she said, sighing. "Enough fear, guilt, and darkness in you to feed me for weeks and weeks. Hmm… what you fear is… yourself! And… for him. Brother. Shall we see what happens? Yesss…"

No!

But it was too late.

Dean called in Meyerson's death and finally managed to slip outside, leaving the man's widow to her grief. Win or lose, Sam would be under radio silence until it was over. Lucy and Wieczorek hadn't heard a peep yet. He started across the brick patio then stopped abruptly when he saw his brother climbing up the handful of steps toward him—holding a butcher knife instead of the makeshift wrought-iron short-spear.

"Sam? What's going on?"

"It's time, Dean," Sam said, a cold glint in his eyes as he turned the knife blade back and forth in his hand.

"What the hell are you talking about, Sammy? Is nightmare bitch dead or what?"

"Of course *you* failed to kill her."

"She was gone already. You got the memo."

"I told him you were useless."

"Told who? What the…?" Dean froze as comprehension dawned. "Oh, I get it. You're not him. You're his nightmare."

"The best version of him."

"In your dreams, pal."

"No. In your nightmare."

Soulless Sam charged, swinging the butcher knife in an arc at Dean's throat. Ducking beneath the blade, Dean swept Soulless Sam's legs. The doppelganger crashed into a deck chair and knocked over an old three-legged barbecue grill.

Shaking off the effects of the impact, Soulless Sam rose up and moved toward Dean, his cold eyes filled with murderous cunning. But Dean had a bigger concern. If he was experiencing Sam's living nightmare, his brother was in real trouble.

He had to end this now.

Though Sam couldn't move, he was somehow aware that Soulless Sam had been unleashed upon Dean, as if he were seeing ghost images of their battle on his retinas. Sam's nightmare was twofold. First, that he would lose his soul again, and that Soulless Sam would cause Dean's death. As he lay helpless on the warden's bedroom floor, that nightmare was happening. Unable to intervene in the deadly fight, Sam could only wait, paralyzed, while the night hag fed on him until all that remained was a lifeless husk.

He had an effective weapon within reach but couldn't use it. The only time he'd had the advantage against the nocnitsa was when she was feeding, when she became focused on nothing but the darkness she craved.

There was nothing Sam could do against her.

So that's what he did. Nothing.

Though he couldn't move, his body was taut with the

need to fight at any cost. He let go of the tension, let it all slip away.

Why fight? She's too powerful. She's in complete control. Can't win. Might as well surrender. Give up and it will be over soon. Won't have to face Dean. Won't have to face our failure. There's no hope…

The night hag noticed his change in demeanor. She leaned forward, nostrils flaring, red eyes glowing with more intensity.

"That's it… *give* it to me… your despair…" she hissed.

Sam closed his eyes, blocking her victory from his view.

She might have won, but he didn't have to watch. All he had to do was give up…

He was utterly still, unresisting, wearing his hopelessness front and center, giving her exactly what she craved. When she began to rock back and forth and make that discordant hissing sound, Sam allowed himself the briefest of smiles—

—and slammed the point of the iron short-spear through her chest.

The nocnitsa shrieked and thrashed as the iron burned through the congealed darkness of her being. Sam sprang up and maintained his grip on the spear, twisting it and redirecting it into the center of her shriveling mass as she tried to recede from it.

With a blast of foul-smelling air, her body burst apart in rapidly thinning tendrils of darkness that flared and burned into bitter ash and then… faded away.

Sam stood, panting, and finally let the iron weapon slip from his fingers.

* * *

Breathing harshly, Dean stood over the corner of the brick patio where Soulless Sam had fallen. Where he had disappeared a moment ago. Raising the iron short-spear, he looked along its length. Of course, the blood had disappeared as well. Noticing movement near the patio door, he looked across the brick patio and saw the pale face of Meyerson's widow staring at him through the window.

Had she seen the whole fight? Or just the killing blow?

Before the body disappeared, had she judged him?

Perception is reality. That's what Sam had said.

"You're wrong, Sam," Dean said, staring down at the previously blood-stained corner of the patio. "That wasn't you. Never was."

Next to a fallen deck chair, Dean's two-way radio squawked. Sam's voice. "Dean. It's over."

Dean scooped up the radio. "Never a doubt."

"I had a few," Sam replied. "On purpose."

Dean frowned but before he could reply, Lucy Quinn's excited voice came through the speaker.

"They're gone! All the nightmares. We're watching through the binoculars and they're all winking out!"

Discretion being the better part of valor, Chief Quinn had already received the first of his rabies shots at County General and had three more deep intramuscular injections to look forward to over the next fourteen days. Harder to accept was Lucy's assertion—not to mention half his department's conviction—that nightmares were coming to life. But… the wolf that attacked him *had* disappeared. And he had seen other things too extraordinary to ignore. He was willing to admit that something strange was happening in Clayton Falls, whether it was a terrorist plot involving hallucinogens, some other kind of biohazard agent or even genetically engineered… creatures.

The latest news was a prison break. But this time Dearborn, the deputy warden confirmed it, though the man had seemed a bit unhinged when Quinn talked to him. And Webb wasn't answering his damn phone. Maybe they'd put something in the water supply. Whoever *they* were. Chief Quinn had no answers.

Driving his cruiser down Bell Street, he couldn't believe his eyes when he saw a large man in pale-blue prison clothes running down the middle of the street holding a bloody meat cleaver aloft and yelling maniacally. Stopping the cruiser and turning on his light bar, Quinn stepped out and stared at the approaching man.

"No. Not this again," he said.

"You can't stop me! I'm invincible! It's my destiny to kill!" the man yelled.

Whatever it was, pretending to be Bartch, Quinn had had enough.

He yanked out his firearm and put a bullet through its forehead.

The body fell to the asphalt with a convincing thud.

The bloodied cleaver spun out of the dead man's hand and skidded to a stop at Quinn's feet. He waited expectantly. But neither the corpse, nor the cleaver disappeared.

"I'll be damned."

* * *

While Dean picked up Lucy Quinn and Jozef Wieczorek at the municipal building and Sam at Alden Webb's house and brought them all to the diner, C.J.'s had cleared out, at least temporarily. The long night was over and the eastern sky had already begun to pale, drawing open the curtain on the majestic mountains to the west. Soon the breakfast rush would arrive. The Winchesters hoped to be long gone by then. Fewer questions to answer once the dust settled.

On her way home after an unexpected double shift, Betsy, their amiable server, handed the brothers two paper bags and two large cups of coffee.

"Cheeseburger and fries, grilled chicken, and a salad for the road," she said pleasantly. "On the house."

Baumbach had caught a ride with another State Patrol cop, leaving Jeffries alone at the diner with Lucy and Wieczorek to say goodbye.

Dean nodded toward Wieczorek. "Back to your regularly scheduled nightmares?"

Wieczorek shrugged. "Good question. I don't know if I still have the Dr. Gruesome gig anymore. Frankly, I'm not sure I want it. May have lost my taste for nightmares."

"People need a nightmare now and then," Dean said. Off their confused looks, he quickly added, "The old-fashioned kind! Helps them appreciate the good stuff in their lives."

"So, I want to thank you for saving my life," Lucy said. "Not to mention half the town." She stepped forward and gave Dean and then Sam a quick hug. "So, thanks!"

"You're welcome," Dean said.

"Couldn't have done it without your help," Sam said, thinking about the friends Lucy had lost and the people he and Dean had failed to save. They knew they couldn't save everyone, but the losses were no easier to accept.

Jeffries hooked his thumb in his bulky cop's belt and shook his head in disbelief.

"You two are unlike any FBI agents I've ever met."

"You've met a lot?" Dean asked.

"Well, no, not personally, but I've heard stories."

"We're specialists," Sam said. "Not too many like us."

"I believe it," Jeffries said, chuckling.

"What about the prison? All escapees rounded up?" Dean asked.

"Only Bartch made it out of the compound," Jeffries said. "And Chief Quinn took care of him. Five killed in the escape attempt, seven others rounded up. Supermax wing's a mess. Survivors will be transferred while the place is repaired."

"If it's repaired," Lucy said. "The protestors will have a new rallying cry. 'No more supermax.'"

"You know," Jeffries said, scratching his jaw. "Chief Quinn will be a bit… livid you guys left before a final debrief. Guess I'll tell him I missed you on your way out of town. Assuming Lucy and Doc Gruesome here back me up."

Lucy punched his arm playfully.

"You mean they left already, Rich? Darn, I was so hoping to say goodbye."

Wieczorek smiled. "Real shame. All three of us missed them."

"Guess that's our cue," Dean said. "You ready, Agent Shaw?"

Sam nodded.

They climbed into the Impala with their bags and coffee cups and acknowledged the waves from the three townspeople as Dean steered the car out of the diner's parking lot.

When they were on I-80 East, Dean said. "Next town, getting the Impala fixed and first motel, I'm sleeping twenty-four hours straight."

"Not worried about nightmares?"

"Used them all up for a while."

Sam stared through the windshield, unsure what to expect the next time he laid his head down on a pillow and his subconscious took control. He was aware of Dean's gaze now and then as the miles rolled by, but said nothing.

Eventually, he had to ask. "What happened with him?" Sam said. "Soulless Sam, I mean. The night hag let me see it. The beginning, anyway. When he appeared and you realized he wasn't me."

"You didn't see the whole fight?"

"Just when he attacked you," Sam said. "What happened?"

Dean stared through the windshield, giving more attention to the minimal traffic than strictly necessary. Sam thought he saw his brother frown briefly. Maybe from the sun glare.

"Like the other nightmares," Dean said at last. "He disappeared."

"Oh."

"That's all it was, Sam. A nightmare," Dean said. "Soulless Sam ain't coming back."

"I know, Dean," Sam said. "Nightmares only make sense while we're having them."

When we wake from a nightmare, we recognize how irrational it was. But Soulless Sam had been more than a nightmare. And Sam's soul had experienced a living nightmare of its own. Who knows what kind of damage that causes, what scars it leaves behind? Maybe you can never go back to who you were.

Dean switched on the Impala's radio and found a classic rock station. The Stones were playing "Paint It Black."

THE END

ACKNOWLEDGMENTS

Thanks to William Nottingham for advice and suggestions on police procedure. (And continued thanks to the Police Department of Logan Township, New Jersey.) For research assistance on various topics that popped up during the planning of this novel, thanks to Jeff Richards and to my wife, Andrea Passarella. For graciously answering my *Supernatural* questions on short notice, thanks to Nicholas Knight. Special thanks to Matthew, Luke, Emma, and Andrea for their suggestions during our nightmare brainstorming sessions. They enjoyed participating in the storytelling process. Much appreciation to Greg Schauer, owner of the genre/indie bookstore Between Books in Claymont, Delaware, for his continued support and encouragement.

Thanks to Cath Trechman of Titan Books for bringing me on board and Christopher Cerasi at Warner Bros. Entertainment Inc. for juggling all the connections that make these books happen. And thanks to Rebecca Dessertine for her early advice and suggestions for this novel.

Finally, thanks to Eric Kripke for creating *Supernatural*, a show I can't wait to watch each week, and to the entire cast and crew for bringing his vision to life.

ABOUT THE AUTHOR

John Passarella won the Horror Writers Association's prestigious Bram Stoker Award for Superior Achievement in a First Novel for the coauthored *Wither*. Columbia Pictures purchased the feature film rights to *Wither* in a prepublication, preemptive bid. Barnesandnoble.com named the paperback edition of *Wither* one of horror's "Best of 2000." At Amazon. com, *Wither* was an Editor's Choice and a horror bestseller.

John's other novels include *Wither's Rain, Wither's Legacy, Kindred Spirit, Shimmer,* and the original media tie-in novels *Buffy the Vampire Slayer: Ghoul Trouble, Angel: Avatar,* and *Angel: Monolith. Supernatural: Night Terror* is his ninth novel.

A member of the Authors Guild, Horror Writers Association, Science Fiction and Fantasy Writers of America, International Thriller Writers, International Association of Media Tie-In Writers, and the Garden State Horror Writers, John resides in southern New Jersey with his wife and three children. He is also a web designer and a webmaster for several *New York Times* bestselling authors.

John maintains his official author website at www.passarella. com, where he encourages readers to send him email at author@passarella.com, and to subscribe to his free author newsletter for the latest information on his books and stories.

SUPERNATURAL™

THE OFFICIAL SUPERNATURAL MAGAZINE

features exclusive interviews with Jared and Jensen, guest stars, and the behind-the-scenes crew of the show, the latest news, and classic episode spotlights! Plus, pull-out posters in every issue!

TO SUBSCRIBE NOW CALL

U.S. 1 877 363 1310
U.K. 0844 844 0387

For more information visit:
www.titanmagazines.com/supernatural